THE CAVALIER

A Twiin Entertainment book

Books to come by Jason McWhirter

Cavalier Trilogy

The Cavalier

The Rise of Malbeck

Glimmer in the Shadow

Published by Twiin Entertainment

www.twiinentertainment.com

Cover art by Cos Koniotis

Map by Jason McWhirter

AUTHOR'S NOTE

This is a work of fiction. Names, characters, places, and incidents are the product of the author's imagination or are used fictitiously, and any resemblance to actual persons, living or dead, business establishments, events, or locales is entirely coincidental.

Praise for the Cavalier

"The Cavalier (Book One of the Cavalier Trilogy) is a descriptively strong story, staying true to the style of similar fantasy novels."
Fantasy Book Review

"The writing is crisp and polished, and the narrative has a good level of description for a fantasy novel. Jonas is a sympathetic character who the reader immediately cares about..."
Sift Book Review

Acknowledgements

Writing a trilogy and publishing it requires a lot of work and help along the way. I would foremost like to thank my wife, Jodi, who put up with my many hours and late nights in front of the computer screen and helped me with guidance and support throughout the entire process.

I would also like to thank my family and friends who were my sounding boards, my editors, and my critics. Without them this series would not have been possible. Specifically, thank you Dad for reading my books and encouraging me along the way. Thanks to my brother, Devin, who always made me feel like my books were good enough to be published. Thanks to my sister, Heather, her husband Jason, and both my nieces, Logan and Delaney, for supporting me in this process. Jason, thank you for your editing and the hours you spent helping me polish my voice. Thank you Beau, Scott, and Aaron for reading my books and giving me advice along the way. Of course I have to thank my final editor, who in this case, is my mother, Linda McWhirter. Thank you Mom for the work you did in helping me put together a written work ready for publication.

I would also like to thank my dog, Meadow, for the long evenings and nights she spent lying next to me while I sat at the computer creating my story.

Thank you Cos Koniotis for your incredible art and helping me through this new process.

Last but not least, I would like to thank all my friends and supporters who came to my Sip and Support party. I appreciate everyone who came to show their encouragement in this endeavor. Special thanks go to the following people: John and Chris McCloskey, Brynne Borhek, Cindi Barton, Dawn and Bill Batey, Nick Sutherlund, Mark and Kathy Johnson, Mike Hunziker, Rick and Debbie Selfors, Linda and Jimmy Collins, Ragan and Clay Masterson, Jamie Radcliffe, and Ben and Liz Zielke.

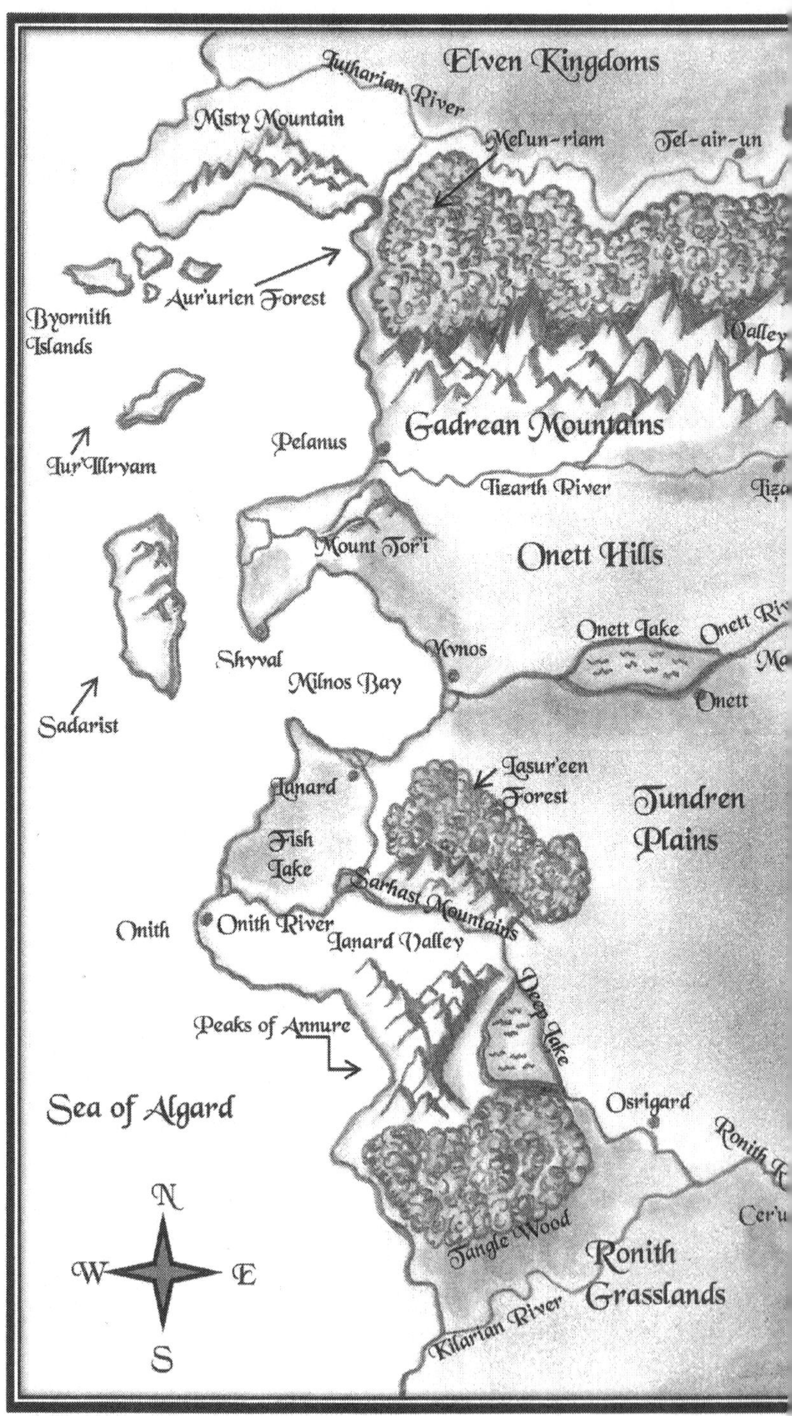
Elven Kingdoms
Iutharian River
Misty Mountain
Melun-riam
Tel-air-un
Aur'urien Forest
Byornith Islands
Iur'Illryam
Pelanus
Gadrean Mountains
Tizarth River
Mount Tor'i
Onett Hills
Onett Lake
Mynos
Shyval
Milnos Bay
Onett
Sadarist
Lanard
Lasur'een Forest
Tundren Plains
Fish Lake
Sarhast Mountains
Onith
Onith River
Lanard Valley
Deep Lake
Peaks of Annure
Sea of Algard
Osrigard
N
W
E
S
Tangle Wood
Ronith Grasslands
Kilarian River

Fown Lake
Longset
Mazgar Forest
Black Lands
The Dragon's Spine
Vanguard Mountains
Dwarf Mount
Torgar
Lyre Lake
Banrith
Tarsis
Lyre River
Tundren Mountains
Tarsinian Plains
Nomad Lands
Cuthaine
Gildren River
Gildren Garrison
Mount Ule
Tuvell Garrison
Nu'menell
Finarth
Tuvell River
Stonestep
Lone Peak
Shadow Valley
Ta'ron
Hills of A'rune
Sithgarin River
Tyvek
Sithgarin Desert
Sith Garrison
Annure
The Lands Of Kraawn
Lake Lar'nam

THE CAVALIER

BOOK ONE OF THE ***CAVALIER TRILOGY***

JASON L. MCWHIRTER

Prologue

Year 5045 of the Kraawnian Calendar, One thousand years after the Great War

Snow crunched under the horse's hooves as the lone rider moved slowly up the mountain pass, his vigilant eyes scanning the rocky cliffs and scattered trees from under the shadows of his cloak. Bitter cold surrounded them, but the man and steed pushed forward through the deep snow, seemingly unaffected by its freezing embrace. It was very quiet; the silent song of falling snow bringing peace and serenity to the area. But this man's heart did not reflect the tranquil setting. No, his mind was focused on his mission, his gloved hand occasionally gripping the bone handle pommel of the magical sword dangling from his hip.

He did not know exactly where he was going. His horse, Suatha, was leading the way. The beast's head was held low, drawn forward by a magical pull. One thing the warrior did know was that evil was near. It always was, wherever he went, for that was his mission in life, to battle the darkness, to bring light where there was shadow. His entire persona radiated with the energy of the gods, making him a beacon to the evil minions of Kraawn, but at the same time giving him the power to combat the dark forces struggling for dominion of all things.

It was not just magic that he possessed, but skill; skill honed from constant years of fighting and training with every weapon. Silver armor, god-made, ensconced his muscled physique, reflecting the soft glow of the sun trying to push through the white clouds above.

Soon he would know his destination, and soon he would face powerful enemies. He could feel it deep within him. The purpose of his mission was so close and he was eager to uncover it, slicing through the dark veil with his silver sword.

His task was important, although he knew not why, but he felt as if the very existence of the beautiful surroundings he rode through depended on it.

6 months earlier…..

Gullanin shuffled his old withered body down the stone passageway, the glow of the braziers doing little to lighten the dark musty hallways of Banrith Castle. He was slightly bent over, his bony shoulders holding up a thick dark gray robe. The wood staff he carried was polished like obsidian. His well-worn robe draped his skeletal figure like a shroud covering a dried and emaciated corpse.

The hall was quiet except for the sliding of his sandaled feet and the rhythmic clicking his staff made on the dark stones. Gullanin's long scraggly gray hair was held back by a silver skull cap. The cap was plain except for a single white eye, the symbol of his dark lord, Gould the Tormentor. Gullanin knew that Gould would be pleased with him, the excitement of this prospect making him smile broadly, exposing yellow rotting teeth, his thin pasty skin stretching from the expression seldom gracing his withered visage.

Turning the corner he came to a large door of thick oak held together with bands of black steel carved into the shape of clawed hands. Two massive orcs stood before the door, blocking entrance to all who were forbidden in this part of the castle. The orcs were thick of limb and their misshapen features appalled Gullanin. These were not ordinary orcs; they were called the Gould-Irin, orcs bred by Gullanin himself, deep in the pits of Banrith Castle. It took him many generations to perfect the breed. He had succeeded in creating impressive beasts that were larger, stronger, and with inexhaustible endurance in comparison to their brethren. Powerful magic and much time were required to create these beings, resulting in the relative scarcity of the Gould-Irin. There would be more, however, once the Dark One returned.

The Gould-Irin were excellent soldiers who did Gullanin's bidding without question. These orcs were guarding the altar room to Gould himself, and only powerful followers were allowed here. The orcs, seeing Gullanin, quickly stepped aside. No one in Banrith questioned Gullanin, especially now that he had found a way to bring their lord back.

Gullanin waved his hand, whispering a word of power. Without even breaking stride the door opened and he walked through, the thick door swinging shut behind him.

The altar room was large and simple, the focus being a massive raised dais roughly five paces in diameter. This dais was as high as a man's waist and the edges were covered with carvings of demons and other denizens of the lower planes. The top was polished black and glistened like oil. The entire floor of the altar room was carved into a giant eye, Gould's mark, and it was painted white in contrast to the dark stone in which it was made. The black round altar was the pupil of this eye, *the eye that saw all* thought Gullanin, as he shuffled into the room.

Around the outer edge of the circular room were six suits of magnificent black armor. At least that is what they looked like. Gullanin glanced at them as he always did. The armor was as dark as midnight and covered in intricate runes and long serrated spikes. The dark helms were also spiked and ominous in appearance, matching the malevolent feeling permeating the entire room.

The armor stood like statues, but Gullanin knew that inside each suit was the withered remains of the black knights of legend. The dark warriors were called Banthras and they were created by his lord during the great wars many years ago. When Gullanin's lord was banished by the long dead Ullis Gavinsteal, the ancient king of Finarth, the Banthras also left the material plane, waiting for their lord to return. Only their shells remained behind.

Normally the altar room was empty, but not today. Today was the day for which they had waited for over a thousand years. Gullanin could barely remember that far back. It seemed that he had been alive forever, the years melting together as memories disappeared and new ones formed. His magic and Gould's power had kept him alive, and today he would be rewarded for his long service. Today his lord, Gould's general on this plane of existence, would rise again and bring darkness to the lands of Kraawn.

Gullanin moved toward the altar where he was greeted by three men, each wearing long robes similar to his, but much different in every other aspect. Gullanin was a wizard of great power; these men were high priests to the Forsworn. They were given their power directly from Gould, Naz-reen, and Dykreel, whereas Gullanin harnessed his power directly from the Ru'Ach, the energy of all things.

Most people lived their entire lives and knew nothing of the Ru'Ach, and some, like Gullanin, spent their entire lives learning about the secrets of the Ru'Ach, and yet knew very little about it. Gullanin understood that everything had energy, and that this energy made up the Ru'Ach. He liked to think of it as a river of energy, a flow that powered everything, and if you had the skill and knowledge, could access it yourself. One thing Gullanin didn't know was how did the gods fit into the picture? Did they create the Ru'Ach, or were they a construct of the Ru'Ach? It was a question that had eluded him his entire long life, and he figured he'd never find the answer.

Janrick, high priest to Gould, moved toward Gullanin with purpose. He was tall and wraith-like, his black robe sparkling with interwoven silver thread.

"Do you have it?" Janrick asked briskly.

Smiling, Gullanin showed his yellow and rotting teeth. He was going to savor this, for it was he who had found the book, not they.

"I do, Janrick," Gullanin said whispering several words of power. Janrick moved away from the wizard, fearful that he was casting a spell at him. There was not a lot of trust between the minions of the Dark One, and why would there be? Personal gain and power was what the Forsworn stood for, and they were rewarded for being ruthless, greedy, and embodiments of injustice.

After a few seconds Gullanin held out his right hand and a swirling form began to materialize at his fingertips. It was square and lined in purple flames. When the flames disappeared, a small leather bound book lay in his hands. It looked old and insignificant.

"That is it?" asked Kane, high priest to Dykreel, not bothering to mask his disappointed tone. Kane was thick of belly, a direct correlation to his favorite past time…eating. He was a sloth, receiving great pleasure from food as well as torturing anyone who was an adherent to the benevolent gods of Kraawn. He lived to hear them cry in pain for their gods' help. In the end they died screaming, seemingly abandoned by their gods. Kane's great pleasure came when the light in their eyes extinguished, the look of despair on their face when their god did not come to save them.

"It is. I hold the book that thousands have been seeking for many lifetimes." Gullanin noticed the skeptical looks of the priests. "Do not judge the power contained in this book by its appearance. I have been studying the book for weeks and have yet to begin to tap its true power."

"Be careful, Gullanin, our lord will not be happy if he knows you sought the power for yourself," replied Cuthare, high priest to Naz-reen. Cuthare was slight of build but Gullanin knew that he held more hatred and malice in that small body than the other two high priests combined. He was ambitious and powerful, and one to watch.

"Cuthare, I had to analyze the book in order to find a way to bring back our lord. That is all I did. Besides, much of the power is beyond even me, and it would take countless years to understand it in order to harness that power. The book will be intact for our lord, that I promise you. It is my gift to him," Gullanin finished, putting emphasis on the word *my*.

Gullanin did not miss the looks of hatred they shot his way. Their jealousy was palpable, and Gullanin knew they would likely kill him now if they learned how to use the magic in the book themselves, but the priests needed him…at least for now.

"Let us start," replied Janrick. "Our lord has waited long enough. Is the vessel ready?"

Gullanin, smiling, whispered another series of words. Instantly more braziers flared to life and a loud noise directed their attention to the ceiling where a strange metal object was being lowered by a thick heavy chain. As it neared the center of the altar it could be seen more clearly. It was a statue of Gould with his arms out wide. The incredible piece was made from some dark polished stone in the shape of a cross, the body of Gould the vertical line, his outstretched arms the horizontal.

Gould was usually pictured simply as a hooded man draped in a black robe, and the statue before them was that exact image, except that it was huge, twice as tall as Gullanin, and strapped to the statue was a naked man. His arms were lashed to the outstretched arms of the statue by thick leather and his legs were tied similarly to the body.

The unconscious man was heavily muscled and covered with many scars, some fresh but most long ago healed. The hair on his head was shaved showing several days of stubble. He was a perfect specimen of a warrior, powerful looking, with a thin waist and wide shoulders. The prisoner was handsome but his visage was hard, like stone.

"He is perfect, as you said," stated Janrick. "How long have you had him?"

"I have been working on him for over fifteen years. It took a while to break him but our lord will appreciate the irony of who he is. He will be very pleased," replied Cuthare. The other high priests smiled wickedly. All three turned towards Gullanin eagerly. "What's next, wizard?" asked Cuthare.

"The procedure is quite simple really, but the spell is very complex and must be recited perfectly," Gullanin said, lifting up the book before him. "Canzar," he whispered. Instantly the book opened and flipped through several pages, stopping on one in particular. "Actually it is not even a prepared spell; it is something that I had to create using the correct phrases found in the book. It took me several days just to find the words, let alone figure out their meaning and the correct order in which…."

"Will it work?" interrupted Janrick. "I care not how you came up with the spell. Will it work?"

"Yes…theoretically it should work."

"And if it doesn't?" asked Kane.

"Then we are in the same place where we started. But, magic is not always exact, there could be some danger to us if the spell does not work," replied Gullanin, enjoying their discomfort.

"Explain yourself," ordered Cuthare.

"The energy of the spell will be released. If it does not bring our lord back, then it might bring something else back," Gullanin explained. "After all, the words used are words for conjuring, mixed with other words of power. If you are afraid, then wait outside while I perform the spell."

The three priests looked at each other, but they all seemed to be in agreement since no one went for the door.

"We need to be here when he arrives. Start the spell, wizard, and make sure there are no mistakes," snarled Janrick as the three priests stepped back so that Gullanin could face the doomed man strapped to the statue.

Gullanin laughed silently. Janrick's words were an empty threat. They were powerful priests but they would be hard pressed to defeat the magic of Gullanin the wizard. Gullanin had an arsenal of offensive and defensive spells that the priests would struggle to counter. But it wouldn't come to a fight, at least not yet. They still needed him.

Gullanin stepped forward and cleared his mind of all thoughts except for the spell that he prepared. The spell was tricky, and there was some danger in using it. He did not lie about that. Gullanin was a powerful wizard, perhaps the most powerful wizard in Kraawn, but much of the book was beyond his powers. Gullanin wished he had had more time to tap the power of the book, but he knew that the Dark One would know if he did, and he did not want to anger him. The book was his gift to his lord.

Gullanin, glancing down at the book, looked at the words one more time, and then he started the spell.

"Athwa Dubel Spudentay"

"Athwa Nostronus Siek"

"Tuatha Lan Andros Kiel"

Gullanin began to say the words louder, and with more force. It was not just the correct pronunciation that made the spell difficult, but he had to use the correct verbal intonation and syntax. The way he said the words, the tone, the pace, the volume, all of which had an effect on the outcome of the spell.

"Dumanostros Mandan'Roh Luthor!"

Raising both his hands towards the altar, he recited the final words. The three priests, who were unsure of what was going to happen, slowly backed away from the focused wizard.

"Vel'Roh Ock Canthree Gyndoe!"

And he finished with his lord's real name in elvish. The first words of magic originated with the elves millions of years ago and it was this language that tapped the true power of the Ru'Ach.

"Ell'eros Tyorthos!"

Instantly the flaming braziers in the room were extinguished followed by absolute silence.

All four of the men waited nervously until Janrick finally spoke. "What is happening?" he whispered, his tone strained from fear.

"I do not know. Now be silent and wait," Gullanin hissed back.

Then, within the ancient stones of the castle, a deep rumbling grew to a crescendo, sounding like a powerful earthquake. All four of the men put their hands to their ears to shut out the piercing noise. As the sound reached its pinnacle, there came a loud clap followed by a bright purple light at the ceiling, above the altar. The light was translucent and it spun clockwise, like a whirlpool.

"It is working!" yelled Gullanin. "I have opened up a gate to the Ru'Ach!" Gullanin unconsciously moved backwards until he and the priests were standing against the wall. As they bumped into the stone, a bolt of purple energy shot from the gate hitting the statue of Gould. The man strapped to the statue shook violently as the energy shot through him, his legs and arms convulsing, his back arching involuntarily. The bolt lanced through him for several seconds before it rescinded back into the gate which disappeared before the four men could blink.

It was deathly quiet and pitch black. They silently waited several seconds before Gullanin noticed a pair of red glowing orbs from across the room.

"Do you see those red dots?" whispered Kane. "What are they?"

"They are eyes," Gullanin quietly replied. As he said that, several more sets of red eyes appeared in five other spots around the room. Then it came to him.

"The black knights; they are awake," the wizard whispered excitedly.

"They are not the only thing that is awake!" a deep booming voice rang out from the darkness. Simultaneously the braziers came to life, spreading their orange glow over the contents of the room.

Standing before them was a tall muscled man, completely naked. It was the man from the statue, but he looked different. He was taller, a full head taller than a Gould-Irin orc, with a bluish tone to his skin. His face was still hard, but it had changed as well. His features were more pointed and angular, his ears almost elvish. His teeth came to razor sharp tips and his eyes were a translucent white. Short, choppy, jet black hair framed a chiseled, but demonic face. The man, if it was a man anymore, was flexing his arms and hands and looking at himself in wonder. His massive striated muscles grew in size as he flexed them.

Then he laughed. The sound was loud and gravelly and full of power. His laughter reverberated in the circular room like an echo. Instantly the four men fell to their knees and bowed.

Gullanin was the first to speak. "My Lord, welcome back to Kraawn."

One
The Meeting

Jonas stumbled down the town's main road, his awkward gait punctuated by the wooden crutch that Gorum the baker made him for his fourteenth birthday, one year ago. His twisted hands could barely hold onto the crutch and the stale loaf of bread that his mother sent him to fetch.

It was a good day for Jonas. The cold winter air and heavy snows kept most people in the warm confines of their homes, which meant there were few people on the street to stare at his crippled and misshapen body as he slowly ambled home.

It was cold, the mountain air freezing him to his bones, his old battered and threadbare clothing doing little to keep him warm. Despite it all, he felt happy. There were no appalling looks from the townspeople, and Jonas's stomach grumbled as he thought about the bread on their table tonight. It was indeed a good day.

Jonas was born a cripple. His bones never grew straight and he struggled to get his muscles to react to his commands. They always tightened up on him, causing him to spasm, twisting his legs and body into unnatural positions. Even his face would contort at times, making it difficult for him to talk. But his mind was sharp and his personality was uncharacteristically gentle and kind for someone in his position.

Despite his twisted and awkward body, his eyes sparkled with an inner light, and if anyone had bothered to stop long enough to talk to him, they would have noticed the intelligence and warmth hidden there. But few took the time to look past his frail and contorted form. Despite his obvious physical handicaps, Jonas's face was handsome with bright eyes and wavy dark brown hair.

Cripples were often abandoned and left to die. It was believed that the goddess of the hunt, Shyann, disapproved of the birth and left her mark upon the child. More often than not, crippled children were seen as a bad omen for the town and the family. In a mountain town like Manson, ones very survival teetered back and forth on the whims of winter storms, wild animals, and roaming monsters looking for their next meal. It was important for the townspeople to believe in something that offered strength and to offer disdain to those who brought weakness. Jonas understood, but it didn't make it any easier.

When Jonas was born, his father, Liam, a reputable hunter, trapper, and warrior, refused to accept the child into his home. His mother had saved his life that day which forever cast a shadow over his family name. She would not allow Liam to abandon him, protecting Jonas and forcing her husband to leave.

His father left the small mountain town of Manson, never to return. It was on that day that he and his mother became outcasts, shunned by most, tolerated by few. It was only the baker, Gorum, who treated them with any kindness. He often traded them old bread for some of his mother's wild onions or various other plants that she grew by their mountain cabin. Gorum became the only positive male figure in Jonas's life.

The sound of horse hooves crunching on the frozen ground brought Jonas from his thoughts. He looked toward the noise just as his crutch slid on the icy path, pitching him hard to the right, sending the stale loaf of bread into the air and cracking his head hard on the frozen ground.

Dazed, he slowly moved his twisted hands around for the crutch, hoping that the bread did not land in any slush or mud that covered the road.

"You okay, son?"

A deep concerned voice came from the road but Jonas couldn't turn his head in that direction until he found the crutch and lifted his tiny frame from the cold ground.

He felt strong hands lift him easily and hold his body upright. Jonas steadied his shaking body before studying the man closely.

He was tall, lean, with the look of a hawk, eyes that blazed with energy and a hooked nose that made him look regal and fierce at the same time. He had long dark flowing hair and his face was covered with the rough growth of a traveler who hadn't shaved in several days. But his hardness disappeared when he smiled warmly at Jonas.

He wore a silver shining breast plate and a wool traveling cloak hung down his back, draping his strong legs. Powerful shoulders were encased in polished steel and his arms and legs were also covered in plates of glittering metal. The man's feet were covered in thick leather riding boots capped with bright metal and everything seemed to sparkle with diamond brilliance. Although he was unshaven, the man was clean and his clothes and armor appeared brand new and of the highest quality, as if he had just purchased everything from a fine merchant's store. There was no sign of mud or dirt typical of a mountain traveler.

The steel breastplate he wore caught Jonas's eye for it was embossed with a silver symbol that looked like a four pointed star on top of a smaller circle. Under the amazing armor Jonas could make out the silvery metal edges of a chainmail shirt.

He looked back at the symbol in the middle of the man's chest for it seemed to draw his attention. It was simple but beautiful, the lines elegant and strong, each point of the star emerging from the circle. Jonas's wide eyes moved down to the man's belt where he wore a magnificent sword and a hunter's knife. The sword handle looked like it was made of a light wood or bone with silver wire adorning the handle. The pommel of the hunting knife was the same, an obvious mate to the sword.

Jonas looked into the piercing but warm eyes of the stranger, trying to smile back, but knowing that his action looked like a sneer, his muscles in his jaw not able to form to his wishes.

"Thank you, sir…..I slipped," Jonas said awkwardly, his deformed mouth making it hard to pronounce the words. Cold weather had an adverse effect on Jonas's ability to relax his muscles, making it more difficult than normal to talk and walk.

Jonas remembered his bread and looked around for it.

"Looking for this?" the man said as he held up the loaf of bread in his hand. "I caught it as you slipped".

Jonas noticed that the man's hands had two identical marks on the top of them, a circle with a four pointed star in the middle, the same mark that was on his polished cuirass.

The man noticed him staring. "Do you know what these are?" the man asked gently.

"No sir, I've never seen anything like them."

"Really," the man said, "do they not teach you about the gods here?"

"I'm sorry sir, I only know of our goddess, Shyann, the goddess of hunting and farming. I have heard my mother mention the High One, but I know little of him."

"Well, that's a start. What happened to you, boy, were you injured or born as a cripple?" the man asked kindly.

"I was born this way, sir. The gods did not want me," answered Jonas, his head hung low in shame.

The man knelt so that his face was close to Jonas's and held onto him with his strong callused hands.

"What is your name, boy?" the traveler asked gently.

"Jonas. Jonas Kanrene."

"Listen to me, Jonas. If the gods did not want you, then you wouldn't have been born and you would be dead already. Remember that. Do not let people's superstitious ideas cover your life with a black cloud. The gods have a plan for all of us, including you. Is it just your body that is afflicted?"

"I'm sorry, sir, what do you mean?" asked Jonas.

"I mean," said the man as he softly tapped Jonas's forehead, "is your head intact? Can you think, or did your brain get damaged along with your body?"

"My head is fine sir. My thoughts are clear, but talking is difficult because my muscles tighten around my face making it hard to move my mouth as I would wish."

"I see," the man said thoughtfully.

The warrior stood up and moved toward his horse, which was the most magnificent animal Jonas had ever seen. It was tall, strong, and its coat glistened as if it was recently cleaned and brushed. The horse's muscles rippled like an ocean's wave as the man leaped up gracefully onto its saddled back.

Jonas noticed a long black bow and quiver of arrows strapped to the side of the horse. He had never seen a more impressive bow. It was wrapped with silver wire and covered with intricate carvings. Everything on the horse shone with brilliance; every buckle, strap, and harness was immaculate. Jonas wondered how a traveler could keep himself and his steed so clean.

To Jonas, the warrior looked god-like sitting erect and strong on the massive back of his warhorse.

"My name is Airos. Remember what I said, Jonas. You are a good boy with a pure soul, for I can see into the hearts of men. It is very rare to lack the taint of evil, especially for one afflicted as you are. You should be proud of that."

Airos rode forward, brought his horse close to Jonas, and, leaning down, he handed Jonas something.

Jonas grabbed it awkwardly and looked at it. It was a shiny gold coin.

"Take that home to your mother. It was nice to meet you, Jonas," the man said with a smile.

"It was nice to meet you too, sir," Jonas murmured, a little stunned by the unique encounter and the heavy gold resting in his palm.

The man nodded his head in farewell, and gently touching his steed's flanks, they slowly trotted down the snow covered road.

Jonas looked at the heavy gold coin in his hand. He had never seen gold before, but he knew the shiny sparkle promised enough food for a month. Jonas forced his muscles into a smile. It was indeed a good day.

Jonas continued to walk down the town's main road toward the north gate. Though Manson was a small town, it did have an impressive log wall that guarded the villagers from the dangers of the Tundren Mountains.

As he patiently made his way to the north end of town, a snowball came out of nowhere hitting him square in the shoulder. Stumbling, he used his crutch to catch his fall. Jonas turned toward the direction the snowball came from only to catch another one in the face. The snowball was mostly ice and it stung fiercely as it struck him on the chin. His head jerked back and he was knocked to the ground. Jonas heard the laughter of boys as he struggled to get to his feet, the pain in his jaw causing his eyes to tear up. He fought back the tears, not willing to give the boys the satisfaction of making him cry.

"Look what we have here, the town's cripple!"

Jonas recognized the voice of the butcher's son, Wil. When he stood up he saw Wil and two other boys walking from a side alley.

Wil was Jonas's age, but much taller, with long black hair. Next to him was Filstar, but most people called him Fil. Fil was short and stocky of limb with curly locks of golden brown hair. Lastly, there was Kohl, the son of the town's mayor, and he was holding a snowball in his right hand. Kohl had a fat face, which matched his large round frame, a visual reminder that his family never went hungry.

"What's in your hand?" asked Kohl with scorn as they strode closer to him. Jonas unconsciously hid the loaf of bread behind his back as he awkwardly stood up.

"Nothing of your concern," Jonas replied. He was hoping that they would just leave him alone, but they seldom did. His real worry was that they would take the bread, or destroy it.

"Really?" Kohl replied. "Maybe we'll just beat you and take whatever you have. How does that sound?"

Jonas noticed that Fil was standing back from the other two boys. He had never had any problems with Fil and he hoped he wouldn't today.

Suddenly Jonas remembered the gold coin he had tucked into his pocket. Losing the bread would be bad, but losing the gold coin to these ruffians was something that Jonas couldn't let happen. Steadying himself he lifted his stout cane before him gritting his teeth in determination. "Don't come near me. I have done nothing to you. Just let me be on my way."

Wil and Kohl looked at each other and laughed. Fil stood back from the others, looking at Jonas with concern.

"What are you going to do with that?" asked Wil through his laughter.

Jonas knew he couldn't really do anything. Holding the stick before him was one thing, but swinging it with enough power to do any damage was another. So he changed tactics. "Do you really want a stale loaf of damp bread?" Jonas asked as he brought the bread from behind his back.

The boys laughed again. This time Fil stepped forward. "Let's go. Leave him alone," he said.

"Why? He's just a cripple," snarled Wil with obvious disgust.

"Which is why we should leave him be," responded Fil.

"You a cripple lover?" asked Kohl.

"No, I just have better things to do than threaten someone who can barely stand and defend himself. Let's go, we need to build the fires in the grange before your father has our hides."

Kohl looked at Jonas and then back at Fil. Finally his face relaxed, dropping the snowball. "You're right, let's go. He makes me sick just looking at him."

Jonas lowered his cane in relief. Wil gave him a disdainful look and pushed him hard as he walked by. Jonas slipped, again falling hard on the snow covered ground. Awkwardly he struggled to get up to defend himself. As he propped himself up on his elbow, he looked up and watched the boys walk off. Wil and Kohl were laughing loudly as Fil brought up the rear, looking back with a troubled glance.

Jonas brushed his wavy brown hair away from his face, slowly lifting himself to his feet. His jaw hurt but he still had his bread and gold coin. Smiling, he shook his head in disbelief. From his perspective, he was actually happy that he came out of that ordeal with just a bruise. It wasn't right, but it was his reality. His happiness was relative to how much pain and scorn he could avoid. Jonas tried to never pity himself, so he shook off the incident and continued his long journey home.

The mile walk to their cabin took Jonas over an hour. His weak frame and the heavy snow hindered his progress. The walk, however, always seemed to go by quickly for Jonas, for he spent his time within the safe confines of his own mind. He watched the birds flying gracefully through the air, and the deer jumping with such ease over the brambles, and wished that he could move like them. Sometimes he would get angry and curse the gods for what they did to him. Today however, he thought about what the man had said. Maybe the gods did have a plan for him, but what would they want with a cripple? Maybe it was a test, as his mother always told him. They would sit at their hearth at night and his mother would tell him that the gods were testing his strength and his resolve, and that if he met their expectations then when he died and went to the silver city of the High One, he would be rewarded with a strong body and a wonderful afterlife. He would be able to meet Shyann, their goddess, and she would show him a life of peace and wonder.

It was a wonderful thought, but it didn't always make his days in Manson any better. I have it better than some, he thought. I am alive, and that is something. I have a mother who loves me and we have a roof over our heads and we are not starving, although sometimes food is pretty scarce. It could be worse, Jonas thought as he emerged from the woods into the meadow that housed their little stone cabin his father built twenty years ago, before Jonas was born.

Suddenly Jonas stopped in mid-stride. Lying in the snow before him was the carcass of a large mountain elk, rare at these times since the snows usually pushed the animals to lower elevations to avoid the harsh winter conditions. A white feathered arrow protruded from the elk's side. The animal had been gutted recently and its innards lay in a steaming pile just to the side of the large beast. The blood was fresh and the animal was obviously still warm.

Suddenly Jonas felt a gentle breeze and then something cold pressed up against his throat as a powerful hand clamped around his mouth. A strong smell of wood fire and sweat washed over Jonas as he struggled in the iron grip. Jonas was shocked by the speed and stealth of the attack.

"You wouldn't be think n' of stealen me kill, would ya boy?" Jonas's assailant hissed in his ear. His breath stank of strong tobacco, similar to what Jonas had smelled from many of the men in town as they smoked their wood pipes. Jonas shook his head from side to side, his eyes wide with fright as the man's blade moved up closer to his left eye, allowing him a glimpse of the glimmering steel. "Are you that crippled boy, Jonas?" the man asked in his ear. The man's voice was soft and raspy but was filled with a quiet strength. Jonas nodded his head up and down in reply. Finally the man released his grip and Jonas turned around to face him.

Jonas recognized the man, for he had seen him several times in the past. He was called Tuvallus, but no one knew if that was his real name. The burly man was a hermit, a hunter and trapper who lived on his own deep in the mountains. He only came into town a few times a year to trade his dried meats and furs for supplies that he needed. He was always spoken of with a mixture of fear and awe, for people feared what they did not know and no one knew much about the strange trapper. But he always came into town with the most furs and meats to trade, a feat that was highly respected in the mountain town of Manson. He rarely spoke and many people thought he was crazy.

The man was tall and wide and he wore a coat of thick mountain wolf furs. His boots were made of leather and lined with similar fur. He needed no hat for his head was draped in a mass of long curly black hair and his face was covered with a thick beard and mustache. It looked as if his entire face was hair, except for two holes for his eyes and one for his mouth. Tuvallus carried a big hunting knife in his right hand and a longbow lashed to his back next to a quiver of arrows. Dangling from his side was a sword, its pommel wrapped in black leather and the cross piece was polished silver like his knife blade; both seemed to be in contrast to his dirty and wild appearance.

"My apologies, boy, thought you might be after me kill," Tuvallus said as he moved past Jonas and continued to dress the elk, cutting away skin and slicing off large pieces of flesh, which he laid out in the snow.

"Are you Tuvallus?" Jonas asked as he moved closer to him. The man simply grunted in response and continued to prepare his kill. "I have never seen a mountain elk this time of year," Jonas commented as he watched the trapper expertly slice into the warm red flesh.

Tuvallus did not respond as he continued to lay out strips of elk meat.

"How did you sneak up on me in this snow? I did not hear a sound until I felt your knife," Jonas said as the man continued to ignore him.

Jonas waited for a response while the trapper worked on the dead elk. Finally Jonas shrugged his shoulders and turned to walk away. His cabin was not too far off; he could see the smoke rising from the chimney into the frigid mountain air. He walked a few paces before turning back to Tuvallus.

"Sir, my mother has a warm fire and she is sure to have some rabbit stew boiling. Would you like to step out of the cold for a while and warm your belly with the best rabbit stew you've ever eaten?"

Tuvallus finally stopped and looked up from the dead elk. His face was completely covered with hair so Jonas could not read his expression. After a few moments of silence he spoke.

"You be invit n' me to ur cabin? A man you don't know, who just put a blade to ur throat?"

"Umm…yes. We don't have lots of food, but it is very good. I can assure you of that," replied Jonas confidently.

Tuvallus shook his head grunting and went back to dressing the elk. Jonas shrugged again and turned back around. He walked a few more paces before Tuvallus called to him.

"Hey, boy!"

Jonas turned around to face the trapper.

"Bring this to your mother," Tuvallus said, tossing a large piece of elk meat toward Jonas. The bloody meat landed in the snow at his feet and Jonas picked it up with a smile. It was wet with blood and still a little warm. Jonas had never had elk meat but he had heard it was the best.

"Thank you, Tuvallus," Jonas said excitedly.

Tuvallus simply grunted and went back to work.

Jonas put the piece of elk meat into the cloth satchel he carried on his back. He had to take out the loaf of bread so the blood from the meat wouldn't spoil it. That was okay though; he could carry the loaf in one hand and still use his crutch since their cabin was so close. Jonas turned around and walked toward his cabin. He smiled, for he had two gifts to give his mother on this day.

Jonas set his crutch down, his hand awkwardly freeing the door latch. The door swung open and the warm air from within covered him like the summer sun.

Lorna, his mother, was adding some spices to their stew that was boiling in a heavy black cauldron hanging over the fire. She was a strong woman with a beautiful face despite the slight wrinkling caused by many years of hard work in the sun. She wore her long dirty blonde hair pulled back and tied with a piece of leather. She had seen over forty hard winters, many of which were laced with bitterness and scorn from her town, but she was content with her life and she smiled often, which lit up her face and made Jonas feel safe.

"Jonas, it's about time," his mother said thankfully. "I was beginning to worry about you."

"I'm fine, Mother. You know it takes me a while to walk back home." He plopped his tired body on the wooden chair that his mother had made him. The seat cushions were made of many rabbit hides stitched together and stuffed with straw. It was very comfortable and Jonas loved to rest in it before the crackling fire.

"Here is the loaf. Gorum said he would love some of your dried rosemary as payment. He said to bring it by tomorrow if you have any and he will get us another one." Jonas handed the hard loaf to his mother and she moved to the wooden cutting board on their table.

"Thanks, Sprout. We'll go into town tomorrow," his mother replied as she cut several large slices from the loaf.

Jonas smiled at the nickname. He always loved how his mother did not focus on his disability; she always tried to treat him as a normal boy, including him in everything that she did. She would wait patiently for him as they picked berries in the forest, tended their garden, or set their rabbit traps. They were all each other had and he loved her dearly. Jonas smiled excitedly as he pulled out the slab of meat from his satchel.

"Mother, look at what I have."

Lorna turned from the loaf of bread to look at the piece of meat Jonas had in his lap. "What is that?" she asked curiously.

"It is elk. I met Tuvallus the hermit on the path here and he gave me a slice of his kill to give to you," Jonas said with a broad grin.

Lorna moved towards Jonas with a beaming smile. "Really? Tuvallus gave you that?" she asked as she took the meat from Jonas.

"He did. I have never had elk meat before. Can we cook some tonight?"

Lorna smiled at Jonas as she put the piece of meat on the table. "Yes, we can have a little tonight with our stew. I'll dry and smoke the rest. This is a great gift, Jonas. I hope you thanked him," she replied as she cut off a few slices of the meat.

"I did. I invited him home to eat with us, but he didn't want to come. Mother, do you know anything about Tuvallus?"

"Not really. People in town say he used to be a soldier in Tarsis. He keeps to himself and not much is known about him," Lorna said as she continued to prepare dinner.

Jonas thought about Tuvallus, the heat from the dancing flames stroking his tired muscles, easing his thoughts as he processed his interesting day.

They sat at their old wooden table eating the rabbit stew and bread. Lorna had fried the elk with salt and onions and it was delicious, the most incredible food he had ever eaten. It was soft, full of flavor, and it didn't have the strong gamey flavor that he was used to in venison. Jonas held his spoon between his thumb and palm; his other fingers didn't usually work well enough to grasp the spoon handle.

"I met a stranger in town today," Jonas said through a mouthful of stew soaked bread.

His mother looked up startled, for it was not common to have strangers enter the mountain town of Manson during the winter. The passes would be snowed in and only the hardiest of men could traverse them.

"What did he want?" she asked concerned.

"Oh nothing, he just wanted to give me this," Jonas said as he brought his hand down on the table and removed it quickly, leaving the gold coin spinning around like a top. It was pure luck that the coin was spinning, as he didn't have the dexterity to do it on purpose. But the effect was dazzling as the coin spun, catching the subtle light in a beautiful dance of brilliant gold.

Jonas smiled as his mom put her hand to her mouth in shock. She quickly reached out and grabbed the sparkling coin, inspecting it closely.

"Where did you get this?" she asked with astonishment.

"I told you, a stranger with paintings on his hands helped me up when I fell. We talked a little and then he handed me this coin and told me to give it to my mother. He was so kind, and he had a sword and bow, and the most magnificent horse I've ever seen," Jonas said excitedly.

"Paintings on his hands? What do you mean?" she asked.

Jonas explained to her the marks on his hands and the symbol on his steel cuirass. Lorna's face lit up in amazement.

"He was a cavalier. I can't believe it. I've heard of them but I've never seen one," she said to herself. "Did he give you his name?"

Jonas looked up as he stuffed another spoonful into his mouth, "Yes, he said his name was Airos. What's a cavalier?"

Lorna looked at Jonas with a huge smile on her face. "This gold coin can feed us well for a month. We'll be able to get through the end of winter with warm food and full stomachs. This is a fortune, son, I can't believe our luck."

"I know, Mother," Jonas said impatiently, "but what is a cavalier? He looked like a warrior."

"I only know what your father told me many years ago. He said he saw a cavalier once in Finarth and they are warriors chosen by the gods to protect and serve the weak, and to serve the greater good of mankind. They are very rare and known to have special powers. The marks on his hands meant that he was a master swordsman sworn to uphold the High One's word. The symbol of the High One is a four pointed star over a circle. Each point of the star represents all four elements; earth, air, water, and fire." His mom paused to look at the gold coin in her hand. "Who you saw was a great warrior, God Marked, and you should consider yourself very lucky to have met him." She looked again at the coin, smiling. "Actually, we should both be thankful that you met him," she said, laughing with happiness.

Jonas, smiling at his mother, happy in her joy, continued to eat his soup, thoughts of the day's events running through his head. "Mother, does the High One have a name? You've never talked about him much."

Lorna got up, hiding the coin in their secret spot under a floor board. "Yes, the High One is called many names throughout Kraawn. But you should not use any of them lightly," she said as she sat back down at the table. "I only know several of his names; we call him Ulren, but I know that in the West he is called Toolm. It is believed that our goddess, Shyann, has a palace in his realm."

"So Ulren is the most powerful of the good gods?"

"Yes. It is believed that the lesser gods all have a place at his great hearth," Lorna said as she ate.

"Is our goddess, Shyann, a lesser god?"

"Shyann is a saint. That means that many, many years ago she was just a normal person like you and me, but she performed a great feat of selflessness and bravery, catching the High One's attention. Ulren rewarded her by granting her sainthood, power, and a place at his hearth."

"What did she do that made her a saint?" Jonas asked before he took a long drink of water.

"I don't know exactly. The tales say she took a small village, like our own, and fought back against an army of boargs, orcs, and other monsters."

"What do boargs look like?"

Lorna smiled, Jonas loved hearing about boargs. "Boargs are strong, fast beasts that inhabit the high Tundren Mountains. It is thought by some that they are related to the big mountain boars that live there. Some think they are the result of a wizard's magic, but no one knows for sure. They have pig like faces with tusks like a boar, sharp teeth, and two great horns that protrude from their bony heads. They are taller than a big man, but they look shorter because they are bent over and their long arms usually rest on the ground. Short, rough hair, covers their muscular bodies, and they are said to be stronger than several men. And I've heard they run on all fours and are swifter than deer. They are ferocious animals that will eat anything they can get their claws on."

"When was a boarg last seen around here?" Jonas asked, never short of questions.

"The last one I can remember was when you were just a baby. Jornath Longhorn went hunting and he never came back. His brothers went out into the Tundrens to investigate and found his ripped and torn body. As they wept over his body, a boarg who was coming back to finish its meal attacked them. Braal, the bigger of the two eventually killed the boarg, but not before he was seriously wounded and his other brother was killed. Braal still has the boarg's skull mounted in his home."

"I hope a boarg never shows up at our cabin. Keep going, Mother, tell me about Shyann," Jonas said excitedly.

Lorna, smiling at her son, drank some more water. "She was just a normal girl that went off to become a soldier, which was rare for a female in these parts. She fought many battles and finally came home to serve her family on their little farm in the Tundrens, not far from here I've heard. I guess they raised cattle and hunted and grew food that they sold in the local markets. There came a year when her village and the other villages nearby were raided by boargs crossing the mountain ranges towards Finarth. This was one of the great wars that you've heard about."

"Yes, I remember. Go on, Mother, what happened?"

"I don't know the details, but the story goes that she trained and united the many mountain towns all across the Tundrens and fought back this horde. Evil men who were trying to unite with the forces of Malbeck led the boarg army and she crushed them, marching her ill-equipped group of hunters, farmers, and herders, to help Finarth combat this evil. I have no idea how she did it, but the stories and songs say that she could inspire anyone. She was good with a sword but her real skill was convincing ordinary men and women that they had something to offer, that their blood was just as strong as another's." Lorna took another spoonful of soup and smiled at her son who had stopped eating altogether, entranced by her story. "I've told you this story before, Sprout," Lorna said as she swallowed her stew.

"I know, Mother. I just really like it. Keep going, please".

"Well, all I really know is that after the forces of Malbeck were destroyed, the king of Finarth knighted her. Then one day, when she was traveling back home to her village, tragedy happened. Her small army was camping deep in the Tundrens and boargs ambushed them in the middle of the night. Shyann's forces defeated them but the cost was great. In the battle, Shyann was mortally wounded. She lay in her tent dying, her men trying everything they could to save her. The next morning when the surgeon came in to check on her, her body was missing. There was nothing in her bed, no body, no clothes, just her sword, bow, and her shield. But the strangest thing about the legend was that in the middle of the tent, a stout oak tree, no more than five feet tall, appeared, and as they cleared the camp and set for home, the men noticed the tree had grown. It grew to the height of ten men with great limbs reaching out towards the sun's rays."

"Is that why one of her symbols is the great oak?"

"Yes, it is," Lorna said as she added more water to their cups from the clay pitcher on the table.

"Where is the tree now?" asked Jonas

"No one knows, but some people think that her tree is somewhere in the Tundrens and her tomb is located there, or maybe it is just a story and it doesn't exist at all. Now finish eating and get some sleep. We have to head into town tomorrow early."

"Okay, Mother," Jonas said, stuffing his mouth with more stew, thinking about the next month without the usual trepidation. The gold would buy meat and other things that would make the last winter months bearable.

***

The morning came quickly. It seemed to Jonas that he had just put his head down to sleep when his mother woke him gently. The aroma of her herbal tea was a sweet comfort that greeted him every morning. She swore that her recipe kept them from getting sick during the winter months. Jonas loved her tea. It warmed and invigorated him after drinking it. Jonas was excited as he drank the tea, knowing that he would need the energy for the walk into town that his mother and he had planned last night over dinner.

The morning was cold, and the harsh mountain air poked and prodded their skin through the gaps in their clothing. The night's new snows made it harder than expected for Jonas to make the mile long walk into town. The heavy, wet snow, grabbed at his feet and crutch, making the walk more difficult.

Finally, after an hour and a half of walking, they entered through the town's main gate. The town was surrounded by a sturdy wall of tall thick logs lashed together and stuck four feet into the ground. The stout gate was built of oak and bound together with bands of black iron. It was open during the day but at night it was shut to keep out the wild animals, and any roaming monsters or boargs. It was rare, but on occasion a hunter would return with stories of mountain ogres, hill giants, and other wild creatures.

Normally, at this time in the morning, the town would just be awakening, but today, the town was already a bustle of activity. The rich smells of Gorum's fresh baked bread and freshly lit hearths wafted down the street as Jonas and Lorna made their way across town. Lorna reached over and held Jonas close to her as the townspeople hurried towards the grange, where they often had town meetings. Several children that Jonas recognized stood by the butcher's shop staring wide eyed at the people moving toward the grange. The feeling in the air was tense; something was wrong.

The butcher's son, Wil, stood against the wall with his two friends, Fil, and Fil's younger brother, Colsen. Jonas stood behind his mother, not wanting the boys to see him and pepper him with their endless barrage of insults.

"What is happening, Wil?" asked his mother.

Wil looked at her with malice. "My father said not to speak with you…that it would bring us bad luck".

"Your father is ignorant and a drunk, now tell me what is happening," Lorna demanded.

Wil was just about to retort when Fil interrupted him. "A cavalier came into town last night and he has called a meeting this morning. He said it was urgent…that the town is in danger," Fil said, barely able to hide his excitement, and fear.

Jonas had always liked Fil more than the rest, and after the previous day's occurrence his respect for him grew. When the kids would yell at him he always noticed that Fil didn't participate, that he just stared at Jonas with pity, the same look that Fil gave Jonas the day before as they left Jonas sprawled out on the frozen ground.

Jonas leaned out from behind his mother. "Was he tall, with long black hair and did he go by the name of Airos?" Jonas asked.

"He did. How did you know that, Jonas?" Fil asked.

Jonas smiled. "I met him yesterday. He gave me a gold coin."

His mother squeezed his arm gently. "That's enough Jonas. Let's see what this cavalier has to say."

His mother gently helped Jonas walk down the street toward the grange. The grange was a great vaulted structure built with strong trees each as big around as a man's waist. It was a large, simple building, big enough to sit at least a hundred people. There was a wooden stage facing rows of benches flanked by two great stone fireplaces with chimneys that rose to the ceiling twenty paces from the floor. Lorna and Jonas entered through the large double doors. The fires were blazing, casting an orange glow flickering across the room.

Airos stood on the stage addressing the confused and frightened townspeople. He was splendid in his shining armor and he had replaced his wool traveling cloak with a long green flowing cape. The cape was made from a light material that seemed to flutter around him as he moved.

Jonas wondered again how he kept so clean, but his thought was cut short as a rough hand reached out and grabbed Lorna by the arm. It was the butcher, Marsk.

"You are not wanted here. Get out and take your cripple with you," the heavy set butcher whispered.

There were a few other people near them that joined in, whispering in fear for them to leave, and glancing at them with frowns.

Lorna held her ground, looking directly into the fat man's eyes. "I have as much right to be here as you do. I am a member of this town whether….."

Lorna was cut off as Marsk grabbed her arm tightly pulling her roughly towards him. "You have no right to be here, now get out," he said, pushing her and causing her to stumble backwards.

Jonas tried to move out of his mother's way but his body refused to react quickly enough. Lorna crashed into him and they tumbled to the floor. Several other townspeople began to taunt them, whispering curses and shooting them shunning stares as Jonas fumbled for his crutch.

Suddenly the entire room lit up with a bright light, and their voices hushed instantly. The light was pure white, and as it washed over everyone the feeling of tension subsided. Though the light was almost blinding, it caused them no harm. Quite the opposite; Jonas felt invigorated and happy as he slowly stood up, the insults becoming an increasingly distant memory. Everyone looked up; the light slowly dissipating from Airos's outstretched hands. To Jonas's eyes it looked like the light just drained into his body.

Airos looked directly at Jonas and his mother as they slowly stood. Jonas saw a hint of a smile before he turned his gaze on Marsk and several others. The change in his expression was so severe that Jonas thought he would draw his sword and strike Marsk down where he stood. Airos's hawk-like eyes pierced Marsk's tough façade, forcing him to look away.

"What is the meaning of this? Is not a woman and her boy welcome in the town's hall?" Airos asked; his voice strong and demanding. Something in the powerful voice stirred Jonas to his core. He felt like he would follow this man to his grave and back. The white light was definitely magic and Jonas thought that maybe Airos was using magic in his voice as well. Having never experienced magic before, he just stared at Airos with awe, his every word reverberating through the hall like a god's voice. Maybe it was a god's voice thought Jonas.

The others felt it too. His voice was magical and commanding and everyone looked directly at him as if in a trance. Airos looked around the room slowly. "What kind of village is this that turns its back on its own townspeople? This boy is a cripple. The gods willed it so, for reasons we know not. Who are any of you to question their will?"

No one said a word as Airos scanned the crowd before finally directing his gaze to Marsk, the butcher. "The poor and the weak should be protected, or we become nothing more than the evil that threatens this town. Am I understood, butcher?"

Marsk, his eyes showing his nervousness, scanned the room. He turned back to Airos trying to match his stare, but to no avail. Marsk, lowering his eyes said, "Yes sir. You are quite right."

"It is not I who am right, but the High One. I am his voice and that is why I am here. Men and women of Manson, listen closely to what I have to say for I am a cavalier of Ulren, the High One. I am his warrior and I fight to protect the righteous and the good of the lands. Airos drew forth his sword with one smooth motion and held it high in the air, the silver blade glowing green and humming as if alive. The crowd was deathly silent as they listened. "I fight the vile darkness spreading through the lands like a plague. I fight this evil on Ulren's demands. He has directed me here, to your hardy mountain town." Airos stopped and sheathed his sword.

Jonas grabbed his mother's hand tightly as Airos's gaze moved over him like a searchlight.

"A small army of boargs approaches your town even as we speak," Airos said bluntly.

The townspeople erupted with frightened responses to this grave news. Jonas felt his mother squeeze his hand tightly as she pulled him closer. *Boargs*, thought Jonas, *what would happen to the town? What would happen to those like him and his mother who couldn't run or fight?* The questions rolled around in his mind.

Airos's powerful voice rang through the hall again, quieting the townspeople. "That is not all. This force is led by a Banthra."

The shock of this news hit the townspeople like a hammer. They all stood speechless, wondering if they heard Airos correctly.

Marsk reacted first.

"Sir…a Banthra?" he asked. "I have only heard of the legends. I thought the Banthras disappeared with Malbeck during the last Great War."

"So we all thought. It seems that the Banthras are back, but we are not sure why. Over the last five years there have been signs of a blackness rising up again throughout Kraawn. There have been mysterious disappearances, animals migrating and leaving the forests, vile monsters crawling from their caves and killing ruthlessly. I have felt it, and even fought it in some cases. The land is being poisoned again by this vileness. This Banthra is yet another sign that evil is stirring again".

Gorum the baker stood up from his bench to address Airos. "Sir, my name is Gorum. Why would a Banthra and an army of boargs be heading to our small town? It makes no sense."

Airos looked at the baker for a few seconds before answering. Gorum looked around, uncertain of the cavalier's stare. Finally Airos smiled and responded. "Ah, good baker, that is a fine question and one for which I have no answer, for I know not why this force threatens your town." Airos paused and looked at the nervous gathering before him. "My guess is that the Banthra is amassing a small army of boargs and that they are moving through the mountain passes to get to the east."

Braal, the only man in Manson who had fought a boarg, stood up. He was thick and powerfully built, his tan face reflecting many years of trapping the harsh lands that surrounded their small town. "Sir, the mountain passes are miles from here. They could just move through them unnoticed. Why go out of their way to come to our town?" Braal asked.

Airos looked at Braal with his intense blue eyes. "You are Braal," Airos said knowingly.

"Yes, sir, I am."

"You of all people can answer that question. That day, many years ago, when you found the body of your brother? Why did the boarg attack you and your brother when you arrived at the corpse?"

"How do you know about that day?" Braal asked uneasily.

"I know about many things. Tell me."

Braal looked at his fellow townspeople. "The boarg was protecting its kill. It was feeding," he said softly, not wanting to bring up the painful memory of that horrible day many years ago.

"That is correct. I believe the Banthra is moving his force to this town so he can feed his army before moving east. You are faced with a dire threat, good people. Your options are few and only the strongest of you can make it through the mountain passes. That means you cannot run."

Jonas's mother spoke up for the first time.

"What are we to do, sir?" Lorna asked with concern, her hand gripping Jonas's in fear.

Airos looked at her, his eyes ablaze with fire, and said two frightening words. "We fight!"

Two
Manson Fights

The town bustled with activity; men strengthened the walls, women and children gathered food stores. Kiltharin, the blacksmith, sharpened axes, swords, scythes and any other tools that could be used as a weapon. Families living on the outskirts of town moved loved ones into the interior. Some built makeshift sleeping barracks in the town's grange, while still others stayed with friends in their cramped little homes.

Gorum offered his small home to Jonas and his mother. Jonas noticed a few stares as they slowly carried their meager belongings into Gorum's home, but not like before. It seemed to Jonas that Airos's words had affected the townspeople's feelings toward him and his mother. Everyone was too scared and busy to worry about a cripple and his mother anyway. They just wanted to survive.

The little home was cozy, clean, and smelled of baked bread. Gorum's bakery was connected to the house through a door in the back. His massive clay and stone oven, built by his father who passed all his skills to Gorum many years ago, took up most of the work shop. The little house had one room with a connected bedroom. Gorum graciously offered them the bedroom which they accepted gratefully.

Jonas stood in the main room looking up at a large old sword hanging above the hearth. The blade was pitted and marked from many battles, and the leather handle was worn and frayed.

"It's seen better days, that's for sure."

Jonas turned toward the voice of Gorum as the baker approached him. Gorum was a big man, round in the face and belly, but strong too, like a sturdy oak.

"That was my father's sword," Gorum continued. "I've never really used it myself, although my father taught me how."

"It looks very old. Is it still sharp?" Jonas asked.

"It soon will be." The dancing flames casted an orange glow throughout the room as Gorum took down the heavy sword. "I guess I need to get this cleaned up," he said as he moved toward the table.

"Are you afraid?" Jonas asked seriously.

Gorum sat down on one of his wooden chairs, the sword resting on his legs. "I am, Jonas," he said. "I am a baker, not a fighter. I would be frightened to fight a man, but the idea of facing a boarg terrifies me." Gorum took up a stone; dipping it in water he began to wipe the stone across the edge of the blade with one long smooth motion. The grating sound of the stone on steel seemed to hypnotize Jonas for a moment. "But we do not have a choice, Jonas. We cannot run. We cannot hide. There is nothing for us to do but fight and hope that the gods will protect us."

"Why would the gods allow the boargs to attack us in the first place? We have done nothing wrong," Jonas asked.

"A good question," Gorum laughed lightly, "but I have never understood the ways of the gods, so it may be hard for me to answer. But I will say this. There is always a balance in the world, Jonas. There is good and there is evil. They both weigh the scale up and down from time to time, but in the end there must be a balance. One without the other would cancel their own existence."

"So you're saying that for good to exist, there must also be evil?"

"I do not pretend to know. But I think it would be hard to define goodness if there were no evil to compare it to," Gorum remarked as he continued to hone the edge of his old sword.

Jonas contemplated the baker's words for a moment before he spoke. "I wish I could fight. I'd stand my ground right next to you, and I would weigh the scale in the right direction."

Gorum looked up at him, smiling, "I believe you would, Jonas. Have you ever heard how Malbeck the Dark One was destroyed?"

"No sir. I do not know much about the Dark One. Can you tell me?" Jonas asked with nervous excitement.

"I only know a little of the tale. The ancient king of Finarth, King Ullis Gavinsteal, defeated him in battle. It is told by traveling bards that the king's armor and sword were enchanted for the very purpose of slaying the Dark One. I've heard several different tales, one of which told that those weapons may have been created by the most powerful elven ekahals for that purpose."

"What is an ekahal?"

"Ekahals are elvish wizards. They are very powerful. When King Ullis killed the Dark One, there was nothing left except a burnt and decimated battle field, no king, armor, sword…nothing."

"What happened to the king and his armor?" asked Jonas leaning forward eagerly.

"No one knows. It is a mystery. Some say that the elves hid the armor and sword, but no one knows for sure." Gorum read Jonas's eager expression and changed his tone. "Remember, son, when the fighting starts I want you to hide. If we are defeated, they will not stay long. They will kill, feed, and then be on their way. There is a good chance that you will survive if you stay hidden. Do you understand?"

"Yes sir. But I still wish I could fight with the rest of you."

"There will be no fighting for you young man," Lorna said, entering the room from the bedroom. The tension of their situation was evident on her face. Her eyes were swollen from crying and she was visibly distraught. Lorna squatted on her knees in front of Jonas and held him at arm's length. "Now listen, son. I want you to do exactly what Gorum has said. You must hide and stay hidden. Do not make a noise until the fighting is over."

"But…"

"You will obey me," she said, ending the conversation. "Gorum, do you have a suitable hiding spot for my son?"

"Don't you want to put him with the rest of the children and elders in the grange?" Gorum asked.

"No, I want him near me and I do not trust how they would treat him."

Gorum nodded knowingly. "I have a place." Gorum stopped sharpening the old blade, setting the sword on the heavy oak table next to him. "But it will be dark and dirty," Gorum replied as he stood. "When the fire is not lit in my clay oven, there is a spot inside where a child could hide safely. It will be full of soot, but that may actually help conceal him and disguise his smell."

They all walked through the back door and into his bakery. The large oven was just to their right, the heat from the clay warming them as they neared it. Gorum opened the iron door and dampened the fire.

"I'll put the fire out now so it has time to cool down. When the fighting starts, that's where we'll put him."

"What about you, Mother? Where will you be?" asked Jonas. The thought of hiding in that dark and dirty hole terrified him. But the thought of being separated from his mother was even worse.

"I will be here, helping where I may. Don't worry son, I will be right here with you the whole time. I would never leave you," Lorna said, another tear dripping slowly down her cheek.

***

Airos checked the gate one more time, making sure the solid oak bar was firmly in place. Satisfied, he moved along the northern wall, reassuring the men as he went. He was wearing his shiny silver breastplate with the High One's symbol embossed on the chest. He wore matching greaves and forearm guards, both covered with intricate runes and symbols. His armor was polished so brightly, that, like a mirror, it reflected everything that was near. A beautifully crafted long bow was strapped to his back and his sword swung gently at his side. All the men looked at him in awe as he passed them, reassuring them with a pat on the back, a smile, and his very presence. He seemed to suck the tension out of the very air and replace it with calm determination.

Airos knew the attack would come tonight; he could feel it. That was one of his many abilities, being able to detect evil, to feel it as it drifted through the air like a poisonous mist. Airos was not afraid, for death had no hold on him. He had given up his own personal desires many years ago to serve a greater good, to serve the High One who had picked him as one of His warriors. And he had served Him well. He would live or die in His service, holding no regrets. He could wield magic and heal the wounded and sick. He could bring forth God Fire at will, an ability reserved to first rank cavaliers, the highest ranking among them. Airos was an expert swordsman and archer; in fact he had never met his equal with a blade.

No, he was not afraid. But he felt a bit of unease, like he was missing something. The question that Braal had asked in the grange hounded him. Why would they attack this town? Was it really to feed? Or was there another purpose?

He continued to ponder his discomfort, checking the southern wall of the town. All able-bodied men, women, and even children, were preparing themselves for the attack. He could see in their eyes that they were frightened, but he could do nothing but give them hope by his presence.

Why would a Banthra be leading the boargs? It makes no sense, he thought. As far as he knew there were only a handful of Banthras that ever walked the lands of Kraawn. Why would they be back? Why would a Banthra be in the mountains to gather a small army of boargs? Surely a lesser minion could handle that job.

One of the few things that gave Airos pause was a Banthra. Banthras were fallen cavaliers, cavaliers who were captured by Malbeck and twisted into his servants many years ago. It was thought that they had all disappeared when Malbeck was defeated, but they had reappeared with dire consequences for Kraawn. Reports of orcs, goblins, trolls, and other monsters, moving from the Black Lands and the Mazgar Forest, have been whispered from city to city all the way to Annure. Evil was definitely growing in the northeast near Banrith, Malbeck's old stronghold.

Traveling bards tell stories of the great wars, over a thousand years ago, when Malbeck had captured six cavaliers. He tortured their minds and bodies until there was nothing of the original warriors left. Airos hoped that the High One had protected their souls; he had to believe that He did, for he had faith in Ulren. Nonetheless Malbeck used magic to twist their minds and bodies into demon-spawn. After many years of this torture the six cavaliers became the black knights of Malbeck. They had the power of a cavalier, but their magic came from the black gods that constantly try to possess the hearts of men. It was not an easy task to create these powerful warriors, but Malbeck was a follower of the Forsworn, the three evil gods of Kraawn, and they had given him great power so that he might rule Kraawn in their name.

These gods represent the dark side of existence. There is Gould, the Tormentor, high evil god of lies, anger, jealousy, and power. Naz-reen is goddess of the dark, stealth, plot, and murder. Then there is Dykreel the Slayer, god of torture and pain. They are the Forsworn, the topic of bedtime stories told by parents to frighten children into being good. But they are no mere story; they are real, and Airos fought their power daily. There was a constant struggle between the good and evil gods of Kraawn, and it was Airos's job to wield his sword in defiance of the evil that would otherwise permeate the lands around him.

Again, the question rolled around in Airos's head, why a Banthra? Why would it come here? He must be missing something.

Suddenly both his hands began to tingle. He pulled off his gauntlets and looked down at the familiar blue glow emanating from both the symbols. The men standing around him looked at his hands, with eyes that revealed their fear.

Braal was among the men nearby and he moved closer to Airos, a large battle axe resting over one thick shoulder. "Is it time?" he asked sternly.

"Yes," Airos said, quickly putting his gauntlets back on and drawing his sword. "Braal, I want you to hold the south wall as we discussed. You must maintain your lines. If you don't hold them off then they will converge on us from both sides. They will breach the wall; there is nothing we can do about that. When they do, and you can no longer hold them off, regroup with my force by the north wall. Our only hope is to stay together. If our forces get spread out then we will be picked off like wounded deer. Do not try to attack the Banthra. No one can defeat him but me. I will sense his presence and hunt him down wherever he goes. If I can kill the Banthra then we may have a chance."

"Yes sir," Braal said, quickly moving off towards the south wall, his men unsheathing their weapons and following on his heels.

This is a hardy group of men, thought Airos, tough mountain men who grew up fighting and surviving, but would it be enough? Airos erased the thought from his mind as his horse galloped towards him, nudging him with her nose. She, like Airos, could sense the approaching evil. His magical steed never ceased to amaze him. Suatha had appeared to Airos on the day that he passed his final trial. She was a magnificent steed that had saved his life many times, for she, like the cavalier, had been given the gift of magic. Suatha could run all day and never tire. She was faster and stronger than any horse and she could sense her rider's thoughts and movements. She would not be swayed by magical fear and together they were a powerful team.

Airos smoothly leaped onto Suatha's back, grabbing the reins and spurring her towards the northern wall. He could feel the energy that came before battle start to rise within him as he neared the gate. The magic in his veins pulsed with power and he smiled inwardly, reveling in the adrenaline rush that always took hold of his body every time he was about to go into battle.

As he rode through the gathering men he yelled, "Our enemy is near! Gather your weapons and take your positions!"

The men, women, and children that had weapons all ran quickly, taking up the positions they had hastily worked out earlier. Airos gathered the townspeople in two lines facing the northern wall and the gate. One line was held back as reserves while the front line carried all the longer weapons they could find or build, pikes, spears, javelins, anything to keep the enemy at arm's length.

Airos rode his horse back and forth before the lines hoping to give them some sense of hope. Everyone was deathly silent. Airos knew that the townsfolk were frightened, and that their fear was paralyzing them now. He had to give them some hope, some belief that they could defeat this threat. Turning his horse to face the men, he held his blade up high, letting the magic flow from his body and into his sword. The god given weapon lit up like a beacon, the magic light piercing the blackness, pushing back the sinking feeling of doom. Airos's voice, lifted by magic, hit everyone like a thunderclap.

"People of Manson, soon these very walls will be climbing with evil and vile creatures that want you dead, that want your children dead! We are here to turn back this pestilence, to protect your homes and families!" His voice and the magic light eased their fears instantly. They all stood up straight and held their weapons before them with new vigor. "I am a cavalier! I am here to fight next to you. To die next to you if that is my purpose! You have the strength to defeat them. I know this; I can see it in your eyes and in your hearts! Fight with me, fight for your life, fight for your homes, fight for your families!" Airos yelled as he turned his horse toward the gate. The large bonfires that had been lit earlier shed a bright light on the entire expanse of the town's walls.

As if on cue, the gate wall began to shake suddenly, and a large gray form pulled itself onto the top of the wooden structure. The boarg squatted in perfect balance on top of the gate, its huge form rippling with muscles as it held itself erect. Two thick, curved horns, sprouted from the sides of its bulky boar-like head. The beast crouched like a cat, its long powerful arms holding its body on top of the wall. The boarg bellowed a defiant roar, exposing long tusks and yellow fangs.

Airos sheathed his sword, grabbed the bow at his side with lightning speed, and had three arrows whistling across the expanse in the blink of an eye. The first arrow struck the boarg's open mouth, while the other two hammered into its neck with enough force to launch the animal off the gate and into the darkness.

Screams erupted in the night from the southern wall as the gate in front of him again shook violently. It has begun, thought Airos, notching another arrow as he waited for his next target.

***

The blood chilling roar jerked Jonas from his trance as he stared into the burning fire. He looked up as the big form of Gorum quickly ran into the room from the bakery.

"Jonas, it is time. I need to get you in the oven." Gorum quickly swept up Jonas's light body as if it were a baby and hurried him into the bakery. His mother was there with a wool sack in her hand, her face streaked with new tears. She bent down and hugged Jonas tightly, her fresh tears wetting the side of his face.

Lorna finally stopped hugging Jonas, holding him at arm's length. "Now listen to me, son. In the sack are food, a knife, and all the money we have including the gold coin. I want you to stay in the oven until either Gorum or I come for you. If neither of us come for you then stay in there until the morning at least."

"Mother, where will you be?" Jonas asked frightened. More screams tore through the night as the attack on the town commenced.

"I will be right here, I promise," she replied frantically.

"I'm scared for you," Jonas muttered.

"I will be fine, now quickly, get in the hole," she said, stroking his face one last time.

Gorum lifted Jonas's tiny form, slowly sliding him into the dark oven. "Remember what I said, Jonas. Stay in the oven, no matter what you hear outside. Do not come out," Gorum repeated, squeezing Jonas's hand one last time before he left. Jonas could feel the soot cover his body and he looked out the mouth of the oven to see his mother's face.

She reached in and touched his arm gently. "I love you, Sprout. Now I'm going to cover the opening with burnt wood to hide you. Push your body as far back as you can."

Jonas scooted his body back until he bumped into the back of the oven. The light from the opening began to slowly disappear as Lorna piled up the wood. Jonas's heart began to beat faster. *I can do it,* thought Jonas. *The whole town is out fighting for their lives and I'm worried about being stuck in a hole. I can do it,* he kept thinking to himself. Finally the last log was put into place and he heard his mother say, "I love you," one more time.

"I love you too, Mother. Be careful," he said before he was surrounded by darkness.

***

Braal swung his huge axe in a ferocious arc taking the boarg in the side of its neck, cutting deep into the beast's collarbone. The boarg's momentum carried him into Braal sending them both flying onto the bloodied snow. Braal scrambled out from underneath the boarg only to feel the crushing weight of another beast land on top of his chest, crushing him as its claws dug into his flesh. He couldn't move as the boarg's face slowly inched towards him, the fetid breath hitting him like a gust of wind. The boarg's mouth was open, its yellowish fangs only inches from his face.

Suddenly the boarg jolted hard, arching its back violently. Braal saw the tip of a spear, dripping with gore sticking out of the boarg's throat. It made a popping sound as it was pulled out. As the boargs hairy body fell to the side, Braal was able to painfully scramble up as he clutched his wounded chest. He saw the young boy, Fil, standing in front of him, holding the bloody spear, his eyes wide with fright.

"Well done, boy," Braal said as he scanned his surroundings. The pain in his chest vanished as he looked around at the carnage. His line was breaking; he could see it as if it were in slow motion. Nearly fifty boargs were attacking the line and more were climbing over the wall as he quickly surveyed the scene. Dozens of townspeople littered the frozen ground, their bodies torn to pieces. There were boargs among the dead as well, but not enough. He turned back towards Fil and saw a boarg bearing down on the boy with incredible speed, running on all fours, covering twenty paces in seconds.

"Get down boy!" Braal yelled.

Fil flattened himself to the ground instantly as Braal's battle axe flew over him, sailing head over end, striking the boarg in the chest. It was as if the boarg hit a steel wall. The axe head buried itself deeply in the boarg's bony chest, sending it somersaulting backwards to its death.

Braal ran over and tried to rip the axe from the boarg's chest. He had to use his foot as leverage before he could pry the axe from the dead body. He hefted his bloody axe and looked around trying to determine what to do. He knew that it was futile to continue to hold their position. His friends were fighting for their lives, but it was obvious to any observer that they couldn't defeat these ferocious animals. Then he remembered Airos's words. "Reserves! Fall back!" Braal screamed. "Retreat to the north wall! Front line, hold your ground!"

Braal ran to the center of the front line and Fil followed. Marsk the butcher intercepted him. His face was covered in blood, and a nasty deep cut stretched the entire length of his thigh.

"If the front line stays, then they will die!" Marsk yelled above the fighting.

"If both lines stay then we all die. I will stay with the front line to give you time to get the reserves to the north wall to join with the cavalier! Now go! Take Fil with you!" Braal ordered.

Marsk looked at Braal with respect and shook his head. "Fil, go with the reserves. Tell Airos that Braal and I stayed with the front line to guarantee your retreat." Fil looked at them both and then ran off into the night joining the retreating men. Marsk returned his gaze to Braal and looked at him seriously. "You ready to die?"

Braal held his bloody axe before him and matched his stare. "I plan on taking a few more with me before I go," he answered with a wry grin.

Marsk smiled as they both raced to help their comrades as they struggled to keep the powerful boargs at bay long enough to give the reserve line time to retreat.

Side by side they fought; sword and axe cleaving into the gray masses of flesh. The boarg's long arms and sharp claws were formidable weapons. One hit from their powerful limbs would send a human flying, usually resulting in more than one broken bone. They were not only strong, but their speed was incredible to witness. The men of Manson were tough men, valiantly fighting for their lives and homes, and yet it was not enough to match the boarg's strength and speed.

Marsk was not a trained warrior, but he fought with the energy and strength of ten men. He was fighting for his home and family and his determination and strength were fueled by the potential loss of all he held dear.

As Marsk struggled to free his sword from the heart of a boarg he had just killed, another creature, with lightning speed, dug its curved claws deep in his leg. Suddenly, Braal's axe swung down, cleaving the boarg's arm off at the elbow. Marsk was momentarily free, but the boarg did not stop. The beast leapt into the air as Marsk retreated, the severed arm still clenched to his thigh. Marsk stumbled back and held up his bloody sword as the boarg landed on top of him, impaling itself on the sharp blade.

The boarg, tougher than any human, continued to move in for the kill. Marsk's arms were buried under the boarg's weight and he could do nothing to stop the bony head from descending. Time seemed to slow down as Marsk closed his eyes and waited for impending death. He felt the hot breath, and then the sharp teeth close around his face. And pain, excruciating pain, as his own blood filled his eyes and mouth. But the pain did not last long. With one quick jerk the boarg ripped his face off. Marsk was still alive, but the pain was gone. All he saw was blackness and then he suffocated in his own blood.

Furiously, Braal swung his axe in a sideways arc with all his strength. The boarg was sitting on top of Marsk with its mouth clamped on the butcher's face. Braal had swung the axe just as the boarg jerked its head up, ripping off Marsk's face. The timing was perfect. The axe hit the boarg in the neck and the strength of the swing carried the axe through flesh, sinew, and bone. The boarg's head landed five feet away with pieces of Marsk's face still hanging from its jaws.

Braal looked down at Marsk's twitching body. He knew that there was nothing he could do for him. Marsk was not a great man, but he had ended his life with dignity and he deserved a better death. Braal turned around to face his enemies, prepared to die with the rest of his friends.

Suddenly a huge explosion shook the ground around him, sending him flying through the air to land heavily on his back. As he slowly arose, he noticed that the forty or so remaining boargs had retreated to the log wall. They all stood, surrounding a huge smoking hole. A ten foot section of the wall was blown inward, the large logs shattered and smoking on the ground.

The remaining fifty men retreated back to Braal. Tired and covered in blood, they glanced around, unsure of what to do. Suddenly all was still. All they could hear was their hearts pounding as a black mist slowly drifted through the hole.

Braal suddenly wanted to flee, to get away from the evil that was stealing his resolve. His men felt it too. But they were frozen with fear, on the verge of running away from the darkness, but they could do nothing but stare at the dark shape slowly emerging through the hole in the wall.

A massive black horse carrying a shrouded rider appeared from the darkness like a wraith. Braal's hands began to shake. His axe dropped to the ground. A dark cape draped the rider's deathly form. Beneath it, he wore fearsome spiked armor as black as night and etched with intricate carvings of demons and other creatures of the dark. Ram-like horns curved down around his ominous looking helm, barely concealing the specter's glowing red eyes which radiated hatred and malice, sucking everything of light into its dark aura that surrounded it.

***

The boargs continued to swarm over the gate like cockroaches. Airos had long ago put away his bow but not before he had killed a score of them as they tried to scale the log wall. Suatha moved up and down the lines allowing Airos to cut a line of death as they went. Suatha would sense the boarg's movement and position Airos for the kill every time, his magic blade easily cutting into the boarg's tough hides.

The men and women around him were not faring as well. The front line was almost decimated, and the reserve line was moving in to fill any slots that opened as the boargs tore someone to pieces.

Airos was quickly surveying the scene when a huge boarg leaped from the top of the wall. Airos sensed the attack and turned just in time to take the full impact of the beast right in the chest, sending them both flying backwards onto the snow covered ground. Airos hit the ground hard rolling backwards to absorb some of the impact. He quickly got his feet underneath him and leaped up with his sword held in a defensive position.

The boarg, now standing, swung its powerful arm with impossible speed. This boarg was huge, two heads taller than Airos, and its fur was more silver than gray. Airos realized he was fighting the leader of the pack. He ducked underneath the swing, launching a series of offensive attacks. The beast was fast, very fast, and it was able to avoid the strikes by dodging them and using the flats of its tough large palms to smack the blade away when it got too close.

Airos drew his razor sharp hunting knife, thinking he may need his skill with two blades to defeat this opponent. He looked to his left quickly to see that Suatha was busy keeping two hungry boargs away from her flanks. A cavalier's steed was no ordinary animal, they were able to think, reason, and use magic of their own. Even riderless they were still formidable in a fight. Suatha's powerful body and hooves were as deadly as any warrior's sword.

Airos was on his own for this fight. He could kill the boarg with magic but he knew that he might need all the strength he could muster when the Banthra arrived. The use of magic always taxed him physically and mentally and therefore Airos had to be judicious with its use.

The huge boarg moved in quickly, both arms reaching to grab him in its iron-like grip. Airos spun the two weapons in a defensive blur, repeatedly slicing into its flesh and narrowly escaping those deadly arms.

The boarg quickly changed its tactics and tried to ram Airos. The huge powerful head charged at him like a blacksmith's hammer, the two horns, both as thick as a man's arm, leading the way. Airos could strike the boarg's head but he knew that their skulls were thick and that it would do little damage. The two horns would impale him before he could kill the beast.

But the boarg had never fought a human as quick and agile as Airos. Instead of retreating, Airos dove forward underneath the massive head and between the legs of the charging animal, his sharp hunting knife slashing across the beast's inner thigh. He continued his roll, rising quickly to his feet to engage the next boarg, not even looking back at the doomed animal as it bled out.

Airos killed four more boargs before he felt it, the evil presence hitting him like an oppressive wave. Suatha felt it too, moving back behind the lines to wait for him. He jumped over dead bodies, many of them women and children, and leaped onto her back, sword held in hand. He looked toward the south wall and saw fifty or so people running towards them. It must be their reserve line thought Airos. There was a young boy carrying a bloody spear running towards him panting with exertion and fright.

"Sir…Braal sent his reserves back to regroup with you! He and Marsk stayed with the front line to keep the boargs back! He told me to tell you this!" Fil yelled through panting breaths.

"Good work, boy," Airos replied.

Just then Airos caught site of Gorum the baker battling a boarg that had breached the front lines. Airos sheathed his sword, drawing his bow and nocking an arrow from a quiver on Suatha's side. In one smooth motion Airos drew back the powerful bow, sighted in the target, and released the shaft. The arrow slammed into the beast's side, burying itself to the feathers. The boarg stumbled to the ground, wheezing for air as its lungs filled with blood. Airos returned the bow to its sheath at Suatha's side as Gorum stumbled backwards; his legs and arms exhausted from constant fighting.

"To me, Gorum!" yelled Airos.

Gorum, seeing safety in Airos, moved quickly towards him carrying his large heavy sword at his side. "Thank you, cavalier," Gorum blurted, his words coming through labored breaths.

"I have to leave you; the Banthra is here, at the south wall. If I do not return I want you to organize a retreat and get as many people out of the town as possible. If you're lucky, the boargs will stay here and feed rather than follow you. I cannot promise you anything, just do the best you can to get as many survivors to safety as possible. If I can kill the Banthra then we may have a chance. If not, then you need to get far away from this town for a while, until they have fed."

"I will do my best, sir," replied Gorum.

"I wish you luck, baker. Now be off and may Ulren guide you," replied Airos as he flicked the reins. Gorum was already running towards the line as Suatha leaped into the night.

***

Braal and his men were paralyzed with fear as the boargs slowly crept towards them, saliva dripping from their open mouths. They could sense their paralysis, and they wanted to tease them, like a cat plays with its prey. Braal's heart began to beat faster and he willed his body to move, to pick up his axe and die fighting, but his body would not obey.

The black rider slowly advanced, his huge horse stepping forward, its massive hooves covered in mangy blood soaked fur, pushing deep into the trampled snow. The horse's cave-like nostrils flared open as steam hissed from them, splattering mucous into the air. The dark steed curled up its frothy lips, exposing large fangs covered with saliva and blood. Red eyes scanned the men before it, hatred spearing every man who looked upon the deadly animal. This horse was no ordinary horse, but a nightmare, a demon, just like its rider. But it was the Banthra's gaze that froze them all and they could do nothing to stop the boargs approach.

"Feed my children, kill them all," hissed the Banthra, his voice sending a paralyzing chill down Braal's spine.

The boargs moved in slowly, continuing to play with the immobilized men. Their jaws clicked open and shut, exposing fearsome teeth.

Braal was not afraid to die, but to die like this was terrifying. *Give me my axe*, thought Braal, *and let me take several of you demons with me.*

A brilliant white light suddenly bathed them all, awakening them and freeing them from the Banthra's spell. Suatha and Airos thundered to the center of the line, white light erupting from them like a star. The men hastily moved back behind Airos, their weapons held before them. The boargs did the same, moving quickly behind the Banthra who had backed away from the light.

The Banthra's scream sent a chill through everyone, and the men looked around nervously, retreating slowly backwards. Airos lifted his sword high, the white light flaring even brighter. As the light bathed the men in its magical warmth, they became invigorated, their muscles no longer tired, their fear erased, new energy and purpose coursing through their veins. They held out their weapons and set their feet firmly in the ground with new resolve. The powerful light slowly dissipated, but it did not totally go away. It was as if Airos and Suatha were outlined in it, a white light that glowed steadily.

"You are not wanted here demon spawn! Your very presence blights this land! Come, and let me send you back to the dark pits from which you were created!" Airos roared.

The Banthra made a rasping, hissing noise, as if it were laughing. "A cavalier; it has been a thousand years since I've had the pleasure of killing one." The Banthra drew a massive sword from its back and held the blade out to the side. The blade erupted with orange and red flames. "Prepare to meet your precious god, cavalier, for you are about to die."

Like a rock flung from a sling, the Banthra bolted towards Airos with its sword held high. Airos and Suatha shot forward to meet the charge. The boargs followed their master and flung themselves forward, pouncing upon the sturdy men of Manson.

The glowing blades of the mighty warriors clashed over and over again, sending sparks and magical energy into the air. The Banthra's devil steed broke through Suatha's defenses and sunk its teeth deeply into the side of her neck. Airos saw the move, kicking the horse in the face hoping to dislodge the dangerous fangs. The Banthra, taking advantage of the sudden opening, swung its sword down and across Airos's exposed leg. The blade glanced across his cuisse that protected his upper thigh and made a shallow cut just above the kneecap. Suatha used her powerful head and smashed it against the demon horse until its jaws tore away flesh and they both pulled apart, circling each other.

The shallow cut on Airos's leg burned with pain. Even a shallow cut from a Banthra's weapon can kill, for the blades and armor of the black knights are cursed. But Airos was a cavalier, and the pain began to subside as he closed the wound with his magic.

"Do you feel it, cavalier, your life nearing its end?" The Banthra hissed mockingly.

Airos laughed loudly. "That is your folly fallen one. I have no fear of death, but you are already dead. You are nothing without the twisted magic that makes you what you are! You are empty!" Airos yelled as he and Suatha leaped forward again. This time Suatha led the charge with her front hooves, and Airos, faster than the eye could see, flung his sword to his left hand.

Suatha's hooves pounded into the Banthra and it was forced backwards, his sword held to the side. Airos, his blade now on the near side of the Banthra, swung it down on top of the neck of the demon horse. The black steed tried to turn its head away from the deadly blade but all that did was expose the side of its neck even more. Eight inches of Airos's blade sunk in just to the right of the vertebrae, slicing all the way through the side of the neck. The devilish horse screamed, staggering backwards, black blood pulsing from the long gash on its neck. As the steed stumbled to the ground, the Banthra jumped from its back to land squarely on his feet.

***

Jonas was not sure how much longer he could stay in his hiding place. It was pitch black and he could hear the screams of the fighting outside. The sounds were all muffled but he could tell that horrible things were happening as he hid away in the safe confines of his hole. He felt like a coward and that did not bode well with him. *But what can I do*, he thought. *I would just get in the way*.

Suddenly a loud noise erupted from inside Gorum's home. Jonas strained to hear what was happening and to recognize the source of the noise.

Lorna stood just to the left of the door of Gorum's home. She was so frightened, more frightened than she could ever imagine, but she was not scared for herself, she was terrified for her son. She could not imagine the deadly teeth of the boargs tearing into her helpless son's body. She would not let that happen. She would die trying to stop it.

In her hand she held a razor sharp bread knife as long as her forearm. She heard the boargs outside ransacking the homes, and she knew it was only a matter of time before they entered Gorum's home.

Suddenly a fist pounded on the locked door. The loud noise brought her out of her reverie. She gripped her knife harder, her heart pounding in her head.

"Lorna, it's me, Gorum, open up the door!"

Lorna let out her held breath, quickly lifting up the heavy oak beam and opening the door. Gorum rushed in and shut the door while Lorna replaced the beam. He was covered in blood and he had a huge claw mark from ear to collar bone, his iron sword was dripping crimson on the wood floor.

"We have to get out of here! We will not win this fight! Get Jonas and let's make a run for it into the mountains. We'll grab as many survivors as we can!" He grabbed a bag by the door that was already filled with provisions.

"Are you sure? Can we make it?" asked Lorna.

"I don't know! But if we stay, we die! That I do know!"

The door suddenly exploded inward, sending splinters and wood fragments into Lorna and Gorum, sending them both sprawling backwards to land hard on the cabin floor.

Two huge boargs entered the room, stepping over the destroyed door, looking around hungrily, their deadly clawed hands scraping on the wooden floor as they slowly looked around, sniffing the air for their next victim.

***

Airos looked around quickly before returning his gaze to the unhorsed Banthra. It was not going well. The boargs were destroying the people of Manson. *I have to kill this Banthra,* thought Airos. *It is their only chance.*

The Banthra lifted its sword in the air and screamed, the screeching noise assaulting the men as they tried to fight, the Banthra simultaneously ramming the blade deep into the ground.

Airos recognized the use of magic and called on Ulren's magic as well, but he was too slow. As the Banthra's blade hit the earth a bolt of powerful energy traveled through the ground towards Airos. The ground erupted in a straight path and struck Suatha and Airos as the Banthra released the full power of the attack causing the ground to explode under Airos.

Suatha and Airos flew backwards landing heavily on the ground five paces away. Airos's body was protected by Suatha's powerful form so the courageous steed took the brunt of the attack. Airos struggled to get up and regain his footing, but his horse lay still, her underside burning and smoldering and one leg broken, hanging at an impossible angle.

Airos's anger burned deep but controlled. He drew his long hunting knife with his left hand, holding his sword with his right he advanced on the approaching Banthra, his piercing eyes pits of boiling rage.

***

Gorum quickly scrambled to his feet, holding his heavy blade out in front of him. Lorna sprang up as well, running to stand next to him with her pitiful knife.

The boargs both hissed, a sound that Gorum now recognized as laughter. Gorum said nothing. He simply looked at Lorna, a silent 'I'm sorry' blanketing his face, and then he attacked the boargs with speed that seemed impossible for his size.

Gorum leaped at the first one, swinging his sword in a sideways arc hoping to kill it with the first blow, knowing that he would never be able to kill them both if he did not dispatch the first one quickly.

But the boarg was just too fast. Its long arm snaked out, grabbing the wooden chair nearby and holding it up, blocking the deadly blade. The blade crashed into the wood, shattering the chair as the boarg used its other arm to open up a gash along Gorum's right shoulder. Gorum stumbled back and saw to his horror that the other boarg had leaped upon Lorna. But he was powerless to help her as the boarg in front of him continued the attack by leaping into the air in an attempt to pin him down with its strong clawed hands and heavy body.

Gorum knew that to retreat was death, so he simply did the thing that was least expected. He rushed forward to meet the attack. But he could not get his heavy sword up in time to cut down the leaping boarg so he punched the animal with the hand that was holding the sword. The boarg and Gorum's powerful fist came together like an explosion, the boarg stopping instantly in the air, its lower jaw and teeth shattering on impact. Gorum felt his fist crumble, the many bones in his hand splintering under the terrible blow. They both staggered backwards in agony.

But Gorum did not feel the pain in his hand as he looked down at Lorna who was struggling against the strong beast that seemed to be playing with her. Its back legs rested on her thighs while the beast's left hand was holding her neck. The boarg was running the claws of its right hand over her cheeks, opening up shallow cuts all over her face. Lorna was screaming and Gorum could see her scrambling to grab the knife that she dropped by her side.

Gorum switched grips, grabbing the heavy iron blade in his good hand. He gritted his teeth, swinging the blade with all his might, but his strength was leaving him and he knew that his left arm held little power. The blade sunk in a couple of inches into the boarg's back.

The boarg roared defiantly, lashing its right arm out with astonishing speed and power, swiping its claws across Gorum's chest and sending him sprawling to the floor with several more deep cuts and a few broken ribs.

Lorna took the brief distraction that Gorum had given her and looked for her knife. She spotted the blade, grabbing it with her right hand just as the boarg returned its attention to her. The boarg was done playing with her. Its left hand was still wrapped tightly around her throat and the beast begun to squeeze harder and lift her face to its open maw. Just as her face was inches from the boarg's mouth, she used her right hand, slamming the razor sharp knife deep into its throat. The boarg howled as she ripped the knife through its flesh, severing the ropey vein that ran up its neck. Dark blood bathed them both but the boarg continued to squeeze her throat with the last remnants of its strength.

Gorum had landed hard, and as he struggled to get up he felt blood gushing from his wounds. As he got to his knees, a powerful weight struck him again, flattening him to his back and knocking the air from his lungs. The boarg with the broken jaw lay on top of him, its jaw crushed and hanging awkwardly to the side. Gorum tried to use the last of his strength to push the boarg off, but the beast was too strong and quick and fueled by pain and rage the beast furiously struck Gorum repeatedly, crushing his face and his throat. The pain was brief and then everything went black.

Lorna used her knife to stab at the fatally wounded boarg's arm, its claws still clutched at her neck. The creature roared with fury and with one last burst of energy, dug its claws deep into her throat. The boarg fell away in death, Lorna's blood covering its clawed hand. Lorna's eyes went wide as she felt the warmth of her own blood pool around her. The boarg had sliced into her neck in several places and Lorna frantically brought her hands to her throat to try and stop the bleeding. But it was of no use, and within seconds she felt dizzy and lightheaded. There was little pain as her life blood gushed from the fatal wound and poured between her fingers. Her last thought was of Jonas as everything faded to black.

***

Fil was terrified. His family and friends were dying around him. He spotted Gorum the baker flee from the fight and head toward his home. He did not know where his family was and he did not want to die alone. Grabbing his spear he crawled out from behind the woodpile that was his hiding place and raced after Gorum. He was thirty paces from the baker's home when he saw the two huge boargs smash their way through the baker's door.

Fil stopped and looked around at the carnage. There were screams everywhere and men and boargs alike were dying all around him. It was obvious to Fil that the town was not going to survive. New anger surged through him and at this point he didn't care if he died; he just wanted to inflict as much damage as possible to the beasts that did this to his home.

He gripped the spear with new vigor and raced toward Gorum's home, running through the damaged door and into the room, attacking the first thing he saw. A boarg, with its back to the door, was sitting on top of Gorum and ripping his face apart with its teeth and claws.

Without thinking Fil ran forward and rammed his spear with all his strength into the back of the feeding beast. The spear point sunk in deep and then lodged against its sternum. The beast howled in pain, standing up and trying to grab the shaft from its back. The boarg turned around stumbling, Gorum's blood coating its face, neck, and claws.

Fil's anger still had not been quenched and he looked for another weapon to finish off the animal. He saw Gorum's sword lying next to him. He grabbed it quickly. Fil was young, but strong for his age. His adrenaline took over and he hefted the sword with both hands and turned toward the stumbling beast. The boarg saw the weapon in his hands and lurched toward Fil hoping to kill the little human.

But Fil lifted the heavy blade and brought it downward with as much strength as he could muster, the sharp iron cutting deep into the boarg's neck, causing the beast to stumble backwards, and ripping the sword from Fil's hands. The animal wobbled on unsteady legs before finally falling to the ground, blood pulsing from the terrible wound.

A horrible gagging noise alerted Fil that he was not alone. He glanced against the wall, noticing a woman on the ground, her throat covered in blood. Fil ran towards her and knelt by her side. Blood had pooled all around her body and it was still slowly pouring from the lacerations at her throat. He noticed that it was Lorna, the mother of the cripple.

Lorna grabbed Fil's arm with surprising strength, looking at him with the last of her life's energy. "Jonas…..in the fireplace…..help him….protect him," Lorna murmured quietly, her voice a soft gurgle. "Promise me, Fil," she whispered, her strength finally leaving her.

Fil held her hand gently. Not knowing what else to say to the dying woman, he said what she wanted to hear. "I promise; I will look after him." Fil stared down at Lorna as she died, her eyes glazing over and her blood smeared hand falling away. Fil did not know Lorna well, but the dying woman seemed to symbolize the entire town, the town that he had loved for fifteen years. He thought about his family and friends dead and dying, and tears began to fall, tears he could not stop as they cascaded down over the Lorna's body.

He went on like that for a few moments, struggling to regain control of his emotions. The torrent of tears slowly stopped as Fil created a mental dam, a dam built of anger and determination. As the tears subsided, Fil gently used his hand to close her eyes. He got up and ripped the spear from the dead boarg. *I'm going to survive this* he thought*; they will all pay for what they have done.*

***

Airos and the Banthra clashed together, their blades creating a blur of magical energy. Airos's skill with a blade was unrivaled, but he had never met a Bantrha in combat before. What Airos possessed in skill, the Banthra made up in magical enhancements. Airos's blades spun faster and faster, creating a deadly barrage of steel that could not be stopped; so he thought.

But the Banthra was there, blocking every slash and lunge. The blackness of the creature began to suffocate Airos as they struggled together. He could feel the vileness seep his energy from him, the Bantrha hissing as he felt Airos begin to slow. Airos jabbed his long sword forward but fell off balance as the Banthra sidestepped the attack, slamming a spiked gauntlet into Airos's side as the cavalier stumbled by. Airos felt the corrupt metal sink several inches into his unprotected side. The sting was unbearable, for the Banthra's weapons were no ordinary steel. They were cursed weapons that created wounds that killed much faster and would not heal without magic.

"What's wrong, cavalier? Does it sting?" the Banthra's gravelly voice whispered. Airos was visibly struggling against the pain as the demon mocked him.

"Ulren, help me fight this abomination," he prayed. As he focused on his prayer, the pain began to subside. His hands began to tingle and the black veil that seemed to cover him fell away and new strength shot through him. The wound in his side sealed itself as the pain mercifully faded away.

The Banthra felt his magic being countered and hissed angrily, swinging his blade down in an overhead chop. Airos flung up his sword and knife in a cross block catching the flaming weapon. He used his sword to slide the Banthra's blade to the side while ramming his knife deep into the Banthra's thigh. The Banthra screamed, lurching backwards, the magical knife ripping from its leg and falling from Airos's hand.

Airos gripped his sword with both hands, and summoning the High One's energy he released it toward the Banthra. "Ulren!" Airos screamed, pointing his sword at the Banthra. Airos's body glowed bright blue for a second, then all the energy burst from the tip of the sword in a powerful bolt of God Fire that hit the Banthra square in the stomach, forcing it to stumble backwards. The Banthra snarled and looked down at a charred burning hole in its bowels, its legs wobbly underneath him.

Braal ripped his axe from the dying beast's chest and looked up for his next victim. He had long ago exhausted all the energy of his physical body and was now fighting with his heart. His anger fueled him; the anger of his brother's death many years ago, the anger of seeing the death and destruction of the town he loved. He knew this new energy would not last forever so he found his next victim quickly.

The Banthra was standing with its back to him not more than twenty paces away. As he looked at the devil warrior he saw Airos launch a dazzling bolt of flame into the demon's stomach. Braal shielded his eyes from the brightness, gripping his axe tighter. He looked back at the staggering demon and his eyes burned with hatred. Braal lifted his axe, charging at the personification of his fury, at the very thing that had destroyed everything he held dear.

Airos saw the charge and screamed inwardly, knowing that Braal's weapon could do nothing. Airos moved in like a striking snake just as the Banthra turned to meet the charge that he sensed behind him. The Banthra held up his sword to intercept the powerful chop of the axe. When the two weapons met the axe exploded in a shower of metal and wood and the Banthra reversed the parry and struck the enraged human in the side, the magical flames of the sword cutting through the man's body as if it were made of air.

Airos saw Braal's body fall away in two pieces just as he leaped forward and rammed his own sword through the body of the distracted Banthra. The blade pierced the black knight through the heart, erupting out the other side in a shower of black blood.

The Banthra lifted his head and screamed into the night. Airos twisted the blade, and called on the power of Ulren again.

"Burn you Forsworn spawn!" Airos yelled through gritted teeth, his power surging through the sword into the body of the Banthra. The Banthra, screaming louder, dropped his sword and grabbed Airos's head with both hands.

"I will take you with me, cavalier," hissed the Banthra. The Banthra's hands began to glow red as he sent his magic into the cavalier. Airos clenched his teeth and continued to pray and channel his magic into the body of the Banthra.

The demon knight lit up like the moon as the blue flame began to flow through it, burning him with fiery pain. As Airos screamed, the demon's dark magic continued to attack Airos's body. They were locked together, fused in a searing struggle for survival. Airos arched his back and screamed louder as the magic burned his core…but he could not let go. If he let go of the sword then the link that was channeling his magic into the demon would be severed and he would be incinerated.

All the men and boargs that were still alive stopped fighting, slowly stepping further away from the glowing combatants. Airos's body became translucent and the red fire filled him and burned from the inside out. They both continued to scream, sending one last burst of energy into each other.

The magic flared and exploded out over fifteen paces before it receded and disappeared. The men and boargs nearby fell to the ground to shield themselves from the blast. Those closest to the battle ended up as charred burning husks. The ground was scorched black around the two dead warriors, their bodies nothing more than burnt and blackened forms, unrecognizable from their previous selves.

There were fifteen men left, barely standing, holding onto their bloody weapons. The remaining fifty boargs advanced on the men, paying little attention to their dead leader, for food was standing right in front of them. The men could barely move, let alone stop the charge of the hungry beasts.

Three
Survival

Fil gripped his spear tightly as he hid under the bed in the baker's house. He did not know that the Bantrha and the cavalier were dead, but he could still hear feeding boargs outside. He had never been more terrified. Fighting and witnessing the massacre was traumatic enough, but sitting and waiting for boargs to feed on his friends and family while he hid, not knowing if a hungry boarg would find him and eat him alive, was more frightening than he could possibly imagine. He wondered how many survivors there were and how many people were hiding like he was? He knew that the cripple was in the baker's oven. Lorna, the boy's dying mother, had told him so. He would honor her wish and do his best to get the boy and any other survivors to safety.

His mind was swarming with questions. Once the boargs left, would the survivors be safe from them? Would the boargs return to feed? Were they better off hiding out in the mountains? Was his family alive? The last he'd seen of his father, Jorm, was at the north gate, fighting as part of the reserve line. His sister, Lara, who was only six, was hiding out with the other children and elderly at the grange. He did not know the whereabouts of his brother, Colson, nor did he know what had happened to his mother, Mell, who he had last seen helping with weapons at the south wall.

His body and mind were exhausted, but he didn't want to risk falling asleep in case a boarg arrived looking for more food. Despite his efforts, his eye lids became heavier and heavier as he struggled to stay awake, the stress of the night taking its toll on the young man. The grunting and growling of feeding boargs grew more distant in his mind as he got sleepier and sleepier. Fatigue finally won the battle. His eyes closed as he fell into a deep sleep, still clenching the blood covered spear in his hand.

***

Jonas did not know how long he had been asleep. He awoke in the dark confines of the oven, soot covering his cramped body and the smell of charcoal and baked bread overwhelming him. He listened intently for several moments, trying to hear sounds of fighting outside. He had no idea if it was morning or still night and he was very frightened. No one had come for him and his heart ached to see his mother, or Gorum, or someone to tell him that everything was going to be fine. What had happened outside? Not knowing and feeling helpless filled him with a deep despair. He had to move, to get out of the tight confines of his hiding place, to get some answers to what had happened.

Slowly he used his wooden crutch to push the wood away from the opening. The wood landed heavily on the floor and light reached into the oven as he knocked more logs out of the way. *It must be morning* thought Jonas, the room lighter than it had been. Slowly he inched his way forward, feet first, until he got to the lip of the oven. He was about two paces up from the ground and he knew he'd have a small fall since his legs probably couldn't catch him. Pushing his body all the way out of the oven he landed heavily on his legs, stumbling to the ground.

"You okay?"

The voice came from in front of him as Jonas struggled to look up and grab his crutch at the same time. He stood up slowly, his cramped legs shaking and his back aching from the tight confines of the oven. Fil stood before him, a long bloody spear in his hand. The boy's face and body were splattered with blood, and at his waist he carried a hunting knife. Fil did not look like the boy he remembered, he seemed to have aged many years in one night.

"I think so," Jonas nodded slowly, solemnly, his eyes huge as he tremulously voiced the question, "Wh-what happened?"

Fil didn't know how to tell the poor boy that his mother was dead and that their town was destroyed. He was never great with words so he just kept it simple. "Everything is destroyed, Jonas. Our town is gone. The Banthra and the cavalier both died in the fight."

"And my mother?" Jonas asked, although he knew the answer even as he asked the question.

"She is dead. Everyone is dead. My family…everyone is gone." Emotions finally claimed Fil for the first time. Tears poured down his face and he didn't fight them, he let them come. He allowed grief to overwhelm him, for he knew that this would be the last time that he would grieve. The tears spilled forth, as he wept unabashedly for each member of his family and for all his friends and neighbors who had perished.

Jonas fell to his knees, his grief grabbing him roughly and weighing him down. He crumpled to the floor and cried in anguish. Fil stumbled towards him and held him in his arms as they both wept, trying to break the dam of pain and grief with a torrent of tears.

***

Jonas didn't know how long he had laid there; time seemed to stand still. The tears were finally gone, replaced with numbness. He was empty, his mother was gone and there was nothing left.

He got up and slowly hobbled into the main room. He looked around at the carnage and saw two bodies against the wall, both with wool blankets covering their forms. Jonas stumbled past them in a daze, walking through the destroyed door into the fresh air.

All around him was blood, death, and despair. The carnage was beyond belief. He had never seen a dead body before, and now they were everywhere, torn and ripped, blood splattering the churned up snow and mud. Some had been eaten beyond recognition. He had to step over bodies, boargs and townsfolk both, some cut with swords and others killed by teeth and claw, the images burning in his mind, finding a permanent spot on his shelves of memories.

Jonas made his way to the south wall and saw two charred forms seared together in death. The snow had been melted in a perfect circle around them that must have been thirty paces in diameter. Jonas saw the cavalier's dead horse, its underside burned horribly and its leg broken at an awkward angle.

As he scanned the destruction he saw faces that he recognized. Braal was dead, cut cleanly in half, many dead boargs surrounding him. Jonas stumbled to his knees and heaved uncontrollably, the contents of his stomach splattering the bloody ground. He knelt there panting for a few moments before he could stand back up, scanning the carnage again. There was Galen the hunter, Mason the leather maker, Jhol, the son of Bain, and many others. Everyone was dead.

As he looked around and made his way through the many bodies, he caught flickers of sunlight reflect off of something. He moved towards the shining object and saw a beautiful hunting knife about as long as his forearm lying on the ground. The handle was carved bone and the blade was so shiny and polished that it almost blinded him, the sunlight sparkling off its mirror like finish. Jonas recognized the blade. It was the cavalier's.

Reaching down he picked it up. It seemed wrong to leave it resting in all the destruction. It was warm to the touch, as if it were alive. He slid the blade into his belt just as he saw Fil move toward him, his face hard and determined, carrying a huntsman's pack on his shoulders.

"We have to go, the boargs may come back and all this blood will certainly attract animals and who knows what else." Fil had a short sword strapped to his side and a bow and quiver was lashed to the pack that he wore. He still held his spear in his hand.

"Where are we going? I can't walk fast enough to keep up with you," Jonas said with apprehension.

"I know. But I will not leave you. We are all each other have now. My plan is to head into the mountains. My father has a cave that he uses during the summer for hunting. I know its location and a mountain lake lies near. The cave has dry wood and a few supplies that are kept there for emergencies. We need to hide for a while and let the winter snows subside before we can travel."

"How far away is it?"

"A half a day's walk. Don't worry, we will go slowly. We have no other options," Fil replied firmly, leaving no room for discussion.

Jonas looked around at the town sadly and then looked back at Fil. Fil's eyes were determined and Jonas knew that he was right. They could not stay here. They didn't even have the time or strength to bury their loved ones. "Okay, Fil. Let me get my things."

***

The long walk was grueling, probably the hardest thing physically that Jonas had ever done. Not to mention the weight of emotions that he carried as an additional burden. He could not stop thinking about his mother, the only person who ever cared for him. His body felt drained, every step weighed down with sorrow. He had walked with his mother in the woods before, but usually no more than an hour or two, and they generally stuck to the game trails.

The first half of the hike went gradually up hill, but they used the game trails available to them which made it a little easier for Jonas. As they climbed higher into the mountains, parts of the terrain became so steep it was almost impossible for Jonas to use his crutch. His hands and feet bled from several blisters and he began to despair that they wouldn't make it by nightfall, for the sun was just starting to set.

"How much longer, Fil?" asked Jonas, exhaustion evident in his voice.

"We are almost there, not much longer. You've done well, but we need to get there before dark. Can you do it?" asked Fil.

Jonas, knowing the sacrifice Fil was making for him, somehow found the energy to reply, "I can."

The sun's comforting light began to recede behind the massive pines as they dropped down towards a beautiful small mountain lake. Fil led the exhausted Jonas to a cave that was nestled on the north side of the lake. The cave was small, about thirty paces deep and fifteen paces wide. In the back corner was a pile of dry wood, some cooking pans, and a tinderbox. Near the entrance was a circle of soot covered stones surrounding several dry pieces of wood lying atop dried moss and small pieces of tinder. The supplies were the same that Fil and his father had left several months ago. Fil's father always taught him the mountain way of leaving the makings of a fire when you left a home, whether it was a cabin, a simple shelter, or a cave. It could make for a comfortable return on a cold day or save the life of some weary traveler in bitter conditions. Fil was thankful for that lesson now. They were both tired and Fil didn't think that he would have the energy to hunt the snow-covered forest for dry wood.

Jonas was exhausted, falling to the ground to rest. Fil quickly lit the fire and the welcome flames leaped up, chasing the cold mountain air away. The heat from the fire bathed Jonas and soothed his tired body, and within minutes he was asleep. Fil gathered up Jonas's wool blanket and covered his body.

"Sleep well, Jonas. You did well today." Fil was impressed with Jonas's grim determination and strength during the hard climb.

Jonas's night was filled with vivid dreams. He dreamt that he was walking along the edges of a frozen lake, the very same lake they were camping by, when he saw a little fawn scrambling on the ice. The ice began to break and crack, causing the deer to struggle more.

Jonas set the crutch down and lay on his belly on the ice. Slowly, he crawled closer and closer to the frightened deer. When he was within five paces of the deer the ice broke and the deer's hind legs went into the water. Jonas struggled closer, reaching out towards the panicked deer, straining to grab its front legs to pull the scared animal to safety. The ice around him began to crack and weaken. He surged forward with one last try to save the deer.

The ice suddenly gave way and he fell into the freezing water. In a panic, he kicked and struggled with the deer, but his frozen crippled limbs couldn't support his weight. Slowly he began to sink into the numbing water.

Everything began to slow. The deer was sinking next to him, just staring at him. Then the deer began to glow a brilliant white and light shot forth from the animal like an explosion.

The panic left him and he found himself lying in the snow at the edge of the woods. He was no longer wet and his body felt warm and comfortable. Blinking several times he saw a glowing form standing before him. The light slowly faded away revealing a magnificent warrior wearing silver armor and a helm with two large deer horns. The warrior was carrying a silver shield embossed with a blue and silver oak tree.

The figure stepped towards Jonas and kneeled at his feet. The soldier took off the great helm to reveal long flowing black hair and a face so beautiful that Jonas couldn't breathe. Her beauty and presence was overwhelming.

"You did well, Jonas," the lady whispered to him. Her voice was soft, but powerful.

"Who are you?" he asked.

"You will know soon enough. Why did you try to rescue the deer?" asked the raven haired woman.

"I don't know. It needed my help. I didn't have time to think about it."

"But you are a cripple. You can barely move," she said with no hint of scorn.

"I was better off than the deer," Jonas replied smoothly.

The lady smiled and touched his arm with her gauntlet covered hand. "Well spoken," she replied, her melodic voice warming him to his soul. "Now, wake up, we will meet again". Her hand glowed brightly as she touched him and Jonas felt a powerful surge of energy enter his body and warm his very soul. He didn't ever want the feeling to go away. The warmth flowed through his body and exploded within him.

Jonas awoke with a jolt, his back arching and his body rigid. He was sweating profusely and breathing hard as he struggled to regain control of his body. After a few moments he was able to relax and he looked around the cave hoping to find the warrior woman. The dream seemed so real, but she was nowhere to be seen, the cave was empty; the fire burning low next to him.

Getting up, he looked around the room for his crutch. Then it struck him. *I just got up on my own!* Jonas screamed in his head. *I didn't use my crutch!* Jonas suddenly stumbled, his right leg giving out on him. As he neared the ground he put out his right hand to brace his fall, and his body complied with his will, his arm lurching out to cushion his decent. He stopped himself from falling, something he had never been able to do. Jonas was now on his knees and he was staring at his hands in shock. He tried to wiggle his fingers and to his surprise they moved slowly, like they were frozen, but they moved as he commanded them too. They were sore and tight, but he could move them, although somewhat awkwardly. Jonas's lips parted and his teeth emerged in a smile of wonder and happiness.

"I can move my hands," he commented to himself with more surprise. Jonas looked around for his crutch and saw it lying next to him. Instead of reaching for it, he used his arms and legs to try and lift his body off the ground. His thin frame slowly rose until he was standing and wobbling on his own feet. He focused on his muscles and willed his body to stop shaking. It took him several seconds but he was finally able to keep his body relatively still. He smiled again, and on a whim he tried to jump. To anyone watching it would have looked pathetic. His body lifted off the ground several inches before he landed on his feet and stumbled to the ground again. To Jonas it felt wonderful and he began to laugh and roll on the ground uncontrollably.

Fil walked into the cave carrying a load of firewood. He looked at Jonas on the ground with bewilderment and concern. Looking around to find the source of Jonas's amusement he asked, "Jonas, what's so funny? Are you okay?"

Jonas stopped rolling around, slowly lifting his body off the ground, smiling the entire time.

Fil stared at him, dropping the wood he was holding onto the ground, his mouth agape with shock. "What happened? You are moving your body! You look different…your face looks different. You look normal…meaning no offense," he replied quickly.

Jonas walked awkwardly toward Fil, slowly placing both hands on his shoulders. "Fil, I am normal. I am healed. Well, I think I am. My body is weak but I feel amazing. I can talk without difficulty, my muscles feel much looser, and…" Jonas noticed Fil staring at his chest. "What is it? Why are you looking at my chest?"

"Jonas, have you seen your chest yet?"

"What do you mean?" Jonas asked as he backed up and looked down at his bare chest. What he saw was shocking. His entire torso was covered with a blue and silver mark, a giant oak tree, exquisitely created and lined with sparkling silver. They both stared at it in awe. It was obviously created by magic; no human could make something as intricate and beautiful as what they saw on his chest.

"In Ulren's name, what happened to you?" asked Fil.

The possibilities came to Jonas in a flash of understanding. The dream, the deer, the dark haired warrior with her gleaming shield bearing the oak tree, and that exact symbol now embossed on his chest. He looked up at Fil with wonder. "I do not know," Jonas stammered in confusion and excitement at the same time.

***

Jonas and Fil sat around the morning fire while Jonas explained to Fil the dream he had and how he awoke with the mark on his chest. Fil listened intently.

"What do you think?" asked Jonas after he completed his story.

"I don't know. It all seems so unbelievable, but here you are able to move your body as it should, with an incredible mark on your chest that just happens to be the symbol of Shyann, our goddess. I don't know why it happened, but I think you've been God Marked," Fil replied as he added another log to the fire.

"You mean like how Airos the cavalier was?" Jonas asked.

"I think so."

"But why me? Why did she mark me?" Jonas asked in wonder.

"I don't know, but I imagine you will find out. I think that maybe we need to take you to a priest and try to get some answers."

"I don't even know where the nearest temple is located. I've never even been more than a few hours walk from Manson," Jonas replied with apprehension. He absently rubbed his hands together, smiling at the simple movement that just last night he could not do.

"I know there is a temple in Finarth. Besides, that is where I want to go when the snows subside anyway. We will travel together. What do you think?" Fil asked.

"Why do you want to go to Finarth? The trip would take us over a month on foot."

"I have nothing left here. I'm going to Finarth to join the king's army. I want to learn to fight. I want a chance to seek revenge on whoever did this to my home. You must understand that," Fil said.

Jonas looked up at Fil and their eyes locked. *I too have nothing left* thought Jonas, flexing his arms in amazement. Learning to fight, to protect the weak, to ride a horse and wield a sword, all things that he believed he would never be able to do. Now it was a possibility, because Shyann had given him a chance. *Airos was right. The gods have a plan for everyone, even me*, thought Jonas.

Jonas looked up at Fil seriously. "I will go with you, Fil. I will search out a priest and I will learn to fight with you." He reached out and grasped Fil's hand in the warrior's hand shake that he had seen the men of Manson do many times. He grasped Fil's forearm tightly while Fil in turn grabbed his.

Fil squeezed his arm firmly and smiled. "After the winter snows, we leave for Finarth." His smile grew wider now that they had a plan.

***

The first part of winter went by quickly for Jonas. He had never felt more alive in his life, but his body was very weak and he still had limited movement. He did not have the muscle strength for running, climbing, or anything too strenuous. The first thing he had to do was train his body to listen to his mental commands, something it was not used to doing. Most of his days were spent hiking in the snow, walking the animal trails, and even running where he could as his endurance grew. His goal was to strengthen his muscles so that they could support him normally and after several weeks he began to feel different, stronger with quicker reflexes.

After a month or so he was able to do basic tasks without getting sore or stumbling. His body was fully healing. He began to push himself by climbing the cliff walls to strengthen his arms, fingers, and legs. Fil taught him how to shoot a bow and hunt, while Jonas taught Fil how to set the best rabbit snares and find wild vegetables and edible plants and herbs, although there was not much of the latter during the winter months. When the snows fell heavily, Fil showed Jonas how to make snow shoes from branches and rope and Jonas used the shoes to continue his long walks through the deep snow.

Jonas hated being cooped up in the cave. Since he was cured he never wanted to be idle again, the idea of not using his new muscles was unthinkable to him. He continued exercising daily as he took in the magnificent scenery the mountains had to offer. As his strength and endurance improved, his skinny frame began to fill out with muscle. Fil accompanied him often, but he did not fully share his desire to walk, run, or climb for no reason.

***

Jonas took his first deer on a cold snowy morning. Hunting was the mainstay of his village and a man's worth was often based on what he could provide. It was believed that the deer and wild game of the Tundrens were provided by Shyann herself, and she rewarded the patient hunter with the most magnificent animals. But because these animals gave them life, and they were gifts from Shyann, all hunters were taught at an early age to respect the animals that provided for them. Young boys accompanied their fathers on the hunts to learn the skills, and to respect nature and what it provided. Jonas had never learned to hunt because he could not physically take part, nor did he have a father to pass on those skills had he been able. But now he was being taught, and he absorbed the knowledge with the enthusiasm and excitement of one who would never take for granted the new opportunity presented to him. Fil was no expert hunter, but he passed on what his father had taught him and it was enough to form a foundation from which Jonas could build.

He had tracked the animal slowly for several hours. Fil had told him that he was a natural and that he had the patience to be a great hunter. He could move quietly and slowly, and his accuracy with the bow was amazing for someone who was just a novice. Jonas didn't tell Fil that he had spent countless hours practicing, shooting the bow when he went out on his many hikes. He could drop a bird out of a tree at thirty paces.

The deer he was following was a huge buck. He caught a glimpse of it through some brambles before it bolted away. The rack was immense, and the large stag held it high with ease.

Jonas was slowly moving from tree to tree, his snowshoes making a quiet crunch as he walked, an arrow nocked to his bow string. His breath came out in billows of steam as he scanned the forest for his target. He had been following the animal for a long time in deep snow, up and down gulches and over logs, and he was getting tired. Luckily for him the deer was actually taking him back towards their cave, which meant that if he actually killed it, he would have a shorter distance to carry the meat. Just to his right he caught a glimpse of the animal as it moved towards some choice buds that had begun to emerge from the undergrowth as spring neared. The buck lifted its big head to feed, exposing its side perfectly. It was a long shot, maybe fifty paces, but Jonas was hopeful that he could pierce the animal's heart. The last thing he wanted to do was wound the magnificent beast and cause it undue pain.

He pulled back on the powerful bow that Fil's father had made, sighted in the animal, releasing his breath slowly as Fil had taught him, and fired. His heart pounded with anticipation as he narrowed his eyes on the path of the arrow. It whistled through the air as the big buck turned. It all happened so fast that it was hard for Jonas to see where the deer was hit, the animal bolted, dashing through the woods and disappearing completely.

Jonas tracked the blood trail up a narrow ridge until he finally found the dead animal at the edge of a cliff face. It seemed to Jonas that the buck had run to this spot, admired its beauty, and decided that this was a good place to die.

The beast was correct. The majestic animal was lying in the snow on his right, and Jonas stood and stared out at the valley below. The snow covered Tundren Mountains glittered in the morning sun. Jonas was suddenly overcome by a flood of emotions. He sat down next to the animal and began to cry. He might not ever see these mountains again. His mother, the only person that had ever cared for him, was dead, frozen, lying in her own blood in Gorum's cabin. He had cried almost daily the first couple of weeks in the cave, but his grief had been tempered somewhat by all the possibilities that were now open to him. The sorrow was fueling his new body. And now it seemed this renewed grief would never go away. Nor did he want it to; he would never forget his mother. Wiping away the tears, Jonas silently wished that his mother could have lived long enough to see him walk and hunt and bring home the meat of his first deer.

He would make things right, he promised to himself. He would take his new gift and do something good. Jonas unsheathed the beautiful hunting knife that he had taken from the dead cavalier. The blade was always bright and razor sharp and much lighter than it should be for a knife that was as long as his forearm. It was the most magnificent weapon he had ever seen.

Wiping away the last of his tears he took the knife and began to skin the deer as Fil had taught him. There was no way he could carry it all back, so he took the best pieces with the idea that he would come back for the rest if the mountain animals didn't scavenge the carcass. He wrapped the meat in the leather skin and stuffed it in his backpack.

Looking down at the dead animal he felt like he needed to say something. After all it was the first animal he had ever killed and Fil had explained to him that a good hunter should always thank the animal for its bounty.

"Thank you. Thank you for giving me your life, and your energy, so that I may grow strong to fight against the evil in the world." It sounded good, and Jonas smiled, walking away through the snow.

The walk back to the cave was peaceful. The snow was falling lightly and the forest was quiet and calm. Jonas was nearing the lake when he suddenly got a burning sensation on his chest, the skin erupting with a fiery pain, causing him to fall to his knees. His mind was assaulted by several flashing images as his chest throbbed.

In his mind's eye he saw the cave entrance, and nearing it was a large form, probably twice as tall as a big man. It was wearing dirty furs that covered a strong hairy body. In its right hand it carried a huge knotted club that was more a log than anything else. The image came and went leaving Jonas holding himself steady next to a tall pine, one hand rubbing his chest where the brief pain had erupted.

Then it came to him; it was a warning! "Fil," Jonas whispered with fear. He quickly dropped his pack, picking up his bow he ran as fast as his snowshoes could carry him towards the cave entrance.

He was panting with exertion as he neared the cave, but he was right. Lumbering towards the cave mouth was a huge ogre. The beast was walking slowly, sniffing the air with its grotesque nose as if it were tracking something. Jonas knew that it must have detected the scent of Fil, the fire, or something that grabbed its attention. Jonas had to warn Fil or he would be trapped inside the cave with no escape route. He had never seen an ogre before, but he had heard from others that they were big and strong and they loved human flesh. They were not often seen but they were known to inhabit the Tundren Mountains. According to the stories he had heard they were not very bright and Jonas was hoping that would work to their advantage.

Jonas quickly and quietly dashed from tree to tree closing the gap between them. He was frightened and his heart pounded in his chest. The monster was huge, but Jonas willed himself to calm down, taking slow deep breaths as he came within bow range of the beast.

Suddenly the ogre turned and sniffed the air behind him. Jonas knew that the breeze was blowing towards him so there was no way the ogre would smell him. Unfortunately the wind direction made it so Jonas could clearly smell the ogre, and it was a strong scent of animalistic musk mixed with the odor of wet and dirty fur, probably from the skins the thing wore over most of its powerful body. Jonas ducked behind a large tree and pulled back tighter on the nocked arrow, ready to fire if need be. Jonas slowly peeked around the tree and saw the ugly beast sniff the air. Large gaping nostrils flared in hopes of detecting a potential meal. Its cave-like mouth was slightly agape, exposing large yellow fangs. Small beady eyes were buried deep in a thick bony brow and its misshapen head was covered in a filthy mat of hair that hung past its shoulders.

The ogre turned around, starting back towards the cave's mouth, its massive tree trunk legs sinking deep into the snow with every step.

Jonas looked around, unsure of what to do. If the monster saw him there was no way that he could out run the beast's long strides in the snow. He would be forced to fight, and that was something that Jonas knew would not end well. Maybe Fil wasn't even in the cave, but that was unlikely and Jonas knew that he couldn't take that chance.

Looking around frantically, Jonas was praying for a miracle. He looked up and got an idea. Quickly he unlaced his snow shoes; quietly strapping the bow to his back he began to climb a large pine tree, holding his breath as he tried to be silent. He pulled himself up to a height of about ten paces. Taking up his bow he re-nocked an arrow, aiming through a hole in the branches. He could clearly make out the beast that was about eighty paces away. It was a long shot but the ogre was huge and Jonas knew that he wouldn't miss its broad back.

He aimed at the center of the ogre's torso and slowed his breathing down, his nerves causing his bow arm to shake and threatening his aim. He closed his eyes and thought of his friend that might be in that cave. Focusing on his rapid heartbeat he concentrated on its rhythm. Taking deep slow breaths the beating of his heart began to slow.

After he calmed himself, he opened his eyes, sighted in the beast, let out a slow breath, and released the shaft with a twang. Quickly he nocked another and before the other arrow hit its mark he already had the second arrow flying through the air. The first arrow struck the beast in its lower back. The ogre bellowed with pain, turning around to take the next arrow right in the hip. Again the beast roared and looked around for its assailant.

Jonas could see that the arrows did not sink in deep, the monster's thick skin and the dirty furs that clothed him served as protection. The beast lumbered through the snow closer to his tree, searching and sniffing the air for its attacker. Jonas could clearly see the beast's eyes blazing with anger as it roared defiantly into the woods.

Jonas's heart resumed its rapid beat and his arms trembled with fear, but he could do nothing else but draw back his bow again and let a shaft fly. This time the ogre saw the movement and looked up in the tree just as the arrow slammed into the side of its neck. Unlike the first two arrows, this arrow sunk in deep, halfway to its fletching, and the ogre stumbled backwards in pain.

Just then Fil came running out of the cave mouth holding his spear out before him, his eyes bulging with fright as he saw the ogre stumbling in the snow not more than thirty paces from him.

"Fil, I'm coming!" yelled Jonas as the ogre turned to face Fil. Jonas quickly began to climb down the tree, dropping the last few paces and landing heavily in the snow, his feet sinking in deep. He grabbed his bow, nocked another arrow and stumbled through the deep snow to get to the clearing by the ogre.

The monster grabbed the shaft sticking from its throat and yanked out the arrow. Blood poured from the wound and the ogre roared in pain as it turned from Fil to face Jonas again. The beast's eyes narrowed in anger and it charged the little human who had caused him so much pain.

Fil took in the scene quickly and did the only thing that he could do. He ran after the enraged monster with his spear point leading the way, screaming in defiance hoping to distract the monster from its charge. It didn't work and Fil knew that he wouldn't reach Jonas in time before the behemoth ran him over and crushed him into the snow.

Jonas stopped in fright, the roaring ogre bearing down on him with incredible speed. Its huge legs pounded through the snow and Jonas felt each step reverberate through his paralyzed body. The thing looked big from the tree, but now its massive size was almost overwhelming. He knew he would be easily crushed. Jonas's fear filled eyes were drawn to the huge tree trunk club that swung easily in its meaty hand.

That thought finally broke through his fear. He dropped to his knee, bending the great bow back as far as he could and taking careful aim. He knew he would only have one shot before the ogre's massive tree club crushed him to oblivion.

Strangely, Jonas's mind calmed and everything seemed to slow down. He breathed slowly, took aim, and waited until the beast was ten paces away before he let the shaft fly. Jonas dropped the bow, unsheathing his hunting knife as the black shaft pierced the charging monster's open mouth.

The ogre's roar was cut short, its head snapping back violently. The behemoth stopped about six paces from Jonas, dropped its huge club to the snow, and grasped for the shaft in its mouth. Jonas could just make out the feathered end sticking several inches beyond its sharp fangs. The creature stumbled around and then it clamped its mouth shut, snapping off the end of the arrow. Its eyes bulged, a look of pain and confusion crossing its face.

Suddenly its back arched and the ogre let out a gurgling roar, turning around and blindly swinging its huge arms at its attacker. Jonas saw Fil yank his spear from the ogre's back, leaping out of the way of the flailing monster and its powerful arms.

Fil and Jonas both circled the ogre as the monster stumbled around in pain. Finally the creature fell to its knees, its eyes rolled back in its head, and the ogre crashed face first into the snow.

Fil and Jonas both looked at each other, their eyes wide with shock and fear, their weapons held out defensively in front of them.

"Is it dead?" asked Jonas, his voice shaking with fright now that the danger seemed to be over.

"I think so," replied Fil as he neared the ogre. Fil unsheathed his hunting knife and slowly stepped up near the ogre's head, which was as big as Fil's torso. Fil kicked the beast hard in the head to make sure. Then he slid the sharp blade under its neck and slit the beast's throat. Blood poured from the wound, soaking into the white snow. "He is now," Fil said as he wiped off the blade on the ogre's fur cloak.

Jonas sat down in the snow, suddenly exhausted. "Is that an ogre?" he asked.

"I believe it is. I've never seen one myself but I've heard descriptions," answered Fil as he sat down in the snow next to Jonas. "Well done, Jonas. If it wasn't for you, I'd be dead. Thank you," stated Fil sincerely.

Jonas looked at Fil, his face ashen with fright as he tried to calm his nerves.

"It was nothing. You would've done the same."

"I mean it. You saved my life," Fil said again.

"It was a lucky shot."

"I don't think so. Like I said, you're skilled with a bow," replied Fil.

Jonas absently stroked the wood bow, his hands still shaking from the adrenaline pumping through his system. "If I didn't have your bow then I think we'd both be dead."

"You're probably right," Fil agreed.

They both sat in silence for a while, taking in what could have happened.

Fil finally got up and placed his hand on Jonas's shoulder. "You know, not many warriors can claim that they've killed an ogre by themselves."

Jonas looked up and smiled. "You stabbed him with your spear. I didn't kill it alone," he replied.

"Yes you did. That shaft in its mouth killed it. I think it just took a while for the stupid monster to know that it was dead."

Jonas got to his feet picking up the bow. "Well, we make a good team anyway," he replied. Fil smiled, picking up his spear from the snow.

"Yes we do," Fil replied as they made their way toward the cave mouth.

"Guess what?" asked Jonas.

"What?"

"I killed my first deer today," Jonas proudly announced.

"Now we can call you, Jonas, the ogre and deer slayer," Fil joked.

They nervously laughed together as they entered the warm cave, both knowing how close they had just come to dying.

***

It took about six weeks for the winter snows to subside and the first signs of spring to appear. The ice and snow began to melt as the temperature warmed. The forest was a bustle of activity as the many animals took joy in the warm sun. Chirping birds flittered from tree to tree while busy chipmunks ran across the forest floor digging and foraging for food.

Although the boys dreaded the thought of returning to their destroyed town, they knew they had to go back into Manson and gather whatever supplies they could find. They needed new clothes, shoes, blankets, and as much food as they could carry. They wanted a second bow and more arrows as well. Then they would start their long trek to Finarth.

Fil was apprehensive about the journey, and though Jonas was also reluctant to return to Manson, he was also excited for the adventure, for the chance to use his body and muscles, and for the chance to find out more answers about his God Mark. On several occasions Fil and Jonas had discussed the night when the ogre had attacked them. They both agreed that something or someone had warned Jonas that the ogre was near. How else could they explain the burning pain on his chest and the images that flashed in his mind? The question was, why were the gods getting involved in their lives? For two small town boys, the thought was overwhelming and a bit unsettling.

***

Manson was as bad as they thought it would be. Patches of snow still covered the ground, but not enough to blanket the many bodies still remaining. It was obvious to them both that animals and other scavengers had taken full advantage of the hundreds of corpses that were left behind. The bodies that had not been taken away by boargs or other larger animals showed signs typical of being in the elements for an entire winter. Luckily the smell was not as bad as it could have been as the temperature was still below freezing for most of the day.

Jonas did not enter Gorum's home. He did not want to see the body of his mother, especially if she had been eaten by winter scavengers. He wanted to remember her as she was, not how she died, and he knew that if he saw her torn and dismembered body that that image would forever be imprinted in his mind. So he avoided the home, as did Fil his own, and they both quickly performed their tasks and departed the town.

After the short re-supply trip to Manson, they began their sojourn east. They pushed themselves hard the first day, eager to get as far away from the town as they could, to distance themselves from the memories of that horrible night. The sun had set and the golden rays of warmth had long dropped behind the tall pine trees, leaving the mountain trail bathed in the cold shadows of dusk. Jonas and Fil set up camp in a clearing just off the trading road. It was still cold and patches of snow decorated the landscape.

"Should we light a fire?" asked Fil, leaning his pack against a fallen log and stretching his sore back.

"Some warm oats would do us well right now," responded Jonas. He, too, took off his pack and looked at Fil, hoping that he would make the decision on whether or not to light a fire. It was always a risk to light a fire at night. They both knew it, but the desire for warm food after a long hard hike began to overcome their caution.

Fil shrugged his shoulders as he dug in his pack for his tinderbox. "Let's light a brief fire, cook our oats, and then we'll put it out."

"Good plan," Jonas agreed. He quickly started a small hot fire while Fil prepared the meal of oats and salt. The food was good and they washed it down with cold mountain water. The oats warmed their bellies and they leaned back against a log and relaxed. The icy fingers of night were creeping into the clearing, leaving them in complete darkness except for the small amount of light radiating from the glowing red coals left over from their fire.

"Should we douse the coals?" asked Jonas.

"No, the light is nice, not to mention the warmth. The light is minimal. I think it is fine," answered Fil, pulling his traveling cloak over his shoulders. Jonas shivered, wrapping his wool cloak around him tightly, hoping to keep the chilling cold away.

They sat in silence for a few moments before Jonas finally spoke. "Fil, will you tell me how my mother died?" Jonas had never worked up the courage to ask Fil about what he saw that dreadful night. He didn't think he could take it, but now he was stronger, and he wanted to know. He wanted to know how she suffered so he would never forget her. The news would be hard to hear, but he was prepared for that.

Fil glanced up and Jonas could just make out the reluctance in his eyes under the faint glow of the coals. "Are you sure, Jonas…you really want to know?"

"I do. Please tell me what you saw."

Fil hesitated. "Okay, but it will not be easy to hear."

"I need to know," was all Jonas said.

Fil sighed. "I will tell you what I saw." He took a deep breath. "The battle was not going well. Everywhere the townspeople were being killed. The boargs were unstoppable. The cavalier had left to fight the Banthra and he gave orders to Gorum to get as many people to safety as he could. So I followed Gorum to his home where I assumed he was gathering up you and your mother. Instead I find a boarg feeding on his remains. I remember feeling so much anger. It all just exploded out when I saw what the boarg had done to Gorum. I went berserk and stabbed it in the back with my spear. The beast jerked away from me and I couldn't remove my spear. It was injured, but it was not dead. The thing's jaw was badly damaged, probably by Gorum, and my spear had pierced its back deeply, but it still came at me. I grabbed Gorum's sword on the ground and swung at its neck as hard as I could. That finally killed the thing." Fil paused for a minute to look at Jonas skeptically. "You sure you want to hear the rest?"

"Yes, please, Fil. I want to know," Jonas responded, his eyes wide with emotion.

"Okay," Fil whispered. "It was then that I heard a noise against the wall near Gorum. It was your mother. She was partly covered by a dead boarg, and I rushed to her side. She held a bloody knife in her hand. The boarg's throat had been cut. She had killed it but she was beyond any help. Her throat had been cut open by the boarg's talons."

Fil stopped for a moment as Jonas wiped tears from his eyes. "Was she alive? Did she say anything?" Jonas asked, his voice catching in his throat.

"Yes, she was barely alive. With her last strength she grabbed my wrist and told me where you were hiding, and made me promise to take care of you. She was not in pain Jonas, she was just thinking of you," Fil said lamely in an attempt to lessen Jonas's grief.

There was silence for a few moments as Jonas regained his composure, wiping the remaining tears from his face. "Thank you for telling me. I'm glad that you did."

Suddenly a low growl emanated from the darkness not too far behind them. Jonas's body went rigid. He reached for his recently claimed short sword lying next to him. Fil reacted similarly, grabbing his spear. They were both up and facing the forest behind them, their weapons held before them in shaking hands.

"What was that?" whispered Jonas.

"It sounded like a boarg," replied Fil, grasping his spear tightly. His voice was dripping with fear but his stance was firm as his wide eyes scanned the darkness.

Just then, another growl came from behind them. Jonas spun to face the darkness holding his sword protectively before him. They were back to back, the darkness of the night sucking away the light as the red embers slowly died. They said nothing, too afraid to talk, and not sure what to say anyway.

Suddenly a loud roar erupted from the darkness followed by a gray shape flying through the air towards Fil. He leaped to the side, jabbing his spear at the attacking boarg. The spear tip hit the beast in the side as the huge beast scattered the remaining coals. The boarg howled in pain as it gripped Fil's spear, snapping it like a twig.

Jonas rolled out of the way of the boarg to come up standing in darkness. Thankfully the moon was out and its bluish glow lightly blanketed the area. It was not much, but it was enough to barely illuminate a second boarg barreling towards him like a charging bull.

Jonas got his sword up just as the beast hit him with tremendous force, launching him through the air. He landed hard on his back. The air whooshed from his lungs as he struggled to get up. Miraculously he had managed to hold onto his sword, raising it in defense against the rushing boarg.

But he was not fast enough. The boarg lashed out with one of its large clawed hands, and Jonas, scurrying on his back, fought frantically with his sword, cutting the beast across the arm. The animal roared, and with lightning speed, used its other arm to grab Jonas's neck. The boarg's strong claws began to crush his throat. The pain intensified as the boarg squeezed, lifting Jonas into the air. He felt himself grow weaker but he still managed to swing his sword down toward the boarg's arms. The boarg batted the weapon away with its other hand. Jonas felt his neck tighten as his airway was slowly choked off. His eyes began to blur and his head swam from dizziness as the boarg brought him closer to its open mouth.

Fil dropped the broken spear and drew his short sword from the sheath at his hip. He was just able to raise the blade as the boarg swung its clawed hand towards his chest. Stumbling backwards Fil chopped his sword down in a powerful swing, cutting the beast deeply across its forearm. But the animal continued its attack unfazed. The boarg roared, lashing out with its other hand, four sharp claws slicing shallow cuts across Fil's chest as he leaned back from the attack. He stumbled further backwards, frantically trying to evade the animal's deadly claws.

Jonas struggled and kicked, trying to free himself from the boarg's iron grip. He managed to grab onto the animals thick hairy forearm with both hands and dug in his fingernails, hoping to break the beasts hold on him, but his efforts were to no avail. The animal kept squeezing and Jonas's vision swam even further as his oxygen depleted brain began to shut down.

Suddenly, the grip loosened, and as Jonas gasped for air, his vision cleared. The boarg had dropped him to the ground. Howling in pain, the angry beast spun around towards the darkness. Jonas, lying on his back and holding his injured throat, could clearly see two white feathered arrows embedded in the boarg's muscled back.

Out of the darkness, came a large fur covered body. In the grayness of night it looked like another boarg, but it wasn't. The form materialized out of the darkness and moved toward the boarg with amazing speed, moonlight reflecting off a glimmering blade. The injured boarg lashed out with a clawed hand but the newcomer quickly ducked under the swing, slicing his glowing blade across the beast's abdomen. Then the savior raced past the dying beast without a second look. Jonas couldn't tell if the warrior's sword was actually glowing or if it was just the reflection of the moonlight off the blade's mirror like finish.

Fil tripped over a fallen log, swinging his sword left and right trying to keep the boarg away from him. He landed on his back and lifted his sword hoping to fend off the attack that he knew was coming.

The remaining boarg lashed out, its dangerous arm only a blur as it easily batted Fil's sword out of his hand. Instantly Fil felt the boarg's tremendous weight as it landed on top of him. He grimaced, struggling under the weight and strength of the animal, feeling the boarg's claws dig into his flesh. The boarg lifted its head towards the moon and roared defiantly, eager to feed on the flesh of its prey.

Jonas followed the warrior with wide eyes as he leaped over the burning and scattered coals, his glimmering blade spinning through the air toward the last boarg who was now on top of Fil.

The boarg's roar was cut short as the razor sharp sword sliced through its exposed neck. Blood spurted like a fountain from the gruesome wound as the animal's head disappeared into the night.

The weight of the boarg disappeared as the beast fell to the side. Fil frantically scooted away from the dead body, wiping its blood from his face and eyes. He didn't know what had happened and he could barely see anything in the darkness. Then a dark shadow of a man stood above him blocking out the moon's light. He carried a shimmering blood stained blade in his right hand.

"Get up, boy. Ya don't need to fear me," the man said to Fil. His voice was deep and raspy. The shadow disappeared as the man moved away from Fil.

Jonas got up slowly, his hand still rubbing his injured throat. The man did not look at Jonas as he began to flick a few of the burning coals back into a small pile.

"Get wood, Jonas, a fire will help chase away de fear that is now gripp'n ur heart," their rescuer said.

Jonas recognized the voice and the burly fur covered form that knelt by the embers. The man had added a few small sticks to the coals and a flame quickly erupted, painting the man's face with an orange glow. His face was covered in hair, but Jonas could just make out a small smile as Tuvallus turned towards him.

"Good to see ya again, boy."

The fire burned brightly and the heat was welcoming. Tuvallus was right; the bright warm flames chased away the fingers of fear that grasped his heart after the boargs' attack.

Tuvallus was heating up some tea in a tarnished metal pot that hung over the dancing flames. The aromatic spices in the tea reminded Jonas of his mother. He lost himself in his thoughts for a moment before looking up at Tuvallus. The man was stirring the tea with a metal spoon.

"Thank you, Tuvallus for saving us," Jonas said.

"Yes, we are in your debt," added Fil with a nod.

Tuvallus looked up at Jonas and Fil. "You owe me nuthin," he grunted. "My appearance was your luck, that is all," he said brusquely.

"Maybe so, but you didn't have to aid us, so we thank you nonetheless," Jonas replied smoothly.

Tuvallus grunted again and nodded his head in acknowledgement. Then, taking a large metal spoon he ladled some hot tea into two cups. He handed them each a cup before pouring some for himself and leaning back against a log. Digging into his pack he pulled out a small wood box with a lid. He tossed the box to Fil who caught it, spilling a bit of his tea in the process. "Healing ointment...clean your cuts with water and dress the wounds with the ointment. It will help rid the wound of infection."

"My thanks," responded Fil as he set his tea down to clean his wounds. "How did you come across us, Tuvallus?" he asked.

"I was hunten when I came across a huge buck, the biggest I'd eva seen. I tracked it for a day and then it jist vanished….no sign…nutten. That is when I saw ur tracks, and the boargs' tracks followun use. The tracks led me here…just in time it would seem."

Tuvallus's speech was fairly primitive. Years of living on his own didn't make for lots of conversation, and in time his spoken language deteriorated, giving him just another reason not to interact much with people.

Fil glanced at Jonas, and Jonas wondered if he was thinking the same thing. Was Tuvallus' sudden appearance just coincidence? Jonas couldn't rule anything out considering what had happened to him. Jonas made a mental note to talk to Fil later in private.

"Tuvallus, I have never seen anyone fight like that. Where did you learn to do that?" Jonas asked.

Tuvallus drank from his steaming mug of tea before he answered. "I was a soldier in the Tarsinian army many years ago. Now, boy, when u goen to tell me what happened to ya?" Tuvallis asked, clearly changing the subject. "The last I saw of ya, you could barely walk. Now you be lookin fine."

Jonas shifted uneasily, not sure how to respond to the burly mountain man. He looked at Fil who shrugged his shoulders and said nothing. So Jonas figured that he would tell Tuvallus the truth, at least half of it anyway.

"After our town was destroyed by the boargs, Fil and I hid out in the mountains until the winter snows subsided. One day I woke up and I could move my body. I was sore, and very weak, but I could move, although I'm not sure how. It took me months to gain my strength. But as you can see, I eventually did." Jonas didn't know what else to say so he just sipped his tea to fill the silent void.

"That's it?" Tuvallus asked.

"Yes, that's what happened," answered Jonas.

"I went into Manson after de attack…not one survived. How did two boys live when no one else did?" He asked bluntly.

"I don't know," replied Jonas.

"I see. Well…I reckon there be more to the story than that, but makes no matter to me. I'll be gone in the mornen."

"Do you want to travel with us, Tuvallus?" asked Fil, hopefully.

Tuvallus grunted again, drinking the last of his tea and laying out his bedroll by the fire. "Good luck on yer travels," he answered as he lay down by the crackling fire and closed his eyes.

***

The journey through the Tundren Mountains was long and arduous, but Jonas relished the hard work and actually welcomed his sore and tired muscles. It made him feel alive. Unfortunately, they soon ran out of food and they had to stop and hunt, set snares, and gather berries, roots and wild onions.

Finally, after three weeks of traveling, they began the descent on the east side of the Tundren Mountains. The trading road was old and well worn. Caravans made the long trek to deliver goods from Finarth, Tarsis, Cuthaine, and Nu-menell, to the western cities of Onett, Bitlis, and Mynos. Merchants brought their wares to Manson and the other mountain towns, and then continued west, finally arriving at the coast and the great Sea of Algard.

Jonas remembered vividly the days when the merchants would come to their town. There would be a week of celebration with lots of dancing and drinking as the merchants sold and traded their products. It was the only chance for the townspeople to buy spices and salted exotic meats from the east, jewelry and pottery from the craftsmen of Finarth, silk and cotton from distant lands, and if you were really wealthy, weapons and armor from the dwarven clans in Dwarf Mount.

Jonas never got to spend much time at the merchant tents because he was always picked on or beat up by the other boys, but his mother would always take him to see the rare goods, listen to the stories and music, and watch the dancers, ignoring the stares, taunts, and ridicule of the superstitious townspeople.

Jonas's heart ached as he thought of his mother, but it was beginning to seem like a distant memory. The attack on their village had only been three months ago, yet it seemed like another lifetime. He had changed so much. Not only was his affliction gone, but his body was growing with strength every day, and he was gaining confidence with every step that he took. No longer was he the little cripple boy who could barely hold himself upright.

It was starting to get dark when they neared a crossroads, one road meandering to the right, while the other lead northeast.

Jonas sat down on a big boulder and took a drink from his water skin. "Which way do we go, Fil?"

Fil looked left and then right. He, too, was uncertain. "We should be heading southeast, which I think is to the right. I'm not exactly sure, but it's almost dark so let's camp here for the night and we'll figure it out in the morning."

"Alright," replied Jonas. "Let's look for a good spot off the main road."

"Lead the way," Fil responded.

They found a small clearing off the main road. It was a good spot, surrounded by large trees and covered in a soft moss. They ate a cold meal of dried venison, sweet salal berries, and some pine nuts that they had collected the previous day.

"We're running out of food," Fil commented tiredly as he laid out his bedroll.

"I know, I think we need to slow down and do some hunting," responded Jonas, absently. He was holding the cavalier's blade in his hand, his mind elsewhere.

Fil looked at him with concern as he lay down on his wool blanket. "You okay?"

"Yeah, I was just thinking, that's all." Jonas looked up at Fil. "To be honest, I'm kind of scared."

Fil got up on his elbow looking at his friend with concern. "What about?" asked Fil, with no hint of mockery.

"I don't know," Jonas answered. "Things have changed so fast. What are we going to do? Neither one of us has even been out of the Tundren Mountains. Now we have no home, no family, and we are heading to Finarth, a city we have only heard people talk about. And this symbol on my chest scares me. What does it mean?"

Fil sat all the way up and looked at Jonas seriously. "I'm scared too. Everything has happened so fast that it is just now beginning to sink in. The symbol on your chest is obviously Shyann's mark, which means she has chosen you for something. I have no idea what her plan is, or why she marked you, but you must have faith that she will unveil her reason to you." Fil reached out and gave Jonas a brotherly pat on his shoulder. "We'll be okay."

Jonas looked up and smiled at his friend. "Yeah, I know, and Fil," Jonas paused, looking up into his friends eyes. "Thanks for not leaving me before, at the village."

"No problem, we are family now, meant to be together. Our destinies are entwined. I can feel it. Now let's get some sleep. I'll take first watch," Fil said smiling.

Four
New Friends

Jonas awoke to a gentle nudge on his shoulder. Fil was kneeling next to him, his finger to his mouth warning Jonas to be silent. Jonas's sleepiness vanished quickly as he saw Fil's worried expression.

"What is it?" whispered Jonas, quietly sitting up.

"A caravan just came up to the crossroads and set up camp," whispered Fil.

"A caravan? How long have I been asleep?" Jonas asked.

"Not long," replied Fil. "What do you want to do?"

Jonas got up and buckled on his belt and hunting knife. "Let's go take a look, see if they appear friendly. Did you get a good look at them?" he asked as he grabbed his bow.

"No, but it looks like a merchant caravan," responded Fil who also buckled on his sword belt and retrieved his bow.

They crept silently through the woods until they neared the crossroads. It was dark, but the clear sky and the bright stars lit the road well. They hid in the trees, blanketed by the shadows of the night, trying to get a good look at the newcomers.

The caravan consisted of twenty wagons pulled by oxen. In the center of the crossroads was a huge fire surrounded by at least a dozen men. Their caravan was large and the only open space available was the road itself, besides, these roads were seldom traveled this time of the year so it was unlikely that they would come across any other travelers that night.

Fil and Jonas moved a little closer to get a better look. One large fire burned in the middle and they saw several smaller fires that were spread out on the road. There were about fifteen men at arms, wearing armor and swords, and equally that number of horses tied to the wagons. Spying on the group they saw a handful of men who wore traveling clothes of high quality and carried no weapons. They did indeed look like traders.

"You're right, looks like a merchant caravan," Jonas whispered in Fil's ear.

"I agree. What do you want to do? Should we ask them if we can join their fire?" asked Fil.

"Let's get a little closer to one of the smaller fires," suggested Jonas.

Fil nodded his head in acknowledgement and they crept silently around the big fire to one of the smaller fires that was separated from the rest of the men. Nearing the glowing blaze they noticed that there was only one figure there, huddling close to the fire, sharpening a thin hunting knife. His face was hooded and they couldn't make out the features underneath. It was dark, but they could see that he had a small, thin frame, and he wore a green traveling cloak, light green tunic, and huntsman boots laced up to the knee.

Suddenly the figure stopped sharpening the blade and lifted his head as if he heard something. Fil and Jonas stopped moving and looked on with interest. The pause was brief, and he started sharpening the blade again. They got to the edge of the wood line, about fifteen paces away, and studied the lone figure some more. He kept sharpening his thin curved blade, but after a few moments, without lifting his head, he spoke.

"Are you going to hide in the woods and stare at me or join me at my fire?" the stranger said in a soft melodic voice, finally lifting his head and turning towards Jonas and Fil. "Have no fear, I will not harm you."

Jonas noticed that he was not a *he* after all, but a woman, with a soft and comforting voice. Jonas and Fil looked at each other uncertainly. They really had no choice now, she knew they were there. Jonas wasn't sure how she could have known; they had been very quiet and were both decent at the art of woodcraft. Fil had developed his skill during the many years of hunting with his father, and Jonas had learned that he was a natural. Hunting and moving silently in the forest required great concentration and focus, and Jonas had learned over the last few months that he had both traits in great quantities.

Stepping from the darkness, Jonas and Fil slowly approached her. They walked into the light shed by the fire. The lady pulled off her hood so they could see her better. She still held her hunting knife at her side, unthreatening.

Jonas and Fil gasped inwardly, their breath catching in their throats. She was beautiful, with long blond hair cascading past her shoulders, a soft but angular face with a petite nose. Her lips were thin, but inviting, with just a touch of pink that contrasted beautifully with her smooth fair skin. But it was her eyes that really held them spellbound. They were larger than normal, oval in shape and sparkling with intelligence and fire.

Suddenly some of the men around the large fire noticed the newcomers. They quickly unsheathed their swords as they approached the lady's fire. The men were led by a large bearded warrior with dark, deep set eyes.

"Who are you? What is your business here?" the warrior asked brusquely advancing on the boys.

"It's okay, Cyn, they are harmless," stated the blond woman. When she turned her head to speak to the warrior, Jonas noticed that her ears were pointed and protruding noticeably from her hair.

"You're an elf?" he asked dumbstruck.

The lady looked back at him smiling. "I'm a half-elf. Now, please state your names and your reason for sneaking around our campfires so the good captain here will put away his sword," she said with a hint of humor.

"I'm sorry lady, but we meant no offense. I am Jonas Kanrene and this is my friend, Fil Tanrey. We are from the mountain town of Manson."

"I am no highborn lady, Jonas. You may call me Allindrian. Cyn, will you please put away your blade."

Cyn looked at her and back at Jonas. "I know this town. Good stout people. How is Braal, the huntsman?" he asked, sheathing his sword.

"Dead," Fil stated bluntly. "Our entire town is gone, destroyed by boargs."

Everyone stared at Fil with surprised expressions, unsure if they heard him correctly.

"That is what brings us here, Allindrian, we have nothing left. We are trying to get to Finarth to join the king's army," Jonas added.

More men moved around the half-elf's fire. A heavy set man wearing a dark traveling cloak stepped forward. His face was slightly round and his head was covered with short curly brown hair streaked with gray. The man smiled warmly at the two boys, holding out his hand in greeting.

"My name is Landon Bylock. I am a merchant and trader from Tarsis and this is my caravan." He shook each of their hands. "It sounds like you boys have been through a lot. Why don't you join us at the fire, take some food, and tell us this tale. How does that sound?" Landon's genuine smile was comforting and Jonas couldn't help but like him.

"We would like that, sir. Thank you for your generosity. It has been a while since we've had a good warm meal," Jonas said.

Jonas and Fil sat around the large fire, eating a hot bowl of flavorful meaty stew, and drinking cold mountain water. Jonas felt awkward being the center of attention, but he was grateful for the food and the warm fire, and he felt at ease with these men. Tough warriors surrounded him, and for the first time in a long while he felt safe.

Jonas began the story. When he got to the part when Airos, the cavalier, appeared, Landon interrupted him.

"I have met Airos once before in Tarsis. He is a first rank cavalier, an amazing man, and almost as skilled as Allindrian with a sword. Where is he now?" asked Landon.

"He is dead, killed by a Banthra," Jonas replied sadly. Landon was taken aback. Even Allindrian looked up with shock.

"What!" Landon asked. "That cannot be, he was unbeatable, and a Banthra you say? I cannot believe it!" Landon exclaimed in disbelief.

"Landon, let him finish the story," interjected Allindrian. "Then we will try and make some sense out of this troubling news."

"Yes, you're quite right, Allindrian. It is just such a shock. Go ahead young man, finish your tale."

Jonas looked at Fil who nodded his head for Jonas to continue. It took Jonas about twenty minutes to tell the tale. Fil interrupted often to fill in the gaps and finally he got to the part where the ogre had attacked their cave hideout. Fil looked at him uncertainly as he skipped over the part about the symbol on his chest, the warning he was given, and the healing that he received. In fact Jonas never mentioned that he was once a cripple. He didn't know how they would react to him being God Marked, and quite frankly, he really didn't know how to explain it. He thought it best to keep that hidden for now until he knew more about it himself.

"So, young Jonas, you dropped an ogre with your bow?" Cyn asked with a hint of disbelief.

"He did. He shot the ogre twice at sixty paces. One arrow hit the thing in the hip and the other in the back. Then he hit the beast a third time in the neck. That is when the ogre charged him and I came out of the cave. I didn't know what to do so I ran at the beast with my spear as the creature charged Jonas like an angry bull. It was incredible. Jonas stopped, nocked another arrow, and dropped to his knee while the ogre charged. When the roaring beast got within ten paces, Jonas loosed the shaft which hit the beast in its open mouth. The ogre's head snapped back and the thing stumbled around. That is when I came up behind it and stabbed it with my spear. The ogre was already dying though. He just stumbled around and then fell face first into the snow. It was amazing. He saved my life," Fil stated proudly.

The warriors around the campfire looked at each other, their expressions revealing a newfound respect for the young boys.

"That is quite a feat, young man; to face a charging ogre with a bow. You have steady nerves. You should be proud; both of you should be," Cyn spoke, his shadowed eyes looking at them with respect.

Landon then spoke up. "You boys have told an amazing story and my heart is heavy for your loss. This is news that must be brought to King Gavinsteal of Finarth. Airos's death is a huge loss to us all…and a Banthra attacking your town, it makes no sense. I guess the rumors are true then," he said sadly.

"What rumors, sir?" asked Jonas.

"The rumors that Malbeck the Dark One is back and that a new evil is spreading south from the Black Lands and Banrith Castle. If your story is true, and a Banthra attacked your town, whatever the reason was, the Dark One must be back. Tarsis borders the Black Lands and Banrith. The fortress of Malbeck has been trouble for the royal family of Tarsis for thousands of years." Landon noticed the boys' confused look. "Do you not know the story of Malbeck the Dark One?" he asked, seeing the boy's bewildered expressions.

"We know very little. We are from a small mountain town, sir. We all struggled to survive every day and had little time for stories of the past. I know of the Dark One, but not anything of detail," stated Fil.

"I see, well, I will have to remedy that. A thousand years ago, the ruler of Banrith Castle was Malbeck Dysander who was a ruthless king. He taxed his people heavily, ruling with an iron fist. Slavery, rape, and murder were commonplace in his kingdom. He became a follower of Gould, as the dark god's creed resembled his own. Besides, he hunted for power, and Gould could provide what he wanted," Landon continued as more than one man around the campfire made the sign of the High One on his chest at the mention of Gould, the tormentor. "Gould gave him power but molded him into his servant. Many years came and went and Malbeck grew in power. He was not recognizable any more. Gould's magic had twisted his mind and body into something else, something dark, a demon capable of wielding god magic."

"What is the difference in god magic and mage magic?" asked Jonas.

"I'll speak to that, good merchant," interjected Allindrian. "God magic is magic freely given from a god or saint. The magic is given to a devout follower to further the cause of the god that grants the power. The elves call the energy of all things the Ru'Ach and we believe that everything you see is made from this energy. Human belief is different and I will not get into that now, but, in the case of Malbeck, he was fed magic from the most powerful of the Forsworn, which is Gould." Again the men all made the warding mark of the High One. Allindrian noticed Jonas and Fil staring at the men when they made the four pointed mark on their chest. "It is believed by some that just mentioning Gould's name, or Naz-reen, goddess of the dark and killing, or Dykreel, god of torture and pain, that you open your heart and soul to their powers. The three together are called the Forsworn."

"Is that true? The opening your heart part?" asked Fil.

"It can be. You see, Fil, there are men of pure heart and soul that cannot be corrupted by the mere mentioning of a name, but these men are few. Airos was one, incorruptible by evil, but almost all men have a speck of darkness in them, a part of them that, under the right circumstances, can let in that evil…anger, jealousy, envy, greed; emotions that can slowly let in the vile filth until the dark poison has completely taken over. Everyone has to be on constant guard for this poison. Naz-reen is the best at this. She uses intrigue and plot over many years to slowly turn the hearts of men black, so they may come to serve her."

"Airos told me that my soul was pure," Jonas said softly as he remembered the conversation he had had with Airos.

Allindrian looked at him with wonder. She stared deeply into his eyes for a few moments as if she were searching for something. Jonas looked away; he could not stare at her without blushing. "That is indeed something, Jonas," Allindrian finally said. "Airos would not be able to lie, and he did have the power to look into the hearts of men. You are indeed a special young man, for having a pure soul is rare, very rare indeed."

There was a long pause before Fil interrupted the silence. "What is regular magic then, Allindrian?" he asked.

Allindrian broke her gaze from Jonas and looked at Fil before answering. "Mage magic comes from nature, from the Ru'Ach, which is everything around us. Everything you see has energy, the trees, grass, rocks, stars.....everything." Allindrian held out her hand and murmured a few quick words. Blue fire leaped from her hand, flickering a foot in the air. Fil and Jonas jumped back in surprise. "This is mage magic."

"You are a sorceress?" asked Jonas in awe. He had never before seen magic.

"Yes, I have some magical power, but not much. I have spent my life studying combat, and if you want to become powerful in magic you must devote your life to the study. Most cannot do it and that is why wizards are very rare. Kings may have court wizards but a powerful mage is rare indeed. My elven blood has made it easier to learn magic, for elves are more connected to nature than are humans. There are words of power that give magic users access to the energy of the Ru'Ach." She closed her hand and the leaping blue flame disappeared. "Since elves are the oldest of the races, we have a stronger link to the Ru'Ach. Our ancient language gives us access to the river of power. Elven wizards, or ekahals, get their power from the Ru'Ach. The ancient elves created magic from the Ru'Ach and all forms of magic use come from the skills that they developed thousands of lifetimes ago. It is not the power that is good or evil, but the person that directs the magic. Certain words and careful study give magic users access to the source of power, which is the Ru'Ach. Elves use the true source, the ancient elven language that is heavily guarded and not taught to outsiders. The common elven tongue is a dialect that we use in daily life. Humans and demi-humans that wield magic use different varieties of this technique by twisting different dialects of the elven language with the common languages. Powerful wizards have studied these languages for years and have unlocked the power of the Ru'Ach. Wizards are always trying to steal words of power from the elven ekahals, who are the most powerful wizards in Kraawn. The term to describe this theft is called Nis'Tai, which means 'dishonorable'."

"So Malbeck used god magic to try and conquer the lands of Kraawn many years ago?" asked Fil.

"Yes," replied Landon. "He also used god magic to create the six Banthras and other lesser minions. He trapped a group of cavaliers who had attempted to enter Banrith and destroy him. The legend goes that he spent years corrupting and twisting their bodies into his most powerful warriors."

"How could one man trap six powerful cavaliers?" Fil asked.

"I do not know exactly," answered Landon. "I have heard that when they entered his lair, where Gould's power was the strongest, that they were somehow shielded from their own god's power. But I don't know if anyone knows the truth of it."

"But if their hearts were pure, how did he corrupt them?" asked Jonas.

"That is a good question," replied Allindrian. "Unfortunately we do not really know how he did it. As I said before, almost all men have a speck of darkness in them. Maybe their hearts were not totally pure. Maybe their energy left their bodies and left a corruptible shell behind. We do not know. All we know is that a Banthra is almost undefeatable, only a powerful cavalier would have a chance at killing one."

"Airos killed one," stated Fil.

"Airos was a first rank cavalier. He was the best. There are only a few first rank cavaliers left now that he is dead. As I said, his death is a huge loss to all that is good," Landon added solemnly.

"So, what are the rumors of Malbeck's return? How was he defeated and how could he be back now after so many years?" Jonas asked.

Landon let out a deep breath and smiled at the inquisitive boy. "That is a long story, young man, a story for another day. Besides, I do not know all the answers to your questions. My caravan is going to Finarth. We are two weeks out and it would be my pleasure to have you both as my guests. Would you like to travel with us?" the heavyset merchant asked, smiling warmly. Jonas and Fil looked at each other, eagerly nodding in agreement.

"We thank you, sir, for your generosity, and would very much like to be your guests," Jonas responded with a smile.

"That is good news," replied Landon standing up from the fire. "Now, let's get some sleep and save some of our stories for the trip to Finarth."

Everyone stood and went about getting ready to lie down for the night.

Allindrian smiled at the boys; her perfect white teeth sparkling in the moonlight. "Come with me, ogre slayers, you may sleep at my fire," the half-elf said with a grin, moving back to her fire away from the others. They followed her and laid down their bedrolls by the flickering flames, basking in the warmth of the little blaze. As Jonas wrapped himself in his wool blanket he looked up at Allindrian who went back to sharpening her knife.

"Landon said that Airos was almost as good as you with a blade. That must mean that you are a very skilled warrior," stated Jonas.

Allindrian smiled at him and her eyes sparkled with something that Jonas recognized as pure confidence in her abilities.

"Will you teach us?" asked Jonas.

"We shall talk in the morning, young Jonas. Now get some sleep. You have had a long day."

Jonas smiled at the lovely warrior and stretched out on his back. He looked up at the sparkling stars, sighed, and closed his eyes. For once things seemed to be going their way. They were with a group of armed men who were willing to take them to Finarth and he was sleeping next to a beautiful half-elf warrior who might teach him how to use a sword. *It could be worse* he thought, as fatigue overcame him and he fell asleep.

***

The first week with the caravan went by quickly, and Jonas and Fil soon fell right in step with the hardy travelers. Landon was a gracious host, allowing the boys to eat with him at night and sharing with them tasty exotic foods, spices, and drink they had never sampled before. One was a thick dark drink that was sweet and bitter at the same time. Landon had said that it was made from sugar, water, and a mixture that was a combination of spices and a ground substance that he called cacao, which came from a bean-like seed in a far off land. They spoke often with the warriors who warmed up to the boys quickly. The men at arms asked them many questions about their recent ordeal and the violence they had faced seemed to help them form a bond with the tough men.

Jonas and Fil wanted to do their part to help with the work on the caravan, for they were taught never to accept charity when they had two good hands and legs. Jonas took that lesson very seriously since it was not long ago that he didn't have two good hands and legs. They helped with the oxen and horses, cleaning and brushing them, and feeding and watering them at night. During the day they would bring food and water to the mercenaries who Landon paid to guard his caravan. They enjoyed and took pride in their work as they slowly meandered out of the Tundrens and into the Finarthian hills. Allindrian mostly kept to herself, tracking up ahead for hours at a time and suddenly appearing out of nowhere to give reports. The boys learned that she was a ranger, trained by the elves in Mel'un-riam, the elven kingdom located far to the west, and north of the Gadrian Mountains.

Allindrian did agree to show them some basic sword fighting skills, just enough to get them started on their own so they wouldn't be massacred if they needed to fight. It was exhausting work, but they were both excited and thrilled and took to the challenge with teeth-gritting resolve. Allindrian was a stern instructor who started their training late in the evening after they had eaten and didn't stop until the sun's rays dipped behind the tall mountain peaks. They used stout sticks, about as long as a long sword, to spar with.

Four days into their march to Finarth, Fil, Jonas, and Allindrian were sparring in a clearing by their camp. "You must get your arms stronger, Fil," Allindrian admonished calmly as she sidestepped his clumsy stroke, smacking him on his left shoulder. Fil stumbled to the ground exhausted, but slowly got back up to his feet, panting heavily. "Swordsmen must first master their strength, not their blade. A strong back, stomach, and arms will allow faster and more powerful strokes, and those muscles are also needed to maintain balance. Your lungs must be strong in order to fight long drawn out battles. And we must not neglect the mind; it is the strongest muscle of all. A confident warrior, who thinks not of defeat, but of victory, is a warrior to reckon with. But you should start with strengthening your body first, and your mind will follow. It is like a home built of wood. The outside may look beautiful, but if the foundation and frame are not strong then it will weather poorly and fall down in a heavy storm."

"Our bodies are the foundation?" asked Fil, readying his stick again, assuming the start position that she had taught him.

"Precisely. It matters not how many fancy moves you have. If you are not strong and fast with powerful lungs, then you will be killed in battle if you face opponents that have mastered their mind and body," Allindrian added as they began to slowly circle each other, their sticks held before them.

Fil was tired and sweating heavily, but Allindrian was calm, seemingly unaffected by the constant dueling. She struck out quickly and Fil parried the stroke, trying the parry she had taught him. Again he was not quick enough and her stick was a blur, deflecting the defensive move and smacking him heavily on his wrist. With a grunt he dropped the stick.

Jonas, who had been watching the session, grimaced as her stick made a solid thud as it struck Fil's wrist. Fil bit back the pain, grabbing the stick from the ground.

"That is enough for now, Fil. Well done. Now, Jonas, it is your turn," Allindrian smiled as she faced him. Jonas stepped into the circle and held up his stick.

In just four days of training, Fil and Jonas had made good progress. They mastered a few training positions, parries, and offensive moves. Their arms were not yet accustomed to the movements that they were learning and they often went to bed at night with sore muscles and bruises from Allindrian's stick. They would hear the warriors laugh every time Allindrian smacked them hard on the body, but, even after a few days, it became apparent that Jonas was much better than Fil with a sword, even if it was just a stick. He was quick and agile, and he did not tire as fast as Fil. The constant running, walking, and climbing he had been doing for the last two months had made Jonas's muscles strong and fast.

Jonas thrived on the physical exertion, often staying up late into the night quietly going through the forms she had taught him. He began to do various exercises to strengthen his arms, stomach, and legs. Allindrian taught him certain movements that he could do alone to build muscle. A tree limb could be employed to pull his body up until his chin was level with the branch or he would lie on his back, lifting his legs off the ground and holding them steady until his stomach burned from the exertion.

This time Jonas hoped to score a touch on Allindrian. He knew that she wasn't really trying, and he wanted to capitalize on that and surprise her with a quick touch. Jonas decided to launch an offensive attack first, before he was too tired and covered with bruises. He moved in quickly with the point of his stick, hoping to bait her to block the false attack. Allindrian swung her stick down to do just that, but Jonas rolled his stick under the parry, trying to smack Allindrian's exposed right thigh.

He thought he had her but she suddenly wasn't even there. She had flipped her stick from her right to her left hand and, effortlessly stepping her leg back from his attack, she swung down, smacking him hard on the right thigh, harder than normal thought Jonas. He jumped back ignoring the instinct to rub his stinging leg.

"Good idea, Jonas. That was a well-executed roll," Allindrian praised him with a slight smile.

The three practiced hard for a while, Allindrian teaching them various moves and forms until the sun dipped its head behind the snow covered peaks forcing them to stop.

"Good work. You are both doing well. I am impressed with your dedication. Keep working on the forms and your strength and you'll become swordsmen yet." Allindrian had barely broken a sweat. She grinned at the two young men, who smiled broadly at her praise.

Allindrian tossed her stick to Jonas who grabbed it out of the air. The ranger smiled warmly at them both and then leaped into the darkness, melting into the forest as if she was never there.

Fil and Jonas blinked, thinking that it was the flickering firelight that was playing tricks with their eyes.

"I hate it when she does that," remarked Fil with wonder.

"Someday, I want to be that fast," responded Jonas.

***

The morning dawned with the promise of a beautiful spring day. The chilling mountain air was slowly being beaten down by the warm spring breeze flowing across the Finarthian hills. The rolling hills were astonishing. They were blanketed with pockets of budding oak trees and elms and the green meadows were specked with blooming mountain flowers. White spring beauties and indigo bluebells were spattered like paint on a green canvas.

Jonas rode ahead of the column on one of Landon's horses. The burly captain, Cyn, rode next to him on his huge warhorse. They were both scouting ahead and Jonas was hoping to spot a nice buck so he could bring some venison to the table.

He still felt uncomfortable on a horse, never having had the opportunity to ride one, and Jonas was constantly shifting in the saddle as he tried to move with the horse's gait. Cyn looked over at him; his sharp eyes twinkling with amusement.

"You haven't ridden much, eh?" he stated bluntly.

Jonas sat uncomfortably with his bow resting across his lap. "No, I never have. My family was poor and we had no horses. Does it show that much?"

Cyn smiled at Jonas. "Make sure you don't ride too long or by morning your legs and backside will be so sore you won't be able to walk. You have to slowly get your body used to the movement. Be firm with the animal; make sure he knows who's in control." Cyn's eyes scanned the forest and grasslands around them.

"What are you worried about?" asked Jonas, noticing Cyn's constant vigilance.

"Nothing in particular, but it is my job to worry. Master Landon pays me well to make sure his caravan makes it to market. There are always brigands and bandits roaming the countryside for easy prey."

"How long have you worked for Landon?" Jonas asked.

"About five years now. I was a soldier in the Annurien army before I was discharged for hitting a superior officer. I went looking for work and roamed the lands for three years before I found myself in Tarsis, where I met Landon."

"Why did you hit your officer?" asked Jonas, curiosity getting the best of his manners.

"I was the captain of a unit that was fighting in a skirmish against the Oshanti tribe, near the edge of the Sithgarin Desert. We were outnumbered two to one and being flanked on both sides. I ordered my men to retreat but my commanding officer, a first rank captain, ordered us to stay while he retreated with a second force. My men and I held the Oshanti back while my commanding officer retreated to safety. Finally, knowing that if we continued fighting we would all be killed, I ordered a full out retreat. I led a hundred men into battle and only fifteen came out of that disaster alive. If we had been allowed to retreat earlier, I would have saved more than half my men. My anger turned to rage as I led my wounded and exhausted men back to camp. I walked into the captain's tent. 'You should have told me you'd planned a suicide mission for my troops,' I said, and then I struck him in the face as hard as I could. I broke his jaw and knocked out some of his teeth. Nothing has felt so good in all my life," Cyn smiled, lighting up his normally stern and battle scarred face.

"They kicked you out for that? Sounds like he had it coming," Jonas said.

"Assaulting a higher ranking officer is punishable by death. There must be strict discipline in an army if you want the soldiers to follow orders. I was saved from execution because this dung-eating aristocrat had made similar mistakes before. The king, King Olegaurd, pardoned me, but I was discharged from the army."

"Doesn't seem fair."

"Not much in life is fair, young huntsman, but I believe you are learning that the hard way."

Jonas and Cyn rode for a while in silence, scanning the countryside for brigands and deer. Hopefully, thought Jonas, they would only find the latter.

"So how good is Allindrian, really? I mean in comparison to other master swordsmen?" asked Jonas.

Cyn smiled broadly at Jonas, exposing his chipped front teeth. "I have never seen her equal. Elves are notoriously great swordsmen, but I believe that Allindrian may even be better than most full-blooded elves, although I have met few elves in my life so I may be wrong. She is a Blade Singer, Jonas. Do you know what that is?"

"No, what is it?"

"A Blade Singer is an elf who has practiced the craft of sword fighting beyond what humans can comprehend. Very few are given the honor of going through the training, although I have no idea what that entails as it is kept a secret. They are given the name because when they fight it is like a dance, and their sword makes a singing noise as it spins through the air. They are trained in their craft for hundreds of years. When they have completed the training, they are given the rank of Blade Singer. It is a great honor, and their skills are never taught to an outsider. The sword she carries is evidence of her rank, for only a Blade Singer carries that particular sword. Some fight with two, but I have only heard tales and have never seen it with my own eyes. The weapons are crafted specifically for each warrior when they graduate through the training."

"Hundreds of years? How is that?" asked Jonas.

"Elves live very long lives. I am not sure why though. I believe that a full blooded elf can live several thousand years," responded Cyn. "Allindrian is half-elf and I've heard they don't live as long, maybe several hundred years, but I'm not really sure."

"But she is teaching us to fight, isn't that against the rules?"

"No," laughed Cyn. "She is not teaching you elven secrets but merely stances and moves that are taught to all beginning swordsmen."

"If they guard those secrets carefully, then why did they teach them to a half-elf? Wouldn't they be reserved for a full blooded elf?" asked Jonas.

"No, elves do not hold disdain for mixed bloods. It is not welcomed or sought after, but if it happens, the elven community fully accepts the half-breed, bringing them into their society. But they are not allowed to marry a pure blood or bear children, so that the elven blood will not be diluted further. If they choose to marry an outsider, then they would be banned forever from the elven lands. I do not know anything about Allindrian's family. She keeps to herself most of the time."

"So why is she here, with the caravan?"

"You like to ask questions, don't you, boy?" Cyn commented amiably.

"I'm sorry, sir," Jonas grinned sheepishly, "but I've lived in a desolate mountain cabin my whole life and this is all so fascinating. I want to learn about the lands and our history, to learn to fight and protect." Jonas wanted to tell the warrior his whole story but decided that now was not the time. He would keep his secret hidden a little longer anyway.

"Worry not, son. I understand. I was not being critical. The elves of Mel'un-riam send Blade Singers out from the forests of Aur-urien to gather information on the happenings of the lands around them, and to combat threats to its people. Their goal is to help maintain balance. They also act as ambassadors for the elven kingdom. They are similar to cavaliers in a sense. Cavaliers are sent by their gods to areas that need their help. Blade Singers randomly roam the lands looking for areas of intrigue, strife, or political unrest. They represent their elven queen throughout the surrounding lands. There are very few Blade Singers, as it is extremely difficult to pass the tests and the training. You should feel lucky to have met Allindrian. She befriended Landon several years ago and has been traveling with us ever since. The lands are alive with unrest now with the rumors of Malbeck's return. There are stories of orcs and goblins amassing in the Black Lands and the Mazgar Forest. Maybe she feels she can learn a lot with us since we travel the many roads of Kraawn so frequently. I am happy her sword is with us. We are much safer because of it."

"You mentioned the elven queen. Do they not have a king?" asked Jonas.

"Yes, they do. His name is Skywise Ell-Runore, protector of the Aur-urien Forest. But my understanding is that all female elves have an affinity with their queen and that she alone directs and controls the Blade Singers. I do not know any details of elven politics. They keep to themselves mostly and I've only met a few in my life, and what I'm telling you is more or less conjecture that I've heard from others." Cyn looked down noticing the pommel of Jonas's hunting knife protruding from his tunic at his side. "That is quite a hunting knife for a young huntsman who lived a secluded life," he stated bluntly.

Jonas felt a little uncomfortable, knowing how his story might sound, but he figured the truth was always the best answer. "It's not mine, or it wasn't mine anyway."

"I gathered that. I noticed that knife earlier. I can't see the blade but the pommel is no ordinary pommel and it is not the knife of a mere hunter. Any soldier can see that." The sound of their horse's hooves on the merchant road filled the pause in the conversation as Jonas chose his words.

"It belonged to the cavalier, Airos. I found it on the battlefield by his body. It was too beautiful to leave in the snow and blood, amongst the dead." Jonas looked up at Cyn. "Should I not have taken it? Should I give it to Landon, or Allindrian, or you? What should I do with it?" asked Jonas.

Cyn smiled, chuckling to himself. "It's okay, son. You did nothing wrong. It would have been a waste to leave that weapon there. Keep it, or maybe return it to the High One's temple in Finarth, it's up to you. I hold no misgivings if you want to keep it. Do you mind if I see it?"

"Not at all," replied Jonas, sliding the blade from the leather sheath and handing it to Cyn. The silver blade shone brightly in the midday sun as Cyn inspected it.

"Amazing weapon. It looks elvish. It must be worth a dragon's horde. I would not readily display it when we enter the city," Cyn advised as he handed the blade back to Jonas.

"When I met Airos, he had the High One's mark on both his hands. My mother said it means that he was a master swordsman. Is that true?"

"It is. I had heard of Airos before, but I never met him in my travels. He was a first rank cavalier, the highest rank in their order. I believe there are only a few first rank cavaliers in the lands of Kraawn. His death is a huge loss and it must be reported to the King in Finarth immediately. If he had a mark on both his hands that meant that he was a master swordsman with both hands, ambidextrous, very rare. He was the best, maybe even a match for a Blade Singer, as you heard Landon say."

"Do you have to be a cavalier to get marked as a master swordsman?" asked Jonas.

"No, not necessarily, it depends on the mark. Some armies offer master rank marks that represent their imperial standards. They are all wizard marks, which makes them very expensive. Some kings give them out to soldiers that pass the master swordsman tests. It is very rare though; to pass the test is difficult and few have the tenacity to train as hard and long as it takes to get that mark. If a cavalier gains the mark then they are God Marked by their god's symbol. I have only met four people with the master swordsman marks. One man is a general in the Annurien army, one was a Halyean cavalier out of Onith, in the west, and another is the master at arms in Finarth, along with Prince Nelstrom."

"Onith? Halyean? I have never heard of them."

"Onith is the capital of King Olek Landibar's lands, far to the west, over the Tundren Mountains. Halyean is the god of sea, the main deity worshiped in the port cities that riddle the Algard coast. It is believed that Halyean is Ulren's brother, but do not take my word for it, the gods are not my strong point."

"What are the tests?" asked Jonas.

"Why?" Cyn laughed. "Do you want to become a master swordsman?"

Jonas paused. "Yes, I do," he said firmly.

Cyn looked at him, shaking his head with a smile. "I see you are determined. It is a fine goal, but a very lofty one. Make sure you are prepared for failure as well as success," he replied.

"What do you mean?" asked Jonas.

"They do not give the mark out freely. You must pledge your allegiance to a kingdom to get the training, or join the school for cavaliers, which is no easy task. Most young men who want to become a cavalier never even make it past the initiation phase, for there are tests of heart and courage that most men cannot pass."

"If that is my destiny I will pass them," Jonas said, his tone firm and confident.

Cyn glanced at Jonas, nodding his head in understanding. "You know young huntsman, part of me thinks that you might," he said smiling. "Now enough talk. I feel like I'm traveling with a woman."

Jonas laughed. They rode on in silence, taking in the beauty of the countryside, each immersed in their own thoughts.

***

On the ninth day they set up camp next to a little stream that flowed under the bridged road to meander through a flowering meadow. A large stand of trees flanked them on the left and the grassy meadow made for a soft welcoming campsite. Landon stepped down from his wagon looking for Allindrian. One of the mercenary guards saw him and rode up to him on his horse.

"You were looking for Allindrian, sir?" asked the blond haired warrior.

"Yes, Janson, have you seen her?"

"She has been scouting for several hours now. She should be back soon."

"Very well, we'll set up camp here."

"Very good, sir," the warrior responded with a nod and rode off to help facilitate the camp's set up. The wagons, all twenty of them, were set up in a semi-circle with the mercenaries forming the other half of the circle. Inside the perimeter were Landon and the other workers and merchants. Fil and Jonas slept in the middle with Landon.

Fil strode up to Jonas as he was adding wood to a fire. "Hey, Jonas," he said, casually sitting down to warm his hands by the flames.

"Aye," replied Jonas.

They sat together quietly for a while, enjoying the warmth of the fire as the rest of the men finished erecting the tents and getting the cooking pots going.

"You still plan on joining the Finarthian army?" asked Jonas, breaking the silence.

"I do," Fil replied looking up at Jonas. "I have nothing left anyway. My choices are limited. I talked with Landon about it and he said that King Gavinsteal is a good king and that he would be a good ruler to fight for. He also said that King Kromm from Tarsis is a ruler worthy of my vows and that he is a mighty warrior king who is unbeatable in battle. But we are heading to Finarth now, so I think I will give King Gavinsteal my allegiance." Fil tossed a stick into the fire and looked at Jonas, who was obviously in thought. "What's on your mind, Jonas? Are you changing your mind about joining with me?"

Jonas looked up at the question. "No…I don't know. I was thinking," he hesitated, "about maybe going to Annure and trying to be a cavalier."

Fil leaned back, startled by the response. "A cavalier? Do you know how hard it is to become a cavalier? Few are accepted and even fewer make it through the training."

"I know. I talked to Cyn about it. You could come with me. We could try together. I know we could do it, Fil," Jonas said, trying to convince himself as much as Fil.

"No, not me, I've never had much faith in the gods, Jonas, and I certainly have less now, considering what has happened to us."

"You blame the gods for what happened to us?"

"Yes I blame them. Our entire town was massacred, Jonas, and for what?" Fil said angrily. "We did nothing to deserve this and the gods did nothing to stop it. I will not put my faith in gods who do not earn it."

"The gods sent Airos to help us, and he died trying to save us. He was a first rank cavalier, Fil. The gods use cavaliers like Airos for their most important missions. They tried to help us. Our town was destroyed and our families killed, but don't forget that Airos killed a Banthra, no small feat in itself and definitely a blow to the evil that is threatening our lands. You can't blame the gods for actions of evil men and beasts," Jonas said with conviction.

"That may be, but I just don't have the faith. I'm sorry. And faith is definitely something you need to be a cavalier. If you want to attempt to become one, then you'll have to do it on your own."

They sat in silence for a few moments and then Fil stood up from the fire. "Let's get some food".

***

That night Jonas's sleep was plagued by nightmares, boargs were again attacking their town, men and women were being torn to pieces. He could hear the horrifying screams of his friends and family which seemed to go on endlessly. In his restless sleep he twitched and kicked next to the smoldering fire.

Suddenly he felt a searing pain in his chest. It felt like hundreds of tiny needles stabbing his skin. He bolted upright, his left hand absently rubbing his stinging chest as he tried to calm himself down, his heavy breathing resonating in the deathly silent night.

He glanced quickly around the camp to see if anyone had noticed him. Why was his chest stinging again? Was it another warning? He looked around trying to shake off the fogginess of sleep that wouldn't disappear.

Something seemed amiss. The air was heavy, almost suffocating. Everyone was sleeping soundlessly and a thick fog was slowly drifting around the camp. It was too still. The usual night sounds were absent. Animals, birds, insects; all were silent.

He got up slowly, grabbing his hunting knife. It was dark, and clouds had moved in to cover the bright moon and stars. He could barely see anything, but the burning embers of the fires reflected a reddish glow on the immediate surroundings. Something was wrong, he could feel it. He felt sluggish and frightened; the fog was floating around them like a wraith as he moved from fire to fire noticing that everyone was sleeping, including the guards who were supposed to keep watch.

The darkness seemed to get heavier and his body felt slow and lethargic. He felt disorientated and his mind whirled with dizziness. Then his chest burst with pain again, a stinging pain that hammered the dizziness away and he began to think clearly.

Something was out there, in the darkness, and it was not good. He had been warned again, like the day with the ogre. Silently he ran to Allindrian's campfire and found her sleeping soundly as well, her silver sword lying across her body. Kneeling down he quietly shook her, but she wouldn't wake up. He shook her again and finally her eyes slowly opened.

"Allindrian, something is happening. Wake up," Jonas whispered, shaking her harder. Her eyes were drifting around until finally they focused on Jonas and she leaped clumsily to her feet, wobbling slightly as if she were drugged. She shook her head to try and clear her mind, then finally she looked back at Jonas and he could tell that she was fully awake, her eyes were alert and they focused with intensity as she realized what was happening.

"Ul anthar Luminos!" Allindrian shouted, holding her hand in the air. From her fist flared a brilliant light that illuminated the entire camp and the meadow beyond. Jonas looked out into the darkness and his breath caught in his throat.

The scene he saw sent a chill down is spine. In the darkness around the camp a group of hulking boargs slowly crept towards them. They had been using the cover of darkness and fog to slowly creep through the meadow and slay them in their sleep.

Allindrian flung the bright globe into the air where it stayed suspended ten paces above the camp. She drew her silver sword, its innate elven magic glowing brightly in the dark night. "Men, awake and fight! We are under attack!" Allindrian yelled, leaping toward the boargs fearlessly.

The camp quickly awakened, the battle hardened mercenaries shaking off the grogginess and rising to the occasion. The boargs attacked quickly and with ferocious abandon. The four warriors who were keeping watch on the perimeter were torn apart like rag dolls. They died horrible deaths as they slowly awoke from whatever dark magic made them fall asleep.

The screams of the dying men were enough to wake all the men, and soon everyone was fighting for their lives. The attack fell upon them so quickly that there was no time for organization or discipline. Lacking a proper formation, they just had time to grab their weapons and stand up before the ruthless boargs were upon them.

The screams of the fighting urged Jonas on, freeing him from the initial fear. With great speed he vaulted onto the seat of Landon's wagon where he kept his bow. Standing up high on the wagon seat, he nocked an arrow, searching for a target. He saw Allindrian leap from boarg to boarg, her silver blade spinning, leaving a glowing blur in its path as it carved into the monsters. He heard the blade whistle and *sing* as Allindrian cut a path of death through a group of boargs. The song of her blade brought courage to his heart and his shaking arm stilled as he sought an enemy.

The ferocious animals sought her tiny form with their deadly claws and teeth, but she maneuvered through them easily, avoiding their attacks and delivering elven steel with practiced precision. Jonas was almost mesmerized by her dance. He had never seen anything like it. She moved like a dancer, her blade singing through the air with impossible speed. The screams of the dying tore his gaze away from her as he quickly resumed his search for a target.

He saw Cyn swinging his huge broad sword back and forth, trying to hold two boargs at bay as his men moved in to help. Jonas sighted in the boarg to Cyn's right and let the shaft fly, quickly nocking another arrow. The shaft hit the boarg in the chest, wounding it enough to give Cyn a quick reprieve, which he used to his advantage.

The boarg stumbled back as a second arrow slammed into its chest. Cyn then focused on the other boarg, swinging his mighty sword down on top of its shoulder just as it was about to leap upon him. His blade sunk in deep, cleaving through heart and lungs.

The second boarg, badly injured by Jonas's arrows, clumsily swung its massive arm at Cyn. It was a killing blow, but Cyn, sensing it coming, ducked beneath it. He lunged forward and lanced the boarg through the abdomen, jerking the blade hard to his right, opening up the beast's belly. The animal howled horribly, leaping back, clutching its gruesome wound, trying to keep its entrails from falling out onto the grass at its feet.

A darkness began to overwhelm Jonas again as he searched the battle scene, looking for a target. Some vile magic was assaulting them a second time. He felt like he wanted to run, his heart began to beat quickly, and the bow began to shake in his hands. The men felt it as well and many began to back up, frightened looks painted across their faces.

Then from the darkness at the edge of the lit clearing, a black horse rode forward carrying a dark rider. The warrior, clad in dark armor, carried a short black spear made of grey metal and his red cape billowed in the air as he galloped into the clearing, scattering boargs and warriors alike. He emanated fear and evil, permeating the men with despair wherever he rode.

The dark knight pointed his spear at a soldier near him and uttered "Atta-Guthor!" The spear head crackled with energy sending a bolt of lightning into the man, launching him into the air and burning a hole right through his chest.

Jonas shook his head, trying to clear it, so he could focus on the evil warrior. He nocked an arrow, lifting his bow, his arms shaking badly. "Give me strength, Shyann," Jonas whispered to himself, trying to aim the shaking bow. In moments his arms steadied and his mind began to clear. He saw the warrior clearly now as he ripped the magical spear from the chest of another mercenary. Jonas fired his arrow and saw the shaft strike the warrior in the shoulder. The arrow deflected off his black armor.

The evil warrior turned towards Jonas, laughing wickedly. He lifted his vile weapon and uttered the same words, "Atta-Guthor!" The bolt of lightning flashed through the air and struck Jonas in the chest, sending him flying backwards to land heavily on his back at the base of the wagon.

Allindrian, who had just withdrawn her sword from the chest of a dead boarg, saw the bolt hit Jonas. "No!" she screamed. She flashed her blade across the throat of the last boarg that was between her and the evil warrior. Blood erupted from the severed throat, and Allindrian, spinning by the dead beast, moved in quickly towards the warrior with the spear. Simultaneously she drew her long hunting knife throwing it side armed at the horsed warrior. The magical elven blade struck the warrior in the leg, sending sparks flying as it penetrated the enchanted armor. The man screamed and angled his weapon at Allindrian.

Jonas slowly got up, astonished that he was still alive. He looked down with wide eyes at his chest and saw that his tunic was scorched and burned, exposing his God Mark, which was glowing with magic. The last remnants of magical energy wavered briefly across his chest before dissipating completely. Somehow Shyann's magic had saved him. Not wasting any time wondering about his luck, he grabbed Airos's dagger that had fallen by the wagon, quickly leaped up and ran to join his comrades. Coming around the wagon he saw Allindrian bear down on the horsed rider, his spear pointing right at her. Jonas was twenty paces away and he didn't know if he could get there in time, but he had to try. He ran towards the horsed rider as fast as he could. Everything seemed to slow down as his mind took in everything around him. He saw Fil out of the corner of his eye throw a spear at the rider just as Allindrian closed the gap between them. The spear struck the rider in the back, but it could not penetrate his magical armor. The impact caused him to jerk forward in his saddle, diverting his spear point away from Allindrian.

Jonas, arriving just in time, jumped into the air, Airos's knife held high, and slammed the blade into the lower back of the warrior. The knife bit in deep, the magical blade slicing through the armor like it was butter.

The warrior screamed, arching his back and dropping his spear to the ground. Jonas was flung backwards as the warrior's horse pivoted.

Simultaneously, Allindrian leaped impossibly high into the air, her elven agility bringing her level with the horsed warrior. Her silver blade arced through the night, slicing across the man's neck and sending his head flying into the darkness. The half-elf ranger landed lightly on the ground as his head made a sickening thump on the grass five paces away.

Jonas got up from the ground quickly, taking in the scene. The mercenaries had regrouped and they were finishing off the last of the boargs.

Allindrian approached Jonas, her sword held low, fire still burning in her eyes. "Are you okay?" she asked in disbelief.

"I think so," Jonas responded, the rush of battle adrenaline leaving his body shaking. He held up his hands which continued to twitch nervously.

"It will pass. It is common after a fight," Allindrian reassured him.

Fil moved up to them both, his short sword in hand. His face, though haggard from fear and exertion, bore a determined look. Jonas was thankful to see his friend was not hurt. "What happened, Allindrian? Were we spelled?" Fil asked.

"We were. That one there," pointing her sword at the dead warrior on ground, "was a cleric of darkness. If it were not for Jonas we would all be dead. He warned me of the attack just in time." Fil looked at Jonas knowingly. Allindrian continued, "I think, young Jonas, that you have some explaining to do. That mark on your chest is a God Mark." Jonas looked down and for the first time remembered that his tunic had been burnt off. "You should be dead," Allindrian stated bluntly.

Cyn had gathered his men and approached the group. He was splattered in blood and had a nasty cut just underneath his eye. It was obvious that he had overheard Allindrian and addressed her comment. "Let's postpone this discussion until we have seen to the dead and wounded. Let's remove this filth from our site immediately," Cyn commanded, approaching the dead warrior.

"No, don't touch him," Allindrian ordered, stepping in front of him. "His armor and weapons are cursed." She used the tip of her sword to move aside the red cape around his neck, exposing the bloody stump and a chain with a pendant. She lifted the blood stained necklace with the tip of her sword. It hissed and smoked as she brought it clear. On a pendant at the end of the chain was a symbol of a spider. Her sword glowed white and the necklace began to glow as well. "Just as I thought. This one was a follower of Naz-reen. Look here at her symbol." Cyn made the four pointed mark on his chest at the mention of the dark goddess's name. She tossed the smoking necklace aside and it burst into flames, melting into an unrecognizable piece of black metal. "The armor and weapons are dangerous as well, only a powerful priest or cavalier can dispel the curse."

"You mentioned her before. Who is this Naz-reen?" asked Jonas.

"Naz-reen is an embodiment of darkness, killing, and strife. You humans think of her as a god, we elves think of her, as well as all of the Foresworn, as a sinister being of great power. She is also known as Bor-zan. She loves intrigue and to slowly build her webs of deceit, hence her spider symbol," replied Allindrian.

"We should not be speaking of her," Cyn said, worrying as he looked out into the night.

Two mercenaries appeared out of the darkness supporting Landon, who was limping badly on one leg. His face was haggard and pale but he smiled with relief as he saw them all. "Thank the gods you all made it. What happened?" he asked.

Allindrian went to Landon to look at his wound. "Is your injury serious," she asked. She looked with concern at the deep laceration on his right leg.

"I'm fine. Just a nasty cut from one of those dreadful creatures. What in Ulren's name were those beasts?"

"Boargs," Fil and Jonas said simultaneously.

Landon nodded his head in affirmation. "That's what I thought. I've heard descriptions of them, but I have never seen one. Thanks to Romul here I might have the opportunity to see another, Ulren hoping I don't. He speared the beast through the chest as he was about to finish me."

"Well done, Romul," praised Cyn. "Take him to Lornan. He needs stitches before he loses more blood."

"Would you like me to see to your wound?" Allindrian asked.

"No, there are men who need it more than I. Use your magic on them if you please," Landon said.

"Very well, Cyn, my magical light will go out in a few moments. We need to get the fires blazing so we can see and take care of our dead," stated

Allindrian, wiping her blade clean and sheathing it in one smooth motion. "We don't have time to bury the boargs but we need to bury this evilness. We don't want some unsuspecting traveler to come across this cursed armor."

"Very well, let's get to work and then we can try to sort all this out," Cyn replied, looking at Jonas with uncertainty. Jonas couldn't help but notice his eyes wander to his chest, which he had already covered with a cloak that he found on the ground.

Eight of the twenty mercenaries had been killed, including Rath, one of Landon's personal assistants. The remaining twelve men joined Cyn, along with Landon, Allindrian, Jonas, and Fil around the large fire to discuss the nights attack. Jonas looked at the remaining men. He felt a deep sense of loss thinking of those who were no longer with them, men he had come to know and respect. Several of the warriors, including Landon, had wounds wrapped in clean cotton cloth, their blood soaking through, staining the cloth crimson.

"It makes no sense," said Cyn. "Boargs rarely come down from the Tundrens and I have never heard of an attack so close to Finarth. And why would a follower of the spider queen be leading them, and why would they be attacking *us*?" asked Cyn impatiently. "Are the Forsworn stealing from trade caravan's now?"

Allindrian replied, "I don't know. I agree; it doesn't make much sense. What could they be after? But I do know one thing; if it weren't for Jonas then we would all be dead." Allindrian looked at Jonas. "Now, I think it's time you told us the truth."

Jonas looked around at all the faces staring at him; some of them seemed unsure, and some a bit frightened. "I didn't mean to deceive you. I just didn't know what to say or how to explain it. I don't understand everything myself." He looked down at the ground, unsure where to start.

"Start from the beginning, Jonas," Landon said. "How did you get that mark on your chest and how did you not succumb to the dark magic like the rest of us, including Allindrian?" Landon smiled at Jonas reassuringly, urging him to proceed.

Jonas looked up at Landon and saw no hint of animosity. He knew these people deserved the truth. He took a deep breath and began his tale. "I was born a cripple. I couldn't move my legs and arms very well, even smiling or talking was sometimes difficult." Jonas went on as the fire burned down, telling his new friends about his life, his mother, and his tough existence at Manson. He told them about the ridicule that was heaped upon him for years and the scorn that the townspeople had held for him and his mother. He told them everything, how he hid in the oven when the boargs attacked, how he and Fil began their journey to Finarth, and finally he told them about his mysterious dream in the cave.

Fil sat next to him, poking a stick into the fire, deep in thought as he listened to Jonas's words and relived the story in his mind.

"And we had nowhere else to go," Jonas continued. "So we waited for the snows to subside before we started our long trek to Finarth. We traveled for several weeks before we got to the crossroads, and met your caravan." Jonas looked up at the men who were now staring at him, enthralled by his story. "And that is when we met you," Jonas finished, not sure of what else to say.

Many moments went by as everyone took in Jonas's story. It was not long, but it seemed like forever for Jonas, waiting for some sort of response, but finally Landon spoke. "Let me see that mark again."

Jonas hesitated briefly before removing his tunic. The blue and silver mark covered his stomach and chest, the silver edges flickering in the firelight and the intricate work was startling. Fil's eyes grew wide, moving closer to Jonas.

"What is it, Fil?" asked Jonas, somewhat taken back by Fil's expression.

Fil looked closely at the mark as Jonas looked at him with trepidation. "The mark has grown, Jonas. It is bigger now. The branches are expanding towards your arms and the trunk of the tree is moving down your stomach," he said with wide astonished eyes.

"What!" exclaimed Jonas, looking down at his chest. Sure enough, Fil was right; it had grown larger. Allindrian moved in close as well, to examine the mark more clearly. She took her hand and gently touched his bare chest, slowly running her long delicate fingers over the edges of the God Mark. Jonas's spine tingled as her delicate fingers traced the edges of the mark.

"That is definitely a God Mark. They are very rare, usually only a cavalier bears the mark of a god, and that is after they have passed the tests, tests that can only be defeated by men of extreme bravery, mental and physical strength, and unmatched martial excellence. I have never known a mere boy, untrained, to have the mark," she said, scrutinizing Jonas's chest further.

"And yet he does," stated Mestus, a tall thin warrior from Tarsis. "Who are we to question the gods?"

"And that is most certainly Shyann's mark. I have seen it many times traveling through the Tundrens where she is worshipped the most," added Cyn confidently.

"What should I do? I need help. I don't know what to do," pleaded Jonas. "I can't express how happy I am that I've been cured, and I thank Shyann for her blessing, but what does it mean? Why did she pick me? What does she want me to do?

"There are many things in life that we have no control over, Jonas," Landon replied. "We live, we try to survive and make a decent life for ourselves, family, and friends, and then we die. Few things are secure or certain. We do not know why Shyann picked you, but I am sure that she has her reasons and that you will know them when the time is right. My recommendation to you is to go to the temple in Finarth with your story and ask for some guidance. You have to be eighteen to start the school for cavaliers, but my guess is that is where you are heading." Landon grimaced as he adjusted the bandage on his thigh.

"Do you really think so? The idea is intriguing but I feel as if it is just a dream, something that I want to reach for but cannot grasp. I do not know if I could do it." There was a part of him that believed the goal was not outside the realm of possibility. He had discussed that very idea with Fil, but hearing the words mentioned by another made it sound impossible and far out of reach for a young boy who was raised in the mountains.

"You do not do yourself justice, Jonas," Cyn responded. "I have known fighting men my whole life. You have a strong heart and you are very brave for your years and lack of experience. You and Fil have both shown your courage and bravery. I have seen grown men, tried warriors, run from less than what we faced tonight. You saved me today with your bow and you both took part in helping Allindrian kill that abomination. I think you have the makings to be a great warrior, maybe even a cavalier," Cyn concluded, looking Jonas in the eyes.

Jonas, not used to compliments, looked away. "I thank you for your confidence, Cyn. It just seems so far-fetched. I can't imagine myself as a cavalier."

"I'm sure Airos felt that way when he was a boy as well," Allindrian said with a reassuring smile.

"They are right, Jonas. I will go with you to the temple and we will see what they say. Then I will join the Finarthian army, hopefully with you by my side," Fil added.

Jonas smiled at Fil, grateful for his support.

"I think we need some rest now. Thank you, young man, for telling us your story. And please know that we hold no misgiving for your concealment of the truth. Under the circumstances, it was probably the right thing to do. Let's get some rest so we can travel with all speed for Finarth in the morning," Landon said as he slowly rose, aided by two of his men. "Cyn, please take care of the watch and make sure that no one is on duty alone tonight. I doubt we can expect another attack but let's be ready for it nonetheless."

"Yes, sir," Cyn replied, and began to give the orders. Everyone settled down for the night, except the guards who constantly scanned the darkness, holding their spear shafts a little more tightly.

Five
Finarth

The remaining four days to Finarth went by quickly and without mishap. The caravan followed the Sithgarin River for several days before they started to meander through various farming settlements. Landon directed the caravan southwest when they reached the smaller Ungard River. The road was well traveled and there were many small homesteads nestled in the Finarthian hills.

As they neared Finarth, on the fourth day, Lanz, one of the caravan scouts, rode to Landon's wagon where Jonas and Fil sat leading the oxen.

"Tell Master Landon that riders are approaching on the main road," the scout said, pulling his lathered horse next to them.

"Tell him yourself. What do you see my friend?" asked Landon, poking his head through the canvas flap on the covered wagon.

"How are you feeling sir?" asked Lanz.

"I'm well. The wound is itching a bit, but other than that I feel fine."

"That is good, sir, means it's healing."

"What of the riders?" Landon asked again.

"I believe they are Finarthian Knights."

"Good. Have Cyn and Allindrian ride next to me when the knights arrive," Landon ordered.

"Yes, sir," responded the scout as he rode off.

It wasn't long before Jonas and Fil made out the long lances sparkling in the midday sun as the knights rode towards them.

"Do we have anything to fear from them, sir?" asked Fil cautiously.

"Oh no, I am well known in these parts and I am a friend of the king. I imagine they will escort us to Finarth," replied Landon reassuringly.

Jonas gazed in awe at the knights as they drew near. There were probably fifty of them, all riding magnificent war horses. They wore sparkling plate armor embossed with the king's standard, a fist within a shining sun. Their billowing blue capes were lined with gold thread and their helms were of the finest quality. Every knight carried a long lance with a wicked silver point. Jonas noticed that they also had shields and swords strapped to the sides of their horses. Their horses also wore protective plates covering their noses and their muscular chests. A blanket of chain mail draped the warhorses to protect their flanks and tough leather saddles were perched like a king's throne on their backs. That's what Jonas thought anyway, looking at the magnificent riders.

He had never seen anything like them. They slowed as they neared Landon's caravan.

"Halt the wagon, son," Landon said.

Jonas pulled back on the reins and they stopped about forty paces from the knights. The knights slowly rode forward, their lances held high as the dust from the road finally settled. The lead knight lifted his visor, handed his lance off to another warrior, and rode forward. He looked like all the rest except that he wore a purple cape while the others were blue.

As the man neared, Jonas could make out his features. His dark hair was streaked with gray, and he wore a dark mustache and beard that made his ice blue eyes stand out. He smiled seeing Landon but it did nothing to erase the hard weathered features of his face.

"Third lance, Lathrin, how are you? How long has it been?" Landon asked smiling broadly.

"Too long, my friend. It is good to see you," greeted the knight. The dark haired knight noticed Landon's leg, his smile changing to a look of concern. "What happened to you, Landon, you are injured?"

"Yes, we were attacked by boargs on the road." Landon's expression became more serious.

"Boargs? You must be mistaken. I have not heard of boarg attacks for many years. Where did this happen?" asked Lathrin.

"On the road from Tarsis, no more than three days ride from Finarth's gate. We have some more troubling news that cannot wait. I must see the king."

"Of course, we will talk more of this when we get you to a healer and a nice comfortable bed. I will escort you personally." Lathrin, seeing Allindrian, smiled warmly. "Blade Singer," he said, nodding his head in greeting. "It is an honor to see you again." Allindrian returned the greeting with a subtle tilt of her head and a gentle smile.

The captain returned his gaze to Landon, continuing to address the injured merchant. "Now, let's get you to a warm bath and a nice soft bed. I'm sure you deserve both."

They rode for half a day before the city came into view. Fil and Jonas were very excited after seeing the splendid knights and they harassed the tired merchant with endless questions.

"Sir, why did you call that knight, third lance?" asked Fil.

"The Finarthian Knights are organized independently from the Finarthian Legion. The knight's leaders are signified by a ranking title and a particular color," Landon explained.

"So the number of lances in their title signifies their rank," Jonas reasoned.

"Yes. Lathrin is a third lance, which means he is in charge of two modrigs, called a ludus," Landon continued. "And that rank is marked by a purple cape."

"A modrig? Ludus? What are they?" Jonas asked, his eyes sparkling with interest.

Landon laughed softly. "Son, let me explain before you sling more questions."

"Very well, I'm sorry, sir, I'm just so…"

"I know," Landon interrupted, "I remember the excitement of youth. As I was saying, a modrig is two hundred and fifty men, while a ludus is five hundred."

"So a second and first lance must be in charge of all of them," Fil reasoned.

"Yes, there are two second lance knights and they each are in charge of an akron, which is a thousand, while the first lance is in charge of all two thousand."

"I see, so Lathrin is a strong warrior?" Jonas asked.

"He is, but it is not always the strongest warriors who make higher rank. They must also be sound thinkers and men of intellect," Landon informed them. "Battles are won for many reasons, just one of them being the ability to fight. There are many other characteristics of a successful army. If things go well here you will both likely learn what I am talking about."

"I can't wait," Fil said excitedly.

Jonas smiled, gazing at the column of knights marching ahead of them.

Fil and Jonas sat in the wagon with mouths and eyes open in wonder. Finarth was huge, and neither of them could imagine a community this large. The lands surrounding the city were blanketed with homes where farmers and herders lived. Landon explained that the land outside the city was cheaper with lower taxes. Inside the city lived the artisans, merchant elite, and the noble families who occupied most government positions.

They received a few looks from the many people along the road, but for the most part the citizens acted as if they were accustomed to seeing merchant caravans and armed knights.

Fil and Jonas looked on, noticing that these people didn't seem much different from the hardy mountain folk they knew. No one was idle and everyone, from children to the elderly, was doing something of use.

As they drew near to the city gates Jonas was amazed at the immensity of Finarth. An outer wall twenty paces high surrounded the city. It was made from thick cut stone, each the size of a wagon. As far as Jonas could see the wall was lined with battlements and armed men walked it with vigilance. But what really amazed Jonas was that he could see an even larger wall behind it. It looked to be over forty paces high, standing like a cliff, impenetrable and indestructible. Jonas, peering ahead of the column, saw that the gate was open and the knights were already moving inside.

"This is incredible," Fil muttered.

"Wait until you see inside those gates," Landon said. "This is just the outer wall."

As they neared the gate Jonas noticed the huge gate house. It looked like it had the strength of a small mountain. The gate itself was built from cut timbers each the size of a large man and laced together with solid bands of black steel. It was so immense that Jonas wondered how it was opened and closed.

But it was the scene beyond the gate that really caught the boys' attention. Landon had not exaggerated. There was an expanse of flat completely empty land well over a hundred paces wide. At the edge of that was a small stone wall about waist high that formed a perimeter around a moat that stretched all the way flush to the inner wall. The stone path they were on led to a tremendous bridge made of stone spanning fifty paces across the expanse of water before merging into an open landing twice as big as the first.

Jonas swept his eyes over the impressive site and for the first time on his travels he was speechless.

"Amazing, isn't it?" Landon said, smiling at the astonished boys. "That there," he said, pointing to the empty land separating the first wall from the moat, "is the killing ground. Anyone that manages to make it over the wall or through the gate, will bunch up here before the moat or bridge where they will face the onslaught of spearmen and archers."

The boys, still speechless, slowly looked around not wanting to miss a thing.

The moat was filled with gently flowing dark water and was easily fifty paces wide. Jonas stood up, craning to look over the side of the bridge to the water below, but it was too dark and deep. The bridge itself was over twenty paces wide and the large column of knights and Landon's merchant caravan easily fit across it.

The wagon came to a halt as the knights were funneling into the large inner gate. Jonas was able to briefly view the face of the gate as it swung open, allowing the knights to continue into the heart of the city. The front of the inner gate was covered in sheets of black steel and in the very center was the Finarthian symbol, the fist in front of the shining sun, made from a silvery metal that sparkled in the sun. The symbol was breathtakingly beautiful and obviously made by a master craftsman. And it was giant, as big around as a frost giant's shield.

"How did they get all this water in here?" Fil asked.

"Master engineers diverted the Talem River. It flows in from the north side and makes a U shaped path around the city where it is then channeled back to its normal course," Landon explained.

"But how," Jonas began.

"Magic," Landon interjected. "It was the court wizard's father who created the moat eighty years ago," Landon continued. "I do not know specifically how it was done, as engineering and magic are not included in my talents."

"What is a court wizard?" Jonas asked.

"The skill of magic is very rare and most do not have the time, tenacity, nor the gold to master the studies needed to wield magic. Most kings can provide the funding and time that wizards require. It is a mutually beneficial relationship, for a king's power increases with a loyal wizard at his side. Usually, as it is here in Finarth, the court wizard is a lord who passes on his skill to his sons so that the connection with the royal family continues. They swear loyalty to their kings and their relationship is a bond of trust. King Kromm of Tarsis also has a court wizard."

"I see," Jonas replied, eagerly taking in Landon's words.

Once they entered the city Jonas was assaulted with so much activity and noise that he couldn't focus on any one spot. His head buzzed with the sounds and smells of the bustling city. People were everywhere, walking the cobble stone roads, buying and selling goods in the markets that seemed to line every street. The buildings were made of stone and wood and some were so magnificent that they had potted plants and flowering roses and other plants that Jonas had never seen. And the massive structures weren't just one level, they climbed as high as trees and many had small balconies and various statues and carvings adorning them.

Continuing on through the main street they arrived at the king's castle deep within the city. The inner castle was made of a white stone, and the thick timber gate was edged and bound in black iron. They entered through the gate into a huge courtyard paved with flat stones. Servants bustled forward, attending to the horses of the knights who had dismounted and were heading towards their barracks. It was routine for them, but for Jonas and Fil everything they saw was a new experience beyond their imagination. Slack jawed, they stared in awe at all the people, the massive buildings and walls surrounding them in an almost suffocating embrace.

The servant boys took the horses to the stables where Landon explained they would be cleaned and fed. Landon told the boys that the inner castle was so big that it had four courtyards all the size of the one they had entered. The king had over two thousand troops living within these walls. These were the Finarthian Knights, the elite of King Gavinsteal's forces. He had another ten thousand troops living within the city walls and he could call on an additional twenty thousand soldiers that were on leave to work their farms and fields throughout the expanse of the Finarthian lands.

Lathrin walked up to Landon's wagon followed by several servants. "My men will provide barracks and food for your mercenaries. Let me take you to a healer and to your room where you can get cleaned up for your audience with the king. I will have a room prepared for Allindrian as well," announced the third lance.

"That is most gracious, my friend. I would like these two boys to come with me. This is Fil Tanrey and Jonas Kanrene."

Lathrin's ice blue eyes gave them a quick wondering look. "Well met. I am Lathrin, third lance of the Finarthian Knights. Tumas here will lead you to your rooms and make sure that you have everything that you need."

A young man, about the same age as Fil and Jonas, stepped forward, smiling and nodding his head in greeting. Tumas was tall and wiry thin and carried himself with confidence. His face was angular but youthful with slightly curly brown hair cut short and immaculately trimmed.

"Very good, Tumas, lead away," said Landon.

Tumas and several other servants guided them and carried their bags to their quarters. Two of the boys helped Landon to the healer while Tumas took Jonas and Fil to Landon's room.

After following Tumas up several flights of stairs and down a couple long hallways, they passed through a strong oak door into a magnificent suite. The day's astonishments continued as they looked upon the most wonderful room they had ever seen. The floors were covered with a shiny smooth rock and the furniture was polished, intricately carved, and of the finest quality. Two glass doors framed in polished wood led out onto a balcony facing the bustling city. Crimson silk drapes covered the windows and billowed gently as the warm spring breeze drifted through the openings. Jonas sniffed deeply, recognizing the smell of jasmine as the warm air wafted around the room.

Tumas set their packs on the floor and smiled at their astonished faces. "It is magnificent isn't it? It is one of the rooms that the royal family uses to entertain other royalty or close friends. I assume you are Master Landon's servants?"

"No, not really, we are his traveling companions. We met on the road from Tarsis no more than three weeks ago," replied Fil.

"I see," Tumas replied skeptically. "I will be here in the castle for most of the evening if you should need anything. I am preoccupied during the day as I am training to become a knight, but there will be other servants here to help you with anything that you need."

"A knight? What is it like? Can anyone train to become a Finarthian Knight?" asked Fil excitedly.

"It is hard work and many long hours of study, but I love it; it's all I've ever wanted. I will have two years of training as an apprentice. Then, when I'm eighteen, I must serve in the regular army for two years. After that, if I've done well, I can continue my training to be a knight. That can take several years. Not everyone can do it. You must be highborn or get a sponsor to apply." Tumas turned to leave.

"Are you highborn?" asked Jonas.

Tumas turned back to face them. "I am. My father is a merchant and landowner. What about you?" asked Tumas.

"No, we are just woodsmen from a small town deep in the Tundren Mountains," replied Fil sadly

"Well you would have to get a sponsor then," Tumas said nonchalantly.

"How do you do that?" asked Fil eagerly.

"You need to find someone of importance, a noble or great warrior to vouch for you, and your character. There are also training fees that need to be paid for the probationary period. If you make it that far, then your training is free. I must be going now. There is a bath already drawn for you in the room to your left. I suggest you get cleaned up. I will have servants bring up some new clothes for you." Tumas opened the door to leave.

"Thank you, Tumas. It was nice to meet you," Jonas said sincerely.

"And you woodsmen. Enjoy your time in Finarth," Tumas said with a smile as he shut the heavy door.

Jonas and Fil looked at each and began smiling until their faces were beaming walls of teeth. They began running around the room, exploring their quarters and investigating the magnificence of the décor. All the furniture was polished wood graced with hand carvings, and everywhere they looked they saw glittering items, like a silver mirror, a set of bronze candle holders flanking the fireplace, and even a set of crossed swords behind a giant silver shield with the Finarthian symbol cast in the middle.

Jonas ran into the bathing quarters first where he saw a huge depression built of the same shiny stone that covered the floor. It was filled with steaming water perfumed with the fragrance of rose petals. There was a big table and drawers next to a magnificent full size mirror. The mirror's frame was built from huge pieces of dark wood. Detailed carvings of vines wrapped around the piece and at closer inspection Jonas could even make out clusters of grapes expertly depicted within the wood.

"Fil, look at this!" Jonas yelled, turning his attention to the bath. He sat on the edge and tested the water. It was warm and inviting, making Jonas realize how dirty and smelly he was. He quickly took off his clothes and leaped into the water, splashing some over the edge.

Fil ran in, his eyes bulging even more. "Is that hot water?" Fil asked incredulously, seeing the steam rise from the gently sloshing water.

"It is," Jonas said with pure joy.

"How did they get it all in here?"

"I don't know. Look at that hole in the ceiling, maybe the water comes from there."

Fil followed Jonas's gaze up to a round hole about the size of a fist. It was positioned directly over the basin.

"I don't know, but this feels amazing," continued Jonas, dunking his head in the water.

Fil picked up a sticky bar from the side of the tub and smelled it. The fragrance of rosemary filled his nose.

"Is that soap?" asked Jonas.

"I think so. Here, give it a try."

Fil threw the bar at Jonas who caught it out of the air. He used it on his wet skin and it began to lather immediately. "It must be. It smells great and it's lathering like soap. It sure smells better than the soap we used at Manson."

"These quarters are amazing," Fil exclaimed, his eyes continuing to inspect the wondrous place.

"The entire city is amazing. I never imagined there could be so many people in one spot or so many buildings, huge buildings," Jonas said, washing his hair with the soap.

"Hurry up, I want to get in."

They both got cleaned up and put on the clothes the servants brought them. They were simple breeches and tunics with a leather belt, but the cloth was a finer weave and not thick and itchy like the wool clothes they wore. It felt so soft on their newly scrubbed skin. They had to continue to wear their leather hunting boots, though, so they scrubbed them clean with one of the towels to make them look decent. They were pretty worn, but they looked presentable once all the dirt and grime was scrubbed from them.

It wasn't long before the door opened and Landon stepped in, no longer limping. Jonas and Fil were sitting in comfortable leather chairs eating a platter of smoked meats, cheeses, and breads that a servant had brought in.

"Ahh, my friends, I can see that you found the bath and food," Landon said, smiling, as he went to the table to grab a cut of meat.

"Yes, sir. I hope that was okay," Jonas said.

"Of course, please, enjoy your surroundings." Landon stood up, rolling his pant leg up to expose his thigh. "Look at this," he said, amazement on his face. "Magic is sure incredible. I've never been healed by a priest before. He put his hands on my leg and chanted. First, a blue light appeared around his hands. I could feel a warm energy that spread from his hands to my wound and my whole leg. I saw the wound slowly close and the skin mend over it. The pain was gone and only a slight tingling remained. There's just a little scar now."

Sure enough, the boys saw that his leg had totally healed, the only evidence of his wound being a faint pink scar about as long as a hand.

"I would have liked to have seen that," Jonas said, examining the scar in wonder. Landon unrolled his pant leg and sat down with the boys.

"Sir, why didn't you have Allindrian heal you?" Fil asked.

"We had other injured men, Fil, men that needed it more than I. Her power is limited and I wanted it directed to my men. Remember boys," Landon said, using the teacher voice the boys had come to love, "when you have power, be it in the form of money, strength, or rank, you must use it with honor if you want to earn respect. Those men saw me suffer through my pain even after I used my own resources to help their comrades. That kind of respect will go a long way."

The boys were nodding their heads, agreeing with what Landon said.

"Sir, you must be really rich or be really good friends with the king to get a room like this. We want to thank you again for letting us travel with you. This place is incredible," Jonas said.

"Yes, I am rich, and I am good friends with the king," Landon laughed. "I have made a fortune trading dwarven weapons and armor from Dwarf Mount down to Finarth and Annure. They cannot produce the prized weapons here so I can command a royal sum for them. King Gavinsteal supplies only the best for his knights."

"I see," said Fil thoughtfully.

"I must change quickly. We have an audience with the king in a few moments," said Landon, standing up and grabbing his bags.

"We?" asked Jonas.

"Yes. I need you to tell your story to the king. Don't worry," Landon continued as he saw Fil and Jonas's apprehensive looks, "I will be there with you. Besides, King Gavensteal is a good and honorable man. I think you will like him. His two sons will be present as well as several priests to analyze your mark. Allindrian will be present as well. No need to fear," Landon continued reassuringly.

It was not long before they heard a knock at the door. Landon opened the sturdy door revealing a man-at-arms who informed him that the king was ready to see them. The soldier escorted them through several hallways and down some stairs until they entered a large anteroom. The room was lined with suits of armor holding magnificent lances, and the walls were covered with intricate tapestries. The tapestries were made from a thick cloth the color of a ripe plum. Gold thread was woven into the fabrics forming symbols and designs of various sorts. Jonas recognized one as the symbol of Finarth, a blazing sun with a fist in the middle. He did not know the others but enjoyed the beauty of the graceful lines and intricate scroll work.

At the far end of the room was a large door covered in a detailed carving. Jonas looked at the carving carefully and it seemed to be of some great battle; men and monsters alike were fighting on a great battlefield. The detail was exquisite and Jonas could even see some of the warrior's expressions as they fought for their lives.

Two guards stood on each side of the door, unmoving as they approached. Jonas wished he could have examined the carving further but the soldier leading them grabbed the solid metal ring on the door, opening it smoothly. For a door so large and heavy, it swung open easily.

"Follow me please," the warrior commanded as he entered the audience chamber. They walked into a large room flanked by huge stone pillars. Stained glass windows lined the walls sending an array of color throughout the room. Intricate stone work covered every base that held up the massive columns. Huge tapestries hung from the walls and placed between each was a polished suit of plate mail, complete with spear and shield. It was beautiful, and Jonas's eager eyes took it all in.

On the far end of the room were steps leading to a great throne made of carved wood and hammered steel. Jonas stared openly at the incredible craftsmanship. The throne was carved into the shape of a huge tree trunk reaching up more than three paces, and all from one piece of wood. Shiny steel covered the arm rests and various other pieces of glittering metal were expertly placed into the carving. In some areas steel was inlaid to form beautiful designs that to Jonas looked like leafy vines. It was strong, powerful, and graceful all at the same time, a fitting spot for a king to rule such a wondrous kingdom.

At the base of the steps was a thick oak table, lined with heavy wood chairs that faced the impressive throne. Each chair was put together with hand carved wood, polished with oil and shining with splendor. Jonas had never seen furniture so beautiful. Everything was sublime and of the highest quality, but it was all very functional and not overly flamboyant.

The one thing that really caught Jonas's eye was the massive painting behind the throne. It was easily fifteen paces wide and ten paces high, covering the entire back wall. It was an impressive painting depicting an armored warrior on a battlefield facing another warrior who wore all black plate armor. They rode huge, muscle bound horses, and carried glowing swords clashing together in combat. It looked so real that Jonas couldn't take his eyes off it as he walked down the short hallway to the conference table.

At the front end of the table sat King Gavinsteal. He was an enormous man, built like an oak tree, his barrel chest and thick shoulders giving him a formidable look. His long hair fell to his shoulders and at the top it was pulled back and tied behind his head. His dark beard was trimmed perfectly. The king's hair was streaked with the silver of age but to Jonas he still looked like a warrior in his prime. He wore a blue tunic embroidered in silver thread with the glittering symbol of the fist in front of a sun. His belt was thick and well worn, carrying a jeweled broad sword swinging gently as he stood to greet his guests. His tanned face was worn and looked like old leather, but his smile was welcoming.

"Ah, Landon, my friend, it is good to see you," the king said in a booming voice. King Gavinsteal stepped around the table to shake hands with the merchant.

Jonas noticed that the others stood at their arrival. He saw two men that were obviously soldiers for they carried themselves as such, wearing swords and bright chain mail shirts under their tunics. One man was middle-aged, with long dark hair and a thick massive frame like the king's. He wore a green tunic over his chain mail shirt that was embroidered with the same symbol. Jonas learned that this was Prince Baylin, the eldest of King Gavinsteal's sons and first in line for the throne. He looked just like his father.

The younger warrior was Prince Nelstrom, the king's youngest son. He was taller and thinner, but still laced with muscle. His strong shoulders and chest held up a black tunic that also had the Finarthian mark. He crossed his muscled forearms and Jonas saw the Finarthian symbol clearly on his right hand. This was the master swordsman that Cyn had mentioned. The man looked hard, like carved stone, and he did not smile, glancing at Fil and Jonas with undisguised disdain.

The other two men were high priests. They wore long robes of fine quality. Each one was made from soft fabric lined with silver thread that flowed around their bodies when they stood up in greeting. Androg was the eldest priest. He had gray hair and skin that hung loosely from his thin face. He wore a silver chain around his neck that carried the four pointed symbol of the High One. Manlin was younger, but his dark hair was still peppered heavily with gray and his weathered face showed signs of aging. What caught Jonas's attention, however, was the silver chain he wore around his neck. It carried a blue and silver symbol that looked almost exactly like the one on his chest. This man must be a priest of Shyann.

Jonas unconsciously rubbed his chest as they approached the king nervously.

"It is good to see you, King Gavinsteal. I thank you for your hospitality, and for the healing." Landon and the king shook hands like old friends.

"Anytime my friend," replied the king glancing at Fil and Jonas. "So these are the two reasons for this meeting? Welcome to Finarth, I am King Uthrayne Gavinsteal."

Fil and Jonas both bowed awkwardly, not sure what else to do.

"It is a great pleasure to meet you. My name is Jonas Kanrene," Jonas said, his voice breaking slightly.

"My name is Fil Tanrey and I thank you for your hospitality, King Gavinsteal." Smiling, the king introduced the others at the table who nodded their heads in greeting. "Come, have a seat at the table and let's hear this important news," the king commanded, moving to the head of the table.

They all sat down and Jonas continued to stare at the huge painting on the wall in front of them. He had to look back and forth to take in the colossal piece of art.

"You like my painting, young Jonas?" the king asked.

"Yes, Your Highness. It is magnificent. I have never seen anything like it."

"I should hope not," the king said, turning to glance at the painting himself. He looked back at Jonas. "Do you know what that picture represents?"

"No, sir, I do not. It looks like a battle."

"Indeed it is, but not just any battle. That painting represents the great battle at the Shadow Plains over a thousand years ago. The two warriors that you see are Malbeck, the Dark One himself, and my great ancestor, King Ullis, who slew him in combat. The battle against the evil that was fought on that day destroyed the battlefield forever. Even today nothing grows there, hence the name Shadow Plains. No one really knows why, but some suggest that when my ancestor killed the Dark One his evil was released, staining the ground and killing it forever. This sword that I carry is a replica of the very weapon that killed him."

Standing, the king drew the dazzling weapon holding it so Jonas could see. It was a huge broadsword, beautifully crafted and each end of the cross piece was gold carved into eagle claws. Each claw was holding a sparkling round stone polished milky white. The hilt was wrapped in silver and the end piece was carved into a fist in front of the sun. The long silver blade bore no mars or imperfections and it looked like it had never been used. The king held the long heavy weapon with ease. "This weapon was forged by the dwarves and imbued with magic by the priests of Ulren. It is not the same blade of course, but it is very powerful."

"It is beautiful, Your Highness," Fil said, eyes wide with wonder.

"What happened to the actual sword that killed the Dark One?" Jonas asked.

"No one knows exactly. Legend says that when King Ullis defeated the Dark One, there was a huge explosion that killed many men, including my great ancestor. The sword and armor were nowhere to be found."

"Come, Father, let us get to business. I have pressing matters to attend to," Prince Nelstrom interrupted curtly.

The king eyed his son, and Jonas did not miss the animosity between the two. "Very well," the king said, sheathing his sword. "Landon, my friend, please tell us this urgent news."

The far door opened again and everyone turned to see a soldier escort Allindrian into the room. Her long forest green tunic flowed at her sides as she walked confidently to the table. She sat down and greeted everyone with a smile.

"It is good to see you, King Gavinsteal. I'm sorry I am late." Allindrian gave a slight bow as she addressed the king.

The king returned the gesture with a warm smile. "Blade Singer, you are always welcome at my table, both for your skill and for your beauty."

Allindrian smiled unabashedly at the king, enjoying his praise.

"You know my sons, Prince Baylin and Prince Nelstrom. This is Androg, high priest to Ulren and this is Manlin, high priest to Shyann."

"It is a pleasure to meet you both and good to see you again, Prince Baylin," Allindrian smiled warmly at the burly man who returned her smile. "And you, Prince Nelstrom, I'm glad you are well," Allindrian added, her smile disappearing along with her warmth.

"Landon, if you will," urged the king.

"I have dire news. It is reported by these two young men that Airos the cavalier was slain by a Banthra," Landon said bluntly.

The room fell quiet as the sobering news hit home.

"That cannot be!" exclaimed Androg with dismay. "He was a first rank cavalier! The best there was! How can this be?"

"Jonas, show them the blade," urged Landon with a nod.

Jonas took out the knife from under his tunic, unsheathed the silver blade, and laid it on the table.

"Where did you get that?" stormed Androg.

"Androg, calm down," Prince Baylin admonished. "These two boys are not thieves or they never would have come here." He turned to Jonas. "Go ahead, son, tell us where you obtained the weapon, for that is most definitely Airos's blade." The prince had an aura of power and confidence, combined with a sense of dignity and honor. Jonas liked him immediately.

Jonas looked around the room and hesitantly began his tale. "Our village was attacked by boargs over three months ago. The force was led by a Banthra," Jonas said, choking on the word.

"A Banthra?" Manlin interrupted. "I don't believe it. They were all destroyed a thousand years ago."

Jonas ignored the comment and continued. "Airos came the night before the attack to help us. He battled the Banthra and killed it, but he died in the process. Their bodies were both burned and fused together in death. I found Airos's knife next to the remains."

Fil interjected. "It is true, your highness. I fought with my family and friends and saw it with my own eyes. Everyone was killed except for Jonas and me."

"I am sorry for your loss. This is indeed grave news. If a Banthra is back then the rumors we've heard of Malbeck's return may indeed be true," the king said thoughtfully.

"How is it that your entire village was killed but two young boys survived?" asked Prince Nelstrom, his tone hard and without compassion.

"Nelstrom, they have suffered greatly and they do not need your accusing comments," Prince Baylin said to his brother. Nelstrom narrowed his eyes at his older brother but said nothing.

"That is not all. There is other news that Jonas must tell. Go ahead, tell them the rest," Allindrian urged.

Jonas, looking at Allindrian, took a deep breath, and told them the rest of the story. He told them everything just as he had disclosed to Landon's men that night after the fight with the boargs.

Everyone at the table listened intently and when he explained the part about his dream and his God Mark their eyes widened with fascination and disbelief. He ended his story with the last battle with the boargs and the destruction of the cleric of Naz-reen.

"That is quite a story, young man. Can you show me this mark?" asked the king. Jonas looked at Allindrian and Landon, both of them nodding their heads urging him to proceed. He stood up, lifting his tunic over his head. Everyone gasped and the two priests stood up in astonishment.

"I can't believe it!" said Manlin, moving closer to Jonas to inspect the mark. "Unbelievable. That is indeed a God Mark and Shyann's symbol."

Androg was looking at the mark closely. "I agree. It is incredible. It is indeed her mark," he said.

Jonas felt strange standing there, his chest bare to all, being inspected by the others.

"I have never heard of anyone being God Marked unless they were a cavalier," the King said in wonder.

"Nor have I," added Manlin. "Shyann *has* marked this young man, but for what reason?"

"To become a cavalier I should think. She has expressed her interest in this young man and even warned him of danger twice, saving the lives of Landon's men. He must go to Annure to train," Prince Baylin announced.

"He is too young. They will not accept a candidate unless they are eighteen years of age," argued Androg. "Besides, he may not even pass the acceptance tests."

"Shyann has accepted him already, why would he not pass?" Allindrian said bluntly. "Jonas, tell the priests what Airos told you."

"You spoke to Airos?" asked Manlin.

"Yes, I was walking home and I slipped. I could not walk very well and I used a crutch and he helped me up and we talked briefly".

"What did he say to you?" Manlin asked.

"He said that my soul was pure, and that I should be very proud because that was so rare. I don't know what he meant but he said he could see into the hearts of men."

"He said that to you? Those words exactly?" asked Androg.

"Yes. I am sure."

"As you can see by his story, he has the character to be a cavalier," stated Allindrian smoothly. "He has fought and killed boargs, an ogre, and a cleric of Naz-reen. I believe he has shown that he has the courage to be a great warrior, the skills will come later. I suggest, good king, that you allow these two men to join your army so that you can train them and keep an eye on Jonas. When Jonas turns eighteen he should go to Annure and train to become a cavalier."

"Watch him? What do you mean by that?" asked Prince Nelstrom.

"If Shyann has expressed an interest in this young man, then that will also draw the attention of Gould, including Naz-reen and Dykreel," replied Allindrian. "A pure soul is like a beacon to the Forsworn, it will bring them to him like flies on a corpse. I'm afraid he will need protection."

The men at the table crossed their chests at the mention of the Forsworn. Jonas processed her words for the first time. She was right. The thought of being hunted by the evil ones was more frightening than he could imagine. His heart began to beat faster as he contemplated the danger he was in as well as the danger he could bring to others.

"You are quite right, Blade Singer. I hadn't thought of that," the king said, standing and walking up the stairs to his throne. He sat down in thought.

Fil looked at Jonas, unsure of what to do. Jonas put his tunic back on and sat down in nervous silence.

"Young men, what are your thoughts on this matter? We are talking about your welfare and yet we have not asked you your own desires." The king's strong voice resonated throughout the hall.

Without hesitating Fil stood up, addressing the king. "I have nothing left your highness. My friends and family are all dead. I would very much like to join your army, and become a Finarthian Knight. I know I can't right away, but some…"

"Young man," interrupted Prince Nelstrom. "A common peasant boy cannot join the elite knights unless you have a sponsor."

"And he does," stated Landon. "I will sponsor them both."

"As will I," added Allindrian.

The young prince eyed them both, unable to completely mask his look of disdain, but he did not press the issue.

"Your Majesty, I do not know what to do," Jonas replied. "My life has changed so much that my mind is whirling with uncertainty. I was a poor cripple my whole life and now I sit in a king's chamber with a God Mark on my chest. It is overwhelming. I have nothing left except for my friend, Fil. I have thought of nothing else other than to do something good with the gifts that Shyann has given me." Jonas looked around the group, making eye contact with them all, even Prince Nelstrom, whose veiled hostility was becoming increasingly apparent to Jonas. He returned his gaze to the king on his throne. "I think that I would like to join your knights, where I can gain the skills to protect the weak and battle the darkness that is spreading. Then when I'm eighteen, with your leave, I will go to Annure to see if my destiny lies there."

Everyone stared at Jonas, most with approval, a few with uncertainty, and one with disdain. For whatever reason, Jonas thought, it seemed Prince Nelstrom would become a problem for him.

"Well spoken, young man. If you are both serious, then approach the throne and swear your allegiance to me," the king commanded.

Fil and Jonas looked at each other and stood, approaching the throne. They stopped on the top stair below the throne.

"Kneel and repeat after me," the king ordered.

Jonas and Fil knelt at the base of the throne.

"I, Fil Tanrey and Jonas Kanrene, of the Tundrens, swear allegiance to the crown of Finarth. I will protect the throne and the people with my honor and blood, unto death."

Fil and Jonas repeated the words.

"And I, King Gavinsteal of Finarth," the king continued, "will protect you both as my vassals. My honor shall be yours through times of peace and war, unto death. Now stand, young men, you are now knight apprentices."

Fil and Jonas stood proudly, looking at each other, trying unsuccessfully to hide their growing smiles.

***

The apprentice knights slept in one large barracks by the north wall. There were around fifty young men between sixteen and eighteen years of age organized into five different training groups. These groups were each given a different color, each with a name. Jonas and Fil were assigned to the blue group, which they later found was the group where most of the commoners were placed. It created fewer problems because many of the highborn apprentices didn't relate well with the commoners.

The barracks were simple but spacious. Bunk beds lined both walls. At the foot of each bed were two small trunks for their belongings. Each bed had a tapestry on the wall above it representing the group to which they belonged. They were all embroidered in their group's colors and insignia.

Fil and Jonas stood at the base of their bed looking up at a blue tapestry. It was edged in red silk and lined with silver thread. In the center was a silver embroidered insignia of a massive set of deer antlers. The horns were spread wide and tall in a protective stance. The other groups were the Eagles, Dragons, Lions, and Boars.

"We're the Stags," said Fil, staring up at it. "I like it."

"Seems fitting, I think Shyann would approve," responded Jonas, looking up at the tapestry in thought. A stag was one of the symbols that represented Shyann, and living in a mountain town their entire lives gave them a deep respect for the wildlife that helped sustain them, particularly the noble stag.

They put their meager belongings into their trunk and took a look around. The barracks were empty now; the apprentices were at the training field. The king had a servant direct them to the barracks immediately after the king and Landon had talked a bit longer. Jonas was obliged to give Airos's blade back to Androg who had insisted that it belonged in the temple of the High One now that the cavalier was dead. Jonas hated to see the weapon go, but he knew that Androg was right.

Jonas sat on his bed, looking around in wonder. Lying on the bed were two blue tunics, each marked with the silver stag horns. He grabbed one, throwing it up to Fil who had climbed to the upper bunk.

"Here you go, Fil."

"Thanks. Should we put them on?" he asked.

"I guess so," Jonas said, taking off his tunic and putting on his new uniform. There was also a plain black belt that he used to cinch up the tunic, and attached to the belt was a small simple knife in a leather sheath.

Jonas put his other shirt into the trunk, adjusted his uniform, and explored his new surroundings. The beds were all perfectly made and the barrack was immaculate. The entire area was simple and clean.

"Can you believe this, Jonas? We're going to be Finarthian Knights," Fil said, staring at the vaulted ceiling from his bed. Jonas noticed that all the beds were arranged in groups according to their training team. Each team had a designated area in the barrack, but there were no lines or walls separating them. The blankets on the beds all matched the color of the team, so you could easily tell which groups of beds were assigned to each team.

"I can almost believe anything now, with all that's happened. It looks like they keep the groups together as much as they can. I wonder what group Tumas is with." Jonas mused.

"I don't know, but I imagine we'll find out soon enough."

Suddenly the far door bolted open and a short stocky warrior stepped into the barrack. He was wearing the gold and silver tunic of the Finarthian guard. The soldier was young, maybe twenty, but he carried himself with confidence, and moved with military precision. He wore a shiny chain mail shirt under his tunic that went to his knees and he carried a short sword and dagger at his belt. Leather greaves studded and lined with metal covered his muscular legs. The young man's cape danced around as he approached the two new recruits. His face was cleanly shaven and his long blond hair was tied back behind his ears with a leather thong.

"Are you Fil Tanrey and Jonas Kanrene?" asked the warrior.

Fil jumped down from the bunk to stand next to Jonas.

"Yes, sir," replied Jonas.

"Good. I am Sal. I was asked by the king to show you around and explain how things work and how your training will progress. If you will please follow me," the warrior said, spinning on his heels and walking away, not looking to see whether or not they were following. Fil and Jonas glanced at each other, quickly running to keep up with the soldier's brisk pace.

As they walked, Sal continued. "As you were told, the apprentices are separated into smaller training units. You will usually train with your unit only, which, by your uniforms, is obviously the Stag team. During the daylight hours you will perform a variety of tasks, from physical training and educational pursuits, to serving the knights that live in the inner castle. You will clean and maintain their horses, clean and care for their armor and weapons, and learn all the other skills needed to someday become a knight yourself," Sal explained, taking them east to a long row of stables. "These are the stables that your team takes care of. Your team leader will organize your work. Do you have any questions so far?"

Sal stopped in the middle of the stables as the two boys shook their heads, indicating that they understood. They were both still busy taking in all the new information and looking around their surroundings. This was to be their new home for the next couple of years and they savored the thought.

The stables were impressive. There were probably at least a hundred horses housed within their walls. Several servants scurried around cleaning stalls, carrying hay, and brushing the horses, work that Jonas knew they would get their fair share of.

A thin older man walked up to them, setting down a bag a grain. He was balding and his face and body showed signs of a lifetime of manual labor. "Good evening, Sal, what do we have here, new recruits?" asked the man.

"Yes, Lars, this is Jonas and Fil, they will be joining the blue team."

"Nice to meet you both. As you heard, my name is Lars and these are my beauties," Lars said proudly, using his hands in a gesture that included the entire stable. "I run this stable and I expect it to be maintained to the highest of standards. Do you know what hard work is?" asked Lars.

"Yes, sir," replied Fil. "We both come from the mountain town of Manson and hard work kept us alive."

"Manson…never heard of it," said Lars.

"It is far to the north, sir, almost a month's travel," replied Jonas.

"What brings you here to Finarth? Oh, never mind, a story for another time. I see that you are busy. I need to get back to work anyway. Good day, Sal. Boys, I will see you tomorrow." Lars picked up his bag of grain and made his way to the feeding bins.

Sal brought them out of the stables, taking them around the outer wall. He explained to them that the inner castle had two walls. Behind the outer wall, the knights lived, trained, and kept their horses. The inner wall surrounded the king's palace and housed the royal family, servants, and guests.

Sal explained that the inner castle was huge with large dining halls and many spacious rooms. Fil and Jonas didn't tell him that they had already seen several of those rooms.

Sal brought them to another barrack, this one much larger and more elegant than theirs. Vines of bright green with purple flowers climbed ornate pergolas that lined the outside courtyard.

In the clearing outside the barracks was a group of warriors, wearing only leggings and boots, their bare skin wet with perspiration. As they neared the group they noticed that two men were circling each other, while a handful watched and cheered. The sweat on their muscular bodies glistened in the sun. Each combatant bore several cuts and dirt streaked their bodies where the dust had mingled with their sweat.

"This is third lance Lathrin's barracks. He has five hundred knights under his command and they are spread out over three different buildings," explained Sal.

"What are these men doing?" asked Fil.

"They are training in hand-to-hand combat," Sal replied matter-of-factly.

Fil and Jonas stared at the bruises and cuts on the faces of the two warriors as their blood was dripping down their bodies, mingling with their sweat. One man was tall and lean and moved like a dancer. The other man was also tall, but much thicker, and looked like a gigantic walking oak tree. Jonas had never seen a man so large, and he was amazed at how quick he could move for a man so thick of muscle.

The burly man moved in quickly trying to grab the smaller man in a powerful bear hug, but the other man, just as quickly, struck him twice with two lighting quick jabs to the face.

The huge man faltered but did not stop. He, too, swung his large right hand towards his opponent, hoping to land a glancing blow at least. The thinner man, sidestepping the punch, grabbed his arm, and using the big man's momentum, he threw him through the air. The man landed hard on his back, forcing the air from his lungs.

"That is enough, Graggis. Let us both get some water," said the tall wiry man, wiping the sweat from his face.

Graggis slowly got up, brushing off the dirt from his sweat covered body. "I hate that throw," Graggis growled.

"You would think you'd see it coming by now," the man laughed good naturedly.

"Who are they?" asked Fil, mesmerized by the warriors.

"That is Graggis, a man you do not want as an enemy."

"But he was defeated by that other man," said Jonas.

"He was not defeated, young apprentice, merely thrown. It would take much more than that to defeat Graggis. The throw angered Graggis and I suspect that is why Dagrinal ended the fight," Sal said, smiling for the first time. "And when Graggis has his axe in hand and he is fighting for his life, it is something to behold. It is like he is possessed."

"The other man is Dagrinal?" asked Fil.

"Yes, fourth lance of Lathrin's ludas," Sal said, looking at them both. In seeing their expressions he added, "A ludas is what we call a group of five hundred men. Dagrinal and another fourth lance split the ludas with Lathrin as their commander. He is working for his sword mark, and he is almost there. He is amazing with a long sword, almost as good as Prince Nelstrom."

Jonas remembered his conversation earlier with Landon and he quickly worked out the numbers in his head. "So, Dagrinal leads his own modrig."

"That is correct, apprentice. He leads two hundred and fifty men," replied Sal.

They spent the better part of the next several hours exploring the castle's inner grounds. Finally they neared the training field, which was located on the northeast section, between the outer and inner walls. It wasn't really a field, noted Jonas, but more like a small circular road. Grass grew in the middle of the dirt road where many apprentices practiced with wooden swords.

A team of eight boys wearing black tunics embroidered with the silver symbol of the dragon were running around the track. Two other teams, the gold team wearing the black marks of the boar, and the white team wearing the mark of the lion, practiced with wooden swords on the grass. The space was large and Jonas doubted he could throw a rock across the field.

Jonas could see one boy, taller than the rest, sprinting far ahead of his other teammates on the track. His strides were long and fluid and he slowly pulled away from his panting teammates. The runner seemed very relaxed and his movements were effortless. Jonas then turned his attention to the rest of the training grounds.

"This is the practice field," Sal continued. "There will usually be two to three teams here at a time practicing sword work, hand-to-hand combat, and endurance training. A large part of your training will be conditioning, both for your lungs and your muscles." Sal walked them across the dusty track.

"Allindrian said that it was important to train your body first if you want to be a great swordsman," replied Jonas.

"The Blade Singer? You talked with her?" Sal asked, stopping and looking at him curiously.

"Well, yes, we traveled with her and Master Landon's caravan. We met with them on the road from Tarsis, that is how we ended up here," Jonas said, unsure if he should say more.

Sal, looking at the boys, obviously wanted to ask more. "Sometime I would like to hear this story. Did you get a chance to see her fight?" he asked, continuing to move forward.

"We did. Our caravan was attacked by boargs," Jonas added.

Sal stopped again, looking at Jonas incredulously. Fil and Jonas looked at each other wondering if they had told too much. "Boargs, you say?" Sal continued skeptically.

"Yes, boargs. Our entire town was destroyed by the beasts. We left to come here," Fil replied, a hint of anger in his voice as the memory of the carnage crept back into his mind.

"I'm sorry to hear that. I did not mean to bring up ill thoughts. Did either of you get a chance to bring justice to their killers?"

"We both fought," replied Jonas lamely, not sure of what else to say.

"But we still seek justice, which is why we are here," interjected Fil.

"I see," said Sal, "I hope that someday you get that chance. What was the Blade Singer like?" Sal asked, unable to hide his excitement.

"Incredible. She was so fast, moving from one boarg to another, her blade spinning in a blur. And it really makes a singing noise when she fights. It was the most amazing thing I've ever seen," Jonas replied with equal enthusiasm, thinking back to that night in the field.

"Count yourselves lucky, apprentices. There are not many who can say they met a Blade Singer let alone fought next to one. They are very rare and unmatched in swordsmanship. I hope that someday I may have the chance to witness one in combat," Sal said as he moved to the training field.

The boys on the field were paired off, practicing various strikes, poses, and ripostes, some of which Jonas recognized from what Allindrian had taught them. These boys were more advanced however, which made sense to Jonas considering that they had been training for many months.

A man wearing a light blue tunic and gray breeches faced them as they neared. He carried a long wooden sword and smiled as they approached. The man was lean and strong and his unshaven face was hard, like granite, with one long scar across his cheek.

"Sal, how's that bruise I gave you?" the man asked.

Sal laughed heartily, shaking hands with the man in the warrior's grip. "Not bad, Master Morgan, but I've been practicing the counter and you won't bait me again."

"We shall have to test your confidence soon," he replied, still smiling. Then he looked at Jonas and Fil and his smile disappeared. "Two new recruits I see. My name is Master Morgan and I will be your weapons instructor for the next two years. At that point, if you have shown promise, then you may be moved up to the advanced classes taught by Master Borum."

"It is a pleasure to meet you, sir. My name is Fil Tanrey."

"And I am Jonas Kanrene. We are very glad to be here."

"Very good. Now I have work to do. I will see you both with your group tomorrow." He moved away to correct an improper strike from one of the apprentices, leaving the boys and Sal watching the training.

"Master Morgan is the best weapons expert we have, next to Master Borum, who I have not seen beaten, even by Prince Nelstrom."

"Does Master Borum bear the expert swordsman mark?" asked Jonas.

"He does. The same as Prince Nelstrom. Let us go now; it won't be long before your group will be at the mess hall. You both must be hungry and you need to meet your group members," he said, leading the boys off the training field.

***

The first year in Finarth was very exciting, but difficult as well. Their long days were split with early morning runs, work in the stables, training, more work, and then more training. They trained with sword, bow and spear. They learned how to ride and take care of a warhorse. They were taught the basics in formation fighting, shield work, and fighting from horseback, which is what the Finarthian Knights were known for. At night they would also perform chores in the castle, cleaning and serving the knights and royalty. Even Jonas hated that work as most of the cleaning revolved around scrubbing the kitchens, including the hundreds of pots and dishes used every day. Three nights a week each team also took classes on writing, reading, and history, the latter being Jonas's favorite.

It was exhausting work, but Jonas and Fil both thrived on it. For Fil hard work was a part of his life and for Jonas it was something that he had never been able to do, so they both took to it easily, quickly gaining the respect of the trainers and teachers.

Jonas excelled even further. He couldn't get enough work. His body did not want to rest. It was as if he were trying to make up for the many years that he couldn't use his crippled form.

At night, he would sneak out and run around the track until he was exhausted and he could barely move. That was the only way he could fall asleep. He was constantly hounded by nightmares and his mind didn't seem to want to rest. He would wake up from restless nights and practice the various sword forms that he had been taught, slowly going over each movement until he had mastered it perfectly. Then he would practice them faster and faster until he didn't have to think about them.

He started to look like a man; his body grew tall and his adolescent frame started to take the shape of a seasoned warrior. The constant running and training strengthened his muscles and gave them that taut look, like a tightly strung bow. His face grew more angular as he lost his boy-like softness. But his shaggy brown hair and his gentle smile tempered the harder edges of his appearance.

Fil changed as well. He grew several inches and bulked up with muscle, becoming stockier than Jonas, and more powerful. Jonas had moved forward in the direction of skill and endurance, while Fil and excelled in strength and power. Like all knights, he trained with a blade, but his weapon of choice was the spear. He learned to use it like a staff and his powerful arms and shoulders could throw the weapon great distances and with immense power. His strong stocky arms enabled him to excel at formation fighting where he used a shield and short infantry blade. It was grueling work to maintain proper shield position while using the heavy cutting blades designed for formation fighting. Strong arms and backs were necessary and Fil took to the skill naturally.

They became very close with the members of their team. They knew that the blue team of the Stag was where most of the lowborn applicants were put. There weren't as many members in their team since it was often difficult for a peasant to get a sponsor. There were eight boys in their group. Calden, a likeable young man just under eighteen winters, was their leader.

Calden was the son of a beautiful herbalist who had befriended a rich lord. Everyone knew that there was a romantic liaison between the two, but Calden's friends said nothing about it to him as it was a sore spot for the young apprentice. Calden's mother was the lord's mistress and it was something that Calden was not proud of. He was not overly skilled in weapons or running, but he was very bright and his personality made him a natural leader. He was tall with red curly hair like his mother. His father was a common soldier who had died in battle when he was born.

Fil and Jonas were saddened to hear that Tumas, the boy they met on their first day in Finarth, was part of the black team, the Dragons. The Dragons were the upper echelon, the sons of the most powerful men in Finarth. They both liked Tumas and they were hoping that they would be on the same team, but he was highborn, and hence were separated

Tumas's group was led by Torgan, a mean, vindictive boy who despised commoners. He was the son of Prince Nelstrom, which put him high on the list for advancement. He was the same boy that Jonas saw running around the track on the first day. He was athletic and handsome and the girls swooned over him.

Jonas and Torgan became enemies early on, for Torgan soon recognized Jonas was his only competition with a blade. Jonas tried to befriend him but it was useless. Torgan viewed Jonas as lowly and not deserving the right to become a knight, and nothing Jonas did could persuade him otherwise.

***

Their second summer of training was exceptionally hot, making the days on the track more grueling than normal. On one of these hot days they were sparring with swords, and the hard work and heat exhaustion had everyone's nerves strung tight.

The blue team and the black team were working hard on their sword forms. Jonas was paired with Titus, the son of a rich lord who was close to the king. Titus was decent enough with the sword and was kind to Jonas. He was one of the few from the Dragon team, other than Tumas, who did not look down on the Stag team.

Jonas had already touched Titus twice with his wooden sword, both killing blows to the chest. Titus was tiring, and sweating profusely, the salty wetness was dripping into his deep set eyes. Jonas was sweating as well, but his muscles still had life, and he danced lightly on the tips of his toes.

Titus came in hard with a powerful downward stroke. Jonas, batting the sword aside, side stepped, smacking him lightly on the leg.

"Good strike, Jonas," Master Morgan said as he walked by. "Titus, go spar with Mulick and bring Torgan here." Master Morgan turned to Jonas who was standing lightly with his wooden sword at his side. "Jonas, you've progressed well. Soon you will have to fight me to get a workout," he said with a sly smile.

"Thank you, Master Morgan," Jonas said, happy with the praise, although doubting he would last more than a few heartbeats with Master Morgan. The man was astonishingly quick and he didn't seem to tire.

Torgan came running up to Morgan, his long powerful legs covering the distance easily. He was wearing the short sleeved Dragon tunic with light charcoal breeches. His jet black hair was trimmed in the usual fashion for royalty his age, short in the back and edges with bangs that were cut straight across the forehead.

"Torgan, I want you to spar with, Jonas. Jonas has improved quickly and he needs a better opponent," ordered Master Morgan.

"Yes sir, Master Morgan," replied Torgan eagerly.

Morgan pivoted, turning to instruct the others.

"Hey dung eater, you ready to feel a sting?" sneered Torgan as soon as Master Morgan was out of ear shot.

"Torgan, I don't know what I ever did to you, but I hold no animosity toward you," replied Jonas.

"It's not what you did, but what you are. You have no right to be here. You are a peasant coward, not worthy to train as a knight."

"If the king sees fit to have us, then that should be good enough for you," countered Jonas.

"Well it's not. Now get that sword up," ordered Torgan, lunging at Jonas. Jonas stumbled back quickly just getting his wooden sword up in time to take the first strike. But Torgan was fast and his sword lightly brushed Jonas's thigh with his second stroke.

"First hit!" Torgan yelled, loud enough for everyone to hear.

And your last, thought Jonas, regaining his composure. They danced around for several minutes, neither opponent scoring a hit. They were both strong and fast and their blades made a rhythmic striking sound, like an axe chopping wood, every time they connected. Jonas had never fought against Torgan before so he was just going through the basic moves, analyzing his technique. Torgan was matching his skill smoothly and was utterly confident in his abilities. But he hadn't fought Jonas yet, either. Nor had he snuck out at night to work on strengthening exercises and to go through the forms until they were second nature. But Jonas had, and this relentless practice for over a year had honed his muscles, his mind, and his sword work. Torgan believed he couldn't be beaten, but Jonas believed otherwise.

Slowly Jonas began to pick up the pace, moving his feet and his wooden sword faster and faster. Torgan matched his speed, but Jonas recognized the slow rise of fear on his face. They were both sweating profusely and Torgan was beginning to tire. Jonas's powerful lungs and muscles, strengthened from constant training, kept him moving lightly on his feet.

Jonas remembered Allindrian's words about fighting a warrior who was stronger and in better shape… *swordsmen must first master their strength, not their blade. A strong back, stomach, and arms will mean faster and more powerful strokes and those muscles are also needed to maintain balance. Your lungs must be strong in order to fight long drawn out battles*

Her advice rang in his head as he picked up the pace. Torgan lunged at him, slightly off balance, and Jonas thought he had him. He smacked his blade down hard but simultaneously he realized it was just a clever feint. Torgan, spinning his blade under Jonas's strike, went to hit his exposed left thigh.

Torgan would have had him if Jonas hadn't reacted on instinct alone. He remembered the move Allindrian had taught him, flipping his wooden sword to his left hand and pivoting his left leg away from Torgan's strike. Jonas was ambidextrous and he could use his left arm as well as his right.

Torgan's blade found only air as Jonas's wooden sword struck him hard in the side. Torgan stumbled forward, but regained his balance quickly, glaring at Jonas with hatred. He launched a ferocious attack, swinging his wooden sword with all his strength. He was angry, which gave Jonas the advantage. He was able to calmly apply basic defensive moves to counter the ferocious attacks.

Jonas waited for Torgan to tire before striking offensively again. Torgan lunged with his sword right at Jonas's abdomen. He was tired and his strike was clumsy. Jonas sidestepped the blade, using his left leg to trip Torgan, who was already off balance, while simultaneously bringing his wooden sword down hard on Torgan's back. Torgan, stumbling, hit the ground with a thud.

Torgan slowly stood, glaring at Jonas with insurmountable fury. Jonas barely had time to react as Torgan, dropping his sword, tackled him. Torgan's body barreled into his stomach, knocking the wind out of him as they both landed on the ground. Jonas got his hands up to his face to protect it from the strikes that he was sure were coming.

Torgan's fists beat down on him repeatedly, but they could not break through Jonas's defenses. Jonas had learned from Master Morgan that if you get into a hand to hand fight, and end up on the ground, that you want to reduce the distance between you and your opponent. It will minimize the damage that they can do to you.

So Jonas, in a brief lull between Torgan's strikes at his face, quickly reached up, wrapped his arms around Torgan's neck, and pulled his head down hard towards him, forcing their bodies together and making Torgan's fists useless. Then Jonas pivoted, arched his neck, and used the ground as leverage to twist their bodies so he was now on top of Torgan. Immediately Jonas let go, leaping away from the enraged boy. By this time a crowd of apprentices had formed and Master Morgan had just made his way toward them.

"You dirty peasant! You don't even deserve to have the chance to fight me!" Torgan screamed, charging a second time.

Master Morgan moved in a blur, striking Torgan hard in the shins with his wooden practice sword. Torgan, bellowing in pain, tripped face first onto the grass, holding his bruised and bleeding shins.

"What are you doing, Torgan?" Morgan raged. "You are acting beneath your station. You are all apprentices to be knights of Finarth!" Morgan raised his voice as he addressed the group. "Someday you may be fighting next to each other, your swords protecting one another! How can you trust each other if you behave like this?"

"I'm sorry, Master Morgan, I did not mean for it to happen. It will not happen again," replied Jonas calmly.

Torgan got up slowly, his anger still apparent as he glared at Jonas with open hatred.

"What happened?" demanded Master Morgan.

"It was both our faults, sir. He scored the first hit and then I scored the last. Our competitive spirit and equal skill fueled our anger and we lost control. I will try to control my anger next time, sir. I apologize," Jonas said in an attempt to cover for Torgan, hoping that that kindness might reduce Torgan's animosity towards him.

"Is this correct, Torgan?" asked Master Morgan.

Torgan eyed Jonas with barely concealed malice. "Yes, sir, that is correct. I am sorry, Master Morgan, for letting my anger control me."

"Good," Mater Morgan said as he turned to the entire group. "Now since you all seem to have so much energy, give me twenty circuits around the track."

Nobody complained or said a word. They dropped their sticks and began jogging to the track, the hot midday sun baking their sweaty bodies as they ran.

Jonas stayed back behind Torgan not wanting to be anywhere near the angry apprentice. He could sense the volatile emotions flow from him like giant waves in an ocean's storm.

Calden, his team leader, jogged up next to him. "It is not wise to make an enemy of the most powerful apprentice here, and heir to the Finarthian throne".

Jonas let out a frustrated sigh. "I did nothing but fight back, and I even covered for him," Jonas said, exasperated.

"Maybe you shouldn't have fought so well," Calden reasoned as they continued around the track.

"Let him win!" Jonas exclaimed in a tone that could not hide his disgust.

Calden raised an eyebrow. "Maybe…I worry for you, Jonas. You do not want an enemy in the likes of him."

"I've done nothing wrong."

"You're right, but sometimes that is not enough," Calden replied.

Jonas, shaking his head in frustration, continued around the track in silence.

Six
Darkness comes

The Greever lifted its bony head from the winged beast on which it was feeding. Its nostrils flared, sniffing the air of his domain, the domain in of which he was the master, the killer that lived to hunt. As its bloody jaws tore rhythmically at the bone and flesh, the demon felt the distant tug of its master's call, a call not heard in ages.

The Greever stretched its nine foot frame to its full height, its long muscular arms held wide, sniffing the air again, feeling the invisible tug of his master's summons, eager for the blood that was soon to follow. The Greever was the ultimate killer, built solely for destruction. It resembled a man, but was much taller and more heavily muscled. Long sinewy arms hung down to its knobby knees. Its powerful legs were shaped like a goat, but instead of dainty hooves, long clawed toes like a dragon bore its solid weight. The Greever's thick leather-like skin was gray and cold to the touch. Its body was completely hairless, except for the thick patch of black hair that covered part of its dog-like head and muscular neck. Sharp bony spikes were imbedded at the back of the demon's elbows, the front of its knees, and the top of its shoulders and head, all of which it could use with flesh tearing devastation. Its red, deep set eyes glowed atop a thick snout above powerful jaws filled with teeth strong enough to break steel. The beast's hands and feet were long and clawed with wicked talons, each the length of a dagger. Tucked into crevices on its back were long leathery wings, capable of carrying the demon long distances. For the Greever did not tire, did not relent from any hunt. At the end of each wing was a long sharp spike that it could wield as a deadly weapon. Everything on the demon was formidable, including its tail, which was as thick as a man's arm and ended in a heavy sphere covered with poisoned spikes. Endowed with lightning speed and power, it could also hunt as quietly as a cat.

The familiar fog began to swirl before it, and the beast entered the mist, eager to be sent to another world, to serve its master, because its master always provided him sustenance, and the Greever was hungry for new flesh.

***

That night Jonas, Fil, Calden, and Bornius, another boy from the blue team, were sitting on their beds quietly discussing Jonas's fight with Torgan.

The black team was on the far side of the barracks and they couldn't possibly hear their conversation.

"I fear you've made a powerful enemy, Jonas," commented Bornius as he changed into his sleeping shirt. Bornius was the son of a farmer and Fil and Jonas liked him immediately. He was a hard worker, kind, and looked to help others before he helped himself.

"Jonas didn't *make* anything. Torgan has had it out for him since he came here a year ago. It doesn't matter what he does, Torgan has made up his mind he hates him," Fil said, sitting on the edge of the bed above Jonas.

"I've tried to befriend him, and even today I covered for him, but it matters not; we commoners will always be scum to him," Jonas said.

"I don't understand how the king, or the other commanders, would promote Torgan to a position of power with such prejudices. How can he be a leader if he can't inspire all his troops, not just the highborn?" asked Fil.

"A lot of the highborn believe the same way he does," said Calden.

"I don't believe the king agrees. He didn't seem that type to me," replied Jonas.

"You've met the king?" asked Bornius incredulously.

Jonas looked up at Fil, forgetting that these boys, their new friends, didn't know anything about their story or how they were sponsored. They never asked so it never came up, and Jonas worked hard to cover his God Mark, which was almost an impossible task, but so far he had been successful in the deception. Master Morgan was privy to Jonas's mark and he helped him in keeping it hidden. When it came to bathing, Morgan would provide time where Jonas could be alone.

"Yes, Fil and I met King Gavinsteal over a year ago. We were both sponsored by Master Landon, a well-known merchant from Tarsis. Master Landon is a good friend to the king. He brings him dwarven weapons and armor to outfit his knights," said Jonas.

"How did you meet this Master Landon?" asked Calden.

Jonas looked up again; shrugging his shoulders, Fil gave him a *go ahead* expression. So Jonas told them their abridged story. He left out information about his mark and the battle they had on the road, but he told them about the destruction of their town and their meeting with Airos.

"I can't believe you met a cavalier. What was he like?" asked Bornius.

"Kind and generous," said Jonas.

"And someone to see in a fight. He was an incredible fighter, and he was inspiring. He made everyone feel like they could win. I've never felt like that before," said Fil.

"Yes, I've heard that cavaliers have the power to inspire courage and push back fear. I've heard Airos was one of the best. I would love to have met him. It saddens me he was killed. And what is a Banthra? I have never heard of one," asked Bornius.

"I'm not sure exactly," responded Fil. "I think it is some sort of demon brought here by Malbeck, a minion of the Forsworn I think, but I never saw it."

All the boys except Fil and Jonas tapped their chests in the four pointed star at the mention of the dark gods.

There was a stir by the entrance and the apprentices that were in the barracks quickly shuffled to attention. Jonas, looking towards the door, saw Prince Nelstrom briskly moving towards them. He wore a glossy black leather breastplate with the Finarthian symbol embossed on it. The prince's breaches were made from supple black leather and a flowing silk cape hung from his strong shoulders. He wore knee high leather boots polished to a glossy black. His dark hair was cut short and his beard was trimmed to a point, giving his face an angular, strong look.

The apprentices near the prince all bowed as he walked with long strides towards Jonas and his friends. Fil jumped down from the bunk and the other boys got to their feet standing at attention, bowing slightly as the prince moved directly to Jonas.

"Leave us," the prince said curtly, staring directly at Jonas.

Fil, Calden, and Bornius quickly walked away toward the other apprentices who were watching intently at a distance.

"Good day, Prince Nelstrom. It is good to see you," Jonas said, matching his stare.

The prince ignored his comment, looking him up and down. His blue eyes were piercing and shone with malice. "I heard what you did to my son," the prince whispered, his voice laced with venom.

"I did nothing, he attacked me…"

"Do not address me unless I ask you to. You are nothing to me, a low commoner who has gotten lucky. Who are you to even consider crossing blades with my son? He is in line to be the king of Finarth and you are likely a bastard son of some common bar whore," the prince continued angrily.

Jonas's eyes blazed with anger and his muscles tensed. A part of him wanted to punch the prince in the stomach.

"What's wrong, boy? Are you angry? Did my words offend you?"

Jonas, controlling his emotions, replied evenly. "No, sir, they did not." The prince smiled wickedly. "Stay out of my son's way. Do you hear me? Don't ever insult him or make him look foolish again. Am I clear?"

"Yes, sir," replied Jonas, his eyes holding the prince's gaze.

"I see you've grown in confidence this last year. That is good. Maybe, in several years, you and I could cross blades. Do you think you could beat me?" the prince asked with an amusing smile.

"No, sir, I do not," replied Jonas evenly.

"Good. At least you're not as stupid as most of your lice ridden kind." Their eyes locked again; the prince turned on his heels and strode briskly from the room.

Jonas let out a deep breath and sat down on the bed. Fil, Calden, and Bornius moved back to Jonas quickly, eager to find out what had transpired between him and the prince.

Fil sat down next to Jonas. "A private conversation with the prince; if only I was that lucky," Fil said, smiling.

"What did he say?" Calden asked with interest.

"I think I've made an enemy of the prince and his son. He told me to stay away from Torgan and to never make him look bad again."

"What! Torgan attacked *you* and you did all you could not to fight," exclaimed Bornius.

"It doesn't matter. He doesn't like me. I will just have to watch myself and make sure that I don't put myself in a position that might create tension between us," replied Jonas.

"That's if Torgan doesn't look for trouble," interjected Fil.

"Blue team! White team! Everyone up, it's time for a night run!" yelled Master Morgan, entering the barracks. "Let's go, move it!"

"Here we go again. Two nights in a row," mumbled Bornius.

"Let's go, Blue Team! Get moving!" bellowed Calden, getting up to put on his boots. All the kids scrambled to put their tunics and boots back on and move out into the cool night air.

***

The Greever flew hard all night. It did not need to rest. Its powerful body was fueled by inert magic, magic born to the beast, and its hunger pushed it relentlessly. The Greever was a demon of a different world, it was born from magic, and the energy of the Ru'Ach pulsed within its veins. Its long leather wings beat the air rhythmically and its piercing red eyes scanned the Finarthian hills for its target. The beast, flaring its nostrils, caught the scent it was looking for. A quick flick of its wing sent it southwest toward the towering city of Finarth.

***

The night's run was long and Master Morgan had also made them do various other training maneuvers and exercises. The boys stumbled into the barracks, tired and sweaty. Even Jonas's muscles felt heavy. They crawled to their beds still wearing their tunics and breeches and quickly fell asleep.

Jonas awoke with a start, his chest itching and tingling. He opened his eyes wide with fright realizing what was happening. He looked around frantically, unsure of what to do. Shyann was warning him of something, but what? He couldn't just wake up the whole barracks.

He silently got out of bed and shook Fil to wake him. Fil, stirring in his sleep, slowly opened his eyes. "Fil, wake up, something is wrong."

Fil's eyes focused as he saw Jonas. "What is it?" he asked groggily.

"My chest, something is happening."

Fil got up quickly, knowing that Jonas's warnings in the past had been all too real.

"The warning is slight, but I can feel it. What should we do?" Jonas asked with concern in his voice.

Fil got up and climbed down to stand next to Jonas. "We need to tell someone," he said, putting on his boots.

"But who? No one will believe us."

"The king will, or Prince Baylin, or even the high priests that know about you," whispered Fil as he buckled his belt around his waist. "We could tell Master Morgan, he knows about the mark."

"We can't go see them in the middle of the night. The guards will stop us."

"We have to try, Jonas. You know what this means. We are in danger."

"You're right. Whatever the warning is, it is probably for me. I should get away immediately so I don't endanger everyone around me."

"You can't do this alone. Let's go," Fil said without waiting for his reply. Jonas quietly followed Fil through the barracks and outside into the cool night.

Fil and Jonas ran to the east, towards the knight's barracks as the Greever landed lightly on the roof of the boys' sleeping quarters. The beast tucked its long leather wings into the crevices on its back sniffing hungrily for the scent of its prey. The demon smelled its target somewhere near, and its maw opened instinctively, saliva dripping from its long fangs. The deadly hunter leaped down to the ground landing lightly by the north entrance, its dark leather-like skin blending like a ghost into the shadows of the night.

Jonas stumbled, his chest flaring with pain. Fil reached out grabbing his arm to steady him. Images flashed in Jonas's mind, images of a great beast entering their barracks.

"Fil! The Barracks! They are in danger!" Jonas said, his eyes wide with fear, seeing the images that Fil could not.

Fil and Jonas glanced back toward their barracks. They were near the knights' own barracks so they wasted no time and sprinted toward the main door. A knight in full armor stood outside the entrance, spear in hand as the boys neared. The knight quickly pointed his spear forward, standing in combat position as he saw the two forms stumble out of the night.

"Who are you?" the knight asked. Then seeing their blue tunics he relaxed a bit and approached them. "What are you two recruits doing out this time of night?"

"Quick, our barracks are being attacked! Raise the alarm!" yelled Jonas.

"What?"

"Do it now!" screamed Jonas grabbing the alarmed knight. Suddenly screams in the distance filled the night.

"What in Ulren's name is that?" asked the soldier looking out into the darkness.

"I told you, we are under attack! Now get help!" Jonas yelled grabbing the knight's sword from his sheath and running back into the night towards their barracks.

The knight dropped his spear, grabbed the horn around his neck and blew the alarm. Fil picked up the man's spear and ran after Jonas. The screeching blast of the horn combined with screams coming from the boys' barracks awoke the battle hardened knights sleeping nearby.

The Greever walked silently through the barracks, its padded paws making no sound on the rough stone. The demon's long claws on its feet were retracted so it could walk quietly.

There was warm flesh everywhere and the Greever's fanged mouth was gaping hungrily. The Greever could almost taste the succulent feast so near. Its long powerful arms reached out as its bony head scanned the bunks for its prey. The demon could smell him; the entire room stank with his stench. To the demon, the boy's goodness and pure heart left an odor that was disgusting, something to be destroyed by tooth and claw.

One of the apprentices to the Greever's right got up slowly; something had awakened him. The Greever stopped not more than two paces away, staring at the boy, its red eyes, like rubies, bright with anticipation. The boy's eyes adjusted to the night and looked directly at the nightmare before him. He shook his head slightly, looking again, his eyes widening in fright as his mouth opened in a scream that never came.

The Greever's right wing shot from its back and the long spike on the tip speared the boy like a pig. The only sound that came from the boy was a gurgle as the demon ripped the spike from him, but the noise was enough to awaken several boys around him who groggily began to stir from their slumber. The Greever's jaws opened wide hissing loudly, its powerful body crouching, ready to attack. And that is what it did.

The Greever tore into the young boys, clawed hands ripping and tearing flesh. The demon was a whirlwind of death, spraying blood into the air, covering the walls with crimson splashes. The barracks were alive with the screams of the wounded and dying, and the Greever relished the cacophonous sounds of his carnage as he savored the coppery taste of blood.

Jonas ran through the doorway and was assaulted with the chaos of death and terror. Blood was everywhere and unrecognizable bodies littered the floor. His heart pounded and fear gripped his body, immobilizing him briefly. Many of his friends were dead, and more were dying as he stood just inside the open doorway.

Then anger filled his body and beat away the fear in his heart. Moving further into the room he desperately looked for some way to help his friends that were still alive. It was dark but he could just make out a large form at the far end of the room ripping and tearing, cutting a swath of death as it moved with unbelievable speed. Jonas heard more screams and hoped that some of his friends had made it out the south door.

He held his sword out in front of him, but it seemed so puny against such a beast. In the murky darkness his eyes swept around the room frantically trying to come up with some sort of plan. Jonas prayed silently, pleading desperately for help from Shyann.

Suddenly Jonas felt his body growing warm with an energy building deep within him. The feeling surprised him, but the screaming in the darkness forced him to focus his mind on the warm flood of energy coalescing inside him; and he prayed, concentrating on his belly where the force was centered. Suddenly his body began to glow. It was as if a white light was slowly growing within him, starting in his belly and emanating outward surrounding his flesh. It was not the explosive light that Jonas saw from Airos, the cavalier, but a softer light, growing in strength the more Jonas concentrated. The light's rays pierced the darkness, beating away the shadows and illuminating the horrible destruction.

The beast pivoted quickly as the light touched it. The Greever didn't like this light; it felt strange and unwelcome, stinging its flesh, but there, standing not more than fifty paces away was its target. The Greever's nostrils pulsed with disgust taking in the horrible smell of its target. The demon hated that smell, hated all it stood for. It wanted him dead. It would take more than light to stop it from ripping the boy to pieces and feeding on his warm wet flesh. The hunter crouched, leaping forward with astonishing power and speed.

Fil ran in behind Jonas, quickly taking in the scene. Jonas's magic light flared brighter, exposing a scene that was beyond Fil's imagination, but Fil didn't have time to wonder about the light or the carnage around him. A huge beast with long arms and blood covered claws was running at them with incredible speed, jaws open, exposing long deadly fangs. He felt fear grip him, but he fought it back, leaping in front of Jonas, and hurling the spear with all his might. The spear took the demon in the chest, the impact stopping its charge momentarily. The beast looked down at the spear jutting from its flesh, momentarily shocked by the power of the attack. But a normal weapon could not harm the demon. The creature simply reached down, ripped out the spear, throwing it against the wall with a clatter. The thick leathery skin around the wound closed immediately and the demon crouched low, hissing at the boy who threw the weapon. Leaping toward him, the Greever snapped its wings forward, the sharp dagger like points piercing Fil through each shoulder.

Fil screamed in pain as the spikes ripped through him, piercing through his back. The Greever used its powerful wings to lift the screaming boy in the air and fling him against the far wall.

Jonas, splattered with Fil's blood, screamed for his friend, a furious anger consuming him. He charged the demon, his god light flaring brighter as his anger surged through him. The Greever hissed angrily as the bright light stung its eyes, forcing the demon to retreat back several paces, covering its eyes with the tips of its wings. The Greever could hear the boy with the sword scream and a few seconds later he felt the minor stings of the sword as it cut its flesh several times. The demon swatted Jonas with its arm, its inhuman strength sending the boy flying through the air, smacking hard against the wall.

"Ulren!!"

The Greever turned toward the new challenge, a gigantic man wearing only leggings, charging from the door. His heavily muscled arms carried a glittering battle axe over his head as he charged. The Greever used its left wing tip as a spear and shot it toward the warrior's midsection, hoping to skewer him. Graggis, a trained warrior and the best axe fighter in all of Finarth, used the flat side of the blade, deflecting the blow and coming in low at the demon. His colossal strength enabled him to easily wield the cumbersome weapon. He swung the axe sideways and across the beast's right thigh.

The beast howled with pain, stepping back from the magical blade, a deep laceration splattering black blood onto the ground. This weapon was no ordinary blade. The demon felt the dwarven magic sting its flesh and it hissed with anger and pain, sending both clawed hands out simultaneously, tearing long deep cuts across the man's chest.

Blood poured from the wounds and Graggis stumbled backwards. More men rushed in through the door with weapons drawn. The Greever sensed that these men were battle hardened warriors, some of whom might possess magically forged weapons as well. The demon looked at Jonas's body crumpled on the floor and back at the men who were flooding into the dark room.

Graggis, seeing the demon turn its head toward the boy, lifted his axe over his head and threw it with incredible speed and strength. Somersaulting fifteen paces the axe slammed into the beast's chest. An eerie howl of pain erupted from the demon as it stumbled backwards. The axe head was buried deep in its chest and the pain was unbearable. With a quick flick of its clawed hand the Greever ripped the weapon from the wound, shuffling backwards away from the knights.

It would take too long for this wound to heal. Its inert magic would be unable to quickly seal a wound inflicted by a magical weapon. The demon could probably kill the boy and the larger warrior, but it knew not what it faced with the rest of the men. The mission could wait. With an angry howl the demon pivoted, racing down the body strewn barracks and leaped out the back door into the night. The beast used its powerful legs to jump into the air, unfurl its wings, and fly into the protection of the darkness. The Greever howled again in anger. The hunt would have to wait for another day.

Graggis was kneeling on the bloody floor using his strong thick arms to hold up his weight. His chest was badly torn and blood was pouring steadily from the wounds to pool on the stone floor.

Lathrin and a handful of knights moved toward him, fanning out into the room, their swords drawn and their faces reflecting disgust and despair as they viewed the carnage clearly for the first time. Most of the knights were wearing leggings and night shirts and not much more as the alarm had awakened them from their slumber. The room was dark again. Jonas's light had been extinguished when he hit the wall, but several of the knights had brought lanterns and they raised them to get a better look at their surroundings.

"What in Bandris's name happened?" asked Lathrin, scanning the terrible scene, his eyes wide with horror. Lathrin and his men were warriors who had fought in many battles, had seen men killed and had experienced the horrors of the battlefield. But this was beyond their imagination. Everywhere, weaponless boys were ripped and thrown around the room like pieces of a rag doll. Body parts and blood were everywhere. Lathrin stumbled forward in shock at the death and destruction around him. "What was that beast?"

"I don't know. It looked to be a demon of some kind. The beast was attacking the boy, Jonas, when I arrived," Graggis muttered through gritted teeth as he slowly stood, pain lancing through his body. Lathrin dropped his sword reaching out to stabilize Graggis's massive body.

"Get a healer in here! Now!" screamed Lathrin. "Dagrinal, report this to the king and warn the castle if they have not already been alerted."

"Yes sir!" Dagrinal, wearing only his night tunic and breeches, raced out the door with his long sword in his hand.

"Sir," Graggis said.

"Yes."

"The boy, Jonas, he was *glowing* when I came in. A white light was shining from him, keeping the demon at bay. It was God Light, like that from a cavalier."

"What! Are you sure?"

"I am," whispered Graggis, stumbling to the ground, his strength finally sapped from loss of blood.

"Get the healers now! And someone get some priests in here!"

***

Jonas slowly opened his eyelids letting his tired eyes adjust to his surroundings. They focused slowly and he saw that he was lying in a large bed. The room was big and richly decorated. His vision swam and the scene blurred; his head throbbed in pain. Dizziness overwhelmed him and everything went black again.

"*Jonas.*" He heard his name whispered as he tried to shed the darkness from his mind.

"*Jonas.*" It came again and he slowly opened his eyes to see Manlin, high priest of Shyann, sitting at his bedside. The priest's face showed concern as he looked down at him.

"Where am I?" asked the weary boy.

"You are well. You are in the king's personal chambers. I am Manlin, do you remember me?"

"Yes, you are a high priest to Shyann."

"I am. Good. Do you remember what happened?" the priest asked.

"It is all a blur."

"It should be. You suffered a massive injury to your head and several broken ribs. Do you recall what happened?" the priest asked again.

Jonas closed his eyes thinking. His head throbbed painfully as he tried to remember what had happened. Jonas suddenly opened his eyes, the memories rushing back to him, and tried to get up. He was very weak and it was easy for the priest to hold him down. "Fil, where is he? Is he alive?" Jonas asked fearfully.

"Yes, he is alive. Barely. But he will make it. He is as tough as mountain stone, but he would have died if we hadn't gotten there to heal him. He was rapidly losing blood from two deep wounds in his shoulders."

"I remember now. A demon attacked us. The beast killed many of my friends and speared Fil with two spikes from its wings. Then it was all a blur. I think I was thrown against the wall or something. Why was I not killed?" asked Jonas.

"Graggis and a handful of knights ran into the room just as the beast flung you against the wall. Graggis fought it and sent it away, but he suffered serious wounds in the fight." Manlin saw Jonas about to ask about Graggis when he interjected. "Yes, Graggis will be fine. I healed him as well."

"That is good. Thank you, sir," muttered Jonas gratefully.

"Thank Shyann."

"I already have," whispered the exhausted boy.

"Can I ask you a question, young man?"

"Of course, I owe you my life."

"You owe me nothing. It was Shyann that saved your life. How did you raise the God Light?"

"You know?"

"Yes. Several of the apprentices that survived said they saw it and Graggis confirmed it."

Jonas hesitated a moment, thinking about what happened. "I don't know. The beast was killing my friends and I didn't know what to do. Then I felt an energy rise up inside me and when I concentrated on it I began to glow. The light penetrated the darkness and it got brighter the angrier I got. That was when the demon charged me."

"Did the demon shy away from the light?" asked Manlin.

"Not at first. After the demon attacked Fil I remember screaming in anger and that's when the light flared so brightly that the demon backed up, shielding its eyes and hissing as if the light stung it. That was when I attacked it with the sword that I had. The blade did nothing and it simply swatted me aside to hit the wall. That is all I remember."

"I see," Manlin said thoughtfully.

"Manlin, why did my blade do nothing to the demon? And Fil threw a spear that went all the way through it. The demon just ripped it out and tossed it aside. We could not harm it."

"A demon that powerful can only be harmed by magic or magical weapons. That is why your light affected it and Graggis's battle-axe hurt it. His axe was a gift from the king and it was enchanted by the dwarves who crafted it. A great gift for his courage," added Manlin.

"How did I bring forth that light?" asked Jonas.

"I don't know, son. The light you called upon was God Light that only a cavalier can bring forth. Even I cannot call it. I have never known Shyann to sponsor a cavalier, nor have I ever heard of someone being able to bring forth the God Light unless they were trained as a cavalier at Annure or another kulam."

"What's a kulam?" Jonas asked.

"They are training facilities for cavaliers. There is one in Annure and several more west of the mountains." Manlin paused as he looked at Jonas. "It seems that Shyann has her own plans for you, Jonas. Now get some sleep. We will talk again later."

***

Jonas awoke several hours later to loud voices outside his door. He sat up in bed just as his door opened. The king quickly walked in followed by Graggis, Prince Baylin, Prince Nelstrom, Lathrin, and Manlin.

"Ah, Jonas, I'm glad that you are awake," the king announced as he approached his bed. Jonas tried to get up to pay his respects but the king waved his hand in a dismissive gesture. "Stay in bed, young man, you have been through a lot."

The king was wearing a blue tunic with gray breeches and draping his shoulders was a blue cape lined in silver. His tunic was embroidered with the silver symbol of Finarth. Dangling from his side was his amazing sword, the blade that was created to replicate his ancestor's ancient weapon, the one that destroyed Malbeck the Dark One.

Jonas looked at the others as they all looked back at him uncertainly; all except for Prince Nelstrom who averted his eyes. The prince's eyes were red and swollen, with dark circles under them as if he had not slept. He wore his customary black clothes with silver thread. He did not look well, thought Jonas. Then it struck him; did Torgan, the prince's son, make it out of the barracks alive?

"I'm glad that you survived, son, but we need to ask you some questions. Will you please tell us your account of what happened," asked the king, who, Jonas noticed, also looked bone weary.

Jonas looked around at the solemn men and took a deep breath as he began his story. It took several moments to relate the events up to the point where he was knocked out.

"It was your chest that warned you again?" asked the king.

"Yes."

"That is the third time now?" asked Prince Baylin.

"It is."

"It seems that these attacks are not just coincidence. They are obviously directed at you, Jonas. You have made powerful enemies," continued the prince.

"What have I done, sir? Why would I have these enemies?"

"It is not you who have made the enemies, but Shyann the Huntress, and Ulren the High One," added Manlin. "Shyann has picked you, for whatever reason, to be her warrior, to wield the light of Ulren. When someone is singled out like you, then you will certainly attract Shyann's enemies. It is possible that all the attacks you have been through have been because they were after you, even the attack on your town. Did you ever wonder why everyone was killed when your town was attacked? If the boargs were just there to feed it seems likely that others would have survived. It also seems likely that maybe Shyann had a hand in shielding you from the boargs. I do not think that a Banthra and hundreds of boargs came to your town to feed. I think they came to kill you, to kill someone who they knew would eventually be a threat to their cause. You are a chosen one; it is obvious to me."

"And to you alone, priest! He is a lucky commoner who was healed by Shyann, and that is it!" spat Prince Nelstrom. "He is no chosen warrior! He has not even been trained at Annure."

Jonas was so focused on what Manlin said that he ignored Prince Nelstrom's outburst. The idea that he brought the destruction on his town and Landon's caravan was too much to bear. His heart ached with guilt and his mind fled from the thought.

"And yet he can bring forth God Light. Can you explain that, my Prince?" Manlin said sternly.

Prince Nelstrom drew his sword and in a blur had its razor's edge resting on the priest's neck. Manlin's eyes widened with fright and then refocused with determination.

"Don't ever talk to me like that. I am your prince. Do you understand?"

The king stepped toward his son, sternly looking him in the eye. "Put your sword away, Son. We are all sorry for your loss. Torgan's death has hurt me too, but it was not the priest's fault," the king said.

"No, it wasn't. It was *his* fault," whispered Prince Nelstrom, glaring at Jonas, his hatred so palpable you could almost feel it.

"No, it was a demon that killed your son. A demon that was sent by someone, someone that we will find," the king said forcefully.

"A demon sent to kill Jonas. If he were not here my son would still be alive," the angry prince countered.

Prince Nelstrom and the king locked stares for several seconds. Finally the prince removed his sword from the priest's neck, sheathing it in one smooth motion. The prince glared at Jonas one more time, and what Jonas saw in those eyes chilled him to his bones. It was a look of despair and death. It was as if he were looking at the very thing that had killed his son. Finally, breaking his gaze, the prince stormed out of the room.

"How many of my friends died, sir?" asked Jonas quietly.

"Nineteen boys were killed, including Torgan. It was a grave night and Finarth will suffer for it for many years to come. Most of those boys were the elite of very powerful families, and all were young men, who no doubt would have become an integral part of the strength of Finarth. They all were a great loss," stated the king solemnly.

Jonas turned his face away, trying hard to hold back the powerful emotions assaulting him as he thought about the loss of so many of his friends. He closed his eyes, fighting back the tears. Eventually anger and determination pushed aside his despair. After a few moments he opened his eyes, searching out Graggis who was standing in the back.

"Graggis, sir, thank you for coming to my aid. I would be dead now if you had not," Jonas said.

"It is my duty. I am only sorry that I did not get there in time to save more of those boys," Graggis replied.

"Sir," Jonas directed his gaze to Manlin. "Do you really think that the Banthra that attacked my town was after me?"

"I don't know, but remember, it is not your fault. We cannot control what evil things happen. We can only do our best to stop them. In fact there is irony in the good deeds done by others. When one does the bidding of righteousness, it attracts the eyes of darkness, which may bring more evil into the light. That, in turn, requires more warriors to fight it. It is a dangerous balance where light and dark are constantly struggling to push the other below the surface. Do you understand?"

"Yes, sir," replied Jonas quietly.

Prince Baylin moved toward Jonas sitting on the edge of his bed. The prince wore a forest green tunic and black breeches. His muscled arms stretched the seams of his tunic. "Son, there is a problem," the prince said softly.

"What is it?" asked Jonas sitting up higher.

"Although it is not true, many people here, including some of the apprentices and the families of the slain boys, think you are to blame, that you brought this evil upon us," replied Baylin softly. "Everyone is talking about how you brought forth the God Light. They don't understand it, and rightly so. When people don't understand something, they fear it."

"I see. In some ways I guess they are right. If I had not been here the demon wouldn't have attacked, and all those boys would be alive. I should leave," Jonas stated bluntly.

"It is not that simple, but," he paused looking away briefly, "you can no longer train as a knight apprentice," the prince said, bringing his eyes back to Jonas.

"But," interjected the king, "I have sworn to protect you as my vassal, as you have sworn to protect me, and I do not take those oaths lightly. It is no fault of yours that tragedy has befallen us. In fact it is our fault. Allindrian warned us that this may happen and yet we did not take proper precautions. I am sorry for that. For some reason, someone, or something of great evil wants you dead, and I assume it has something to do with Shyann and her interest in you. I cannot have you stay here, nor can I send you away alone." The king got up, pacing in thought.

"What should I do, my King? Tell me and I will do it. Many people have died because of me and I will not let their deaths go unanswered, nor will I be the cause of further unnecessary death. I am determined to fight this darkness, my Lord. Whatever evil fate awaits me, I will face it head on, alone if need be," Jonas said evenly.

The king stopped and looked at him. Jonas noticed that he looked even more tired than when he entered the room. His weary eyes were laced with red, surrounded by dark coloring from lack of sleep. But they still held the intensity that Jonas noticed when first they met. "Well said, and spoken with courage, which by all accounts you do not lack. You are now seventeen winters, right, son?"

"Yes, sir."

"In one year you will be eligible to apply for training as a cavalier at Annure. That means we need to find a place for you for a year. I will not abandon you. In fact, I am asking a favor from a friend that I have not seen in a long while, someone that can protect you and continue your training," the king informed him.

"Father, of whom do you speak?" asked the prince.

The king, looking at his oldest son, took a deep breath. "Kiln," he said bluntly

"What! Kiln? He left Finarth over fifteen years ago. Do you even know where he is?" asked Prince Baylin.

"Sir, with all due respect, Commander Kiln left your service in disgrace and without leave. He is not fit to protect Jonas," added Lathrin, speaking for the first time.

"I agree, Father. The stories are old but if they are anything close to the truth then he is not fit for this task."

"I know where he is located. He sends his men to the markets once a year. I have had trackers follow them over the years so I think I know his location. He was a good friend of mine…"

"A friend who left you and broke his oath. It is not right," the prince interrupted.

"You do not know the whole story, son." The king sighed heavily, "No one does."

"Sir, I'm sorry to interrupt, but who is this Kiln?" asked Jonas.

The king looked at Jonas. "Kiln was my general, Jonas. He was unbeatable. We were best friends that grew up together, but he was a commoner and I, of course, was not. We trained as knight apprentices just as you and Fil have. He is the best warrior I have ever seen, and his mind, as well as his body, is an instrument of war. I have never seen his equal with a blade. Anyway, when I became king I appointed him general first class, high commander of the Finarthian army. We won many battles together, fighting the orcs and ogres from the Tundrens, the bandits from Numenell and the raiding tribes from the Flatlands and the Sithgarin Desert. He simply did not lose. He became a legend, here in Finarth and all over Kraawn. Warriors sought him out, challenging him with blade and axe, but he was never beaten."

"What happened to him, my Lord? Why did he leave?" asked Jonas.

"I think maybe it is not my place to tell that part of the story, but he left my service. I know the truth of it, but no one else does. He could not stay here any longer and he lost the taste for war. He traveled far to the lands in the east for several years before returning and hiding out in the mountains with the riches he had earned in my service, carving a life out for himself deep in the Tundrens. By all accounts he is a recluse, and keeps to himself."

"And you think Jonas will be safe with him?" asked Lathrin.

"I do. He has at least ten men that work for him and I will send a handful of knights to stay with Jonas. Besides, Kiln can teach him things that we cannot."

"Sir," interjected Manlin. "It is obvious that Shyann, the Huntress, has marked this boy. That mark has put him in danger, a danger that all cavaliers know well. They are constantly hunted by the Forsworn, but cavaliers are trained for that, and this boy is not. I suggest that he stay with me in Shyann's temple."

"It is true that Shyann has marked him, but his presence here is a danger to everyone and there is no way that we can hide him from the populace for a year. The word would get out and there are some very powerful people that blame him for this tragedy. It just wouldn't do to have him here." The king looked back at Jonas. "Son, we have not asked you what you think. It is important that you have a say in your own destiny. What do you think?"

"Sir, what if Kiln will not take me?" asked Jonas.

"I will write a letter to Kiln myself, the contents of which will be more than enough to convince him to accept you in his care."

"Sir, if you think it is a good idea then I will do it. I do not want to cause more problems here. I want to train to be a cavalier, and if going to stay with Kiln puts me one step closer to that goal, then so be it."

"Then it is settled. Now we need to put together a team to take Jonas into the Tundrens."

"I will head that team, Father," ventured Prince Baylin crossing his arms and standing firmly. "After all, it should be someone from the royal family who presents the letter to Kiln. Besides, I was just a young boy when he left and I would like to see him again. I remember very little about him."

"And I will be by your side, my Prince," added Graggis.

"Good. Baylin, pick eight others from our knights. Pick men that have experience in the mountains, for the journey will be long and hard."

"I will, Father."

"Jonas, can you be ready in two days?" asked the king.

"Yes sir," Jonas said confidently.

Seven
Kiln

I can't believe you're leaving," Fil said as Jonas pulled himself into his saddle. The king had given Jonas a glittering coat of chain mail and new traveling clothes of high quality. The new tunic he wore was blue with the symbol of Finarth embroidered on the chest. His black breeches were made of softened leather and his boots were made of the same material and of equal high quality. A gray wool traveling cloak draped his shoulders and at his belt was a long sword and hunting knife, all gifts from the king. His ash wood bow was strapped to the side of the horse next to a full quiver of arrows.

He had never worn such fine clothes nor had he ever received gifts from a king. It amazed Jonas at how fast things were changing for him. Just two years ago he was a cripple living in a small mountain town where he had traveled no more than a half day from where he was born. Now he was a traveler that could ride a horse, wield a sword, and use magic to some degree, not to mention he was receiving gifts from the king of Finarth. It was hard for him to believe. Even so, the cost had been steep, and he wished his mother could be here with him, to see him sit proudly on his steed.

"I will miss you, Fil. Good luck with your training," Jonas said, reaching down and taking Fil's hand in the warrior's handgrip. Jonas was feeling very anxious at leaving his friend behind. They had been through a lot together and the parting was not easy. But both knew that they had different paths, at least for now.

The entire blue team was there to see him off, except for Bornius and Litus, who were killed by the demon. The other teams had lost more boys on that dreadful night. Jonas's team was bunked closer to the south door which enabled more of them to get out before the demon tore into them.

Bornius's death sat heavy on Jonas's heart as the young man was kind and carried a lot of promise as a knight. They had kindled a strong friendship over the last year and he missed him greatly. Jonas felt guilty. He knew it was his fault that the demon had come that night. In fact he had learned that is was very possible that the deaths of his entire village were his fault, including his mother. High priest Manlin had suggested that that could be the case, that all the attacks that have occurred around Jonas had been directed at him. If that were true, although he was unclear why the Dark One would target him so, that meant that he had a lot of blood on his hands. He was carrying a big load of guilt on his shoulders and he didn't know how to deal with his emotions. Mostly he was angry and a large part of him was glad he was leaving. He didn't want to endanger anyone else, plus he wanted to move, to ride, to train, anything to occupy his mind away from the guilt.

The last week had been difficult for Jonas. He had wept for his friends that were killed and he was trying to deal with his friends who survived. Some were cold to him, obviously blaming him for the tragedy. Others, like Calden and his other teammates, were friendly and treated him with new respect. They asked him questions about the demon, his God Light, his meeting with the king, and where he was going.

Fil's wounds were healing quickly thanks to Manlin. His shoulders were very sore and it would be several more weeks before he could start training again.

"You be careful, Jonas. Remember, I will not be there to watch your back," Fil said with a smile.

"I will. I will see you soon, my friend," Jonas replied, not really knowing if it were true or not. He was saddened to think of his journey without Fil. He had been with him ever since his mother died and the reality of his departure without him made Jonas realize how important he was to him.

Prince Baylin rode up to Jonas, addressing him seriously. "Are you ready, young Jonas?" he asked. The prince looked magnificent. He, too, wore the blue tunic of Finarth, but it was laced with silver and gold thread that glittered in the morning sun. A shining chain mail shirt and matching metal greaves and wrist guards completed his uniform. He was prepared for hard traveling, and hard fighting if need be.

His men rode up behind them all similarly outfitted. With them were Graggis and eight other men, all hard looking men who were forged from the many battles they had fought. Sal, the young knight that showed them around on their first day, was there and he nodded his head at Jonas as he rode up. There were also Jorm and Nogris, two brothers who were known for their woodcraft. They had been hunters and trappers as young men before they joined the Finarthian Knights. Next was Dagrinal, fourth lance, who rode up on a large and magnificent warhorse. The last four were all young knights recently accepted into the order. There was Largress, Togin, Gar, and Piap. Finally there was the king's tracker, Beorth, who knew the Tundren Mountains intimately. He was dressed in light woodsman's clothes and high leather boots. The horse he rode was smaller, lither, unlike the bulky horses the others rode. Beorth was outfitted with a long hunting bow and a thin rapier dangling from his hip. The man was thin and wiry, his un-kempt hair and beard giving him the look of a man from the mountains.

"Be careful, Jonas," warned Calden, walking up to him to shake his hand.

"And you, my friend," replied Jonas with a smile.

"Let us go," ordered Prince Baylin riding forward followed by the rest of the men. Jonas smiled one more time at his friends, locked eyes with Fil, and rode off into the morning sun.

***

The first two weeks of travel were easy and without incident. The terrain made for easy travelling. Expansive meadows of grass with spotty patches of trees could be seen as far as the eye could see. The grassy hills they rode through were gentle and allowed the traveler a clear view of the expansive sky to the east and the craggy peaks of the Tundren Mountains to the west. They had headed south through the Finarthian hills and across the Bitlis River that flowed into the Sithgarin River, which meandered all the way to Lake Lar'nam. Jorm and Nogris, their scouts, always rode ahead of the group. Beorth rode with the main group and his knowledge of the area allowed him to estimate that they had about two weeks of travel before they would veer west into the Tundrens towards Kiln's location.

***

They were resting one night around a fire they had built alongside the main road to Annure. The topic of discussion was how they would find Kiln's location.

"Actually finding Kiln's compound will be another story," explained Beorth to the others as he sat on a log by the fire to eat his stew. "I do not know its exact location since we only followed Kiln's men part way there." Beorth was one of the king's scouts who had been the given the task of finding Kiln several years back. "We will have to do some scouting to find it."

"Understood. Nogris and I can help with that. It shouldn't take us too long to find it if you can place us in its proximity," mumbled Jorm as he shoveled hot food into his mouth.

Jonas smiled inwardly as he looked at all the faces sitting around the fire. He liked these men and he appreciated their help in getting him to this mysterious Kiln. These were men of honor and courage and he was enjoying their company.

"I hope my father was right and that the letter that he gave me will be enough to convince Kiln to give Jonas shelter," added the prince.

"If not, we'll just have to convince him," added Graggis with a smile, patting his axe blade.

Baylin laughed out loud at the confident warrior. "Graggis, we were all young when Kiln was general. In fact we were not even of age to join the apprenticeship. Have you not heard the stories about Kiln the warrior?" he asked.

"Some, but I only know of the legend. And he is just a man. Legends are just that, fables and exaggerations to make people feel safe. I am confident my axe would prevail," said Graggis as he drained the last bit of his ale.

"No, he is not just a man," Baylin said seriously. "He is the best swordsman in all the lands, maybe the best ever. My father told me many stories about him when I was younger. It is said that he is a warrior unmatched, even better than both Master Morgan and Master Borum."

"I don't believe it. I had heard stories about his bravery in battle but I had not heard that he was marked as an expert swordsman," interjected Dagrinal.

"He is not marked. I remember asking my father when I was a boy why he was not wizard marked. He said that Kiln did not believe in advertising ones abilities to one's enemies. He also thought it was just arrogance to get the mark."

"That's why Dagrinal wants to be marked. He wants to impress the wenches at Pygon's Inn," Graggis said, chuckling.

"Prince Baylin, how do you know he is better than Master Borum? I had thought that no one could beat our weapons master," asked the young blond warrior, Piap.

"Master Borum told me many years ago, and so did my father."

"He sounds like an interesting man. I am looking forward to meeting him," said Dagrinal.

Jonas looked around at all the faces and noticed Sal eyeing him curiously.

Finally the young knight spoke up. "So, Jonas, do you think you are a cavalier?" Several of the warriors glanced at each other, obviously wondering the same thing.

"Sal, I told you that you were not to speak of it," said the prince with authority.

"I'm sorry, my Prince, but we are all wondering what he is, what he can do, and since we volunteered to protect him, I think it fair that he explain himself to us," Sal replied, losing some of his steam as the prince's gaze hardened.

Prince Baylin addressed Sal, a calm authority lacing his words. "Fair? You are a Finarthian Knight, you follow orders! You do not have the right to question…."

"Sir, it's okay," interrupted Jonas.

The prince stopped abruptly, swinging his gaze to Jonas. The weight of that look caused Jonas to look away like a scolded child. He was not used to being in the presence of great warriors, let alone royalty and an heir to a kingdom's throne. "I'm sorry for interrupting," was all Jonas could mutter.

"Son, let me tell you something. It is not Sal's right to question me, or any of his commanders. Sal is young and ambitious, but not wise in these matters. The chain of command must be followed at all times. If I specifically told them not to question you, then I expect that order to be followed. Do you understand?"

"Yes, sir, I do," Jonas said.

The prince turned his piercing blue eyes to Sal. "Do you understand, young knight?"

Sal dropped his gaze, looking at the ground. "Yes, sir, I apologize."

"Good, but with that said, I happen to agree with you both. The king ordered me to tell you all not to question Jonas, that it was his business, and that what had happened to him was something that maybe he didn't want to continue to bring to the surface. But he said nothing about Jonas freely giving information. I agree with you, Sal. You all have sworn an oath to protect this young man, and yet you know nothing about him and what happened to him other than the rumors. So, young Jonas, I will not order you to tell the story since my father has forbidden it, but if you are willing, then I think they are ready to listen. What do you say?"

"Yes, my Prince. I will tell them," Jonas replied.

All the men stopped eating and looked at Jonas expectantly. He began his tale as he had in the past. He was getting good at telling the story and the words flowed easily from his vivid memories, memories that, Jonas was afraid, had been burned into his mind. He ended the long tale with the attack of the demon and how Graggis had saved them.

"I guess you're good for something other than belching, eh Graggis," added Dagrinal, chuckling at his own remark. The men laughed heartily at the joke.

"You might have been there earlier to help if you hadn't been so busy snoring," said Graggis, throwing a small rock at Dagrinal.

"I was dreaming of your mother," Dagrinal replied, smiling as he batted the pebble away.

Everyone laughed together and Jonas felt at home. The camaraderie of these men was contagious and it calmed Jonas's turbulent thoughts.

"That is an amazing tale, Jonas," said Gar, a quiet young warrior from Ta'Ron. "I am sorry for your losses."

"Thank you, Gar," added Jonas gratefully.

"Jonas, may we see the mark?" asked Sal.

Jonas shyly looked at the prince who nodded encouragement. He stood up slowly and took off his cloak, lifting his tunic and chain mail shirt over his head. He stood baring his chest in the cold night air. His muscled torso reflected the orange firelight and the God Mark could clearly be seen. The men moved closer, staring in awe at the beauty of the design. The silver edges of the mark glittered like diamonds.

"Jonas, have you looked at your chest lately?" asked the prince, eyeing him curiously.

"No. Why do you ask?"

"The mark seems to have grown since I saw it last, unless my eyes are playing tricks on me."

Sure enough, the prince was right. Jonas saw that the mark had spread slightly over his shoulders and down his arms. It had almost completely covered his stomach and chest. The mark must have been expanding slowly as Jonas had not noticed it until the prince pointed it out. It was a piece of art to look at and even Jonas's breath caught in his throat as he gazed at the symbol.

"It is amazing!" Sal exclaimed. "I have never seen anything like it."

"It makes a wizard mark look like a child's drawing," added Dagrinal.

Self-conscious, Jonas put his tunic back on and sat down by the fire.

"Do you think you will become a cavalier?" asked Graggis.

"I don't know. Shyann has a plan for me and I think the plan will unfold as she sees fit. I want nothing other than to be a warrior that fights against that which threatens us. I would like to be a cavalier, if that is my destiny."

"It is a hard life, Jonas, never knowing where you're going or where you'll be. Forming relationships is almost impossible and the constant threats and challenges a cavalier faces can wear one down. It is a tough road to travel, and few can do it," Prince Baylin said.

"I do not know you well, Jonas, but you seem a fine young man," Graggis addressed Jonas seriously. "You are brave, and from what I've heard, do not lack skill. I saw you stand up to that demon with nothing more than a sword in your hand and courage in your heart. I think you'd make a fine knight, or cavalier, and Shyann wouldn't have picked you if she didn't think so too."

"I thank you Graggis," Jonas said modestly. He felt uncomfortable with the conversation and the focus on him, so he turned to Dagrinal. "Dagrinal, my sword training was cut short. Would you mind sparring with me when we have time? I would be grateful to learn from you."

"It would be my pleasure, Jonas. Master Morgan told me that you were the best among the apprentices and you have potential to be a master swordsman."

"I want to learn all that I can. I would appreciate your help."

"How about now?" asked the tall swordsman standing up from the fire.

Jonas smiled. He stood up and drew his sword in response.

***

The terrain began to change as they headed farther west towards the Tundrens. Rolling grasslands gave way to forested hills, and the peaks of the massive range slowly grew larger. Their horses made good time through the grasslands but progress slowed as they moved deeper into the mountains. The terrain grew steeper and they had to carefully pick their way through rocky trails. Their pace was hampered as the horses stumbled occasionally, making the slow progress dangerous as well.

It was on the second night in the forested mountains that they sat around their fire to discuss how to continue their journey.

"Prince, I think it is time that we leave the horses. We will need to take to the game trails now and the horses cannot navigate them," Nogris informed them, throwing more wood on the fire.

"Do you agree, Beorth?" asked the prince.

"Yes, my Lord," affirmed Beorth. "I was going to suggest that myself."

"Then so be it. Largress, Togin, I want you to stay with the horses until we return. We will need them to get back to Finarth."

"Yes sir," they both said.

"How long should it take us to reach our destination?" the prince asked Beorth.

"It is hard to say. It is summer so the trails will be open. We do not know the exact location so we will have to scout the surrounding area."

"In your estimation, how long will that take?" asked the prince.

Beorth chewed on that question for a few seconds before responding. "Probably five or six days. Then it may take another several days to scout out Kiln's exact location."

"Okay. Largress, Togin, give us three weeks, one to get there, one to get back, and one for some extra time in case something happens. If we have not returned after three weeks then take the horses back to Finarth."

"Yes my Lord," they replied.

"Let's get some sleep. We have a long hard trek ahead of us," added the prince as he got up and moved to his bed roll. Jonas lay down on his own blanket and looked up at the mountain sky. He could make out pockets of the night sky through the dense trees. The stars sparkled in the clear sky as a soft breeze rustled the leaves. Jonas felt at home here, and he closed his eyes drifting off to sleep.

The next four days of their journey were more difficult, though there were no complaints from the hardy men as they carried their heavy packs over boulder strewn switchbacks. Jonas loved the strenuous activity and the landscape was breathtaking, reminding him of his home, or at least what used to be his home. The game trails were fairly clear and the summer sun kept things warm and dry. They slowly gained in elevation, continuing deeper into the mountains.

On the fifth day of their march they decided to camp next to a cascading waterfall that plunged heavily into a placid pool. On the far end of the pool the creek continued down the mountain, carving a shallow rift through the earth. Soft green moss covered patches of ground that otherwise was flat rock. The moss was thick, a perfect bed for their blankets. They lit the cooking fire and roasted some venison from a deer that Beorth had killed early that morning. They couldn't carry the entire animal so they cut the choicest pieces, which were roasting over the hot fire. The fat, dripping into the hot coals, sizzled with small eruptions of delicious aromas.

Jonas and Dagrinal were sparring on a large flat rock that jetted out over the pool. The stone was over four paces wide and twice as long. Jonas had learned much from the warrior over the last couple weeks and they had quickly developed a strong friendship. Dagrinal emphasized to Jonas that good swordsmanship was a combination of balance, strength, and speed. He said that most men were lucky to possess just one of those characteristics, but very few possess all three in enough quantities to become master marked.

Jonas and Dagrinal circled each other, as they often did when sparring. Jonas lunged at Dagrinal, attacking him with lightning quick strikes, but Dagrinal was there every time to counter them. His agile footwork on the flat rock always kept him in the correct defensive positions. Dagrinal smiled confidently as he picked up his speed, changing from counters to attacks. Jonas backpedaled, trying to counter his impossibly quick moves. After various exchanges, Dagrinal smacked Jonas twice with the flat of his blade, once on the thigh and the other on his side.

Jonas lowered his sword in frustration. "I just can't keep up. You're too fast!" Jonas said with frustration, sweat dripping freely off his nose.

"Of course I'm too fast, Jonas. Don't get frustrated. I've been using the sword for over twenty years. How long have you?"

"Almost two years."

"Exactly. Listen, no one starts off an expert at anything. It takes time. You are by far the best swordsman I've seen for someone your age. You are better than most trained soldiers. It doesn't matter how good you are, there is always someone faster, stronger, and more skilled. To you I seem unbeatable, but when I fight Master Borum, I feel just as you do now. Do you understand?'

"Yes, sir, I think so."

"You need to remember, if you want to become a master swordsman worthy of the mark then you must also possess patience and tenacity."

"I will remember that," said Jonas lifting his sword again. "Let's keep going."

"You certainly have no problems with tenacity," laughed Dagrinal, lifting his sword in response.

Suddenly Jonas felt the familiar sting on his chest. His eyes grew wide in alarm as he looked about frantically.

"What is it, Jonas?" asked Dagrinal with concern.

Jonas grabbed his chest feeling the familiar sting again. "We're in danger," he replied seriously.

Prince Baylin, who was sitting by the fire, hearing Jonas's words, stood up quickly. "What is it?" he asked.

Jonas moved toward him quickly, scanning the forest surrounding them. "We're in danger! Someone, or something, is coming!"

"To arms, men!" ordered the prince loudly.

Everyone reacted quickly, forming a hasty perimeter. Beorth, Jorm, and Jonas grabbed their long bows, nocking arrows and scanning the forest for any threat. Jonas's heart was beating fast. He was frightened, not just for himself, but for these men who had sworn to protect him. What manner of threat was this? Was the demon back? That thought alone caused fear to explode inside him sending a deathly chill down his spine. His chest tingled one more time, this time more severe.

"I believe the threat is near, my Prince," Jonas said, his voice quivering with fear. Dagrinal touched his arm lightly, reassuring him with his presence. Jonas looked at these men, all standing ready, swords and bows out, their intent eyes searching the forest for any threat. These were good men to die with if that was his destiny. He lifted his bow, searching the forest, trying to focus on something, anything other than his shaking bow arm.

Suddenly a huge boulder sailed through the air crashing into Nogris's back. Jonas heard Nogris's bones break and his body shatter like dry wood as it was launched into the water behind them.

Jorm screamed for his brother and everyone dove behind whatever cover they could find. But there was none. Several more boulders landed around them, crushing rocks, logs, whatever they hit.

Piap dove to the ground just as a huge rock landed on his right leg, crushing it into pulp. His screams filled the evening air.

Everyone looked on the opposite side of the little pool where the rocks had come from and saw three hill giants push through the dense forest. Each giant was more than twice the size of a man. They were thick and stout like trees and covered with coarse black hair. Their appearance was similar to an ogre, but Jonas thought they seemed less animalistic. Dirty furs draped their waists and they wore nothing on their thick calloused feet. They were human-like except for their massive size and the long canines protruding from their thick lips. Each of the giants carried a club that looked more like a limbed tree. With their strength and size they would be formidable weapons.

The giants growled ominously, stepping into the water and moving towards them with hunger in their eyes. Their long strides and height enabled them to push their large bulk through the little pool quickly.

"Form up, use the bows!" yelled the prince. The hardy warriors quickly reacted to the attack. Jonas, Beorth, and Jorm stepped to the edge of the rock face pulling their powerful bows back. The strong bent wood and taut bow strings sounded like the creaking of an old barn door. They fired at will, each arrow thudding into the thick hides as if they were hitting tree trunks. The arrows didn't seem to slow them down much. In fact they looked like little needles sticking from their colossal bodies.

A crunching, cracking noise, like wood being split, alerted the prince that someone, or something was now behind them. Prince Baylin, Graggis, Dagrinal, and Sal all turned to face the new threat.

Three more giants pushed their way through the dense forest. They easily pushed the trees out of their way, the wood splintering like twigs. They lumbered into the clearing, logs in hand, eyeing the four warriors. One huge giant, easily several heads taller than the others, mumbled something unrecognizable. The deep baritone voice seemed to shake the ground they stood on. The other giants growled in understanding, approaching the warriors with saliva dripping from their mouths. Their intent was obvious.

Jonas had no time to wonder about the sounds behind him. He continued firing his bow at one of the giants. The twang of his bow sounded with each beat of his heart. His fourth arrow took the beast in the eye finally slowing it down. The giant roared in pain and swung its tree-like club into the water with frustration, splashing water all over the place as it stumbled around in the pool. They were only fifteen paces away now so the water splashed over the three bowmen. The flat rock they were on was a full pace above the pool's surface, which put the giant's heads even with the top of the rock. The giants would have to climb up the rock, which would expose them to an attack.

Jonas fired his last arrow into the stumbling giant before dropping his bow and drawing his sword. It was a good shot and the close range drove the arrow deep into the giant's throat. The beast roared again, its anger apparent as it continued swinging its club wildly. The injured, and apparently dimwitted beast, swung its club at an unseen foe and hit a nearby giant in the side of the head. That giant stumbled, roaring in agony and grabbing his smashed and bleeding nose.

Graggis faced the giants, his axe held in front of him. His bulging arms flexed as he clenched the axe handle firmly in anticipation of battle. He smiled eagerly for the challenge. "Come on tree swingers; let's see how you handle my axe."

One of the giants stepped toward him swinging its thick club in a sideways arc. The giant was huge and strong, but not very quick.

Graggis roared defiantly, diving forward under the club, and rolling up right by its tree trunk legs. The bewildered creature looked down as Graggis swung his magical axe with all his strength into the beasts exposed thigh. The blade sunk in deep and blood erupted from the giant's severed artery. The giant grunted in pain trying to bring the end of its club down on Graggis's head. Graggis sidestepped, swinging his axe into the giant's hand, the razor sharp blade severing the giant's thick fingers. The beast dropped the log, roaring in surprise. The giant's bloody fingers fell to the ground like thick summer sausages.

Prince Baylin and Sal flanked another of the behemoths as it stormed toward them. The screaming giant kicked out with its right leg trying to crush Sal. The beast's huge foot glanced off of Sal's side as he dove out of the way. Sal grimaced with pain as he felt several ribs crack. But he was a Finarthian Knight and it would take more than a couple cracked ribs to take him out of the fight. He landed, rolling back up into a fighting crouch just in time to see the beast's massive foot descending upon him.

Suddenly the giant howled and its foot stopped as he stumbled backwards. Prince Baylin had struck the beast several times across the back of its hamstring, his magical blade slicing through the thick skin easily, scoring several deep wounds.

Dagrinal faced the third giant on his own. He slowed his breathing and calmed his beating heart as the giant bore down on him. Where Graggis fought with rage and power, Dagrinal fought with calm precision. He lifted his sword calmly and began his dance. His lithe strong body kept him constantly moving, his razor sharp sword inflicting numerous wounds, a blur of pain gradually slowing the giant. The giant roared in agony and frustration as it tried to crush the dancing swordsman. The beast bled from many gashes along its legs and torso but it still swung the huge club with power.

Beorth and Jorm also dropped their bows and drew their swords as the two remaining giants, riddled with arrows, moved towards the rock edge. The third giant had finally succumbed to the arrow in its eye and throat, sinking below the surface of the pool.

"Go for their arms as they try to climb the rock!" yelled Jorm. Beorth and Jonas readied their swords as the giants neared. One of the giants surprised them by throwing its club like a spear.

"Look out!" Jorm cried diving to the side. Beorth tried to dodge the log but it was too long. The heavy log clipped his shoulder sending him sailing into the air. Jorm looked up just as the second giant, its chest even with the rock edge, swung its massive club downward, hoping to crush the human who lay sprawled before him.

Jonas looked on with horror. He screamed loudly, willing the log to stop its decent. Jonas felt something shift within his mind, something that he could not explain. In a flash, he saw the scene in hues of colors; everything around him had a distinct glow, or aura. It was like a murky soup of color, everything connected somehow. Jonas didn't know how, but as he willed the club to stop, it did. It was like all of Jonas's will and desire flew from his mind and grabbed the club.

The giant's club froze in mid-air as the giant looked on dumbfounded, not sure why its club wouldn't move. Jonas stood with his sword in one hand and his other arm outstretched toward the immobilized club. He concentrated on the log, keeping it still. His head began to ache but he continued to focus on the club. He willed the log backwards, toward the giant's face, and the log obeyed, smashing into the surprised giant's nose. It was almost as if he were a puppeteer and the log was his puppet, connected by invisible strands of energy that only he could see and control.

Jorm was a warrior who had fought in many battles, and he learned long ago to never falter or think about one's luck while fighting. He simply took advantage of the situation that was presented to him. He jumped up as the giant struck himself in the face with its own club, swinging his razor sharp sword across the throat of the bewildered creature. The blade hissed through the air slicing across the beast's throat, parting it easily. Blood erupted from the wound dousing Jorm in red splashes. The dying giant stumbled backwards falling into the pool, turning the crystal clear water a crimson hue.

The bleeding giant fighting Graggis shuffled backwards, kicking out its massive leg trying to batter the man with the painful axe. Loss of blood had slowed the beast and its movements were clumsy, but it got lucky as its left leg clipped Graggis in the hip, spinning him backwards. Graggis gritted his teeth from the pain of the kick but managed to stay on his feet and hold onto his axe.

The giant took advantage of the small reprieve by reaching down with its good hand and grabbing its club on the ground. The huge creature lifted the club easily, chopping it downward, hoping to crush the skull of the man that had caused him so much pain. Graggis quickly regained his footing just as the club was descending toward him. As the club came down, Graggis bolted forward with his axe over his head.

"Ulren!" Graggis screamed as the giant's club smashed into the ground, narrowly missing him, his axe head taking the beast in the groin. The magical blade bit in deep and the giant roared in agony. The giant dropped to its knees, never before feeling that kind of pain.

Graggis stepped back, yanking the blade from the grisly wound. The screaming giant brought both hands to its groin as its eyes rolled back in its head. Graggis growled swinging his mighty axe at the giant's throat, which was now at eye level. His powerful swing brought the axe through the giant's thick neck, severing it cleanly all the way to the beast's spine. Thick red fluid showered Graggis as he stepped back, the giant falling backwards, choking on its own blood.

Sal and Prince Baylin were taking turns inflicting damage. Sal's movements began to slow as his broken ribs were taking their toll. This giant was strong, and he was not giving up easily. Sal sliced his sword across the giant's calf as the beast swung its club at Baylin. The blade stung the giant and it kicked its leg backward hoping to connect with the blonde human again. Sal's tired body could not react quickly enough and the giant's heel took him in the chest sending him sprawling to the ground. The wind was knocked out of him and several more ribs cracked from the tremendous force of the kick.

Dagrinal continued to enrage the bleeding giant he was fighting. The beast bled from dozens of wounds, none of them critical, but they were slowly sapping the strength from the behemoth.

Jorm, covered in the giant's blood, turned to see the last giant climb up onto the rock ledge. Beorth, dazed from the thrown club, was slowly struggling to get up.

Jonas looked on as the hairy beast reached out with its gnarly hand, grabbing Beorth by the head. The man screamed as he was lifted into the air.

"No!" yelled Jonas, as he and Jorm bolted towards the giant with swords leading the way. The giant swung the screaming man at the charging humans. Beorth's legs struck Jorm and Jonas solidly, sending them flying backward onto the hard rock. Jonas and Jorm looked on as the giant grabbed Beorth's legs, his other hand still holding his head, and pulled with all his might.

Jonas tried to stop the giant's movement, just as he had the club, but as he concentrated on the beast, his head exploded with pain, causing him to pitch over. He reached up, grabbing his throbbing skull, agony lancing through his head.

Beorth's head ripped off like he was just a rag doll. Blood spewed from the headless body as it dangled in the roaring beast's hands. The giant dropped the head to the rocks below flinging the lifeless body into the mountain pool.

Jonas struggled to get up and grab his sword, shaking away the painful pounding in his head. Jorm leaped up in anger just as a score of arrows mysteriously flew from the woods slamming into the giant. They both looked around, wondering where the arrows were coming from. The giant stumbled around on the rock; many arrows embedded in its flesh. Finally the sheer number of arrows ended the beast's life, causing it to fall and topple off the rock ledge into the water.

The same fate awaited the remaining giants fighting Baylin and Dagrinal. Black shafted arrows peppered the monsters until they looked like pin cushions. They, too, stumbled around before finally succumbing to the massive amount of arrows and falling dead to the ground. None of the deadly arrows struck the tired warriors.

Dagrinal, Graggis, and Baylin slowly retreated backward towards Jorm and Jonas.

"What is happening?" asked Dagrinal, his crimson stained sword held before him. They were scanning the wood line before them, bloody and tired, but holding their weapons with determination.

"I don't know, but if they wanted us dead then we would be. Lower your weapons," ordered Prince Baylin.

After several seconds of waiting, a lone cloaked figure emerged from the trees. He wore a long green hunter's cloak and his face was hooded in secrecy. He carried a long black bow in his right hand and a quiver of arrows was lashed to his back. "Who are you?" the man said in a commanding voice.

Prince Baylin stepped forward speaking with authority. "I am Prince Baylin of Finarth. These are my knights, along with a young knight apprentice."

"You are a long way from home, Prince Baylin. What brings you here?" asked the bowman bluntly.

The prince gritted his teeth, not accustomed to such forward questioning, and took a deep breath. This man had saved their lives, and Finarth had no dominion over land this far into the Tundrens. "I am on the king's errand, in search of a man. His name is Kiln. I have given you my name; it is customary to now give yours."

The man slowly brought his hand up lifting off his hood. The warrior's black hair was peppered with gray; his eyes were shadows and cold and his face looked as if it was chiseled from stone, with skin that was tanned and weathered.

As if on cue, eight more men silently emerged from the forest like wraiths. The sun was just beginning to set and the tree's shadows covered the cloaked men.

"I am Kiln."

***

It was hard for Jonas, watching Jorm grieve for his dead brother, seeing the pain that Piap was in, his leg crushed by the giant's rock, and watching Sal grimace every time he moved. Again he felt like he was to blame. These men were here because of him.

Jonas's head ached, a dull throbbing pain deep in his brain. Why was he able to stop that log and why did it cause such severe headaches? More questions that nagged at Jonas.

The newcomers helped bury Nogris and Beorth before the sun set and the darkness of night made it impossible to see. They dressed each other's wounds next to a large warm fire built with the very clubs that caused so much destruction. Sal, Baylin, Jonas, Graggis, Dagrinal, and Jorm sat on one side facing Kiln and his eight woodsmen. They were all lean fighting men, most middle aged and several peaking even that.

After a quick meal of venison, cheese and water, Prince Baylin procured the letter that his father had written for Kiln.

"I thank you and your men for coming to our aid. How did you know we were here?" asked the prince.

"We did not. The giants have been getting bold and they have been raiding my cattle for food. We have been tracking them for several days and they led us to you," answered Kiln, his voice low but resonant with authority.

"I see." Baylin got up, handing the sealed parchment to Kiln. "Kiln, this letter was written by my father and given to me for safe keeping until I could find you. Now that I have found you, it is yours. It will explain our presence and our purpose."

Kiln glanced at him curiously before breaking the wax seal and unrolling the parchment. The two groups of men glanced at each other across the fire as Kiln read the letter. Finally, after many minutes, Kiln lowered the parchment directing his cold gray eyes toward the prince. "Have you read this letter?"

"No, I do not know its content. My father said that it was for your eyes only."

"I see." Kiln directed his hard gaze at Jonas. "Let me see the mark."

Jonas looked at the prince for affirmation. Prince Baylin nodded his head and Jonas lifted off his tunic and chain mail shirt exposing his bare chest. Jonas stood so that the mark could be clearly seen. Kiln and his woodsmen leaned in close staring at the extraordinary mark. Even in the darkness Jonas could clearly see their eyes sparkle with interest as they gazed at Jonas's chest.

"You may put your shirt back on," Kiln said, rolling up the parchment he had just read. "Son, I would like to hear your story. Would you mind repeating it to me and my men?"

"No, sir, I don't mind." And so Jonas began his long tale again. He kept it short and to the point, but he didn't leave anything out. There was something in this man that required honesty and truth. He felt that Kiln would recognize a lie no matter how subtle. The story went on for many minutes before Jonas got to the part about their journey into the Tundrens to look for Kiln. "That is it, sir. That is what happened to me."

"You've had it hard and I'm sorry for that, but it seems that you have been given a gift, no one can deny that. The king has asked that you stay with me for a year. Is that what you want?"

"I don't know, sir. I don't know you or your men. But the king is a good man and if he trusts you then I must as well. You are all putting your lives in danger for my sake and for that I am grateful. I will not be a burden, of that you can be sure," answered Jonas honestly.

Kiln smiled at Jonas. "That is a good answer and one that shows honesty. You obviously understand that if I take you, that I put my men and myself in danger. That demon that attacked you will probably be looking for you again."

"Yes, sir, I do understand. I will face my destiny alone if need be, but if people are willing to help then I will accept their generosity with my own sweat and blood as payment," replied Jonas.

"Well spoken, and with courage, the latter of which you do not lack or the king would never have sent you here. Prince Baylin," Kiln said, turning his attention to the prince, "do you wish to know the true story of what happened between your father and me?" asked Kiln.

"I do…sir," replied the prince.

"Very well. Many years ago your father and I were knight apprentices together. We became good friends, the best, and when he became king he brought me up through the ranks quickly. I was the best commander in Finarth and when I was thirty years old he appointed me high commander of all the armies of Finarth." Kiln paused slightly and then added. "What do you know of your mother?"

The question startled the prince momentarily. "She was a commoner, the daughter of a metal smith. My father met her in his twenties and married her a few years later. She bore him two sons, me and my brother, Prince Nelstrom. She died when I was six giving birth to my brother. I do not remember much of her."

"Yes, that is mostly true. What you do not know is that I loved your mother with all my heart. I was going to marry her, but your father met her through me and fell in love with her as I did. This all happened after I was appointed general," added Kiln, deep in thought as the memories came back to him.

"I do not believe it!" stormed Baylin, standing up defiantly.

"Sit down, Prince," said Kiln coldly, his stern eyes penetrating Baylin's fury.

The prince hesitated, and then obeyed, sitting back down.

"It is true," Kiln continued. "Your father used his position to take her away from me. I could do nothing. I tried to uphold the oath I took to him and Finarth, but it was impossible. I could face anything in battle, but watching Cassandra with the king ripped my heart from my body every day. Then you were born and that caused more pain than I thought was imaginable. Cassandra and I still loved each other, but we tried to create distance between us so we could honor our oaths given to your father. But we couldn't do it. One night, a great and terrible night, we came together in passion."

"I cannot listen to this!" bellowed the prince, his anger taking over again.

"But you must. Your father asked it in this letter. He wants you to know the truth," Kiln insisted. Jonas watched the prince pace back and forth before finally sitting back down on the log. "After dishonoring my position and my king, I left Finarth forever. I knew that I could never stay, that I could not control my love for her, nor hers for me. I broke my oath, and I will never forgive my weakness, but I believe that your father, my friend, broke his oath to me, the oath of friendship. He took the woman I loved, when he knew that she loved me more." Kiln lifted the rolled parchment. "And I'm glad to finally hear the good king apologize to me, to recognize the wrong he did."

Baylin looked directly at Kiln. "He said that in the letter?"

"He did. There is one other thing, Prince," Kiln added.

"What is that?" Prince Baylin asked.

Kiln looked directly at the distraught prince. "Your brother, Prince Nelstrom, is my son."

This time the prince didn't get angry or emotional, he just sat staring at Kiln. "My brother is not my father's son?"

"No, he was conceived the night I was with your mother. I did not know this until now."

Jonas listened intently, things becoming apparent now. In his mind's eye he pictured Prince Nelstrom, realizing how similar he looked to Kiln. The jet-black hair, the cold eyes and rock like features.

"I see," replied the prince.

"It is my recommendation, and the king's that no one need know about this. It would do nothing but cause scandal. Do you agree?" asked Kiln.

Baylin was looking into the fire deep in thought. Finally he directed his gaze toward Kiln. "I do. I would like an oath from everyone here that no word of this will be spoken," Baylin commanded, addressing his men.

"Yes, sir," replied Sal.

"You have my oath, sir," stated Graggis.

"And mine," put in Dagrinal.

"You have my word, my Prince," stated Jorm with a nod.

"I will not say anything, sir," added Jonas.

"Good. Now let us get to business. Will you take Jonas for the year as well as two of my men?" asked Prince Baylin.

"I must ask my men their opinion, Prince. I hold no dominion over them. Allowing the boy to stay will very likely put them in danger, which I will not do unless they agree to it."

"I understand. Let us camp separately. You can discuss it with them and give me your decision in the morning."

Kiln stood, as did his men, "Until the morning, then." The men silently disappeared into the night making camp on the other side of the pool.

It wasn't long before a fire could be seen glowing brightly on the other side of the water. Finally Jorm looked directly at Jonas asking him the question that had been nagging him ever since the fight.

"Jonas," Jorm said, "I owe you my life and I thank you for that." Jonas looked at him a little uncomfortably, knowing where this was going. "But, I don't understand how you did it. How did you stop that log from crushing me?"

Jonas looked around unsure of how to answer the question. The others were looking at him as well.

"What do you mean, Jorm? Jonas, what happened?" Dagrinal asked.

"I'm not sure. One of the giants was going to crush Jorm with its club. I couldn't do anything to stop him so I just screamed and willed the club to stop. And it did."

"The club stopped in midair?" asked Graggis incredulously.

"It did," Jorm added. "I thought I would be killed. Then the club just froze. And you should've seen the giant's face. He didn't know what was going on. Then the club flew back and smashed him in the face several times giving me enough time to get up and cut its throat."

"How did that happen, Jonas?" asked Dagrinal.

"I don't know. I saw Jorm about to die and something broke free within me. I felt it in my mind. I just willed the club to fly back and hit him in the face. I visualized it happening and it did. Everything in my vision blurred briefly, but I could still make out the scene, each shape was a different color and everything felt connected. It was just a flash as I willed the club to stop, then it went away and my head pounded with pain. I'm not sure why it happened."

"I do." Everyone looked at Prince Baylin who was staring into the fire. Finally he turned his dark eyes on Jonas. "You're a cognivant."

"What! You think so, sir?" asked Graggis.

"What is a cognivant?" asked Jonas.

"A cognivant is someone who can use their mind to do certain things. Each cognivant has different powers, some can levitate, control objects with their thoughts, or even read people's minds. They are extremely rare, even more rare than wizards," added the prince. "The elves call cognivants, IshMians. Not much is known about cognivants, but the elves believe that IshMians can access the Ru'Ach with their minds. They do not need words of power as a wizard does. We know very little about cognivant gifts, but their powers are usually limited to the skills that I mentioned. A cognivant's power is known to surface around adolescence or times of severe distress, which would explain why it has surfaced for Jonas on both accounts."

"Is that why my head hurts so much?" Jonas asked.

"I don't know. I have never actually met a cognivant, but it makes sense that if your mind is the tool that accesses the power, that it may cause headaches, especially if the power has just surfaced and you have no practice with it. Maybe, as you learn to master this power, the headaches will go away, or lessen at least."

"It seems you are gaining some powerful tools to battle that which threatens you," added Graggis.

"Jonas, since we are talking about power, have you ever tried to heal anyone?" asked Sal.

"No, I wouldn't know what to do."

"I think maybe you should try to heal Piap. He will not make the trip as he is I'm afraid. What do you think, my Prince?" asked Sal.

"I was thinking the same thing," said the prince softly as they all looked at the bundled form of Piap.

He was wrapped tightly in blankets and his face was pale and sweating. The pain from his crushed leg had caused him to pass out and he was still unconscious.

"Jonas, I think you should try it. Piap will surely die if nothing is done," stated the prince.

"I will do as you ask, my Prince. But I do not know what to do, or how to do it."

"I have seen priests heal, and I even saw a cavalier heal once. They lay their hands on the injured and pray. I'm not sure what they said or did, but the wounds mended," the prince said as he rose and approached Piap. He slowly un-wrapped the blanket from the dying warrior who moaned with pain as his body moved.

Jonas moved over to Piap looking down at the damaged leg. His entire knee and most of his thigh was smashed. It looked like someone had dropped a large rock on a giant tomato. The wound was horrible and Jonas knew that Piap would die if he didn't at least try.

Jonas knelt by the man putting both his hands on his leg. Piap groaned with pain as he lay unconscious. Jonas began to pray to Shyann. He didn't know what to say so he just asked for her power to save this man who had fought with so much courage.

Instantly, in his mind's eye, he saw the interior of the damaged leg. The vision rose so quickly that he nearly released his grip. He could see shattered bone, ripped flesh, and torn tendons and blood vessels. He concentrated on putting the bones back together. He could feel his body grow warm as magic flowed into Piap's leg. Jonas was ecstatic as he felt Piap's bones begin to mend. He kept praying and sending Shyann's power into Piap, visualizing the ripped and torn flesh healing itself. He didn't know how long he prayed, but his body and mind began to tire and finally he released Shyann's energy and fell over, nearly fainting. Graggis caught the young man as his eyes slowly fluttered open.

"Did it work?" asked Jonas in a whisper, his strength all but drained.

"It did. You've been praying for a long while. I think you need some sleep." Graggis gently laid him down on the ground by the fire. Dagrinal brought him his bedroll, putting it under Jonas's head.

"You did well, now get some sleep," added Dagrinal with a smile. Exhausted, Jonas closed his eyes and sleep overcame him immediately.

***

Jonas's dream came quickly that night. He found himself lying on the ground under a massive oak tree. The tree's trunk was as wide as two men and its huge thick limbs reached towards the clouds majestically. Jonas slowly got up, looking around. The forest was thick and beautiful and smelt of summer. Sunlight shone through the dense tree limbs sending fingers of light to warm the luscious mat of moss and leaves that covered the ground. Little brown birds chirped and fluttered from branch to branch looking for food.

He stepped back to get a better look at the magnificent oak tree. It was amazing, colossal, and bigger than any tree he'd ever seen. The tree's green leaves fluttered in the gentle breeze and the sound was mesmerizing. Jonas sensed a power, something old and natural. The tree hummed with energy, Jonas could feel it, although he wasn't sure why.

"Do you like it?" a familiar voice whispered behind him.

Jonas turned towards the soft voice seeing the same female warrior that he saw in his first dream. This time she was wearing fitted black leather breeches and a flowing white blouse that clung to her graceful but strong form. Her feminine attributes were obvious to Jonas, but she also emanated regal power and strength. At her side swung a magnificent long sword and a hunter's knife. She smiled warmly at Jonas, stepping closer to him. Her long black hair cascaded over her perfect features and her welcoming smile made Jonas feel safe. "Do you like my tree?" the lady asked again.

Jonas snapped out of his trance, answering her with awe. "I do, my lady. It is the most beautiful tree I have ever seen. Who are you?"

"You don't know?" she asked boldly.

"Are you my goddess, Shyann?" Jonas asked dumfounded.

"Very good, my young warrior. It is good to see you again." Jonas fell to his knees bowing his head. "Please get up, Jonas. I do not need you to grovel at my feet. I am no queen."

Jonas lifted his head, slowly standing up. "But you are a god."

"In a sense, although the words god and goddess were made by men. I may not be exactly what you define me as, but that is a story for another time, my young warrior," Shyann said. "Do you know why I cured you, why I marked you and why I have helped you along your travels?"

"I do not…my…"

"Just call me Shyann."

"I do not, Shyann," Jonas said softy.

"You have a pure soul. Your heart is pure, as Airos told you. Do you know how rare that is?" she asked.

"I don't," Jonas replied.

"Extremely rare, almost non-existent. There is evil growing in Kraawn, Jonas. The side of the righteous needs a new hero, someone pure of heart and soul, someone who can't be corrupted by power and greed, someone like you, Jonas. Do you understand?"

"I think so."

"You have lived up to all my expectations, and then some. I am glad that you are here with Kiln. He can teach you much. Will you fight this evil with me? Will you serve the forces of good?"

"I have desired this my whole life. I want nothing more than to battle this evil and bring your light to where it is needed."

"Good. Keep training. Practice with the sword. You will grow stronger and I will grant you more power as your body and mind gain in strength and wisdom. Be ready, for I will call upon you again."

"I will be ready, Shyann. Thank you for your faith in me."

"No, Jonas, thank you for yours," she said smiling. Her body began to glow brightly and Jonas had to bring his hands to his face to shield his eyes.

***

Jonas awoke early in the morning, his eyes wide, his body rested and rejuvenated. He felt like he had slept for a week. He felt more at ease than he had in a long time. Shyann wanted him to serve her, to serve something big, something important; he knew that now. He smiled; his purpose was clear, and it made him happy. He had never had any goals, any real reasons to get up in the morning, but now he did; now he could do something that would help Kraawn. Not only was he healed, but now he could help heal the lands he lived in, and that made him happy.

It was still early, the sun not yet over the mountain peaks, the gray morning quiet as the forest animals slept. Jonas buckled on his sword belt and walked down toward the creek that flowed from the southern end of the pool through a beautiful clearing filled with wild mountain flowers intermingled with large flat rocks.

As Jonas neared the clearing he saw a man, wearing only his breeches, balancing on his head, his knees resting on his elbows. His bare chest was broad and muscled and covered with coarse black hair.

As Jonas got closer he realized that it was Kiln. He sat down on a rock, about twenty paces away, and watched Kiln balance, not moving a muscle, his eyes closed. Jonas couldn't believe the man's concentration and balance.

After about a half an hour of standing on his head, suddenly Kiln's eyes flickered open and he pushed up with his arms so that he was balancing just on his hands. Then in one smooth motion he flipped up to his feet, slowly standing up straight, his posture perfect.

"You have patience, young man, to sit there for so long to watch a man do nothing," Kiln said casually as he approached Jonas. Kiln walked with the grace and dexterity of one much younger. His shoulders were wide and his arms strong and muscled, his powerful chest tapering to a small waist covered with bands of muscle.

"You knew I was here?" asked Jonas.

"Yes, in that meditative state I can see most things around me."

"But your eyes were closed."

"You can see with more than just your eyes," Kiln said.

"What were you doing, sir?" Jonas asked with interest.

"That is called the Ty'erm. In the Sharneen language it means 'the position of power'."

"Who are the Sharneen? I have never heard of them," asked Jonas.

"They are a foreign people that live far to the east. Their lands border the Sithgarin. They are a nomadic people that live for war and conquest. I spent several winters with them after I left the service of Finarth."

"What does this Ty'erm do?"

"It is used to sharpen the mind and body. You practice calming the mind and body so that you can focus and see things as they are. Some Sharneen priests use it to get closer to their gods. I found that it works well in combat."

"How, sir?"

"You like to ask questions, don't you, boy?"

"I'm sorry, sir, but this interests me. If it helps in combat then I would like to learn it."

Kiln stared at Jonas as if he were trying to look inside him. After a few seconds of silence he answered Jonas's question. "In the state of Ty'erm you can control your mind and body, slowing everything down. Your senses are heightened, improving reaction time, strength, and enabling you to react with instinct and not emotion. It is a mental exercise that I've practiced for many years. I can now do it at will."

"Can you teach me this?"

"That depends. You must be mentally strong and very patient. It takes time to master."

"I see," Jonas said, pausing and looking back toward the camp in hesitation. "Sir, what did your men say about granting me asylum?" Jonas asked slowly.

"What do you think they said?" Kiln replied, redirecting his question.

Jonas thought about it for a moment before answering. "I think they said yes."

"Why would you say that?" Kiln asked again.

"Those men would follow you to the front door of the Forsworn. I could see it in their faces; and I think you want me to stay, which means they would agree to it."

Kiln stared at Jonas for a moment before lifting the edge of his lip in a slight smile. "You are a good judge of men, Jonas. You're right. We have agreed to take you for the year, but it will not be easy. We work hard, and life here is difficult and dangerous."

"I am a hard worker, sir, and I will not shy away from danger. You can count on me," Jonas replied with sincerity.

"I believe that I can. That is why I chose to accept you. Besides, there is something bigger going on here, something bigger than me and my men, something that includes you. I have been secluded for a long time. I think it's time to come out of hiding."

"Sir, will you teach me to fight and to master this Ty'erm?"

Kiln looked at Jonas with his cold gray eyes, his face a mask of stone. Jonas wondered what he was thinking. "I will, young man."

***

Jonas felt like a ball, which had been bouncing around from place to place, from one group to another. The last two years had been a whirlwind of danger, death, sorrow, friendship, and excitement.

He was sorry to see Dagrinal, Graggis, Sal, Jorm, and Prince Baylin go, but he was happy that Piap, now healed, was able to walk on his own. Jonas felt good about healing him, although he still needed much training to master the technique; but it was a start. He tried his healing again on Sal's ribs and it went a bit faster and it didn't seem to drain him as much. He could not tell if it was because he was getting better at it, or that Sal's wounds were not as serious, but either way, it made Jonas feel better that both the men would be walking home more comfortably.

Kiln agreed to take Jonas with him, but Jonas only. They would not take any of Prince Baylin's men, a subject that caused a brief debate. They did not have room for more men and Kiln felt that the king's warriors might cause conflict within his group. In the end, Kiln and his men left with only Jonas.

His new comrades led him many miles deeper into the Tundrens, until they entered a small narrow belt of rolling hills that Kiln called Shadow Valley, since most of it fell under the shadows of the tall Tundren peaks. It was beautiful though, the undulating hills of the valley covered with lush green grass and wild flowers. It was here where Kiln raised his cattle.

They meandered through the valley until they neared Kiln's home. The structures were simple; one large house built of stone and thick lumber sat in the middle of a flat clearing surrounded by four smaller stone and thatch roofed cabins. There was also a large wooden barn and several fenced areas containing sheep, goats, and chickens. It was a farm, similar to farms that Jonas had seen, but as they neared the structures, Jonas noticed some small differences. Each building was built of solid stone and thick rough cut timbers. The support beams that held up the roofs were massive and thick, capable of withstanding deep heavy snows. Also, each window had shutters made of solid wood laced with iron that could be shut from the inside. The doors were all oversized and made of stout thick wood connected with black iron. Kiln and his men had obviously worked very hard over the years to build this farm, and Jonas was impressed. The Tundrens were dangerous and it became apparent to Jonas that these men were ready to confront whatever threat faced them.

There were eight men that lived and worked with Kiln. Kiln's foreman was an older man, in his late fifties, named Lambeck. Jonas learned that Kiln had met Lambeck many years ago at Numenell and that Kiln had acquired his services as a scout. Lambeck had been in trouble with the law and he took Kiln's offer with relish, but considering the payment that Kiln offered, he would have taken the job regardless. Lambeck had gotten in a bar brawl in a small village on the outskirts of King Gavinsteal's lands and accidently killed a young man. He was found guilty by the local magistrate. It turned out that the lady he was courting that night was the daughter of the magistrate, and that the young man who attacked him was the man her father had picked for her to marry. Luckily for Lambeck, the young lady rescued him that night and he fled as fast as he could. That was many years ago and he ran into Kiln soon after, forming a bond of friendship immediately. They had a lot in common when they met. Lambeck was running from the law and Kiln was just running, trying to get away from his previous life. They traveled together and as a team they were unstoppable. Lambeck was a master scout and woodsman and his skill with the bow was unmatched.

There was also Jondris and his younger brother Lark, who were both outlaws from Finarth. They had been arrested for stealing the king's cattle fifteen years ago, but they escaped into the Tundrens. The king's knights hunted them for a while but later gave up as the two brothers were forced to hike deeper into the Tundrens, where Kiln found them. Kiln enjoyed the irony of hiring two thieves who stole from the king. They were good men, who had experienced hard times and needed to eat. Kiln would not condemn them for trying to survive.

Diomond was a tall barbarian from the Highlands. He was of the Veor Tribe located in the Highlands southwest of Tarsis. He was cast out from the Veors after he had fought with the battle lord of his tribe. Their rules are harsh and their justice even harsher. Diomond had gotten drunk and tried to bed the battle lord's sister. She slapped him and in Diomond's drunken state he hit her back. The battle lord was furious and demanded a bare handed feud fight, which was his right. If you lose a feud fight, then you were banished from the Highlands forever. The battle lord was called the battle lord for a reason; he was the best fighter of the tribe. Diomond lost the fight and left his tribe, never to return, wandering the countryside, until he ran into Kiln ten years ago. Diomond was gigantic, almost seven feet tall, and his long blonde hair framed a weathered tanned face.

The other four were recent additions to the group, all wandering vagrants and displaced farmers that now stood as tall proud men. Kiln gave them purpose and confidence, and he taught them how to fend for themselves.

They all loved him as a father and great friend. There was Ballic, Corman, Wil, and Anders. Anders was only twenty one years of age, the youngest and newest addition from Finarth.

Jonas enjoyed his time with these tough mountain men, and Shyann was right, Kiln had a lot to teach him. Jonas continued to thrive on the strenuous activities, and the work on the farm made him think of his mother, which usually brought smiles, but sometimes tears. He spent many hours with Lambeck training with the bow, and with Kiln working with the sword. Lambeck was the most incredible archer he had ever seen. In three seconds he could place three arrows in the same hole at eighty paces. He taught him many techniques on speed, breathing, and how to make proper bows and arrows. Jonas loved it and he learned, as Fil had told him a year ago, that he was a natural. As his strength increased so did his speed, power, and accuracy, and it wasn't long before he could hit a fleeing rabbit at fifty paces.

Kiln was an anomaly to Jonas. On rare occasions he could be jovial and fun, but most of the time he was cold and seemed to lack emotion, especially when he fought or trained. It was several months before Jonas even touched a sword. They spent the early mornings running through the mountains. Jonas could not keep up with Kiln, which surprised him. Jonas thought he was in great shape and that he would be able to outrun a man who must be in his early fifties. He was mistaken. Kiln moved quickly through the mountain trails, and his powerful legs carried him up the rocky steep terrain like a mountain goat. But Jonas struggled on, keeping within eye sight of the warrior at all times. His legs gained muscle and his strong lungs could keep him running all day. Kiln taught Jonas how to strengthen his arms and legs and how to stay supple and flexible as his muscle mass grew. Kiln would push him until he was exhausted, and it was in this state where he taught him the skills of Ty'erm.

One early morning they ran to the edge of a rock cliff and below them they looked down at Shadow Valley. They had been running for two hours, and Kiln had pushed him hard, running up steep slopes for most of the exercise. Jonas's legs burned with the exertion as they stopped at the cliff edge, both sweating profusely and sucking in deep intakes of fresh mountain air.

"Well done, Jonas. You have been working hard. Now, let us try Ty'erm again," suggested Kiln, sitting on the smooth stone.

"Sir, why do we keep practicing Ty'erm when I am exhausted? Wouldn't it make more sense to try something this difficult when I'm rested?" asked Jonas, sitting down near Kiln.

"Jonas, to achieve the mental state of Ty'erm, you must be able to focus without distraction. When you are exhausted, your brain tries to shut down, which means you are concentrating on less, enabling you to enter the state of Ty'erm more easily."

"I see," said Jonas a little frustrated. They had been practicing the mental exercises for two months now and Jonas had seen little progress.

"Jonas, don't forget that it takes most people many years of practice to enter Ty'erm. You are progressing quickly, much faster than I had anticipated. Now get into position."

Kiln easily lifted his body into a handstand, balancing smoothly for several moments with his eyes closed. Jonas too lifted his body with his strong arms, holding the position, his eyes closed, concentrating only on his body. They had been practicing core strength exercises for several months. Kiln showed him various positions that helped stretch, strengthen, and relax the body. Jonas's balance and strength improved immensely and he could now hold the handstand for a while with little shaking.

Finally, Kiln spoke softly. "Now drop into the position." Kiln and Jonas both lowered their bodies smoothly until their heads were resting on the ground and their knees dropped to balance on their elbows. "Now, concentrate on your breathing only. Just focus on your breathing until your mind is free."

Jonas thought of his breathing, each breath coming in and out. He focused on his chest expanding, over and over again. Don't think of anything else thought Jonas, just breathing in and out. He had gotten this far before but usually his mind began to drift to other things and he could not enter the meditative state. This time he began to feel different. He went inside his body and saw his lungs expand slowly as they filled with air. He saw his blood flow through his arteries and feed his muscles. He concentrated on slowing his heart rate and breathing, so his body could enter the relaxed state needed. He saw his heart beat slowly, pumping blood through the various chambers, and willed it to slow down even more. It did, and his body relaxed, his mind seeing only blackness.

Jonas lost track of time, but eventually he began to see a light, and he followed it. His vision began to clear and he saw himself on the rock ledge, in the tripod position, Kiln next to him. He was assaulted by all the sounds and smells that he didn't notice before. He felt invigorated and alive. He could hear the ants crawling around the rocks and he could smell the pollen on the bee as it flew overhead. It was an incredible feeling and Jonas didn't want it to go away.

But it did, and in a flash. One minute he was seeing and hearing everything, and the next he was slammed back into his own mind. The conscious link he had achieved to Ty'erm was tenuous, and it had come and gone quickly. His eyes fluttered open adjusting to the morning sun that was now rising over the tall snow covered peaks. Jonas lifted his body in the air flipping down into the sitting position that Kiln had taught him, both legs crossed and his back straight. He was looking right at a smiling Kiln who was sitting similarly.

"You were out for quite some time," Kiln said.

"Really? It didn't feel like it. I felt like I could barely hold on to it."

"You will have more control as you practice," Kiln promised.

"It was amazing, Kiln. I did it. Not for very long, but I did it! It was the most incredible feeling," Jonas said excitedly.

"I know. Wait until you can do it at will. We will keep practicing, Jonas. You have done well."

"Thank you, sir, for teaching me," Jonas replied, his eyes sparkling with joy.

***

Many weeks went by, but for Jonas it felt like he had lived with this group of men his entire life. He felt so at home with these men that it was hard for him to imagine not being with them.

Kiln stepped up his training and they began to use practice swords. Kiln did not believe in using wooden swords for he felt they did not have the weight and feel of a real blade. Kiln and his men trained often and they had long ago taken two swords and dulled the edges and blunted the tips so that they might use real steel.

Dagrinal was right, there is always someone better. Kiln was the most incredible swordsman he had ever seen. Jonas was not sure that even Allindrian could beat him. Kiln fought with sword and dagger for he was ambidextrous, just like Jonas. Kiln urged him to spar with two weapons, which of course, was much more tiring and difficult. Learning to fight with two blades was like starting all over again. They would spend every morning running, stretching, and meditating, while the afternoons were spent working the farm and tending to the cattle. The evenings were used for sword play, which Jonas enjoyed the most. He excelled quickly. His tenacity and drive to work as hard as he could pushed him to gain new abilities and skill. Jonas learned quickly and after a year of training he could best everyone, except Kiln.

***

It was a cold night and Jonas, Kiln, Lambeck, Diomond, and Anders all sat by Kiln's hearth sipping a thick coffee from Annure. They could only get the coffee once a year when Kiln's men made the long trip, so it was rationed out sparingly, usually on cold winter nights. The rest of the men were already in their cabins tucked into their warm beds.

Jonas had yet to bring up the fact that he was a cognivant. He had enough on his mind already without trying to worry about that, but he felt that this was the time to talk about it, and maybe these men would know something about it that might help him.

"Sir, do you know anything about cognivants?" Jonas asked.

Everyone looked at Jonas, wondering what would bring up a question like that. Kiln took a sip of his coffee and said, "Why?"

"Well…" Jonas paused taking a sip of the warm black drink. He had always been direct and truthful so he figured why stop now. "I am one."

"What! You're a cognivant?" asked Lambeck skeptically.

"I am. I found out during the fight with the giants last season."

"How did you learn this?" asked Kiln, now interested.

"I stopped one of their clubs in mid-air and forced it back into its face," Jonas replied, remembering back to the fight.

Kiln took another long sip of his coffee while the other men looked at Jonas with wonder.

"What else can you do?" asked Diomond.

"I don't know. I haven't tried anything. I was hoping that someone might know something about it. I'm not really sure what it is."

"Cognivants are called IshMians by the elves. They are extremely rare and they can be very powerful. This is indeed a useful weapon if you are so gifted," Kiln said.

"Try to move something," Ballic suggested.

"I don't know. I have never tried it since the battle, and that just sort of happened," replied Jonas taking another sip of his coffee.

"Move my cup," Kiln said, setting his empty cup on the table.

"Really, you want me to try?"

"How else will you know what you can do?"

"Okay, I'll try," Jonas said, setting his mug down and staring at Kiln's cup across the table. He slowed his breathing, concentrating on the mug of coffee. He imagined the cup lifting in the air. He kept looking at it but nothing happened.

"Look at the cup and imagine that you are actually lifting it. Pretend that your hand is touching it, and that you can lift it. Try again," ordered Kiln.

"Okay." Jonas thought back to the fight with the giants and tried to remember how it happened. He and his friends were in danger, and it was the threat that awoke the power within him. He thought about what it felt like, and what he saw in his mind's eye when the power erupted.

Jonas looked again at the cup, visualizing his hand reaching across the table and touching the mug. He slowed his breathing down like he had been taught and focused on the energy to lift the cup. In a flash he could see in his mind the energy between him and the cup, and he could touch the energy with his mind. It was a strange realization as Jonas suddenly made sense of what he was seeing. Everything around him was made up of the same energy, everything was touching everything. With that thought in mind he lifted the cup in the air holding it two feet above the table. The four men looked on with eyes wide.

"Now, move it about the room," ordered Kiln quietly.

Jonas concentrated on the connection between his mind and the cup. In his mind's eye the link was energy that he could actually see, just like he did during the fight with the giants. Jonas knew that no one else could see the link, but he could.

Jonas's head began to ache slightly as he concentrated on the spinning mug. He spun the cup through the air easily. It whipped around the room with great speed before he brought it right above Diomond's head.

"Don't even think about it, Jonas," Diomond said playfully as he kept his eyes on the cup above him.

Jonas smiled and set the cup back down on the table. He had a slight headache and he absently reached up to rub his temples. Everyone looked at Jonas and grinned with excitement. It was infectious and so he forgot about the minor headache and smiled back.

"Gentlemen, we are in the presence of an IshMian," declared Kiln grandly as if he were introducing royalty.

***

The wound in the Greever's chest had healed, but it had taken a long time. The beast would not forget that magical axe that had cut through its muscle and bone. It had been a long while since the demon felt that kind of pain, but it would take more than that to stop the hunter. The demon feared nothing, except for its master, Gould the Tormenter.

The Greever also knew that the man who had summoned him, if you could call Malbeck a man, was Gould's general in this world. The beast knew that its master had plans for this pitiful plane of existence, and that this powerful man, or demonoid, for he was definitely part of the evil that created him, was its master's link to this land called Kraawn.

Malbeck was furious that the Greever had not accomplished its task. But instead of sending the demon back to finish the hunt, he had sent the Greever on another hunt, one that it relished. This new task promised the beast plenty of blood; blood that tasted better than most since it pulsed with the white light of the Ru'Ach. The demon loved the feeling of that pure light being extinguished by its claws and teeth. These were hunts worthy of its powers.

***

"Alright, Jonas, try and stop the rocks as we throw them!" yelled Lambeck as he and Kiln gathered up a handful of stones about thirty paces away.

"Okay!" Jonas yelled back beginning to calm his mind. It was easy for Jonas to concentrate on one stone and stop it, but it got more difficult when he had to concentrate on several.

They had been practicing his IshMian skills trying to figure out the extent of his power. They had learned quickly that it was a skill, something that required practice and mental strength. They also learned that his power was also tied to his ability to enter Ty'erm. As that skill progressed, so did his IshMian powers. It was like his brain was a muscle, the more he used it the more power he could draw upon. Any expenditure of this power caused him headaches, and the greater the use of the power, the greater the severity of the pain. It was difficult to do it quickly but he was getting stronger and faster the more he practiced.

Jonas had learned the hard way that if he tried to focus on each object individually that he couldn't stop them all. He still had several bruises on his body from stones that made it through his mental barrier. Jonas had learned that he could actually create an invisible wall of energy that could block a larger amount of objects. It was a strange feeling for Jonas, one that he couldn't really explain. He began to learn things about the world that were strange concepts to him. In his mind's eye he could see that everything had its own energy, including the air that connected everything together. Jonas thought that he must be actually seeing the Ru'Ach, the energy of all things. That is how he could control objects and even people, he learned. With his mind he could actually touch everything around him. The farther away the object, the harder it was, the more objects there were, the harder it was. The more powerful the person, the harder they were to control, which caused more severe headaches. If he used his skills for a long duration, or concentrated heavily on something large or far away, it would also cause him severe headaches. They got so bad a few times that he collapsed in pain, his head swimming with dizziness. It was a powerful skill but not without its drawbacks.

The rocks flew in quickly, one after the other. Jonas held up his hand and concentrated on creating an invisible wall of energy. In his mind's eye the particles in the air in front of him spun into a translucent wall of force, and the rocks smacked against it silently to fall to the ground. He could have held them in the air but it would have taken more energy, and caused a more painful headache. The rocks kept flying and Jonas continued to hold up the energy barrier.

Jonas smiled inwardly, thinking back at the rocks that had broken through his barriers in the past, and came up with an idea. He concentrated harder as more rocks flew at him. He held a handful in the air until Kiln and Lambeck exhausted their collection. It was a strange sight to see ten rocks floating in the air as if they were stuck in something. Jonas smiled outwardly sending a burst of energy into the rocks. They bolted back towards Lambeck and Kiln like they were flung from a sling. He could have directed the rocks anywhere he wanted, but he didn't want to cause them too much pain.

The look on their surprised faces was payback enough when the rocks flew back towards them. They both turned covering their heads as the rocks landed around them. One hit Lambeck in the leg and a second smacked hard into Kiln's back. Jonas laughed out loud at the two men who were cowering like children.

"They sting, don't they?" laughed Jonas as both the men stood up glaring at him. Soon his laughter was contagious and both men were fighting back smiles trying unsuccessfully to look mad. Jonas's head ached from the exertion but it didn't stop him from losing himself in laughter. It had been a long time since he laughed like this and it felt good. It wasn't long before everyone was laughing, the sound bringing warmth to the chilly mountain air.

Jonas continued to work on his skills as a cognivant, and his training with Kiln and Lambeck progressed daily. He continued to grow in strength and confidence. His body was lean and hard; any residual fat long ago burned from his muscled frame. He could now fight for a long while before Kiln was able to score a hit with either of his blades.

Jonas had thought himself good with a bow, but after training with Lambeck he realized that he was just a novice. Lambeck continued to teach him how to track and survive in the wilderness and how to shoot with speed and accuracy. He had set up a training course for Jonas to help sharpen his skills. There was a trail through a thick neck of woods near their home and it was here that the archer set up a shooting course. He made human targets out of old clothes and straw and positioned them in various concealed locations. He was able to rig a couple to spring up on bent sticks that he would trigger by releasing various ropes. They were crude set ups but they were adequate enough for the element of surprise.

But for other simulations he had Ballic, Anders, Wil, and Cormac help by positioning themselves behind various large trees, randomly holding out training dummies as Jonas moved through the course. They complained bitterly about the job, not thinking it wise to be holding targets for Jonas's arrows.

"What if he misses?" asked Ballic as he reluctantly took position behind a nearby tree. He held a crude bust of a man on the end of a long thick stick.

Lambeck laughed handing Cormac his dummy. "Keep your arm behind the tree and it won't matter."

"Easy for you to say since you'll be safely out of the way," muttered Ballic.

"Don't worry, the arrows don't have barbs so we can withdraw them easily enough," Lambeck said, continuing to goad the young men.

Lambeck got everyone positioned behind various trees and bushes and ran back to where Jonas was waiting at the head of the trail. "Okay, Jonas, nock an arrow and proceed when I yell it's okay. I'm going to get in position now."

"Very well," Jonas said, adjusting the quiver on his back.

"Remember, quick shots. Do not wait to aim. Practice on visualizing the target and releasing the shaft in easy fluid movements."

"Okay, I'm ready."

With that Lambeck ran back down the trail taking up position behind some bushes. He had three different lengths of ropes on pulleys that all converged on his position. He could release any rope at any time and a dummy would spring up along the trail near Jonas.

Jonas lightly moved down the trail, an arrow nocked and angled to the side, eyes searching the area for targets. It was only a sloppy training course, but nonetheless Jonas's pulse began to race and his heart was pounding in his chest. He took several deep breaths trying to calm his nerves. And of course that is when the first dummy sprang up behind some bushes.

Jonas pivoted smoothly to the right, drawing back the string and firing quickly at the moving target. Since the bust was on a bent stick it continued to sway back and forth after it was released. Jonas's arrow seemed to be on target but the dummy was shaking so badly that it missed it by a finger's length. Jonas swore softly, quickly drawing another arrow and launching it towards the target again.

Just as he released the second shaft he heard movement to his left. He kept moving forward as he drew again, pivoting to his left and finding his target. He released the shaft, shuffling forward to take cover behind a tree. He knew that in a real combat situation the enemy might be returning fire and that it was important to take cover when it was available.

Lambeck had taught him to always move, always look for cover. Never stay in one spot, even if it was only a few feet to the left or right. If you are stationary you offer an easy target for an enemy. Sometimes the difference between life and death was just inches.

Jonas glanced back at his first target noticing that his second arrow was embedded in the dummy's chest. He drew another shaft, nocking it quickly before stepping from behind the tree and moving quickly but surely down the trail. The second target he had hit swayed gently back and forth and Jonas noticed that his arrow had stuck into a wood branch under the bust. He swore softly as it was not a killing shot. It would have hit a man in the groin or a leg, enough to maim him temporarily, but not necessarily enough to take him out of the fight.

But Jonas had gotten control of his nerves. He was focused, his heart beat smoothly, and his bow arm was steady. Slowly he breathed, his eyes scanning the forest in front of him like those of a hunting cat.

Right in front of him, no more than five paces away, sprung a third dummy. Jonas drew back firing just before he dived to his right over his shoulder so he wouldn't damage his bow. In the real world an enemy that close would surely have a weapon with which to fire, so any hesitation would have cost Jonas his life. His aim was true and his arrow hit the bust dead center, penetrating all the way through and disappearing into the woods.

But Jonas didn't have time to relish his skill as the two trees in front of him came alive with movement. He noticed two different dummies peek out from behind the tree. They did not extend very far from the protective cover of the tree, which caused Jonas to chuckle slightly as he thought of the complaints from Ballick and the rest of the men who were charged with holding the dummies.

Jonas fired quickly, shuffling forward so as not to stay stationary, and drawing another arrow. His first arrow took the closest dummy in the face, but just as Jonas fired his second arrow the last dummy ducked back again behind the safety of the tree. Jonas's arrow flew by harmlessly as the dummy popped back out on the other side. But Jonas had already strung and drawn back a third arrow just as the dummy reappeared. Jonas's bow twanged as the shaft was released. The range was close and the arrow slammed into the bust knocking it from the grasp of whoever held it. Jonas heard a surprised yelp from someone behind the tree and he guessed it was Anders.

Then Jonas heard a screaming charge from behind him.

Jonas spun, simultaneously drawing another shaft, and saw a wooden bust of a man running at him with all speed. The dummy was made of planks of wood and it came complete with outstretched arms, legs, and even a head. It was made extra wide so the person holding the dummy from behind was completely shielded.

From the sound of the scream it must have been Lambeck. He was only ten paces away and charging him with wild abandon. Jonas released the shaft, smiling at the satisfying *thunk* the arrow made when it struck the dummy dead center.

Jonas's eyes grew wide as the dummy kept coming. Hastily he fumbled for an arrow and got it nocked and drawn as the wooden dummy slammed into him, sending him flying backwards to land on the soft leaf covered ground.

The wind was knocked from his lungs and he was gasping for air struggling to get up. The wood dummy appeared above him just as a foot came down on his chest, pinning him to the ground.

Lambeck popped his head out from behind the dummy smiling down at Jonas. The other men had emerged from their concealed locations and surrounded Jonas with equally beaming smiles. They seemed to enjoy Jonas's precarious position, as if they had been there themselves, which Jonas reasoned they had.

"What did you just learn, Jonas?" Lambeck asked.

"That a man is not dead until you *know* he is dead?" Jonas replied finally reclaiming his breath. The men around him laughed at the joke.

"Exactly. A charging man may not fall with one shot. I've seen men die from just that scenario because they assumed the dying man was out of the fight. To their own demise they learned that lesson the hard way."

"Good lesson, Lambeck. I will remember it," Jonas replied, getting up from the ground.

"Well done, though. Good movement and foot work, and your aim was true, except the first shot. What happened there?" Lambeck asked.

"I was shaking, nervous anticipation I guess."

"That happens. The only way to get rid of that is through experience, and the only way to get experience is…"

"To survive!" all the men, including Jonas, said in unison.

Lambeck laughed with the men, enjoying the camaraderie together.

Jonas was also taught how to shoot from a galloping horse. They spent many evenings hunting wild boar and deer and hiking the mountain trails that spider webbed the peaks around them

It was on one of these excursions that Jonas, Kiln, and Lambeck came across some tracks that worried them. They had been hunting for several days in the mountains when Lambeck, who was in the lead, motioned for them to stop moving and be silent. He squatted down, inspecting something on the ground. Kiln, who was just behind him, moved up slowly while Jonas scanned the open grasslands that blanketed the tall peaks. The scenery was filled with meadows of grass and wild flowers, dotted with pockets of trees and surrounded by boulder strewn cliff faces. They were high in the Dragon Spine, a small range of jutting peaks that Kiln had named many years ago. A fitting name thought Jonas, for the sharp peaks looked like the spiked spine of a dragon. It was a difficult climb that took them several days but it was one of the best locations to hunt the nimble footed mountain goats.

Kiln moved up beside Lambeck to see what had grabbed his attention. On the ground was a series of impressions that crossed the game trail, disappearing into the tall prairie grass that draped most of the high mountain landscape. They were tracks that looked like human feet but much larger and tipped with claws.

"Fresh tracks, maybe an hour old," Lambeck commented, tracing the outline with his finger.

"Gnoll track?" asked Kiln, his expression cold.

"Yup. Must be some of One Eye's vermin," replied Lambeck.

"This far east? Seems unlikely," Kiln replied in thought.

"It's been a hard winter, maybe it's a hunting party looking for food, or even a raiding party finally getting bold enough to claim our cattle and attack us."

Jonas quietly moved next to the duo to find out what was happening. "What is it?" he asked.

"Gnoll tracks," replied Lambeck.

"Way up here?" questioned, Jonas. Just two years ago Jonas would not even know what a gnoll was, but he had learned at Finarth that they were tall furry creatures with dog-like snouts and mouths filled with sharp teeth. They spoke a guttural language and sometimes allied themselves with orcs or goblins. They were strong and formidable warriors but not very common.

"We've long known of a band of gnolls living several days west of here. The group is led by a big gnoll that we call Chief One Eye. It's a small group that has not ventured close to us, as of now anyway. These tracks were probably made by a scout."

"What are we going to do?" asked Jonas.

Kiln looked at Lambeck and smiled. "We follow the tracks and kill them."

"Just the three of us?" Jonas asked, a hint of concern in his voice.

"More than enough for gnolls," Kiln replied, standing up confidently. "Lead the way Lambeck."

Lambeck guided them for several hours, stopping now and again to inspect a blade of grass or a smudge on a moss covered boulder. The clues were invisible to Jonas, but not to Lambeck, who was the best tracker in Kraawn according to Kiln.

It wasn't long before Lambeck, who was a good fifteen paces in front of Kiln and Jonas, suddenly crouched, his body tense and alert, and motioned for Kiln and Jonas to stop. Lambeck slowly lifted a hand, drawing forth an arrow from his quiver and silently putting it to string.

Jonas and Kiln followed suit, scanning the countryside around them. They were standing in a beautiful meadow and just beyond them was a small glade of trees into which Lambeck was staring intently. It was dusk and the sun's rays were beginning to disappear behind the tall Tundren peaks, casting shadows and pockets of darkness within the stand of trees. Lambeck scanned the pine trees for several seconds; Jonas's heart was beating faster as the tension within him grew.

Then Lambeck motioned for them to follow slowly, advancing into the thicket of trees. As they moved into the glade, Jonas picked up the sounds of guttural laughter and growling ahead of them. He glanced at Kiln who obviously heard the noise as well. The sounds got louder as they quietly made their way through the pine trees. The ground was littered with a soft bed of pine needles that cushioned their footsteps, making their approach perfectly silent.

They moved up beside Lambeck who was squatting down behind a fallen log. The noise was now very clear, sounding like a large group of men talking and laughing, except in a language that Jonas could not understand and in voices that were deep and raspy.

Jonas and Kiln joined Lambeck, following his pointing finger with their eyes through a hole in the tree branches. Below them, in a moss covered clearing surrounded by trees and rocks similar to the ones that they now hid behind, were a group of mountain gnolls sitting around a small fire. Jonas had never seen a gnoll before and he stared at them with wonder.

They were built like men, but much bigger with bodies covered in dark brown fur. Their arms and legs were thick and strong and they stood on fur covered feet with toes capped in wicked claws. Their hands were also human-like, but with longer fingers tipped with sharp claws. Odd pieces of clothing, furs and leather, and miss-matching pieces of plate mail adorned their tall frames.

But it was their faces that held Jonas's attention the most. Their heads were large and bony, with sloping foreheads and dark beady eyes sunken into a jutting brow ridge. Long snouts covered with short hair gave them a look similar to dogs. Yellow teeth lined their dangerous looking jaws, and the sounds that emerged from the beasts were loud, deep, and guttural. Gnoll features were all very similar and it was hard to tell them apart.
Jonas noticed that most of them carried swords and long crude spears. The ugly creatures brought a shiver of fear to Jonas as he looked down upon them. They were eating large chunks of cooked flesh that they were pulling from a side of beef that was roasting on a spit over the fire.

"What do you want to do?" whispered Lambeck, looking at Kiln questioningly. All three of them dropped down behind the log to quietly discuss their plan.

"There are fifteen of them," Kiln said softly. "They are eating my beef which gives me reason enough to deal with them. Besides, they are more than likely a scouting party. We must take care of them," Kiln said, looking at them both, his eyes intense and determined. "Jonas, you ready to test your skills?"

Jonas looked at them both, seeing already that they had made up their minds. "We're going to attack all of them?" he asked.

"We are. I feel bad though, doesn't seem fair does it?" replied Kiln with a smile as Lambeck let out a choked laugh.

"We're just going to kill them?" asked Jonas.

"Jonas, they are gnolls," Kiln said as if that was enough to condemn them. "They would attack and kill you in your sleep if they could. And it would be you over that roasting pit instead of my cattle. This group probably has orders to steal my cattle and to do reconnaissance on our home. It is a scouting party that is probably going to report back to One Eye with information on how to attack us. We cannot let that happen. It is better to attack this group now, while we have the advantage, and potentially stop any future attacks against us."

"Well, if you put it that way," Jonas said with an unconvincing smile as he began to pull arrows from his quiver. He tried to show some bravado but inside he was shaking with fear. He had never really fought anyone, or anything, in a premeditated fashion before. Any combat experience he had was derived from defending himself from attacks directed at him. It was one thing to fight back on instinct, but quite another to plan an attack against an unknowing, and formidable opponent. "What is your plan?"

Jonas silently crept through the trees, moving from trunk to trunk to get to the left side of the glade. Luckily for the men the gnolls were in a clearing that was completely surrounded by rocks and trees, and in the dead of night the three warriors could easily flank the scouting party. And the air was still; no breeze this night that would alert the gnolls with their smell, especially over the intense aroma of the cooking meat.

The plan was simple. On Kiln's signal they would pepper the group with arrows from above and then move in quickly in the confusion and finish them off. Jonas was nervous; his heart was beating loudly in his head. But he also felt an excitement, a rush of adrenaline coursing through his veins as he thought about the battle to come. These beasts were gnolls, evil by nature, and it was a similar evil that had destroyed his town and his friends in Finarth. They were here to do them harm, and Jonas would not let that happen. At least that was the rationalization that Jonas used to convince himself as he neared his position on the left side of the glade.

He moved up behind a large rock and looked down into the clearing below him. The gnolls were about forty paces away, separated from the men by a gentle hillside of rocks and trees. It was a perfect spot. Jonas could fire his arrows into them and then leap down the boulder strewn hillside into the clearing with his sword in his hand. These beasts were huge and ominous, but Jonas had trained hard and he was ready. He was confident in his skills and eager to test them, but nonetheless his heart still beat with nervous energy and his hands were shaking. Jonas took a deep calming breath and withdrew three arrows from his quiver, leaning them against the rock that hid him. Then he nocked a fourth. He would need to make his shots count so they could even the odds before they jumped into the clearing with swords drawn.

Jonas looked down at the large creatures, waiting for the signal. He glanced at the gnolls nearest him picking out his targets. He remembered Lambeck's teachings and began to take slow deep breaths, calming his nerves so that his aim was accurate.

He leaned out, spotting his first target. There was a large gnoll who had his back to Jonas ripping off a piece of flesh from a bone he was holding in his greasy clawed hand. The thing's thick neck was exposed and that was the spot that Jonas focused on as he drew back his long bow. He breathed slowly, looking down the straight shaft and focusing on the little spot at the base of the beast's skull. The signal would come soon, and Jonas waited, concentrating on the task at hand. Closing his eyes, he focused on his breathing and heartbeat. It took him a few seconds before he was in the state of Ty'erm. His eyes fluttered open and everything was much more acute. He could hear the crackling fire as if it was right next to him and all the sounds and movements seemed slow in his mind.

Suddenly a gnoll howled, falling into the fire with a dark shaft protruding from the back of its head. The rest of the gnolls stood still, staring at their comrade in shock as his face burned in the hot fire.

Jonas released his shaft, reaching down quickly and sending two more arrows whistling into the night as his first arrow hit its mark. His target arched backwards, a bloody shaft erupting from its throat.

Everything happened quickly as arrows rained down on the beasts. The surviving gnolls immediately grabbed their weapons, leaping away from the fire to face the invisible threats around them.

Jonas pulled back his long bow sighting in his last target, a tall gnoll who had leaped up from the fire and drawn a wicked looking serrated sword. The beast roared defiantly as he ran toward the rocks where Jonas was hiding. Jonas looked down the shaft, leading the beast as Lambeck had taught him. He let out his breath, releasing the arrow smoothly. The arrow took the gnoll in the chest launching it hard onto its back. He was out of the fight, permanently.

One of the gnolls was not as stupid as the rest and it quickly grabbed a dead comrade throwing the body on the burning fire. Immediately the fire was smothered and the glade was blanketed in darkness.

Kiln released his last shaft as the light disappeared. The stars were out but the trees surrounding the glade blocked much of their bluish glow, making it very difficult to see if his arrow had hit his mark. He swore softly, drawing his long sword and hunting knife. Gnolls can see in the darkness, but he and his men could not. "Jonas, we need light!" Kiln yelled across the clearing.

Jonas had just drawn his long sword as Kiln screamed across the glade. *Light, they needed light.* Jonas had not drawn forth any light since the fight against the demon in Finarth, but they needed light now and so he had to try. Jonas prayed to Shyann and asked her for strength to fight these foes. He prayed for her light and concentrated on bringing it forth, just as he had when he fought the demon.

Jonas felt warmth rise up within him as Shyann's power instantly erupted from his body. It felt like he was filling up with light and all he had to do was let it loose, and that is what he did. White light burst forth from his body slamming back the darkness in the clearing. His God Light was so bright that it easily covered the entire camp site.

The remaining six gnolls shielded their eyes from the light as the three men jumped down from their hiding spots.

Lambeck had seen more than fifty winters but he was still in better shape than most men half his age. He had fought in different places all over Kraawn and he had been a hired tracker and hunter his whole life. The elements in which he lived had forged him into a tough fighting man and the gnolls below would not deter him.

He jumped easily over fallen logs and rocks with his long sword in his right hand. Jonas's light clearly lit the scene for him and he thanked him silently as he charged the nearest gnoll.

The beast was covering its eyes with its hairy forearm and in its right hand was a large war axe. The gnoll was temporarily blinded but he was still able to make out the leaping form of the man attacking him from the woods. He got his axe up just in time to block the downward strike from his assailant, but he couldn't block the man's booted foot as it kicked him directly in the groin.

The gnoll howled in pain, instinctively lowering its axe and grabbing its injured crotch. That split second action was the gnoll's last as he looked up just in time to take the swordsman's blade in the face, splitting its shocked expression in two.

Kiln's location was about five paces above the ground. He was hiding behind a tree that grew from the edge of a small cliff overlooking the clearing. It was a long drop, but Kiln was in the state of Ty'erm and he moved with the agility of an acrobat.

He jumped off the small cliff, landing hard in the clearing right beside two unsuspecting gnolls. As he landed he rolled forward, bracing and cushioning his fall. The roll took him right by one surprised gnoll who was holding a spiked mace in his hand and was turned away from Jonas's light. Kiln came up to his feet smoothly, his long sword whistling in the air, slicing into the gnoll's arm as the creature brought it up in front of him to block the lighting fast strike.

The second gnoll recovered quickly from Jonas's light and swung its heavy broad sword at Kiln's back. Kiln knew the gnoll was there and sensed the beast's attack. He ducked under the heavy blade, stepping backwards into the beast, simultaneously reversing his grip on his knife and slamming the razor sharp blade into the belly of the gnoll as the beast stumbled forward. The knife sank in deep and Kiln spun away, ripping the sharp knife through the gnoll's bowels as he used his deadly long sword to spear the other injured gnoll right through its left eye. Both gnolls fell to the ground dead as their crimson blood dripped freely from Kiln's blades. If you blinked twice you would have missed the kills.

Jonas jumped from boulder to boulder, his agility bringing him easily into the clearing. His body glowed brightly and the two gnolls in front of him stepped back from the light.

One gnoll, in desperation, flung its war club at Jonas, trying to extinguish the painful light. Jonas had only a split second to react, using his cognivant powers to stop the club just before it hit him in the face. He focused on the club, wrapping it in energy. It floated in the air for a moment before Jonas used his mind to reverse the direction of the club, sending it somersaulting back towards the astonished gnoll. He felt the familiar dull ache in his head as he used his powers, but it would not be enough pain to significantly affect him. The club hit the gnoll in its forearms as it brought them up to deflect the weapon.

The second gnoll, still slightly blinded by the powerful light, lunged forward, jabbing at Jonas with a long spear. Jonas, trained by the best warrior in Kraawn, reacted on instinct. Instead of retreating, he swayed to the side spinning around the spear point toward the enraged gnoll. The beast's eyes grew wide in astonishment as Jonas, using the momentum of his spin, swung his sword through the air, slicing a shallow cut across the gnoll's forehead.

The creature stumbled backwards, frantically trying to wipe the blood away from its face as it poured into its beady deep-set eyes. But Jonas did not let him go that easily. As his sword sliced across the beast's forehead he used his left hand to yank the spear from the wounded gnoll's grasp. As the blind gnoll stumbled backwards, Jonas spun the spear in his grip so the tip was pointing toward the beast, and jabbed the long weapon forward, lancing the gnoll in the throat.

Jonas pulled out the spear point and the dying creature fell to the ground just as the second gnoll recovered from Jonas's initial attack and tried to run away into the protection of the night. Jonas spun the spear around again so that the bloody point was facing the fleeing beast. He used his long arms and powerful legs to throw the spear with all his might. It was a left handed throw, but the distance was not so great.

The spear shot through the darkness, hammering into the beast's back. The power of the throw launched the gnoll to the ground and the dying beast slowly tried to crawl into the cover of darkness. The doomed creature made it about two paces before the fatal wound took its toll and it dropped face first in the dirt.

Jonas spun around to survey the scene. It was all over in a matter of seconds. Kiln moved toward him calmly holding both his blood-covered weapons. Lambeck was busy searching the dead gnolls and yanking his arrows from the corpses.

"Nice work, Jonas. Your light saved us," Kiln said. Jonas let the light draw back into him until it was nothing more than a slight glow surrounding his body. "Can you hold the light a bit longer while we get the fire lit again?"

"I can."

"Lambeck, get the fire going and let's get these bodies dragged out of the clearing. I'm hungry and my beef smells good."

***

They saw no more of One Eye's warriors, but nonetheless Kiln made sure that the areas surrounding his home were scouted regularly. They also had to continue surveying their cattle to make sure no more animals were being stolen.

With all of this happening, Jonas's training continued. Kiln began to train him in hand to hand fighting. Jonas had learned a little during his time with the knight apprentices, but again he realized the hard way that he was still just a novice. He spent many evenings training with Kiln and the other men, and most of his time was spent flying through the air to land hard on his back.

Kiln was unstoppable, his speed and strength with the sword carried over in hand to hand combat as well. It was the Sharneen, a war-like tribe that lived far to the east, who had taught Kiln their secrets of combat. Kiln explained to Jonas that they were a small people, slight of build, with narrow eyes spaced wide, but they trained their bodies to have great power and speed. Kiln learned much from them, and they from him. He trained their chiefs in formation fighting, while they taught him secrets of the blade and hand to hand fighting. These were the secrets that Kiln now taught to Jonas.

"Jonas, the key is balance. Always be on the balls of your feet, so you can move quickly in either direction. You want to use an opponent's energy and momentum against them," Kiln explained. "If they punch you, don't retreat or shy from the punch as most fighters do. Move into the punch and redirect their energy so you are in control."

Kiln showed Jonas how to redirect an attack to one's advantage. He taught him how to throw an opponent and how to immobilize him with wrist locks, submission holds, and pressure points. Jonas learned that there was a difference between fighting to avoid hurting someone, and fighting to maim or kill an opponent. Jonas learned that the throat, groin, sternum, kidneys, and joints were the locations to direct an attack to completely disable an opponent.

Kiln built a wooden frame of a man for Jonas to practice his strikes. He taught him how to strike without hurting himself, how to use his palms, the sides of his hands, his shins, knees, elbows, and forearms as weapons. The strikes hurt at first, but after a while the pain subsided as his body adapted to the hits. After months of training he began to build up calluses from constantly hitting the wooden dummy. Jonas's powers were substantial, but they had their limits, therefore he was happy to learn any skill that would help him survive.

"I think I will have to make a new wooden dummy for you," commented Kiln as he walked up to Jonas. Jonas had been practicing on the dummy for an hour and he was sweating heavily. The dummy was indeed in bad shape; the wood had taken a beating, especially in the strike points that Jonas constantly worked. Months ago his hands would be bleeding, but not now. They were strong, the striking areas covered with thick skin. He stepped back from the dummy and took a long drink from his water skin.

"Your form has improved," Kiln complemented Jonas.

"Thank you, sir," replied Jonas as he set the water skin down. His upper body was bare and there was a layer of glistening sweat that covered his lean muscular torso. His God Mark shone brightly as the mountain sun reflected off the silver and blue etchings. It had grown some, now covering most of his torso.

Kiln sat down on the wood fence that penned in his sheep. "Do you know how long you've been here, Jonas?" he asked softy.

"Yes, sir. I have been so absorbed in my training that time has meant little to me. Do you want me to leave?" asked Jonas, wondering where Kiln's questioning was going.

"You have been here for over two winters, Jonas, surely you know that."

"Yes, sir, I do."

"Do you not want to go to Annure as you previously planned?" asked Kiln in a fatherly voice.

"I do, sir. I know I've been here longer than was previously arranged. It's just that I've never felt more alive and at home than I do here, with you and your men. I do not want that to go away."

"I see," Kiln said with understanding. "I, too, have enjoyed your company, and your friendship. You are gifted with skill and power that I've seldom seen. But it is not your destiny to stay here secluded in the mountains with me. Take it from someone who knows, seclusion does not solve your problems."

"I know, sir. I have known that all along. I guess that is why I was trying to stretch this time out as long as I could. I know that once I leave here, that my life will be filled with constant struggles." Jonas wiped his dripping brow with his hand and looked up at Kiln, his long sweaty brown hair glued to his forehead, and his deep brown eyes filled with emotion.

"I understand. Are you afraid?" asked Kiln.

"I am, but not for me. I'm not afraid to die, I realize that now. I should have died years ago with my mother." Jonas hesitated for a moment. "I'm afraid to fail. I'm afraid I am not strong enough to serve Shyann. I've been weak my whole life and this power is new to me. I wonder if she picked the right person."

Kiln laughed and shook his head. "Jonas, trust me. She picked the right man. You have a pure heart. I've been around fighting men my entire life, and believe me, she did not fail in her choice. You are on your way to being one of the best swordsmen I have ever seen, and you have powers that will get you through the tasks ahead. I can feel it."

"Sir, do you have faith in the gods?"

Kiln paused for a moment before answering. "I have faith in myself and my friends, nothing more."

"I see. Do you ever feel like praying?"

"Jonas, the gods are real, I will not deny that, but I question many things, all of which keep me from praying to anyone. I rely on myself. My success or failure will fall on my shoulders only. Praying means you are relying on others. That can be dangerous for a warrior. Do you understand?"

"I do, but what things do you question?" Jonas asked, leaning on the railing as he put on his cotton tunic.

"I question the gods' motives. Who they are and what they want. The world we live in can be a terrible place. I have seen awful things and I wonder why the gods would allow it. Why does a poor farmer, who can barely feed his family, slaughter a lamb before and after the farming season as a gift to his god? Does his god require it? If so, why do they not help these people live a better life? There are many things about religion that makes no sense to me, Jonas."

"Perhaps the gods don't have the power to change everything."

"Maybe, but why do the priests preach the opposite. And why do many of these same priests live a pampered life in their big temples paid for by the coin and sweat of the poor. The system is corrupt, Jonas, and I will not give my allegiance to a god that allows that to happen."

"Maybe the gods don't have total control over what happens here. Maybe corrupt men created the corrupt system, not the gods. Maybe the gods struggle to do right in this world, but their power is not inexhaustible. Or maybe they allow man to do as he will to test his character. Shyann is good. I can sense it, feel it, everything about her resonates hope and courage. Isn't that something to believe in?"

"For you, yes, she chose you to help her. I believe she chose well. But there is no place in my heart for the gods. Besides, there are too many *maybes* in your argument. I believe in what I can see and hold in my hands, my friends, honor, courage, and my sword. I do not deny the god's existence or their power, but their purpose and their role in our lives is unclear to me. And until I have clarity, I will continue to pray to no one."

"I see. It is a difficult topic of discussion. As you said there are many unknowns when it comes to the gods. But I feel good about believing in something other than my sword and myself. I am Shyann's ally against evil.

Shyann's purpose is linked to mine, I can sense it, and until I feel differently, my sword will uphold her will."

"I respect your principles, Jonas. As I said, Shyann has chosen well."

"Thank you, sir. I owe much to you. You have taught me things that I never dreamed of knowing."

"I want to thank you too, Jonas," Kiln replied.

"For what?"

"For awakening a part of me that was dead for many years. I tried to escape something that I couldn't face. I tried to bury a part of me that has always burned like an ember deep in my soul. I am a warrior Jonas, pure and simple. My skills are being wasted away in this mountain retreat because I was not strong enough to face my fears. I do not want to die up here. I want to die with my sword in my hand. You have made me realize this, and I thank you for it."

Jonas smiled warmly at Kiln, unaccustomed to seeing any hint of emotion in the hard man. "I knew you were not all ice and muscle," grinned Jonas.

Kiln smiled and stood up. "Don't tell anyone."

"I won't. I wouldn't want to ruin your reputation."

"A reputation that I will have to repair when I leave here with you," Kiln said seriously, the hint of a smile slowly emerging.

Jonas looked at Kiln in surprise. "Really! You're going to leave with me?"

"I am. As soon as this winter is over, we leave for Annure." Now Kiln was smiling openly, and Jonas couldn't help but laugh in excitement.

***

The winter was long and cold and Jonas grew frustrated as he was not able to train as usual. He continued to hunt the forests around him with Lambeck when the weather permitted. There were no more gnoll signs, and the winter days melted away without any major incidents.

He exercised with Kiln inside the barn, keeping their muscles strong, and training with sword and fist. But he felt locked up, not being able to run the hills and climb the steep cliffs that surrounded them. At the same time, Jonas was excited because each day took him closer to when the snows would subside and he and Kiln would venture out into the unknown.

***

When that day arrived it was like a huge weight had been lifted from his shoulders. He had been penned up for months thinking of what was next in his life, thinking of Annure and the conflicts to come.

Finally the day came, and Jonas felt conflicting emotions, happy and excited to depart, and yet apprehensive to leave his mountain home and his new friends. He had spent over three years with these men and the thought of leaving them was not easy for Jonas.

Everyone had gathered to say good bye in the cold morning air. The sun had just risen over the steep peaks and the dripping of the melting snow broke the stillness of the quiet dawn. There was still snow on the ground but many of the game trails were now clear and passable.

Kiln was wearing his customary light chain mail covered with his thick wool tunic and on his shoulders hung his dark green traveling cloak. He wore dark breeches and thick leather boots. At his waist dangled his long sword and dagger and he carried his long bow in his hands. Kiln hefted his backpack to his shoulders and looked at Jonas with a nod.

Jonas was similarly outfitted with thick wool traveling clothes and at his belt hung his sword and dagger. Jonas adjusted the straps of his pack and looked at Lambeck and the rest of the men, unsure how to say good bye. Kiln had given the compound and most of his money to Lambeck. Except for what he now carried on his back and a small pouch of gold and silver, enough for their travels, he had nothing.

"Good luck, Jonas. May the High One watch over you," Lambeck said, reaching out and shaking Jonas's hand in the warrior's grip.

"And you as well, Lambeck, thank you for everything. I owe you much," replied Jonas, their eyes locking.

Lambeck nodded his head and stepped back. Jonas shook everyone's hand and said his good byes.

"Lambeck, you've been a good friend to me over the years, as have you all," Kiln said, addressing the group. "I count myself lucky to have spent so many years with you. Take care of my home for me," he added as he went to each man to say his good byes. Kiln did not shed a tear, but Jonas saw more than one eye glisten with moisture from his men. "I will be back again. If I am to die then I want to be buried here in the mountains. If I live then I will walk these hills with you again. Either way I will be back. I promise you that. Until another day!" he shouted as he and Jonas started the long walk down the valley.

***

The first few days of travel were slow but without incident. Snow still covered some sections of the trail, making their descent down the Tundrens a bit arduous.

On the third day Jonas spotted a huge stag in the forest, standing at the crest of a tree dotted hill. It was standing absolutely still and looking directly at them. The deer was massive, almost the size of a horse. Its rack was gigantic. The span of the impressive horns was as far apart as a man is tall. At first he thought it was an elk, but then he noticed the horns, which distinguished the animal as a buck, despite its impossible size. Jonas had never seen anything like it. It was standing amongst the trees, head held high with no sign of fright, eyeing them both as they walked along the game trail. It was as if the deer was expecting them.

Jonas immediately thought back to a conversation he had had with Tuvallus, the mysterious mountain man who had rescued him and Fil. He recalled the man saying that he was tracking a huge buck, the biggest he had ever seen, and then it had just disappeared. That was when he had spotted the boarg tracks that had been following Jonas and Fil. Tuvallus had arrived in their camp just in time to save them both from the attacking boargs.

Jonas smiled to himself momentarily as he thought about the possibility that Shyann had had her hands in that rescue. Was this stag another warning? Or was it something else?

Jonas motioned for Kiln to look to his right, towards the animal. Kiln stopped and looked up into the woods and spotted the magnificent animal. His eyes widened and his hand automatically reached for his quiver.

"No," Jonas whispered. Something inside him told him that this animal should not be shot, that it was standing there for a reason.

"Why not?" Kiln asked incredulously.

"I don't know. I just feel like we shouldn't shoot it." Just as Jonas spoke the deer flicked its head as if it were saying, *come here.*

Jonas and Kiln looked at each other in wonder as the animal flicked its head one more time before leaping through the brambles and over the crest of the forested hill.

Kiln looked at Jonas and shrugged his shoulders. "What now?" he asked.

"We follow it," replied Jonas with certainty as he ran after the majestic animal. Jonas and Kiln had to run quickly, leaping over rocks and snags as they tried to keep the buck in their sight. The stag stopped several times, looking back to see if they were still following.

"It's leading us somewhere. Are you sure we should be following?" asked Kiln as he ran effortlessly beside Jonas.

"Yes. It wants us to follow; I can feel it," Jonas panted as he jumped over a fallen log.

The two men followed the deer for several hours before they came to the top of a small hill overlooking a clearing. Down in the clearing was the largest, most magnificent oak tree that they had ever seen. Its base was probably thirty paces wide and its thick branches, each the size of a large tree, reached over a hundred feet in the air. It was colossal. Kiln and Jonas stared at the tree with wonder.

The huge deer looked back at them, flicked its head again, and disappeared behind the enormous trunk. Jonas sensed something special in the clearing, an aura of pure goodness that emanated from everything, especially the tree. It was like an oasis of pureness.

Kiln looked at Jonas in amazement. "What is this place? It is beautiful, and I feel something…different, like an overwhelming sense of peace. I can't explain it. It feels like a sanctuary."

"Trust your senses. We are looking at Shyann's tree. I recognize it from a dream. This is the place where she was buried," replied Jonas, his face a mask of wonder, similar to that of a child looking at a cavalier for the first time. Jonas looked at Kiln and smiled broadly, unable to hide his excitement. "You are looking at a sacred place. I'm willing to bet that no human has ever set eyes on this tree. Let's go, nothing can harm us here," Jonas said as he walked down into the clearing.

As Jonas entered the clearing, he felt a magical pulse deep in his body. It was brief, like a flash, and then it was over. He was standing at the base of the tree looking up into the branches. It was so big that his eyes could not encompass it.

Kiln moved next to him. "Did you feel that, Jonas?" he asked.

"I did. I think it was some magical barrier that we crossed." Jonas stepped around to the backside of the tree where the deer had disappeared. He slowly ran his hand over the bark of the tree. Jonas felt the magic within the tree hum and pulse with life. It was an incredible feeling and his body felt alive. A sense of calm surrounded him and a flood of warmth surged through his fingers and into his body. He tingled everywhere and he had an overwhelming feeling to laugh, which he did. The scent of lavender filled the clearing and the gentle chirping of small forest birds created a peaceful symphony of sound.

As he neared the back of the tree he noticed a large opening at the base of the trunk. It was shaped like an inverted V and at the bottom of the opening was a set of stone steps that went down, underneath the oak's root structure. The deer was nowhere to be seen.

Kiln approached him. "Do we go down?" he asked.

"Yes," replied Jonas, mesmerized by the magic of the place.

Jonas led Kiln down the dusty stone steps. Vines and roots draped the walls as they went deeper into the ground. The air smelt of wet moss after a morning rain. The passage was dark, but as they stepped from the last step onto a stone floor, the room instantly lit up as torches ensconced on the walls flared brightly.

Kiln looked at Jonas in surprise.

"It's okay. We are supposed to be here. No harm will befall us in this place. Don't you feel it?" Jonas asked, his eyes scanning the room.

"I do. I just wanted to make sure that you felt it too," answered Kiln with a smile. There were six torches lighting a round room about twenty paces in diameter. The floor was covered with thick dust and completely empty except for a massive stone sarcophagus resting in the middle.

"Is that what I think it is?" asked Kiln.

"I think so," replied Jonas in complete awe. He slowly stepped toward the stone coffin. The entire structure was carved with intricate designs. On the lid was etched a beautiful oak tree that looked similar to the mark on Jonas's chest. The sides of the stone coffin were covered with carvings of Ulren's four-pointed star. The work was intricate and the lines graceful and smooth, obviously the work of a master craftsman.

Jonas put both his hands on the coffin closing his eyes in prayer. He recognized the gift that they were given in being allowed to see this place and he wanted to thank Shyann for the honor she had given them.

"Jonas, look," Kiln said with wonder.

Jonas opened his eyes to see a shining silver set of chain mail lying on top of the coffin. The metal shirt sparkled in the torchlight like diamonds. Resting on top of the chain mail was a metal breastplate that was covered with Shyann's silver and blue oak tree. The symbol was perfect, the lines clean and fluid. The blue and silver sparkled in the light, causing the cuirass to glow as if it were alive. There were metal greaves, faulds to cover the hips, wrist guards, thigh guards, and shoulder plates. Each piece of the armor had a mirror like finish and was covered with intricate etchings of Shyann and the High One.

There was also a leather belt that carried two magnificent swords. The handle of each blade was carved from the horn of a deer and capped with shiny steel. The scabbard was hardened black leather enforced with polished steel and covered with intricate carvings and runes. The belt buckle was shaped in the image of the silver and blue oak tree of Shyann. The polished metal sparkled with beauty.

Next to the chain mail shirt was a long black bow and a quiver of matching arrows with silver and blue feathers. The leather quiver was lined with silver and stamped with more symbols, some of which Jonas recognized as Ulren's and Shyann's symbols, as well as others that didn't look familiar. The tips of the bow were capped with carved white deer horn and the handle was also deer horn wrapped in black leather.

The item that really caught his eye was the silver helm resting at the head of the coffin. There were two deer horns jutting from the shiny steel. The entire helm gleamed and every inch of it reflected the god-like presence that Jonas felt when he gazed upon it. Jonas just gazed in awe at the treasures, his mouth agape.

"Where did all this come from?" Jonas asked.

"When you touched the coffin, they just appeared," answered Kiln, moving a bit closer. "Is this really Shyann's grave?"

"Yes, it is. I can feel it. I can sense her all around us." Jonas reached out and grabbed the handle of one of the blades. It felt warm to his touch and the handle felt like it was made to fit his hand. He slid the blade out with one smooth motion. The metal rang and hummed as he held the sword up in the torchlight. The blade was polished silver and curved slightly at the end. Both sides were razor sharp and there was writing etched in the middle of the blade.

Jonas brought the blade closer to his face so he could get a better look. He felt the power pulse within the sword and the energy vibrated in his head. The sword was extremely light and perfectly balanced. Jonas looked at the script carved into the blade. He recognized it as elven and he tried to pronounce it.

"Tanaii…"

"Tanai' Kay Des-tai," interjected Kiln as he stepped closer to analyze the blade.

"What does it mean?" Jonas asked.

"It is elven. It means *the path of righteousness*, a fitting saying for a blade. I think your goddess has given you some powerful weapons, Jonas."

"Should I take them?" Jonas asked, unsure.

"Yes. All cavaliers are given weapons by their god when they pass the tests at Annure."

"But I have passed no tests," Jonas said skeptically.

"It seems that Shyann does not care. Take the gifts, Jonas," Kiln said. Jonas looked at Kiln who was nodding his head in affirmation. "Go ahead."

Jonas slid the blade back into the scabbard and laid down the sword belt. He lifted off his traveling cloak, tunic, and old mail shirt and dropped them to the floor. He then noticed that in a neat pile near the armor were new breeches made of dark fine leather, along with a blue tunic made of the same soft material. There was also a long shirt made of thick soft cotton, and black leather boots that laced up to the knees. They were magnificent, fit for royalty, and Jonas quickly discarded his old clothes for the new. The leather and soft cloth felt warm and comfortable as they caressed his skin. He reached out and lifted up the shiny chain mail shirt. It was light and warm to the touch as well.

"It is so light," Jonas said in wonder.

"It is magic. You will barely be able to feel that shirt and yet it will stop a spear thrown by a giant. A magnificent gift," Kiln said.

Jonas dropped the sparkling shirt over his head and it seemed to shrink to his form, looking like a normal shirt of metal. It was so light that Jonas could barely feel it. Next he put the breastplate over his head and buckled it at the sides. It, too, fit perfectly, as if it were made for him. He buckled on his shoulder guards, greaves, and wrist guards. He put his new tunic in his backpack and lifted his green traveling cloak from the floor and put it back over his head. He then unbuckled his old sword and buckled on his new ones. The twin blades hung lightly at his side and the belt fit him perfectly.

Lastly, he reached out and grabbed his new bow and quiver. He buckled the quiver to the side of his pack and held the long black bow firmly in his hand. He felt magic within the bow as well, and the grip fit his hand perfectly. There was no doubt in Jonas's mind that these were indeed gifts from Shyann.

"You are looking more and more like a cavalier every day. Now all you need is your steed," Kiln said with a smile.

Jonas looked down at his breastplate, his swords, and his bow and grinned from ear to ear. "This all feels so right, like they were made for me."

"I think they were, my friend."

Eight
Startling Events

Lathrin, third lance of the Finarthian Knights, led fifty of his knights off the main road towards the farm. A report had come in several days ago that there was a massacre at one of the farm settlements near the outer limits of the king's land. Lathrin and his men were sent out immediately by the king to investigate the attack.

Lathrin led the column of knights toward a lone farmhouse, their sparkling lance tips flashing as the setting sun shone against the jostling weapons.

A middle aged farmer wearing old worn out clothing approached them as they neared his home.

"Good day, sir, I am Lathrin, third lance of the Finarthian Knights. We have come to investigate the massacre," he said as he stopped his warhorse next to the man.

The man eyed the soldiers uneasily before replying. "Two days ago in the middle of the night my family and I heard horrible sounds, like a battle of some sort. There was screaming and horrible screeches, sort of like a wild animal. But it didn't sound like any animal I had ever heard. We saw a very bright light shine in the field but it didn't last long. We didn't know what it was. But in the morning I took my sons out into the field to investigate and saw the killings."

"How many dead?" asked Lathrin.

"Four," the farmer replied.

"Where did this happen?"

The man turned, pointing into a field beyond his house. "It's a short walk away, just follow the fence line and you will see it. I don't know what will be left now with the scavengers and all. Sir, it looked like one of the men killed was a priest or maybe a cavalier. I have never seen one myself but he carried Ulren's symbol. I didn't touch anything; it had the feel of evil."

"I see," Lathrin replied. "Thank you. We will go have a look." The farmer nodded and watched the horses thunder into the field.

It didn't take them long to find the carnage. Lathrin could see the four forms ripped and torn to pieces even at a distance. Their dark blood had soaked into the ground, staining the otherwise beautiful grassland.

Lathrin dismounted and told the others to do the same. "Don't touch anything," he ordered his men. "Just look for any clues as to what may have caused this."

Lathrin walked to one of the corpses on the ground. A large buzzard flapped its wings angrily as he approached before it was forced to fly away. The body's chest was ripped open and it was missing an arm. The man's face had been torn off as well. Lathrin covered his nose from the stench as he knelt by the corpse. The dead man was a warrior, that much was obvious. His metal chest plate had been ripped off and thrown to the side and his sword was lying about ten paces away. Lathrin could see four deep cuts, like claw marks, covering his right thigh. It was obvious that claws and teeth of some sort ripped open the man's chest.

"What did this sir?" asked Pelimus, a veteran knight of twenty years.

"A beast of some kind. Something big and powerful. What of the other bodies?"

"Looks the same, sir. They were killed with tooth and claw. There are no other bodies about so whatever attacked them left no trace," he said as he averted his eyes from the gruesome scene.

"Sir!" yelled one of his soldiers.

Lathrin stood up looking over his shoulder. About forty paces away one of his men was motioning for him. Lathrin and Pelimus jogged over to see what he was so excited about. "What is it, Caros?" asked Lathrin as he neared the warrior.

"Sir, I think you should look at this," Caros said as he stepped aside to reveal another corpse. Lathrin looked down at the body and saw another mutilated corpse, this body worse than the others. His entire chest cavity had been ripped open and his entrails spread over the grass. The body was clawed repeatedly until most of the warrior's arms and legs had been ripped of skin and flesh, exposing white bone underneath. The only thing left untouched was the man's face, and Lathrin knew that face.

"I can't believe it, that's Hilius, cavalier to Bandris."

"I thought so," replied Caros. "I found this lying nearby." Caros held up a silver necklace carrying a pendant marked with Bandris's double bladed battle-axe. It was the cavalier's religious symbol. "What could do this to a cavalier, sir?" asked the uneasy warrior.

"I don't know, Caros," Lathrin said kneeling next to the mutilated body and shaking his head sadly. They have been getting reports from scouts and travelers that cavaliers from Annure, Tarsis, and all the eastern lands of Kraawn, have been attacked and killed over the last year. The king had ordered his officers to keep the reports secret, but eventually word had spread through the troops and to the people of Finarth. It wasn't long before it became common knowledge that something was hunting and killing cavaliers.

The people were becoming frightened and restless and the king had no answers for them. The only thing they did know was that an evil was awakening; there was no doubt of that. The knights of Finarth had been constantly roaming the lands trying to find the killer, or killers, but to no avail. Whatever was killing the cavaliers was eluding them.

"Bury these men," ordered Lathrin. "Then we head back to Finarth. The king must be given word that another cavalier has been killed."

***

"How can this be!" bellowed the king, standing up angrily from the table. In audience was Lathrin, Prince Baylin, Manlin, high priest to Shyann, and Alerion, the king's wizard.

"I don't know, my Lord, but I am not mistaken. I have met Hilius on several occasions. It was he, and he carried Bandris's symbol," replied Lathrin.

King Gavinsteal turned around and looked up toward the back wall at the huge painting depicting the Dark One being defeated by his ancestor, King Ullis Gavinsteal. He gripped his sword handle tightly as he looked at the black figure of Malbeck. *Is it possible that Malbeck is back?*

"Sir, if I may speak?" asked the aging wizard. Alerion's head was bald and his chin was speckled with gray and black hair that was trimmed to a sharp point. The wizard wore an ordinary blue tunic and gray breeches, and at his shoulders hung a heavy blue cloak lined with expensive silk.

"Of course, Alerion. What have you found out?" asked the king, turning back around to address the men.

"My Lord, I have been exhausting all my power to try and gain information as you requested. I have magically contacted the court wizards at Annure, Ta-ron, and Tarsis. So far, there have been six cavaliers killed."

"How is this possible?" whispered Manlin. "Are you sure, Alerion?"

"Yes, unfortunately I am. Lapeen, Tary'an, Osandris, Rian, Katliss, and now Hilius," added the wizard.

The king sat down heavily in his chair. "Katliss was slain? But he was the last first rank cavalier," moaned the bewildered king.

"I do not believe it. What could do this?" muttered the shocked priest.

"It could only be a demon or beast of great power," answered the wizard. "It could be the same one that attacked Jonas and the knight apprentices. All six of the cavaliers were killed in different locations, but in the same way. Also, I have received an urgent message from King Kromm."

"What is it?" asked the king.

"It is reported that a large army is forming at Banrith castle," Alerion continued. "Tarsinian scouts have reported that orcs, goblins, boargs, and other monsters have been pouring from the Blacklands and the Mazgar Forest by the thousands." Everyone sat in silence taking in the wizard's words.

"Father, there can be no doubt now," interjected Baylin. "Over three years ago a Banthra attacked a small village that happened to be the home of a small boy. Soon after that same boy was attacked on the road by a priest of Naz-reen and then attacked by a demon in our very castle. Now six cavaliers have been killed by a demon and a monstrous army is building in Banrith, the stronghold that used to be the home of Malbeck himself before he was killed a thousand years ago. Father, it is happening again. The evil in the lands is growing in power and preparing the road for invasion. What better way to do that than to take out the ultimate threat to them, the cavaliers who protect our lands from this evil."

The king sat silently for a moment, contemplating everyone's words. "Have we heard anything from Jonas or Kiln?" asked the king, looking up at Alerion.

"No sir. No word."

Suddenly the chamber's double doors burst open. Everyone looked down the hall to see a young soldier running toward them. He was dirty and sweaty and flanked by the door guards who let him in.

The king got up immediately, moving toward the stumbling scout. "What is it, Tuarg?"

"Sir, I'm sorry to barge in on you, but I have urgent news," sputtered the man through panting breaths.

"Go ahead, what is it?"

"Sir, I was scouting deep in the flatlands along the Tuvell River when I saw an approaching army."

"What!" stormed the king in disbelief. "Who was it?"

"Sir, they bore the colors of Lord Moradin, but there were Sithgarin tribes with him as well."

"How many?"

"I'm not sure. We were spotted by boargs and Keltick was killed. I barely got away, but I think there must have been thirty thousand or so. My Lord, the Tuvell Garrison was destroyed to the man."

The perimeter of the king's land was marked by several garrisons. These garrisons served two purposes, one, to protect the local people that lived in the king's lands and paid taxes but were far away from Finarth, and two, to act as a warning bell to any approaching threat. These garrisons were located by the only bridges big enough to move an army over the expansive Sithgarin River

"Bandris's axe! We had five hundred men at that garrison!" the king roared. He moved back up the stairs to his throne and sat down heavily in thought. "Lathrin, call a war council. We meet in one hour."

"Yes, my Lord," replied Lathrin as he got up from the table and strode down the long hallway and out the double doors.

"Good work, Tuarg. Rest now and be ready to scout again tomorrow," ordered the king.

"Yes, sir," the tired scout replied, turning to follow Lathrin out the door.

"Father, Lord Moradin would not attack us openly unless he was being forced to, or being paid a lot of gold. He has always been a thorn in our side but he does not have the power to confront us directly. Do you think Banrith has something to do with this?"

"I do," replied the tired king. "Something is happening at Banrith. Evil is spreading from that land again." The king directed his demanding gaze toward Alerion. "Alerion, I need some questions answered, and soon. Is Malbeck back? What sort of evil is rising from the North? What are we going to be fighting and how do we defeat it?"

Alerion stood up and gripped his staff that was leaning against the table's edge. "I will do my best, sire," replied the wizard with a nod as he walked out of the king's conference room.

"Manlin?"

"Yes, my Lord?" asked the high priest.

"Go to your temple. Pray to Shyann, use her power to find out anything for me, any information that would be useful."

The priest stood up. "If she wills it my Lord, then I will have some answers for you." Manlin turned, following the wizard down the hallway.

"Father, it's a ruse of some sort. The army at Banrith attacks Tarsis, while this new army attacks us. Neither army can come to aid the other. Simple divide and conquer strategy."

"My thoughts exactly," the king replied. "Baylin, send out riders immediately to our allies and ask them to send their soldiers. Tell them to meet our army at the Lindsor Bridge as soon as they can mobilize their forces. How long to march an army from Numenell?"

"I'd say about eight days," replied the prince.

"Okay, go, my son. Send out the riders and then meet me back here as soon as you can for the council. I will need you."

"Yes, Father," replied the prince, bowing as he departed.

***

The Greever loved the night. It was his favorite time to hunt and the darkness did nothing to hurt his vision. He could see just as well in the pitch black of a moonless night, as he could in the day, and the dark trees below him glowed with a shimmering green. The demon saw things in auras of color, greens, reds, blues, and oranges, depending on the heat signature they put out. But everything had energy, this, the demon knew, so everything had a color.

His master had been pleased with his work lately, and the Greever loved these recent hunts more than any other. The feeling of ripping the flesh from a cavalier made the demon shudder in ecstasy. But these warriors were not easy prey, they caused him great pain over the years, wounds that stung and magic that hurt its flesh. The Greever had felt similar pain before, not too long ago, when the big human cleaved its chest open with that silver axe. The demon wouldn't forget that warrior, his stench, and it would hunt him down for the pain that he caused.

But this was the hunt that the Greever had been waiting for, the one that started it all. He still remembered the smell of the young man that he had almost killed over two years ago. The smell of his pure heart coated the demon's nostrils. The pulsing goodness within the boy was a bright light to the Greever, and the beast wanted nothing more than to extinguish it.

The Greever beat its long leathery wings and its nostrils pulsed with life, hunting the air for the stink of the man. The hunter knew its prey would be close; its master told it where to go. The Greever would not fail this time, nor would it stop until it found this human and ripped the life from him and ate his bloody heart. The beast's jaws opened instinctively, its tongue darting out beyond its razor sharp fangs, hunting for the metallic taste of blood. It wouldn't be long now, thought the demon, flanking to the right toward the dark peaks of the Tundrens.

***

"Fil, have you heard?" asked Calden excitedly as he ran through the barracks toward Fil who lay on the upper bunk.

"Heard what?"

"We are mobilizing, we're being invaded. Scouts came in today and said that an army approaches us as we speak."

"What!" exclaimed Fil, jumping down from the bunk. Fil had worked hard over the last few years. He was powerfully built, short and solid, with legs and arms thick with muscle.

When the knight apprentices turned eighteen they all moved to the soldiers barracks beyond the inner wall. It was there that they had to serve two years before they would become full-fledged Finarthian Knights. The king believed that before apprentices could become knights, they had to learn how the common soldier lived. King Gavinsteal believed that you learned valuable lessons in the regular army and that you couldn't really learn how to lead men unless you knew how the common man lives, fights, and thinks. That wasn't a problem for Fil, Calden, or a few others, but most of the knights were highborn, and they really had no idea how most people in Finarth lived. Fil believed it was a good lesson for them, although most of the knights resented it. "What army?" asked Fil.

"Lord Moradin from Stonestep, along with several tribes from the Sithgarin."

"You're kidding," Fil's eyes widened in surprise. "Why would they be marching on Finarth?"

"I don't know," replied Calden. "Lord Moradin has never openly attacked us. He always hid behind politics and banter while bandits and tribes staged attacks on us from his own city."

"Why would he risk an open attack?" asked the bewildered Fil.

"I don't know, but we are to mobilize with our modrig immediately," Calden replied, excitement evident in his voice. "Hopefully we'll get some answers there."

Fil was scared, nervous, and excited all at the same time, and he could tell that Calden felt similar emotions. They had both trained for nearly three years and now the time had come to test their skills.

"You ready for this, Fil?" Calden asked.

"I am," responded Fil confidently.

***

Jonas and Kiln traveled hard for several days, and it wasn't long before they entered into the thick forests that covered the base of the Tundren Mountains. Kiln had told Jonas that once they came down from the mountains it would be five days to Ta'ron and then a full week to Annure.

The weather was good, which allowed them to push hard through the forest. The warm fall sun was shielded partly by the canopy of green trees that rose above them. The game trails were numerous, allowing them to push through the dense forest and onto the rolling plains without mishap.

Jonas stood high on a hill looking down across the rolling grasslands.

Kiln joined him. "Ta'ron is southeast of here. It shouldn't take us long if we run," he said, smiling.

"Run? But you've lived over fifty winters, surely you couldn't keep up," replied Jonas, who enjoyed their good natured banter.

"Only one way to find out," Kiln said as he jumped off the small ledge and sprinted down the grass covered hill.

"Go ahead!" yelled Jonas. "You'll need a head start anyway!" he laughed as he jumped off the ledge and ran after the sprinting warrior.

They ran the rest of that day, slowing their pace down to a jog and resting only for water and food. Their packs and armor slowed them down a little, but they were both in such great shape that their strong lungs could carry them all day. Jonas's magical armor hindered him little, and even his new metal chest plate didn't seem to weigh much more than hardened leather.

The sun started to set and Kiln slowed down to a walk. "We should camp here. I don't like being in the open like this, but there are no trees for as far as I can see," Kiln said, scanning the vast plains of grass.

Jonas looked ahead of them and couldn't make out anything except more gently rolling grasslands. "I guess we don't have a choice," replied Jonas, taking off his pack and laying it down on the grass.

They scrounged up some dry sticks and twigs from nearby shrubs to build a fire; the warm food would do them good after the long run.

They both settled down by the flames as the sun set, giving way to a clear moonlit night. Kiln had prepared some warm oats with salt and they cleaned their plates with milt, a hard corn bread used by the soldiers in Finarth. The hearty warm food in their bellies, combined with the crackling fire and the chirping of the crickets, had a relaxing effect on the tired warriors.

Jonas looked up from the fire, gazing at the sparkling stars above them. It was a beautiful night, the air was warm and still and the bright moon and stars gave the countryside a bluish glow.

"It's so calm out here," Jonas said softly. "It's like time is standing still and all your worries no longer exist."

Kiln looked at Jonas and then followed his gaze to the sparkling dots of light. "I spent many evenings doing just this, looking at the stars above the craggy peaks of the Tundrens. Wondering what I was doing with my life, wondering how Cassandra was, how my king and my men were faring. A warm fire and a calm summer night have a way of making you look within yourself."

Jonas looked at his friend and mentor. "What are you going to do, Kiln?"

Kiln looked at the glowing red embers as he thought about the question. "I'm not sure, but I think you came to me for a reason, Jonas. You've brought me out of the trance that I've been living in for twenty years. I think my lands are in danger and that the people of Finarth need a general again."

"Do you think Malbeck, the Dark One, has returned to Kraawn?"

"I'm not sure, but some evil is back; you, of all people, know that. Banthras were created by Malbeck so it makes sense that he might be back. Someone or something of great power may have brought them back, I know not. But your village was attacked by a Banthra and I don't think it was by chance"

"What do you mean?"

"Jonas, your village was attacked by a Banthra, you were attacked by boargs, twice, and a powerful agent of Naz-reen. And then you were attacked by a demon. I agree with the king in saying that you are the target. The evil that stirs is afraid of you, and they want you dead," Kiln finished with emphasis.

Jonas looked away from the warrior, got up, and stirred the red-hot coals with a stick. Being a target of such enemies was not an easy thing to grasp, but Jonas had thought about it much and he could not argue with the logic. Shyann had obviously picked Jonas as her champion, and in doing so had made him an enemy of her enemies.

"But what can one person do, what can I do?" asked Jonas, confused.

"The power of one, Jonas, think on it. Malbeck was one person, and what did he do a thousand years ago? The king's great ancestor, King Ullis Gavinsteal, slew Malbeck in battle, and he was only one person. I have used my skills in war to turn the tide of a battle and bring us victory where we should have suffered defeat. I have seen a farmer with a sword stand his ground in war and instill courage in others who would have run, which in turn affected the outcome of the battle. He was just one person whose own actions greatly affected the world around him. The list goes on. Jonas, never underestimate the power of one person."

Jonas nodded his head and stirred the coals some more, thinking about what Kiln had said. "I won't," he said after a few moments.

"I hope not, because I am a good judge of character. You are the type of man that shoulders that power and responsibility; you will change Kraawn, Jonas. I can feel it."

Jonas felt the weight of Kiln's words on his back. If it were his destiny, then he would carry that weight, with both swords in his hands.

Jonas looked up again and saw that dark clouds had begun to drift across the sky, eclipsing the moonlight and bathing the area in darkness.

Kiln looked up as well, noticing the change in light. "Strange those clouds would move in so quickly," he said. Jonas frowned, looking around; something didn't seem right. Kiln noticed his expression and spoke with concern. "What is it? Do you hear something?"

"No, that is the problem. There are no more crickets," Jonas said as he stood up. Then he felt it, the familiar tingle on his chest. It was Shyann's warning. Jonas instinctively brought one hand to his chest, a move not missed by Kiln.

Kiln quickly slid his blade from its scabbard, the ringing of steel echoing in the still night. "What is it?"

"I'm not sure, but something evil is near, that much I know," Jonas replied, his voice tense, as he quickly donned his helm and reached down to grab his new bow. He gripped the bone handle tightly and planted six arrows in the ground next to him. "Put out the fire," whispered Jonas as he moved toward the flames.

"No! Whatever is out there can see in the dark, but we can't. Leave the flames; the light might hinder its vision," Kiln said as his eyes sought the threat. Jonas and Kiln stood alert, looking for the danger that was surely near. "I don't like this, Jonas. I can't hear or see anything."

"I know. It is near, I can feel it," Jonas whispered as he hunted for any signs of an attacker. Suddenly his chest flamed again and some intuition within Jonas told him to look up.

A shadow flew at them from the darkness, completely silent, its long leathery wings making no noise as the deathly form came at them like a falling stone. Jonas quickly grabbed an arrow and had it flying at the beast just as he dove to the side, out of the way of the attacking demon. The arrow struck the beast as it landed in the flames, sending sparks and a shower of burning embers into the air.

Kiln had seen Jonas's move and flung himself blindly away from the fire. Both warriors rolled backwards, leaping to their feet, their silver swords glistening with magical energy.

Kiln's long sword was also a magical blade, a priceless weapon that he took from the hands of a dead Sharneen chief. Kiln told the story one night to Jonas as they sat by his warm hearth. Long ago he had been challenged by a Sharneen chief, a chief of a tribe that was feuding with the tribe he was living with. The Sharneen rules are simple, accept the challenge and fight to live, or decline the challenge and be stoned to death as a coward. Kiln accepted the challenge and defeated the warrior, raising his status within the tribe and giving him weapon rights to the slain warrior. Kiln explained to Jonas that there was nothing more valuable to a Sharneen than the weapons that they collected in combat, and that one's wealth, position, and power as a warrior was measured by the amount and quality of weapons that he possessed.

Kiln held the weapon in front of him, the blade glowing green in the pitch black. The blade was unique as the shape was not common. The base of the blade was narrow and its length curved slightly like a scimitar as it came to the tip. It was thin and as long as a long sword but the Sharneen weapon was as strong as any infantry cutting blade. The Sharneen blade smiths were some of the best, and that, in combination with the magic of the blade, made the sword nearly indestructible.

The demon sat on top the burning coals. The flames were now extinguished and the red hot coals did nothing to the creature as it leered at them with its red glowing eyes. Jonas had landed to the demon's left and had come up gripping both his swords before him, their twin curved blades glowing bluish in the dark night. Jonas had dropped his bow in the grass and his arrows were scattered on the ground in front of him. The demon swung its bulky head back and forth before stopping and locking gazes with the young warrior. The beast's long dark wings were held wide, the sharp bony points hovering menacingly before them.

"Finally, I get to kill you," hissed the demon, its words barely recognizable as it spoke through its tooth filled jaws. Its deep voice sent a chill through Jonas as he looked at Kiln to his left.

Jonas recognized the look on Kiln's face; he had dropped into Ty'erm, the mental state that prepared his mind and body for battle. Jonas quickly calmed his beating heart and entered into the state of Ty'erm as Kiln had taught him. His nerves calmed and his senses became enhanced. His breathing slowed, and he could hear his heartbeat. His senses were now so acute that he could pick up the subtlest nuances of sound or movement.

"You did not kill me at Finarth, and you will not kill me now," Jonas answered the demon. He was gaining confidence as he prayed to Shyann and as he felt the warmth of magic flow into his body. He smiled inwardly, feeling strangely at ease, knowing that Shyann was with him, whether he lived or died.

The beast flicked its tail in agitation and Jonas noticed the long sharp spikes that covered the twitching appendage. "I have killed many of your brethren, but you are the one that I've longed to destroy," rumbled the beast, its voice the epitome of evil.

The Greever stared at the two warriors, its red eyes carrying the weight of its hatred for all that is good. The beast began to growl, a low menacing sound that reverberated through their bodies. The sound was entrancing and Jonas's sword tips began to slowly sag as his eyes began to close. The resonating sound got louder and Jonas felt his body teeter on the edge of consciousness.

Suddenly light flared within his mind and his body tensed, dispelling the demon's magic. Jonas's eyes sprung open and the demon roared in defiance. Jonas glanced to his left and saw Kiln swaying back and forth, his sword point touching the ground. The beast was using magic, using its voice to spell them. Shyann's magic had freed Jonas from the demon's grasp, but Kiln was still in danger as his eyes fluttered, barely maintaining consciousness.

The demon swung its tail in a powerful arc at Kiln as it shot its wing tips toward Jonas. Jonas screamed, hoping to wake up Kiln, and brought up his swords in desperation, trying to deflect the deadly wing points. His magical blades created a wall of razor sharp steel as he retreated quickly from the attacks.

Kiln felt dizzy and tired, the low growling from the demon resonating in his mind like a mother's lullaby. But Kiln was strong in spirit, and in the state of Ty'erm even a powerful demon would have a hard time spelling the mentally tough warrior.

Kiln snapped his eyes open as Jonas screamed, and he lifted up his blade as the beast's tail barreled into him like a spiked boulder. His blade deflected the powerful stroke slightly, but the sharp spikes still raked deep cuts across his shoulder and the momentum of the strike sent Kiln flying backwards.

He landed hard on his back, the impact of the fall not noticed as the pain of the three cuts shot through his body. The lacerations burned agonizingly; Kiln knew that these were no ordinary wounds, that the demon's tail must be poisonous. He rolled around on the grass, moaning with pain as the poison found his blood stream and began to do its work. Kiln used his powerful mind, concentrating on dismissing the pain and pushing it aside so he could stand and fight this demon. He sought his center, focusing on it, willing his heart rate to slow and his breathing to relax. He pushed away the pain, attempting to ignore the effects of the poison. Gritting his teeth he grabbed his sword, lifting himself to his feet.

Jonas, seeing Kiln so severely wounded, was filled with fury. He dug deep within himself and brought forth his God Light with a brilliance that he did not think possible. He shone like a star. The beast hissed, retreating slightly, giving Jonas a quick reprieve from the deadly and ferocious attacks of its spiked wings and claws.

Jonas attacked without hesitation, despite the sinking feeling that filled his mind knowing that Kiln had been grievously wounded. He fought with all the skill that he had been taught, ducking and pivoting as his two glowing blades spun a glowing weave of steel.

The demon hissed in anger as he felt the sting of the magical blades, and the blinding brilliance of Jonas's light. But the Greever had his own magic and he brought it forth with malice. Suddenly the area around Jonas was blanketed in darkness; a blackness so thick and dense that it extinguished his God Light. Jonas couldn't see anything, and he backed away with his swords spinning defensively in front of him, while the Greever could see as if the sun were shining brightly. The demon beat its wings once, and springing with its two powerful legs, it flew through the air above the deadly blades and landed on top of Jonas.

The impact of the demon sent Jonas flying onto his back, and the full weight of the beast crushed the air from his lungs. Jonas felt the bite of the demon's long talons trying to gouge holes through his magical armor and chain mail. Jonas struggled, but his arms were pinned by the demon's powerful legs.

The beast's claws ripped at the exposed flesh on his arms, his vital areas saved by the magical armor. The razor sharp claws tore through Jonas's clothes but could not find his flesh through the armor.

Jonas lay there, blinded by the darkness, his heart pounding with fear. Terror gripped him and he almost succumbed to it until he remembered Kiln's teachings and once again entered the state of Ty'erm.

The demon hissed with frustration when his front claws could not break through Jonas's rib cage, his armor shielding heart and lungs from the deadly talons.

"I'll just feed on your face first," spit the demon as its maw opened, moving toward Jonas's face in the darkness.

Jonas closed his eyes, concentrating on the demon on top of him. He could feel the familiar energy in all the air particles around the beast so he focused his mind on these particles, creating a mold of energy around the demon. Then he froze the particles. Suddenly the demon couldn't move its body, its deadly jaw only inches from Jonas's unprotected face.

"Feed on this!" yelled Jonas, directing a pulse of energy into the particles surrounding the demon. The demon flew backwards as if it were flung from a catapult, the sphere of darkness surrounding Jonas leaving with the beast.

The Greever reacted quickly, flinging its wings out wide and beating at the still night air. The demon hovered in the darkness forty paces above Jonas.

Jonas stood up slowly, his head aching from the tremendous amount of energy that he was forced to expend to hold the powerful demon. Jonas brought forth his God Light again. The bright light flared powerfully and lit up the area around him. Jonas saw movement to his right. Glancing over he could see Kiln's form stand shakily, his sword held before him.

Jonas was relieved that Kiln was not dead, but the relief soon vanished as he looked back up into the air just as the demon bore down at him from the darkness. Jonas brought up his blades once again fending off the attack with desperate defensive maneuvers.

The demon hovered several paces off the ground, its long leather wings beating powerfully, sending gusts of wind and dust into Jonas's eyes. The beast's claws lashed out again and again trying to bring down the expert swordsman.

Jonas fought with all his strength, relentlessly blocking the deadly claws and attacking with lighting quick jabs and ripostes, scoring numerous hits to the beast. But the Greever was a hunter of another world and its strength and power was nearly inexhaustible.

The Greever then changed tactics; it landed softly, and with one smooth motion sent both spiked wings and both sets of claws in for the kill.

Jonas reacted quickly, spinning his deadly blades in a deflecting barrage of steel, but he couldn't block both wings and claws. A powerful claw broke through his defenses and penetrated the gaps on his helmet, just missing his eyes. The razor sharp talons cut two shallow lacerations across his forehead. The pain was intense as evil magic penetrated the wounds, but Jonas, in the state of Ty'erm, was able to ignore the pain, and concentrate on the task at hand. Jumping back quickly he tried to focus on the demon, but his face stung and his eyes were filling with blood, making it almost impossible to see anything. Through a haze of blood Jonas caught the blur of a spiked tail before it crashed into his head.

Kiln screamed defiantly as he saw the beast's tail strike Jonas with tremendous force. Jonas's head snapped to the side violently and his horned helm flew into the air. The powerful tail had launched Jonas into the air, spinning him around like a top to land on his side.

Kiln ran forward without hesitation, his magical sword in his right hand as he quickly drew his long hunting knife from his scabbard with his left hand.

As the Greever's tail hit Jonas, the demon pivoted quickly, sensing and hearing the threat from behind. The puny human moved in faster than the demon thought possible. Kiln's razor sharp blades danced left and right and scored several hits on the Greever's arms as it tried to swat the deadly weapons away. The demon howled from the pain and shot both its spiked wings forward in attack.

Kiln saw the spikes approach with lightning speed, but Kiln was the warrior of legend and he was able to follow their trajectory as if they were in slow motion. Kiln turned his body sideways just at the last second and both spikes shot to either side of him. Kiln, reacting rather than thinking, dropped his knife and shot that empty hand forward towards a spike. In the slow motion state of Ty'erm, Kiln could see his left hand wrap around the dark gray spike. He was hoping that the demon would react instinctively when he threw its spikes out for an attack by pulling them back toward its body. He guessed right. The demon pulled its wing tips back just as fast as it had shot them forward. Kiln gripped tightly as the demon yanked the deadly swordsman right toward it.

The Greever saw the warrior's move but it was too late. The swordsman crashed into the demon's body, his glowing sword leading the way. Roaring in pain, the Greever felt the magic blade pierce its abdomen, erupting out the other side with tremendous force. Kiln dropped to the ground, trying to roll backwards out of harm's way, but the demon was too fast. The beast shot both clawed hands forward, grabbing Kiln by his shoulders. Kiln's struggles were futile against the powerful demon. He felt the monster's claws dig in deep as he was lifted into the air as if he weighed no more than a child. Kiln gritted his teeth against the pain as the demon brought him to eye level. The Greever's beady red eyes pulsed with hatred and its long yellow teeth dripped with saliva.

"You cannot kill me, human." The demon spit out the last word with hatred. The beast's claws continued to dig in deeper but Kiln didn't cry out.

"Maybe not, but I can cause you pain," he gasped as he reached out with his hand and twisted the sword that was still buried to the hilt in the demon's stomach. The demon roared in pain and Kiln could smell its hot fetid breath on his face.

Just then he felt a searing pain in his back. His head shot backwards as his back arched violently. He could feel his lungs start to fill with blood. He looked down, seeing the demon's tail underneath him. The beast must have snaked its tail between his legs as it held him in the air. The demon couldn't get a powerful swing from that position but it was enough to bury the spikes in his back deep enough to puncture his lungs. Kiln coughed, struggling to breath, spitting blood from his open mouth.

The demon threw Kiln aside like a piece of garbage. But Kiln was an experienced warrior and he learned long ago to never let go of his sword, no matter how grievously he was wounded. So Kiln held onto the hilt of his sword as he was thrown aside, yanking it from the demon's body. The Greever stumbled backwards as black blood poured from the horrible wound.

Jonas's head rang, throbbing with intense pain. He shook off the dizziness, struggling to get his feet underneath him. If it weren't for his magical helm he would be dead, the demon's tail would have crushed his skull like a ripe melon. He staggered to his feet, the fogginess in his head slowly clearing. His face was covered with blood and he still couldn't see. He closed his eyes and used his powers to locate the monster. He was an IshMian and could see the demon's energy within his mind, allowing him to see the glowing outline of the demon's form.

Jonas stumbled again trying to get his bearing. He could make out two forms fighting, one obviously the demon and the other must be Kiln. Jonas's spirits lifted as he saw his friend, but they soon plummeted again as he watched Kiln's desperate attack, and moments later his body flying through the air to land unmoving in the grass.

The beast was hurt, for Jonas could see the different shades of temperature on its body and its wounds were lit up with an orange glow. But the damage Kiln did wasn't enough to stop the monster. The demon swung around and turned its attention to its real target. With lightning speed, the demon's long bony body, outlined with blue energy, moved in like a glimmer of death.

Jonas couldn't move quickly enough and again felt sudden and immense pain as one of the beast's sharp wing spikes drove in deep into his upper hip, just above his thigh greaves. He screamed from the pain, yelling in his mind for Shyann's help.

Instantly Jonas's body flared with blue fire. Jonas didn't really know how the power came. It wasn't like he was praying. He just asked for help, or maybe that wasn't the correct way of explaining it. He willed the power forward, and it came. But this time it was different. It was a new form of magic. Burning flames erupted outward from his body like an explosion, striking the demon and scorching its flesh. It roared in pain and leaped back from the fire, ripping its long spike from the deep wound in Jonas's hip. Bright red blood gushed from the puncture wound and Jonas stumbled backwards, still blind from the blood that was pouring into his eyes. He didn't know where the fire had come from, and even though he figured the magical flames came from Shyann, he did not have time to ponder the question. Jonas used his cloak, frantically wiping his face so he could see. He was able to clear enough blood from his face to allow him to view, through a blur, the scene around him.

The Greever roared in pain as its thick skin turned black from the God Fire. The demon glared at the dangerous warrior, its lips curling up in a smile, exposing long dirty fangs. The warrior was stumbling on one leg, blood pouring from the gruesome wound on his hip. The pitiful human was frantically wiping the blood from his eyes trying to find the stalking hunter. The Greever, though badly wounded, knew that it had this one defeated. The beast licked its dripping teeth anticipating the taste of the warrior's blood.

Suddenly pain shot through the demon as arrows slammed into its back, into the joint connecting its left wing to its shoulder. The Greever spun towards the new attacker to see a brilliant light around eighty paces away coming at him like a shooting star. The demon crouched low, hissing in anger, and tried to flap its wings. The left one burned in pain and wouldn't react to its commands. The arrows must have been magical as no normal weapon could have harmed him so seriously.

As the light came closer the Greever saw that it was a female warrior on horseback illuminated with powerful God Light. The cavalier held a long bow drawn back tightly, a silver tipped arrow pointing at the monster.

"Time to die, demon," whispered the red haired warrior. She let the arrow fly, nocking another quickly. The arrow whistled through the air leaving a streak of blue magic in its wake. The sharp point slammed into the demon's muscled chest. The arrows, blessed by the gods, burned deeply into the demon's body, causing excruciating pain.

The Greever was getting weaker; the wounds from the deadly swordsman, the young cavalier, and now this female warrior, were taking their toll. The beast needed to destroy this new threat quickly. Using its powerful legs, the hunter from another world sprinted toward the horsed woman with astonishing speed.

The female cavalier sent another magical arrow into the chest of the charging demon. The shaft struck the demon in the upper shoulder, causing it to stumble slightly, but it didn't stop the ferocious charge. The Greever closed the gap quickly and the cavalier dropped her bow and drew forth her long sword.

Suddenly a form rose from the tall grass directly in front of the charging demon. It was the man that the beast thought it had killed. The beast could not stop its momentum, realizing too late that the man was still holding his glowing green sword. That was the last thing the beast felt as it barreled into the man.

Kiln held the sword in front of him like a lance and the demon hit him hard. The impact felt like a smith's hammer swung from a frost giant, the power of the charge driving the point of the magical blade through the demons thick chest, slicing through the protective bone plating that covered its heart, and burying the sword to the hilt, completely cleaving the beast's heart in two. Kiln and the demon somersaulted through the air, landing heavily in a tangle of claws and limbs.

Jonas could barely make out the events as he stumbled dizzily towards the light, leaving crimson stains on the tall grass behind him. He saw the demon charge a horsed warrior, but it was all a blur as the blood in his eyes still affected his vision. His head ached and his temples pounded like an army's war drums. The use of his cognivant powers had weakened him tremendously. The loss of blood caused his vision to blur even more, and his body felt too heavy to bear. Jonas finally succumbed to his wounds, falling face down in the bloody grass, his mind a whirlwind of visions and thoughts. He rolled over on his back and tried to stay conscious. The last thing he remembered before darkness overcame him was the vision of a lovely face framed in red hair leaning over him.

***

Jonas slowly opened his eyes struggling for consciousness. His vision swam and his head was clouded with pain. His eyes managed to focus on a flickering orange light which helped to bring him out of his sleep and into reality.

The light became a burning fire. Jonas was lying next to it and wrapped in his sleeping blanket. Sitting by the fire was a beautiful red haired woman who was gazing intently at him. He remembered seeing her briefly before he lost consciousness. She was wearing magnificent polished plate armor that reflected the dancing flames off its silver surface. A dark blue cloak was pulled tightly over her shoulders.

"How are you feeling?" she asked; her voice was soft and filled with concern.

"I feel weak and tired, and my head hurts."

"Understandable, you lost a lot of blood and you suffered severe injuries to your head. I'm glad I was able to heal you. I feared you would have died."

Everything came flooding back to Jonas in a rush of memories, and he bolted upright, frantically searching for Kiln.

The female warrior moved toward him and gently placed her hand on his chest. "It's okay, the demon is dead, and your friend is alive." She paused. "Barely."

Jonas looked around and saw Kiln lying on the ground, wrapped in blankets on the other side of the fire. "What happened and who are you?" asked Jonas, dizziness overtaking him and forcing him to lie back down.

"Your friend killed the demon as it charged me. I didn't see your friend until he rose up from the grass and lanced the demon through the heart.

The wound in his back should have killed him, and yet he stood up in front of a charging demon and killed it. The beast hit him hard, breaking both arms and several ribs. He was filled with poison and he lost a lot of blood. I don't know how he survived at all. He never should have been able to fight a demon that was that powerful. He was lucky his blade was enchanted and that he managed to pierce its heart. He must be very strong."

"It was not all luck, and yes, he is very strong. Will he make it?" Jonas asked hopefully.

"I don't know. I will need to link power with you to heal him correctly. I don't have the power alone to heal such serious wounds. I merely stopped the bleeding and eliminated the danger of the poison."

Jonas looked at the amber haired warrior intently. "How do you know I have power?"

"You're a cavalier," she said bluntly.

"I am no cavalier."

"What do you mean? I saw your God Light, and that mark on your chest is a God Mark, for no human could make something so beautiful. You must be a cavalier."

"What I mean is that I have had no formal training. I passed no tests and attended no school."

"What? How can that be?" she asked with surprise.

"It's a long story for another time. More importantly, what is your name and how did you happen upon us in our time of need? We owe you our gratitude. We would not be alive today if it were not for you."

The woman smiled warmly, immediately reminding Jonas of Allindrian. She had the same sharp features, minus the elven ears and almond shaped eyes, and her smile lit up her entire face. Jonas analyzed the woman as she stared at him from across the fire. Her long red hair was tied back at the top of her head by a leather cord, which kept it out of her eyes. Light freckles dotted her creamy complexion which accentuated her full red lips. Yet the line of her mouth and jaw created an image of strength as well as beauty.

"My name is Taleen. I'm a cavalier to Helikon."

"I am Jonas Kanrene. I thank you again for saving us. You're from the lands west of the Tundrens?" Jonas asked, remembering from his classes at Finarth that Helikon was what the people in the west called Bandris, god of war, honor, and courage.

"I am. I am from Osrigard along the Ronith River."

"I'm sorry, I've never heard of it. Where is that?"

"It is directly west of here, over the Tundrens, through the Tundren plains and across the Ronith grasslands. It took me eight weeks to get here."

"Why have you traveled so far?" Jonas asked. "You are a long way from home."

Taleen looked at him with interest. "For one who wields the power of a cavalier, you know very little about them."

"I told you, I was not trained to be a cavalier. The mark and powers just…sort of…appeared," Jonas added lamely.

"God magic does not just appear, young warrior, but that discussion can wait. Cavaliers travel to where their god directs them, and their god's bidding becomes apparent as they near their destination."

"You traveled eight weeks because your god directed you here?"

"Yes. Helikon needed me here…to help you, it would appear."

"You traveled that distance just to help me?"

"I did. Something is happening, Jonas, that you might not be aware of. That demon that your friend killed has been destroying cavaliers all throughout Kraawn."

"What! How many?"

"I'm not sure, but I don't think there are many left. Maybe none at all, except for you and me."

"But I'm not even a cavalier."

"I don't know how to explain that, Jonas, but Helikon brought me here to save you, of that I am certain. As you must be aware, there is a growing source of evil in the lands, an evil using great magic to destroy the cavaliers. I believe that the source of this evil is paving a path for invasion. A second Great War is upon us. And it's up to you and me to help win this war."

Jonas looked into her determined eyes. "I will not shy from that task, Taleen, but I need to go to Annure to get some answers."

Taleen stared at Jonas for a few seconds before looking into the flickering flames of the fire. The dancing fire bathed Taleen's features in an orange glow, and Jonas couldn't pull his gaze from her stunning face. She looked back into his eyes. "I agree. You need to get some answers. It may be that Annure will have them. I will travel with you. But for now, get some rest. I will watch over your friend until you regain your strength."

Jonas had forgotten how tired he was, and at the mere mention of the word *rest* his eyelids began to drop heavily. He wrapped the blanket firmly around himself and let his eyes close in exhaustion. "Thank you again, Taleen," Jonas muttered as his tired body shut down completely and he fell into a deep sleep.

"Thank Helikon, young cavalier who is not a cavalier," Taleen replied as she watched the young man fall asleep.

***

It took most of the day for the Finarthian army to mobilize, but the king insisted that they begin their march immediately, even if it would be dark in several hours. Fil had never seen anything like it. The entire city was a bustle of activity as the army packed up supply wagons and the officers prepared their modrigs.

It was hard to believe that Prince Moredin was actually marching an army towards them. The prince ruled a large lawless city called Stonestep which was located along the trade routes that snaked through the dangerous Sithgarin desert. Stonestep was no friend to Finarth, and it was commonly known that the lands there were used as a staging base for brigands and raiders to poke their thieving fingers into Annure and Finarth. But Prince Moredin had never openly raised a sword against Finarth, nor had he ever allied himself so obviously with tribes from the Sithgarin. Why would he do so now? What was causing this rash behavior? Everyone was asking the same questions as they prepared for war.

There were two ludus's in a modrig and two modrigs in an akron, an akron being a thousand men. Ludus's were further split into five pandars; each pandar was led by a lieutenant.

Finarth had roughly twenty akrons, not including the Finarthian Knights, which were considered a separate unit. Each modrig was led by a corporal and each akron was led by a third rank general. It was a hierarchy that seemed to run smoothly. Next in rank came the second rank generals that each controlled five akrons. Following that was the first rank general, or high commander, who was in charge of the entire Finarthian army, including the knights. The king, of course, commanded them all. Fil had never met the high commander, but he had learned from Tanus, the corporal of their modrig, that his name was Volnos and he was an aging veteran of many campaigns.

Fil marched in line next to Calden, his friend and fellow knight apprentice. There were no other apprentices in their modrig or even their akron. They had been spread out to different units. It was organized that way for a reason, forcing the young men to interact with different people and establishing relationships with soldiers from various backgrounds.

Each of the soldiers wore a hardened leather breastplate lined with circles of steel over a shirt of heavy chain mail. Their forearms, thighs and shins were protected by leather reinforced with steel plates. Each footman soldier was issued a short infantry sword, stabbing spear, and a steel shield, all designed for formation fighting.

Fil gripped his spear with anxiety, wondering if the rest of the men felt the way he did, eager, yet frightened at the same time. He scanned the men around him and saw no hesitation in them. They were mostly middle aged veterans who had fought and survived many battles, which was why his akron was a front line unit. Calden, marching next to him, gave a sidelong glance at Fil.

"I can't believe we're going to war," Calden muttered to Fil. "Are you nervous?"

"I am," replied Fil. "But this is what I want. I want to avenge my family."

"You think that Moredin's army is led by the same evil forces that destroyed your town?"

"I don't know, but Tanus told us that the king thinks this army is being backed by Banrith Castle. And if that is so, then they are somehow linked to the Banthra that attacked my village. I will get my revenge, Calden," Fil said fiercely. He gripped his spear so tightly that his thick knuckles turned white.

"I hope you do, my friend, and I will be right beside you."

Fil smiled at Calden, taking comfort in his friend's presence. Fil's mind wandered to Jonas, and wondered how he was faring. He missed him dearly, but he realized that their paths were now different, and that Jonas's calling would take him to different places. It saddened Fil that he might not see his friend again. What if he died in this battle? What if Jonas was already dead? It was a frightening thought, but certainly a possibility considering the enemies that were hunting him.

When Fil had heard that cavaliers were being killed all throughout Kraawn he immediately feared for his friend. He even went to Shyann's temple in town to get some guidance. The priests couldn't really help him. All they said was the normal religious rhetoric. That it would be Shyann's will whether he lived or died, that type of thing. Fil couldn't understand that belief system and that was why he had such little faith in the gods. Was it just a game to them? What right did they have to decide someone's fate? Who were they to decide who lived and died? And did they really have that power anyway? Fil did not deny their existence, just whether or not the gods lived up to most people's expectations. Fil didn't think so. He often wondered whether or not they deserved his allegiance at all.

The sound of a galloping horse brought Fil out of his thoughts. He looked over his shoulder and saw a heavy warhorse gallop by. The dust from the road billowed around them as the warrior quickly rode down the column.

It was Tanus. Fil recognized his blue billowing cape and his unique silver helm. Fil had learned that years ago Tanus had taken a small group of warriors to a tiny farming settlement on the outskirts of their lands, almost to the edge of the Tundrens. The village had been raided by a small pack of boargs and the leader of Tanus's akron had sent him there when he was a young officer. The story went that his entire pandar, which was fifty men, had been slain, except for him, and that he had killed the last of the boargs by himself, his men dead around him. Men tell the tale as if he had been surrounded by snarling boargs, and in berserker frenzy, Tanus had killed them all. No one really knew for sure what happened as he never spoke about it.

Tanus then cut the horns from the pack leader and had the king's blacksmith fashion a helm from them so he would never forget the men that died. The helm was crafted from bright silver steel and etched upon it were beautiful, intricate patterns. The great curved horns gave him a menacing look and when he flipped down his visor, all you could see was the dark slits for his eyes and two massive horns curving outward. It was said that it had cost him a season's wages to have it crafted and when Fil looked upon it he could believe it. It was truly an amazing piece of armor, more fit for royalty than a common soldier.

Fil shuddered every time he saw Tanus's helm. The horns created a flood of memories that he would just as soon forget. But Tanus was an honorable man, and a great warrior, and Fil was happy to be serving under him.

***

Jonas awoke the next morning feeling refreshed and rejuvenated. He stood up, and looked around the camp. Kiln was still wrapped in blankets and unconscious. Jonas inspected his own wounds quickly and was surprised to feel only slight scarring on his face and arms where the demon had clawed him. The painful wounds were almost totally healed. The only reminders left of the horrible battle were the lines of pink tissue where the wounds had been closed. He lifted up his tunic and saw a similar mark on his hip. There was a round spot above his pelvic bone that was pink and tender to the touch, but other than that he felt fine.

Jonas looked around for his armor and weapons. He found them lying on the ground near the smoldering fire. Lifting up the chest plate he inspected the damage. He frowned with curiosity at what he saw. The silver chest plate was glistening as if it had been recently oiled. The silver embossed symbol of Shyann sparkled in the morning sun, and there was not a mark on it. Jonas then picked up his helm to see what damage the demon's tail had done to it. It was perfect, no dents or scratches, and it shone with brilliance.

"How can this be?" Jonas whispered to himself.

"And you say you're not a cavalier," came a soft voice behind him. Jonas turned around to see Taleen ride up on a magnificent horse. He hadn't even heard the animal as it trotted through the tall grass. The large animal's chestnut coat glistened in the sun, accentuating its powerful muscular body.

It reminded Jonas of Airos's steed. The horse wore plated steel on its chest and sparkling chain mail draped its massive sides. A black leather saddle shone as if it were just crafted and brought from the tanners shop.

Taleen was just as beautiful. She wore fitted black breeches and laced up riding boots. Her shins and thighs were covered with bands of silver steel, each of which was carved with intricate runes. A thick sword belt of black leather circled her thin waist and a silver cuirass covered her chest. The center of her cuirass had a carved symbol of Helikon, a double bladed battle axe.

Intricate runes and symbols wrapped around her molded chest plate, forming perfectly to her feminine but strong body. Her muscular arms were bare except for black and silver wrist guards. A sturdy long bow was tucked in its sheath that hung from the side of the horse. Everything about the pair was perfect. They both glistened and sparkled as if they had recently been groomed by some invisible servant.

"I don't understand," Jonas said, taken back by their magnificent appearance, trying not to stare at Taleen's beauty.

"A cavalier's armor, steed, and gear are always clean and polished. No matter how much damage my equipment takes, I wake up in the morning to find it perfect and clean. Look at yourself, Jonas."

Jonas looked down at himself, his eyes growing wide as he noticed his own clothing and armor in the same pristine condition. His breeches and tunic were perfectly clean, with no blood or rips anywhere. His chain mail shirt sparkled and his boots were free of any dirt from their hard travels.

"But this has never happened before," he said in amazement.

"It's not my place to know why, but it seems you are gradually being given the powers of a cavalier. That much is clear," Taleen stated.

"I have come to understand that. The problem is I've never had the opportunity to talk to another cavalier, so I don't know what powers I may have, or may gain."

"Now you do," she smiled. "But first, let us see to your friend."

Taleen dismounted and strode through the tall grass to Kiln. Jonas couldn't help but follow her swaying hips as she walked. He briefly felt ashamed at himself that he was looking at her in that way while his friend was lying unconscious nearby. He quickly moved by her as she knelt next to Kiln.

"How is he?" Jonas asked.

"He'll be fine. He should have died but he is a strong one. I need your help, Jonas, if we are going to heal him enough to travel anytime soon. I don't have the power to heal wounds as serious as he sustained. Do you feel up to it?"

"I've only healed one person before and I don't really know how I did it, but yes, I will do whatever needs to be done to help Kiln."

Taleen's expression changed briefly at the mention of Kiln's name. "Did you say his name is Kiln?"

"I did. Do you know him?"

"Kiln from Finarth?" Taleen asked, a hint of wonder in her voice.

"Yes, the same. Do you know him?" Jonas asked again, a little confused at her reaction.

"Only of him. He is a legend even in the West. He was once a great general who fell from grace, as the story goes."

"He still is a great general, and he did not fall from grace," Jonas replied with a little more edge to his voice than he wanted.

"Relax, Jonas. I meant no insult. I am only repeating what I've heard."

"I know, I'm sorry. It's just that he's been such a great friend to me over the last few years. He is good man."

"And a strong one, no doubt. It is said that he cannot be beaten with a blade. No wonder he was able to hold his own against that demon."

"Now that is one rumor that is true. He is incredible to watch." Jonas smiled as he thought of his friend and all the combat training they had done.

"Well, let us restore him to his talents. All you need do is hold my hand and call upon Shyann as you did when you last used her healing power. The power will be there, you just need to bring it forth. I want you to channel her energy into me and I will take care of the rest. Don't stop the flow of magic until I release your hand. Do you understand?"

"I do," replied Jonas.

Taleen smiled, reaching out for his hand. Her touch sent a tingle down his spine. Her hands were calloused but warm, and the way her thumb lay on his thigh made Jonas's face flush. *Concentrate on healing, you idiot,* Jonas told himself.

It took him a moment but he was finally able to concentrate on the task. He fervently prayed to Shyann, asking her for her help in healing Kiln. Instantly he felt the familiar heat within him. The magical energy surged through his body and rushed into Taleen's hand.

He felt her body jolt as her hand gripped his harder. Jonas just fell within himself and let the power fold into her. He didn't know how long he was praying but suddenly Taleen let go and the connection was broken. Shyann's power receded within him and Jonas slowly opened his eyes.

Taleen was staring at him wide eyed.

"What is it?" he asked with concern.

"I have never felt that kind of power. I thought your energy would consume me."

"I'm sorry. I didn't know. I thought that the more I gave you the faster Kiln would be healed."

"Theoretically true, but the wielder of the power has to be able to control the energy. I barely had the strength to wield your power, Jonas."

"I'm sorry, Taleen. I truly didn't know."

"I know. I should have explained a few things to you before we tried that."

"Can you teach me how to control my power?" Jonas asked.

"I don't know, but I think we need to at least discuss it, so you have a better understanding of the powers gifted to cavaliers."

"I would like that."

"Are you going to just sit there and talk with the beautiful lady, or help me up," mumbled Kiln.

They both looked at Kiln with astonishment.

"That was fast. Here, let me help you," Jonas said as he helped Kiln to his feet. Kiln stood up slowly, arching his back to work out the kinks, and stretched his arms and legs to loosen them up. His body was sore and his mended wounds ached, but he felt great considering.

"I feel as if my insides are burning, but it's a pleasant feeling, a feeling of warmth and energy," Kiln muttered in disbelief as he inspected the wounds. There were only small pink scars to remind him of the horrible injuries that almost killed him. "How can this be?"

"Taleen and I healed you," replied Jonas. Kiln looked at him and then looked at Taleen, his hard features suddenly broken by a gentle smile.

"I am Kiln. We are deeply indebted to you. You're a cavalier to Helikon?"

"I am. How did you know I'm from the west?"

"We call Helikon, Bandris, but the western symbol for Bandris is different, longer in the blades with different markings. I recognize that symbol on your cuirass."

"You are very observant."

Kiln continued to look at Taleen and Jonas felt a twinge of jealousy. "I take it that it was you who came to our aid last night?"

"It was."

"Again, we are in your debt," Kiln said for a second time.

"No, you are in Helikon's debt. He sent me here to find this young man."

"I see." Kiln looked at Jonas with concern. "How did you fare, Jonas? I don't remember much after that demon lanced me in the back with its spiked tail."

"I was hard pressed. I fought it with God Light and my blades, but the beast had magic of its own and countered mine. He injured me badly before Shyann came to my aid again and helped me burn it badly with flame."

"It's called God Fire. Not all cavaliers have such a gift. Most are not strong enough to wield that power," interjected Taleen.

"I sent God Fire into the demon and that forced the beast back. It was just about to attack me again when Taleen came to our aid. The demon then charged her."

"And that is when I lanced it with my sword, a second time," added Kiln remembering.

"You stabbed it twice? I couldn't see with all the blood in my eyes but I knew you were battling it. How did you counter the demon's spell?" Jonas asked.

"I don't know. I broke the demons trance just before its spiked tail slammed into my side. I was able to get my blade up to deflect most of the power, but it still cut me, and the pain was severe, far more than it should have been for those wounds."

"It was poison. You never should have been able to counter the spell or fight off the poison. Your spirit is very strong, Kiln, only a cavalier or powerful priest would have been able to counter that demon's power. However, charms and spells of the mind can sometimes be countered by mentally strong and disciplined warriors, which I assume is why you were able to do so." Taleen spoke with obvious respect in her voice.

Kiln, uncomfortable with the praise, looked away, stretching his tired limbs some more. "Jonas, I'm sorry that I couldn't finish the beast," he said regretfully, lifting both hands towards the sky to loosen his sore muscles.

"It was not your fault, general, anyone, including a cavalier, would have a slim chance against that beast by themselves," Taleen commented as she went to gather her backpack.

"You know who I am?"

"I do. I recognized your name."

"Really? My name is known in the west?" Kiln asked.

"Your name is known to all warriors, sir."

"My name or my disgrace?" Kiln retorted bitterly.

"A little of both I'm afraid," replied the cavalier as she dug out some provisions from her pack.

"I see." Kiln stared at Taleen for a moment with his cold gray eyes, but she held his stare, her bright blue eyes showing no hint of judgment. Kiln's face softened as he picked up his pack. "We can talk more later. I see you're hungry as well. Let us eat breakfast."

Taleen simply nodded in affirmation.

"Yes, I am starving," added Jonas as he went to his pack.

They ate a warm breakfast of boiled oats mixed with honey that Taleen had brought with her. They used a sweet brown bread to clean the wooden bowls. Jonas was famished after expending so much energy and the food did wonders for his tired and sore body. They finished off the meal with cups of boiling water that Taleen had mixed with several herbs. It tasted very similar to the drink that Jonas's mother used to make him in the morning, and that thought made him smile as he sipped his tea.

The trio was quiet as they ate; the only sounds came from the chirping birds that flew back and forth over the grasslands, eating their morning breakfast of bugs.

Finally Kiln broke the silence. "Since you are a cavalier, I assume that Helikon sent you here for a reason."

Taleen took a slow sip of the warm brew before answering. "He did, but I do not know the exact reason. I can assume it was to help Jonas against the demon, but I cannot know for sure."

"What does Helikon ask of you now?" Kiln asked.

"I'm not sure. A cavalier's travels are not always clear. Our gods give us information when they think we need it. I will travel with Jonas to Annure until I am called elsewhere."

"Do you talk with your god?" Jonas asked.

"No, cavalier's do not actually converse with their gods. Usually messages or intent is sent through their steeds or passed to the cavalier with mental pictures, like waking dreams, some of which can be unclear at times," Taleen explained. "I do not even think that priests or clerics actually converse with their gods."

"I have met Shyann," Jonas said.

Taleen paused for a moment and looked at the young warrior. "You mean you have seen her, talked with her in person?" she asked skeptically.

"Yes, well not exactly. I have spoken to her in my dreams. But it is real, as if she were standing right in front of me. It is like a waking dream," Jonas said, trying to explain the few times he had spoken with Shyann while he was asleep.

Taleen looked into the fire for a few moments before speaking. "That is something, Jonas. I will admit that I envy your personal connection with Shyann. I have never heard of that happening before. I would very much like the opportunity to speak with Helikon, as you have with Shyann."

"The games gods play," Kiln muttered.

"Indeed, at times it seems so. The truth be told we know very little of the gods we worship. All I know is that there is good and evil in the world, and if Helikon fights against that evil, then he is worthy of worship," Taleen said.

"Why ask to be worshipped to begin with?" Kiln asked no one in particular. "Isn't that a sign of arrogance? It seems that even the good gods want power, which to me is the root of greed, the very foundation of despots and evil. Is the line between the benevolent gods and evil ones so defined, or is it sometimes blurred? I often wonder if the world would be a better place if no one believed in either."

No one spoke for a while as they digested the warrior's words. Finally Taleen spoke up.

"Whether people believe or not has no bearing on whether the gods exist. They either do or they do not. We get our power from somewhere, be it gods or something else, and as long as I believe, and feel, that my power is being used to make the world better, then I will continue to believe in something. Your disbelief, or repudiation, whatever you will call it, does not confirm or deny their existence," Taleen argued.

"I disagree. If no one believed, or worshipped the gods, they would have no power over us; therefore their very presence in our world would slowly disappear. Do you think that the people before us believed in the same gods as we do now?" Kiln asked.

"I do not know, no one knows," Taleen said.

"Exactly. One thing is certain though. Our presence is but a blink in the life of our world. Therefore it is highly probable that the people before, and after us, have had, and will have, other beliefs. They will believe in other gods, in other religions, and they will be no more right or wrong than you and your beliefs. To me, these contradictions confirm that to worship gods is to believe in something that is just an idea, an emotion, and nothing more. I think the elves have it right, that there are no gods, that the magic of the universe comes from the Ru'Ach and these so called *gods* are just beings of great power that somehow have found a direct connection to this energy," Kiln said.

"Love is an emotion," Jonas said, deep in thought. "It seems to me that some ideas are worth living for, and fighting for."

Kiln looked at Jonas but said nothing, clearly thinking about the simplicity of his words.

"Always a difficult conversation," Taleen said. "I suggest we move on to more pressing matters."

"Agreed," Kiln confirmed.

"Taleen," Jonas said. "Can you help me understand the powers of a cavalier? I have never had the chance to actually talk to a cavalier in depth. I do not know the full extent of my powers and I think it would aid me greatly to know what I am capable of doing."

"Yes, I can, and I agree. If you've never been formally trained then you need to learn some basic knowledge about cavaliers." Taleen took another sip of her hot drink before continuing. "A cavalier has several basic powers. They can dispel fear and evil, they can dispel magic, and they can bring forth God Light which, in itself, has several powers. God Light can dispel magic and fear and bring pain to creatures of darkness. This same light can also create an aura of confidence to bring hope to those who have none. Some can even use their voice as a tool of power, quieting crowds, bringing hope and strength to those who hear them. That is a rare skill typically only granted to first rank cavaliers.

"I heard Airos use that power at a town meeting. It was impressive. Everyone was transfixed to his every word as if he were a god," added Jonas.

"Airos was a first rank cavalier, which would explain that power," interjected Kiln.

"It is unfortunate that he was killed. His death was a huge blow to our cause." Taleen paused to take another sip of her brew. "A cavalier also has powers of endurance, allowing them to fight for many hours without tiring or eating. They can heal the wounded and sick. The most powerful tool that a cavalier can wield is God Fire. God Fire can be used in several ways but only the strongest of cavaliers can wield this power. This power is reserved to first rank cavaliers only. That is why I was so surprised to hear you say you used fire against the demon. It is unclear to me how you could do so when you've never been trained. The number of first rank cavaliers that exist is small, and I don't even know how many of them have been killed."

"Killed? What do you mean?" asked Kiln. Jonas had forgotten that Kiln was unconscious when Taleen had told him that cavaliers were being murdered throughout Kraawn.

"The last two years have seen many of our cavaliers destroyed. Hunted down by a demon, or demons, we're not sure. It is very likely that the same demon that attacked you here was doing this killing. It is possible that there are no more first rank cavaliers, except for Jonas."

"How can I be the highest ranking cavalier when I've never been trained?"

"And why do the gods not give all cavaliers these powers?" Kiln added.

"Our land is being attacked," Taleen said sadly. "Perhaps the gods reasoned that there is no time to train you. Maybe you are needed now and your strength and constitution is enough. Not all of us have the constitution, the physical and mental capabilities of using and sustaining some powers. I would imagine that if Helikon granted me the power of God Fire that the first time I used it I would be burned to a crisp. Jonas, there is something inside of you that gives you strength. That *something* allows you to wield power that I cannot. Hopefully Annure can help answer some of these questions."

"So this demon that we fought last night has been killing other cavaliers," Kiln muttered to himself.

"The beast told me last night that it had been killing my brethren. There can be no doubt that the demon was referring to cavaliers," added Jonas.

"This is grave news," said Kiln.

"It is. Cavaliers have been our shield against evil for thousands of years. Without them, we are vulnerable. I do not know how many are left besides Jonas and me. I hope that Annure will have that information," Taleen said hopefully.

"What is the training like at Annure?" asked Jonas.

"I did not train there. I trained at Rohindrin on the coast of Algard, but the training should be the same. The first step for a potential candidate is the purity test. This test is done by the high priests that represent your god or goddess. I do not know exactly what they do at Annure, but at Rohindrin you sit in the center of an altar room while six high priests circle you. They pray and ask their god or goddess for their blessing in accepting you into the training. If you are deemed pure of heart and soul, then you will be admitted. Very few people pass this test. There are many people that try to become cavaliers for the wrong reasons. Your thoughts and desires cannot be hidden from the gods. After you pass that test then you are trained in weapons, combat, and many other advanced skills."

"Like what?" Jonas asked with interest.

"Like horsemanship, movement of armies, sieging of a city, politics, royal etiquette, languages, history, reading and writing, and so on."

"That must take a long time."

"The first part of a cavalier's training takes five years. Once that is completed then they move on to the tests of strength."

"Physical strength?" interrupted Jonas.

"No, strength of body and mind together. The amount of magic that a cavalier can control is directly related to their constitution. It is not totally understood, but there are some people who can withstand more than others. They need to determine the strength of each candidate. This is what determines the ranking. There are first, second, and third rank cavaliers. Third rank cavaliers have the power of God Light and dispelling evil. Second rank cavaliers, like myself, can bring forth God Light, heal, and dispel evil, while first rank cavaliers have all of those powers plus they can wield God Fire. God Fire can be used in many different ways, and the strength of the user will determine what they can do. Each cavalier, even within their ranking, has certain ranges of power. Some are more powerful in certain areas than others, but always a cavalier is trained in combat. If they pass the tests then they will be marked as an expert swordsman, their God Mark covering their hands." Taleen glanced down at Kiln's hands and her eyes twinkled with interest.

Kiln did not miss the brief look. "You expected a mark?"

"I did. I had heard you were the best."

"I think such marks are signs of vanity. Besides, why warn an enemy of your skills," Kiln replied.

"In most cases I would agree with you. But the cavalier's mark is not a mark of vanity. The God Mark is designed to uplift men and women and ensure their confidence in the cavalier. The mark is a deterrent for evil and violence, a warning so to speak.

"I do not see a mark on your hands, Taleen," Jonas said curiously.

"I could not pass the master swordsman tests. I am good, but not that good. My skill is with the bow," replied Taleen with no hint of arrogance. "Anyway, if the candidate has passed the tests of combat and magic then they must be put on trial."

"Trial? What do you mean?" asked Jonas.

"The cavalier candidate must prove their faith by passing several tests. The first one is a test of pain. If a candidate makes it this far, there is high probability that he or she will fail here. The candidate is tortured by high priests of their faith."

"What! Tortured, by their priests?" This time it was Kiln who responded with disbelief.

"Yes. To ensure the faith of the candidate, they are tortured for five days. Their bodies are cut, burned, and broken, with the idea that at the end of the fifth day their god or goddess will heal them. The Forsworn are constantly hunting and looking for ways to corrupt or destroy cavaliers. If a cavalier is captured, the tortures that they would endure at the hands of that evil would be incomprehensible. This test will help prepare them for the possibility of that happening. If they keep faith through that intense ordeal then they will pass the test. If not, then they will be healed and released from training, never to be a cavalier."

"And you went through that?" Jonas asked in amazement.

"I did. The hardest thing I've ever done."

Jonas and Kiln both looked at Taleen with newfound respect.

"The next trial is called the Balnock, or dream test. The candidates are put into a trance by their priests. In this trance they are assaulted by various demons and monsters and the candidates must use their powers to defeat them."

"Are the demons real?" asked Jonas.

"No, but they seem real. In that state everything feels real, including pain. If you die or retreat, you fail that test and are released from training forever."

"How long does it take a candidate to pass all the tests and become a cavalier?" Kiln asked.

"It takes around six years. As you can imagine, very few make it through all these tests. Candidates must prove themselves in purity, combat, and faith, which very few can do. If we lose all our cavaliers, then it will take too long to train more. We cannot die, Jonas."

"I don't plan to," Jonas said seriously. "What about a cavalier's steed? I had heard that they are granted a steed from their god."

"After the cavalier passes all the tests and they are officially recognized as a cavalier, they will usually get their steed, armor, and weapons, but these gifts are given by their god and there is no set rule as to when this happens. I can see that you have already received your armor and weapons. The steed may come at any time. Kormac, my horse, came to me the night before my first mission."

"And they have powers as well?"

"Oh yes, the cavalier's steed has powers of strength and endurance. They can run continuously without tiring. They can fight and sense evil as you do. They, too, are always perfectly groomed, their armor and coat glistening like it was recently polished and brushed. It is believed that a cavalier should instill strength and courage in others and to do this they must look the part."

"We will travel to Annure to get some answers. At that point I may leave you and head to Finarth. I have some unfinished business there," said Kiln.

"I would like to accompany you to Finarth," replied Jonas hopefully.

"We'll see, my friend. You may have a different calling. The council at Annure may have other plans for you."

"But I swore allegiance to King Gavinsteal."

"That may be, but your calling as a cavalier supersedes any prior oath to a king."

"He is right, Jonas," Taleen interjected. "Cavaliers have no allegiance to any one king or land. Their allegiance is to their gods and to all the people of Kraawn. King Gavinsteal knows this and would not hold you to your oath."

"I see," replied Jonas, saddened at the thought that he might not be able to see Fil anytime soon. He had missed his friend over the years and hoped that he fared well.

Kiln suddenly stood up, buckling on his sword belt. "Well, I think it's time we are on our way."

"I agree," added Taleen as she also stood. "To Annure, and answers."

***

Alerion prepared for the summons with infinite care. The demon he was calling was a pit fiend named Ixtofin, and even though Alerion knew the beast's real name, he must prepare the spell precisely or risk being torn to pieces by this powerful denizen from another plane.

Alerion was a powerful wizard whose real skill was in conjuring. He was not a battle wizard, and although he did have some offensive spells, his skill was in finding and retrieving information. One of the best, though most dangerous, ways of doing that was to conjure beasts from other planes of existence, beasts that were made of magic that could get information in ways that Alerion could not.

Alerion's chamber was spacious and lined with book shelves filled with old leather bound tomes. Large thick tables of oak lay about randomly, all littered with various beakers, parchments, books, dried herbs, and other items for magical use. To an observer the room would have looked unkempt, but Alerion knew the exact whereabouts of every herb, parchment, and magical component.

The center of the room was empty and that is where Alerion knelt, drawing a four-pointed star with a circle around it. Alerion was not a follower of any one god, but Ulren's symbol was one of the strongest symbols to use for conjuring. Using a stick of lime to draw the symbol exactly, he made sure that there were no gaps in the lines.

He got up and locked the large oak door, placing the heavy beam down in the locked position so no one would accidentally enter while he was summoning the pit fiend. It could be disastrous if that happened. They could spoil his concentration. Or worse, Ixtofin could use his powers to assault the mind of someone mentally weaker or unprepared, and possess their body temporarily, just long enough to destroy the symbol which acted as the demon's prison on this plane. A demon cannot leave the interior of the symbol, which was why it was so important that the symbol be drawn perfectly with no gaps.

When the door was locked, Alerion lit four candles made of red dragon fat, a substance so rare and expensive that very few wizards had the means to acquire it unless they were court wizards to a rich king, as was Alerion.

Alerion was kneeling five paces from the symbol as he opened his most prized possession, his book of spells. He had used the spell before, but Alerion did not get to where he was by being careless and impatient. The words must be recited exactly or he would not be able to access the magic of the Ru'Ach and summon the demon. The ancient words he guarded with care and magical wards because if they got into the wrong hands the power of the book could be used for evil, which Alerion would not allow. The wards, spells used to protect the book, were designed to incinerate it if anyone but him opened it. It would be devastating to lose the book, but it would be far worse knowing that his life's work was being used for dark deeds.

Alerion took a deep breath and began to recite the words slowly and exactly. Words of magic were much more difficult to use than people suspected. Not only did they have to be read correctly, but the inflection and tone must also be perfect for the Ru'Ach to be tapped. His words rolled off his tongue smoothly and perfectly. His voice gained in tempo and power as he read the ancient words from the heavy book.

Slowly a mist began to form at the center of the symbol. The swirling smoke-like mist drifted upwards, meandering back and forth in a cylindrical shape.

Alerion did not look up or falter from recitation of the spell; it could mean certain death. The pit fiend would rip him to pieces and he would stand little chance in stopping the demon. He might also permanently transport the pit fiend to their own plane. Alerion could not let that happen. He continued reading from the book, his voice now booming with power in the large stone room.

Suddenly all the braziers in the room flared and were suddenly extinguished, leaving only the four candles in each corner of the symbol shedding any light. The air felt heavy and dark and Alerion knew that Ixtofin was entering their realm.

After reciting the last word of power, Alerion looked up at the drifting smoke. He heard a deep rumbling, like the slow growl of a huge dragon, and the mist began to change and take on the shape of a figure. Alerion could just make out the form of two large bat-like wings slowly opening and expanding to reveal the upper body of a giant muscled torso. The mist slowly materialized into the upper body of the pit fiend, while its lower body was a tendril of smoke that was connected to the center of the symbol.

Ixtofin's body was colossal, with heavily muscled arms extended wide as if it were stretching. The demon's clawed hands opened and closed, the massive muscles on its forearms rippling and flexing with each movement. The demon raised its head slowly, exposing two black horns curving upwards. Its mouth opened revealing black fangs as long as fingers. Red eyes, glowing with fury, were set deeply in the demon's thick bald head. Tendrils of smoke drifted from the demon's red scaly skin as if it were burning from an immense internal heat.

Alerion felt his resolve flutter as Ixtofin's eyes flared with malice, centering on him with obvious hatred. The demon's voice was gravelly and deep, shaking the very floor. "What do you want, human?" spat the demon.

Alerion knew that the demon would tear him to pieces if it could, but as long as his magical barrier held, and he was strong enough to manage the magic, the demon would have to answer his questions.

"Ixtofin!" Alerion bellowed. "I need information." Alerion purposely used the demon's real name. Knowing the beast's magical name gave Alerion some control over the demon and it reminded the pit fiend that he was in control.

The demon growled at the use of his name, the noise causing Alerion's eardrums to vibrate. "You have two questions."

"Three, you will answer three questions," ordered Alerion with confidence.

The demon roared, shooting its giant hands toward Alerion. Alerion did not move or flinch, concentrating on the task at hand. Sweat dripped from his forehead as he focused his mind on the magic around the barrier. Ixtofin hit the magical barrier and was repelled back toward the center of the symbol.

"You know you cannot break through my defenses, Ixtofin."

"You will make a mistake, wizard, and when you do I will be there to rip your arms and legs from that pitiful shell you call a body. Now ask your three questions so I can leave this place," rumbled the angry demon.

Alerion had thought about his questions carefully. He had prepared for this extensively but there was no telling how the demon would react to his wording or how much the beast would answer. It was all a risk and nothing ever went as planned when you dealt with creatures and beasts from other planes of existence. "Has Malbeck the Dark One returned to Kraawn?"

"Yes and no," replied the demon.

"Explain," ordered Alerion.

"I answered the question, now proceed to question two." The Pit Fiend spoke slowly, its deep and powerful voice reverberating off the stone walls around them.

"You did not answer the question," replied Alerion. "And if you don't finish the answer then I will give your true name to every powerful wizard in Kraawn and you will spend the next thousand years being summoned by wizards for their own petty desires. Now answer the question!" ordered the wizard, his powerful voice echoing in the chamber.

The demon's beady eyes narrowed in anger and it looked as if it were about to attack again, but the fiery demon just flapped its wings in frustration and spoke with a thunderous voice. "When Malbeck was destroyed a thousand years ago only his physical body died. Weapons of steel could not permanently destroy Malbeck's evil essence, which drifted through the Ru'Ach in limbo, between planes of existence until a powerful follower of his found a way to bring him back. So yes, he is back, but he is not the same as he was. His time within the Ru'Ach changed him, making him more powerful."

Ixtofin stopped talking abruptly, staring at Alerion with open hatred. Suddenly Alerion's mind flared with pain as the demon tried to assault him mentally. Alerion instantly brought up a barrier to ward off the attack and the pain in his head abated. He should have been more prepared for the demon's attack. The beast always tested Alerion, trying to find a hole in his defenses, but Alerion was busy trying to process the new information and his mind had wandered. *It would not happen again* he thought.

"How did they bring him back?" Alerion asked, using up question two.

Ixtofin eyed him menacingly for several seconds before answering. "They found the Shan Cemar."

The words hit Alerion like a hammer. "What!" Alerion yelled, momentarily losing control. "That cannot be," he continued, quickly refocusing his attention on the demon. "The Shan Cemar has been hidden for thousands of years. Even the elves do not know its hiding place."

"Not anymore," the pit fiend hissed, taking pleasure in Alerion's distress. "The Shan Cemar was found. The followers of the Dark One have been looking for it for a thousand years and their resolve has paid off."

Alerion couldn't believe what he was hearing. The Shan Cemar was a book that held words of power written in the ancient elven tongue, the true language of magic. The book had been hidden thousands of years ago by the ancient elves and most people just thought of it as a legend, a tale told in taverns by traveling bards.

But Alerion knew that the Shan Cemar was real and that many adventurers and powerful wizards had been trying to find its location for many life times. He simply couldn't believe it had been found. The power in the Shan Cemar was beyond Alerion's imagination, and he knew that if Malbeck had the book in his possession then the good people of Kraawn were in serious danger.

"How do we kill the Dark One?" asked Alerion whose head was spinning with fear and unanswered questions.

The demon hissed as smoke and fire flared from his nose and mouth. "You must find the IshMian that has the blood of Finarth pulsing through his veins."

The response was brief and to the point, which startled Alerion. Alerion wanted to ask the demon more but he knew that if he broke the rules that his magic would weaken, giving Ixtofin the chance to break through his defenses.

"You are released to return to your burning planes. Now be gone with you, Ixtofin." Alerion read the last few lines of the spell and the pit fiend's form began to dissolve slowly into mist again.

The last thing that Alerion heard was the rumbling laughter as the swirling mist disappeared into the floor. Immediately the braziers lit and flared to life again, shedding the flames orange light throughout the room. Alerion stood, closing his book.

"An IshMian," he repeated out loud as he set his book down and strode out the door.

Nine
Annure

Jonas had thought that Finarth was a wondrous city, but he was dumfounded when he looked up at the gates of Annure. The city walls were shining white and shot up towards the clouds like a god's palace. There were no shacks or small homes speckling the land before the city. Spacious green grasslands, uncluttered by habitation, flowed right to the base of Lake Lar'nam where the city sat nestled into the water's edge. At least ten round towers rose to the clouds, with the flag of Annure jutting from each one, all flapping in unison as the gentle breeze blew in off the expansive waters.

Kiln explained to them that Annure was a major port city and because of that they were able to charge high tariffs on goods imported into their lands. Lake Lar'nam was immense, like a fresh water ocean. It took weeks to sail across it, and many large trading ships went down in the turbulent winter storms.

Annure was a rich kingdom which brought many travelers throughout its lands every year. To live in Annure was costly, but the wages were higher than its neighboring towns. Good jobs were hard to find but if you managed to find work then you could live a good life in Annure. There was a high demand for dock workers, and since the pay was good, competition was steep.

Taleen had left her horse several miles from the city where it could graze in the grasslands. She explained to Jonas that a cavalier's steed did not need to be stabled, that her steed would be there when she returned, refreshed and eager to travel.

"Will Kormac be okay out here by himself?" Jonas asked when Taleen left her animal standing in the middle of the field.

"He will. He can take care of himself."

"But he's not even tethered," Jonas said, a little unsure about whether the horse would still be there when they returned.

"A cavalier's steed does not need to be tethered, Jonas. Kormac will be here when I return." Taleen smiled, seeing his expression of doubt. "Come, Jonas, let us see this Annure."

As they neared the huge black gate Jonas stared up at the towering round buildings that seemed to poke holes in the clouds. The colossal gate was covered with sheets of black iron, in stark contrast to the white walls surrounding it. Jonas had never seen anything constructed in such size and strength.

"It would take a dragon to break through that gate," Jonas said, awestruck by the sight.

"Indeed it would," replied Kiln who was also staring in admiration at the seemingly indestructible wall.

There was a small caravan of six carts entering the gate before them. The caravan was flanked by guards, several on horseback. They all easily managed to fit through the expansive entrance. It looked like a merchant's caravan and that thought momentarily brought Jonas's mind to Allindrian and Landon. What were they both doing? Would he see them again?

Jonas was deep in thought as they entered the open gate. Two guards wearing the green of Annure stood on each side of the entrance. The Annurian royal crest, a ship sailing with the sun setting behind it, was embroidered in gold on the front of each tunic. Jonas was amazed at the intricate embroidery of the crest. They were works of art probably worth a small fortune.

Kiln saw Jonas's eyes and answered his un-asked question. "Annure is a very rich kingdom. Not only do they earn high tariffs, but the mountains surrounding the kingdom are filled with precious minerals. King Olegaurd has several rich and productive mines in the area bringing in gold, silver, and lots of iron ore."

"They must. If every guard is dressed like this, then the king must have a large treasury indeed."

Annure was an open city and Kiln told them that they would not have a problem getting inside. Some cities were strict on who came and went, especially during certain times of the night. Annure had a strong city watch and the rules within the city were strictly enforced. It was not a place that welcomed pick pockets and thieves. The strong security made the city a welcoming environment to traders and anyone who was interested in honest work; therefore the city gates were open to all, as long as they walked the line of the law.

As they walked past one of the guards, Jonas noticed the man's eyes sweep over them and widen slightly as he recognized the symbols on Jonas's and Taleen's breast plates. The middle aged man was outfitted with a long chain mail shirt under his green tunic. He also wore a long sword dangling from a black leather sword belt cinched tight at the waist and knee high leather boots plated with pieces of shiny steel. Each guard held a long sharp spear with a thick wooden shaft.

The guard near them bowed slightly as they passed, and Jonas couldn't help but notice that the guard was staring at Taleen and himself, focusing on their breast plates which bore the marks of their gods.

"Welcome, cavaliers," the man announced. Jonas and Taleen nodded as they walked by the soldier.

"It seems I'm in the presence of royalty," Kiln chuckled behind Jonas.

"Kiln is nearly right, Jonas. As a cavalier you will be welcomed everywhere and people will treat you with deference, but it comes with a price. You will also be asked to do things that may or may not be within your power. When the world has high expectations of you, it can be easy to let people down. We are not gods, but some people don't seem to understand that."

"True words, Taleen," agreed Kiln.

"I can't believe they recognized me as a cavalier," Jonas said as they entered the main entrance to Annure.

"Look at yourself. If you were standing here three years younger, watching yourself walk through these gates, what would you think?" asked Kiln.

Jonas looked down at his immaculate clothes and shining armor. The symbol on his sparkling breast plate glittered like fish scales in the sun. His legs and wrists were covered with mirror-like metal guards all decorated with intricate designs. His incredible horned helm was strapped to his pack. That unique piece alone would draw someone's attention. He wore two beautifully crafted swords at his belt and on his back was a black leather quiver also decorated with intricate symbols. The black shafts that jutted from the quiver were perfectly crafted with silver and blue feathers, which obviously did not come from nature. The gloss black long bow he carried in his hands was obviously built by a master craftsman. They were truly magnificent weapons.

"I see what you mean," Jonas said, looking around him for the first time. Annure was bustling with activity. There were people everywhere, walking up and down the many streets lined with shops and markets of all kinds. Annure reminded Jonas of Finarth, except Annure was much cleaner and had more of an open feel.

Jonas took a deep breath, smelling the fresh air blowing in from the lake waters. The streets were spacious and all the structures were built from the same white stone that was used to create the immense walls that protected the city. It gave the place a god-like look and Jonas immediately felt safe here.

"We need to procure rooms and find out where the kulam is located," Kiln announced as he, too, took in his surroundings.

"What's a kulam?" asked Jonas.

"That is what the cavalier training facilities are called," Taleen answered. "Let us ask a guard where good rooms and food may be found."

"I agree, but let's look around a bit first. It's been a long time since I've been in a city like this and I wouldn't mind exploring some," said Kiln.

"I'd like that," added Jonas, not able to hide his enthusiasm.

Kiln led the way and Jonas and Taleen followed closely. They walked down the main street looking at everything around them. It was loud with people shouting and selling wares everywhere they went. Jonas saw a large variety of fruits and vegetables and meats of every sort. He saw expensive cloth, beads, and intricately carved furniture that he had never seen before. The fragrance of exotic spices, baked bread, and fresh flowers mingled with the clean air that continuously blew in off the lake.

Everyone passed curious glances at the trio at first until they saw the two cavaliers. Most people then quickly bowed their heads and muttered a greeting with a smile.

They walked by an alley and Jonas noticed a small boy huddled in the shadows. He was young, maybe eleven winters, and he wore dirty clothes. But it was not his clothing that caught Jonas's eye. It was the crutch that lay next to him as he sat watching the people walk by, despair surrounding him almost palpable. Jonas noticed that his right foot was twisted and deformed, and in his right hand he held out a small tarnished cup, hoping that someone would stop and drop in a copper coin. His greasy hair was ratty and dirt covered his cheeks in patches.

Jonas stopped, kneeling by the boy. The boy's sad eyes widened slightly as he looked upon the magnificent cavalier.

"Hello, son, what is your name?" Jonas asked softly.

The boy hesitated for a few moments before answering. His voice was shaky. "My name is Piton, sir. Are you a cavalier?"

"I am. What happened to your foot?"

"I was born like this," the boy hesitated. "Is it true that cavaliers can heal?"

"Yes, some of us can," Jonas responded.

"Can you? Can you heal my foot, sir?" the young boy asked bluntly.

Jonas looked back at Taleen and Kiln who stood behind them, their faces reflecting concern. Jonas knew they could not heal an inherited deformity, but it pained him to admit it to the boy. "I'm sorry, Piton, but we cannot heal the type of injury that you have. Your bones in your foot have a certain shape to them and I cannot change that. Do you understand?"

Piton lowered his head in dejection and nodded his understanding.

It was heart breaking to Jonas, but he could do nothing. Perhaps that was the hardest part. Despite his power and strength, he could not help this little boy. "Where do you sleep, Piton?" Jonas asked.

The boy used his hands to gesture into the alley. "I usually sleep in the streets. Sometimes I can find a bed in one of the temples. It's not too bad, except for the winter. It can get pretty cold."

"Where are your parents?" asked Jonas.

"I never knew my dad, my mom died of some sickness a year ago."

Jonas reached into the leather pouch at his side, fingering the gold coin that was there. It was the coin that was given to him by Airos, and he had kept it to remember his mother by, but this boy needed it more than he did.

Besides, it felt right to Jonas. The coin had been passed to him by a cavalier who recognized his need, and now it was being passed from another cavalier to another cripple. The boy was in desperate need and this was the only thing Jonas could do to help him.

Jonas lifted out the gold coin and handed it to the young boy. Piton held the heavy coin in his hand and his eyes lit up with astonishment as he realized what it was.

"Is that gold?"

"It is, Piton, given to me years ago by a cavalier," Jonas said.

"Thank you, sir. I have never had gold before." The boy dropped his cup, reached for his crutch and struggled to stand up.

Jonas reached down, lifting him to his feet. That simple act brought a flash of an image to Jonas's mind, an image of Airos lifting him from the ground when he had slipped on the ice four years ago. Jonas smiled as he looked at the boy's beaming face. Piton smiled broadly. No amount of dirt on his face, or lack of food in his stomach, could crush the boy's joy. It wasn't so long ago where the simple act of another had given Jonas a similar feeling of happiness. It warmed Jonas's heart to see the young boy smile so.

"Promise me you will buy food and warm clothes for the winter. I am a cavalier and I will know if you don't."

Piton smiled and his body shook with excitement. "Oh, don't worry, sir. I will not waste it. I will do as you ask. Thank you."

Jonas squeezed the boy's shoulders before standing up. "You're welcome, young Piton." Then he turned and rejoined his friends on the sidewalk.

Taleen smiled at him warmly but she said nothing about the boy. She knew that there was nothing else they could do. There were likely hundreds of boys like Piton in Annure and many more living in less prosperous cities.

They continued to explore the lively city. At first, Jonas liked the attention, but it began to wear on him as the day progressed. People were continuously greeting them, diverting his attention from the many wondrous things that the city had to offer.

Kiln led them into a small shop that sold various weapons, knives, and armor. Two armed guards stood at attention inside the store keeping a watchful eye over the store's products. The room was small but immaculate. The walls were lined with glittering weapons of all sorts. Glass cases were filled with small jeweled knives and silver and gold jewelry made with precious gems.

Kiln approached one of the guards who looked at him curiously. "Excuse me, soldier, might you answer a few questions for a traveler?"

The soldier saw something in Kiln that all fighting men see in him, strength, courage, and possible danger. He glanced at Jonas and Taleen, then suddenly smiled, his stoic demeanor melting as he became the young boy that he was. "Yes sir. I would be happy to help you if I can."

"Might you know where we could find an honest establishment to get a good room and food for the night?" asked Kiln.

The warrior glanced quickly at Taleen who smiled back. The man flushed slightly, fidgeting with his sword belt. "I do. I would recommend the White Unicorn. If you follow this main street down to the fourth road and then take a left, you will see the inn on your right. It has the best food in Annure and the rooms are clean and spacious. It is costly, but the innkeeper, Bomm, will probably give you a deal considering who you travel with. May I ask you your names, cavaliers? You are a rare sight lately, even in Annure."

"My name is Taleen, I am a cavalier to Helikon."

"Helikon?" asked the young warrior, not recognizing the name.

The other soldier had moved closer to the group to hear the conversation. He was a bit older and heavy in the shoulders and belly. "Helikon is who we call Bandris," interjected the older soldier.

"Oh, that is good, a warrior's god. I pray to Bandris often," added the young soldier.

"I hope that his prayers follow you into battle, young man," added Taleen with a smile. "This is my friend, Jonas. He is a cavalier to Shyann."

"Nice to meet you both," Jonas said with an awkward smile.

The older soldier's face showed a little confusion. "Shyann? I have never met a cavalier to Shyann. Are there many of you?"

"No, I am the first," replied Jonas.

The big man smiled warmly. "I am glad that you are here. We have heard some disturbing news, that cavaliers are being killed. We have not seen any cavaliers at Annure for many months now. You are both a welcome sight. Is there anything else that you need?"

"Yes," replied Kiln. "Where is the Kulam?"

"Oh, of course. Go to the northeastern section of town, near the docks. Ask anyone and they will point you in the right direction. You can't miss it. It is a beautiful building."

"Thank you for your help," Kiln added.

"Anytime, sir. May I ask your name?" the older soldier asked.

Kiln had already turned, moving toward the front door. "Kiln, of Finarth," he replied, striding through the wooden door.

Jonas glanced at the two men and noticed the shocked expressions on their faces at the mention of Kiln's name. *It seems that cavaliers are not the only famous people in Annure* thought Jonas. He smiled and followed Taleen and Kiln out the door into the street. He was excited about the prospect of sleeping in a warm bed and eating a hot meal.

The trio arrived at the White Unicorn easily enough. The front door was thick and plain but above the door was a sign with a majestic white unicorn painted on it.

They entered the door, looking about the large spacious room. The ceiling was high and vaulted; maybe twenty paces at its peak. To the right was a giant stone fireplace that was as wide as a man is tall. The day was still warm so the fire was unlit. The stone chimney rose up the wall disappearing into the roof.

The bar was straight ahead and it ran the entire length of the room. A burly man with a bushy mustache worked behind the counter washing thick clay mugs. There were many sturdy wood tables and benches sporadically placed throughout the room. A set of stairs on the left led to a landing on the second floor. Jonas could see at least six doors above that, each leading to an individual room.

As he looked up his eyes were drawn to an incredible chandelier. It was huge and constructed of numerous sets of antlers. The massive racks were intricately entwined and interwoven. There were countless thick candles set into metal bowls to collect the wax. There must be a hundred candles thought Jonas.

There were only a couple patrons at the bar since it was the time between lunch and dinner. Kiln strode up to the bar and Jonas and Taleen followed. "Excuse me, barkeep, is Bomm around?"

"You're looking at him," replied the heavyset man as he looked up from the counter. "What can I do for you?" Bomm had a large friendly face that was completely devoid of hair except for his bushy mustache. His face glistened with perspiration and his cheeks were slightly flushed from his work. He had the look of an old burly warrior who had put on some extra pounds.

"My friends and I need two rooms and food," Kiln replied.

"No problem at…" Bomm stopped in mid-speech as he looked at Jonas and Taleen, "all. You're cavaliers. It is good to see you both. I am Bomm and I own this place." The big man reached out, shaking each of their hands.

"I am Taleen, cavalier to Helikon."

"My name is Jonas." Jonas could not quite bring himself to say he was a cavalier. It didn't feel right considering that he had not been through the same training as Taleen.

That omission did not sneak by Bomm and he eyed Jonas curiously, but something told him not to press the issue. Bomm finished by shaking Kiln's hand.

"And I am Kiln, of Finarth," Kiln said.

Bomm's hand stopped in mid-shake and he looked at Kiln with surprise. "General Kiln?" He slowly released Kiln's hand.

"The same, but just Kiln now."

Bomm looked at Jonas, Taleen, and then back to Kiln. After a few seconds he recovered from his surprise. "Well, it seems I have some esteemed guests tonight. We don't have much warm food available yet. The kitchen is getting prepared for dinner, but I can get you some dried meats, bread, and the best cheeses from Cer'une if you're interested in that."

"That will do nicely," Kiln replied.

Bomm walked over to a back wall, removed two sets of keys, and handed them both to Kiln. "You can take room three and four. Why don't you get settled in your room and I will have Wes, my son, bring up some hot water so you may refresh yourselves. Would you like the meat platter in your rooms or down here?"

"Down here is fine. When will the dinner crowd arrive?" asked Kiln.

"Around sunset."

"Thank you. We will be down momentarily to eat. How much do we owe you?" asked Kiln.

"Nothing, your presence here is payment enough."

"We thank you for your generosity," Kiln said, tilting his head down in a barely perceptible bow.

"It is my pleasure, sir," Bomm replied with a smile.

Jonas and Kiln took room three while Taleen took room four. The rooms were large and clean just as the soldier had promised. Each room had a large glass door that opened up onto a narrow balcony that looked at a garden courtyard. It was just after mid-day and the sun's rays shone brightly through the door, spreading shadows throughout the room.

It wasn't long before they heard a knock at the door. Jonas went to the door and opened it. There was a young boy standing in the doorway holding a steaming bucket of hot water.

"You must be Wes?" Jonas said kindly.

The boy was young, maybe ten, and his round freckled face shone with the vitality of youth. His sandy blonde hair draped his head like a mop. The boy's eyes were wide and sparkling with excitement. "I am, sir. Are you really a cavalier?"

Jonas laughed, looking around the room like he was going to tell the boy a secret. "I am, young man, can you keep that a secret?" Jonas whispered.

"I sure can, sir," whispered the boy in return. "But won't people know you're a cavalier just by looking at you?"

"You may be right, young man," laughed Jonas. "You are very observant."

"Thank you, sir. If you need anything you just let me know. I am really tough and my dad taught me how to punch."

"I will certainly look for you, Wes, if I need help. Now why don't you put that water in the wash basin."

"Yes, sir." Wes stepped inside, moving quickly to a large copper bowl sitting on the table. He poured the hot water into the bowl and laid down two clean towels next to it. "There you go, sir." Wes looked at Kiln for the first time and walked over to him boldly. "I am, Wes, sir. Are you a warrior too?"

Jonas choked back his laughter while Kiln smiled down at the boy. "I am, young Wes, but I am no cavalier."

"I want to be a warrior also, but my father just wants me to work here."

"Your father runs a good establishment. It is a noble profession and you should be proud to have that opportunity."

"Yes, I guess so. Well I better get back to my chores. I have a lot of work to do before the dinner rush. It was nice to meet you both. Oh, father said that your food is ready." Wes turned and walked out the door. Jonas looked at Kiln and they both laughed.

***

The dried meat was exquisite; cured with exotic spices that made Jonas's mouth water. He washed it down with some hearty ale before stuffing a thick slice of white cheese in his mouth. The food was delicious, better than anything he had ever tasted.

"What's the plan now?" asked Jonas, reaching for another slice of cheese.

"I say we go to the kulam and try to get those answers you came for. Then we come back here for dinner. After that, your guess is as good as mine," replied Taleen.

"I agree. Let's go to the kulam first. See if we can find anything out about Jonas, the demon that attacked us, the missing cavaliers, and whatever they know about Malbeck. What we learn will decide our next course of action."

"What do you think will happen to me?" asked Jonas.

"I don't know," Taleen replied. "They will probably want to test you. It is unprecedented that you would have the powers of a cavalier without going through the training. I imagine they will have a lot of questions for you as well."

"I would really like to travel to Finarth with Kiln."

"That may or may not be possible. You may get a calling, or the council may request that you stay here for more testing. I do not know," Taleen responded as she finished the last piece of cured meat.

"What of you, Taleen. What will you do?" asked Kiln.

"If I get a calling then I will go where I'm directed. If not then I will stay with Jonas. Something tells me that we need to stay together."

Kiln nodded his head in agreement. "I agree. Let us go to the kulam and get some information. It is a waste of time to speculate until we know what the council will do with Jonas."

They found the kulam easily. It was a huge stone temple, as big as a small castle, and at least three levels high. The building was surrounded by a well manicured lawn. It was an oasis in the middle of the bustling city. The center part of the temple stood fifty paces high with sharp spires rising towards the clouds. The entire façade was covered with carvings of gods and their symbols, Shyann's great oak, Ulren's four pointed star, Bandris's axe, and many more.

There was a main door located at the center of the impressive structure. It was made from a solid white stone over ten paces high. The symbol of Ulren was carved into the stone and the seam that split the double doors was so thin that it was barely visible. It gave the door the appearance of a solid piece of flat rock.

Flanking the large temple were two large buildings that appeared to be two story barracks or warehouses. There were several entrances along the fronts of these buildings, and the entire kulam was made from the same white stone. Taleen explained that the center building was a temple representing the various gods of the realm. The outer two buildings were the training facilities and living quarters for the potential cavalier candidates.

They walked up the stone stairs that led to the white stone door. As they neared the door its marvelous craftsmanship became apparent. The polished stone was covered with a detailed carving of Ulren's symbol, one that was so intricate and the lines so graceful that it was obviously done by a master craftsman.

"It doesn't even look like a door. You can't see the seam or the hinges," Jonas said, running his hand over the smooth stone.

"This must have been created by dwarves. No one else could do this," added Kiln.

Taleen reached out and grabbed what looked like an impression in the middle of the door. There were two impressions on each side of the middle seam and once your hand was inside you could firmly grip an inner edge giving you the leverage to pull. She pulled hard expecting the door to be heavy and cumbersome, but she almost fell backwards as the door, a foot in thickness, easily swung outward on invisible hinges that made no sound.

"Incredible," muttered Taleen.

They stepped into a large interior room covered with polished stone. Jonas looked down and saw a large mosaic of Ulren's four-pointed star on the floor. The mosaic was made from different pieces of marble ranging from colors of white to black. The symbol itself was gray and black while the background was white in contrast. There was silver inlaid writing over the top of the symbol that Jonas thought was elvish.

Taleen read it out loud. "Araste makatar nih daia dadutha dandis"

"What does it mean?" asked Jonas.

"Some must live by the blade to stand against the shadow," interpreted Kiln. Jonas liked the saying, smiling as he contemplated its meaning.

They stepped across the symbol into the entryway. Sunlight shone through colorful stained-glassed windows highlighting a large double door before them. The walls were lined with expensive tapestries and paintings. There were wide cathedral hallways on their left and right, each ending with extravagant stone stairways leading to another level. The hallways were lined with thick stone columns and statues of magnificent warriors in various poses.

"This place is beautiful," muttered Jonas in awe. Taleen approached the large double doors in front of them. The doors were made of thick oak and in the center was an inlaid carving, presumably created from a softer wood. The carving brought a smile to Jonas as it was clearly Shyann's oak tree.

As Jonas glanced around the incredible room he noticed it was covered with many different carvings. Parts of the ceiling, walls, and stone columns were covered with impressive carvings so detailed they seemed to be alive. He saw Ulren's four-pointed star, Bandris's double bladed battle-axe, Shyann's oak tree, Inis's rose, and the symbol of Nomis, God of farming and weather. His symbol was a scythe. He noticed the trident head symbol of Halyean as well.

Taleen walked up to a large metal gong that was placed next to the door. She grabbed the wood mallet and hit the gong once, the sound reverberating through the halls and echoing off the tall ceiling.

"That won't go unnoticed," said Kiln.

A few minutes later as the trio was inspecting the expansive entry, the door in front of them opened, and an old man appeared, wearing a long gray robe of fine cotton. Tall and thin, his straggly gray hair draped a face that looked like a dried out grape. He held a carved wooden cane that supported his bent body as he walked. Around his neck was a silver necklace that bore the symbol of Halyean, god of the seas. The man's face was passive as he ran his eyes over the trio standing before him.

"Good evening, priest, I am Taleen, cavalier to Helikon. This is Jonas Kanrene and Kiln from Finarth. We seek a conference with the council."

The old man fixed his gaze on Kiln first and then Jonas. His eyes lingered on Jonas for a while and suddenly Jonas felt something jab at his consciousness, something subtle but intrusive. It felt like light tendrils were slowly wrapping around his brain, looking for something.

Jonas reacted on instinct. He threw up a cognitive barrier and reached out mentally towards the old man. "*It is not polite to enter one's mind without permission.*" Jonas was shocked that he was actually conversing silently with the man.

The priest's eyes flared briefly with astonishment but he quickly regained composure, smiling softly. Jonas was equally shocked. He had not known that he could mentally speak inside the minds of others. Another of the cognivant powers of which he had not been aware.

"Forgive me Jonas Kanrene. I did not know you were a cognivant. It is standard policy to probe the minds of any that wish entrance into the kulam. Guests do not even know of the intrusion, unless of course they are cognivants, which is so rare that it has yet to happen, until now of course. Rest assured that I do not intrude in their minds for more than the few seconds it takes me to ascertain their purpose here." The old priest smiled warmly at them all. "I am Rayall, high priest to Halyean." The priest looked at Taleen, bowing his head slightly. "It is good to see a cavalier. I'm afraid we have not had a cavalier here for many months."

"So I've heard. Thank you Rayall, it is good to be here," replied Taleen.

Rayall looked at Kiln, nodding his head in greeting. "General Kiln, your reputation precedes you. I did not know you were still alive."

"Alive and well, Rayall," replied Kiln.

"And you, young man. What brings a cognivant who looks like a cavalier to a Kulam?"

"Sir, meaning no disrespect, I would like to tell that story to the entire council. That is why I am here." Jonas wondered if maybe he was able to speak inside the priests mind because he too was a cognivant. He made a mental note to ask the priest about it later if they had time.

"I see," replied the old man. "No offense taken. I think that you three are of sufficient interest to bring the council together. If you will please follow me," Rayall said, slowly turning and walking through the large double doors.

The three kept up with him easily as he slowly ambled through a huge temple. The ceiling was at least forty paces high and the walls were built of the same white stone. Rows of benches lined the floor along the aisle that led to a large altar. Light shone through expansive sky lights lining the ceiling. Behind the altar was a stone statue of Ulren reaching all the way to the ceiling. His muscular arms appeared to hold up the stone roof.

Jonas immediately understood the artists meaning. The High One was holding up the temple with his bare arms, symbolic of his strength in holding up all that is good. The walls were lined with statues of all the gods.

Jonas's eyes were immediately drawn to a female warrior at his right. The statue was twenty paces high and she stood gracefully holding a long sword and shield. She wore no helm and the artist captured her beauty perfectly. Her chest plate was decorated with the very same symbol tattooed on his chest and embossed on his own armor. From the folds of her cloak to the waves of her hair, the statue was stunningly lifelike. The work was incredible and Jonas could hardly believe that a person could create something so beautiful.

They walked to the end of the aisle and the priest motioned for them to sit on a bench. "Please have a seat. I will assemble the council. Someone will come to summon you when they are ready."

"Thank you, Rayall," replied Taleen. The priest nodded his head and moved across the floor to a wood door on the far wall.

"This is amazing," whispered Jonas as he gazed at the magnificent temple.

"It truly is. I've never seen anything so beautiful," added Kiln.

"This is a temple to all the benevolent gods of Kraawn. My Kulam is very similar. All the followers of all the gods are welcome here. There is Helikon," Taleen said, pointing to her left.

Jonas followed her finger to a statue of a powerful warrior wearing only a leather and metal skirt, accentuating his muscular chest and powerful arms. In his right hand he held a thick broad sword and in his left he held onto a shaft tipped with a long sharp blade. His face was bearded and long wavy hair hung down to his strong shoulders. *He looks every bit the warrior's god* thought Jonas.

"This is Inis, the wife of Ulren," Taleen continued as she pointed at another statue.

Jonas looked upon a beautiful lady wearing what looked like a thin cotton robe that clung to her perfect form. Her long hair was swept back from her face by an invisible breeze. In one hand the goddess held a bouquet of roses and in the other she held a basket of food.

The sun shone through the ceiling in such a way that it lit up each statue like a spotlight. The architecture was truly incredible, allowing the sun's light to purposely highlight each figure.

"Inis is the goddess of beauty, passion, and kindness," Taleen said as she continued her explanation of the gods.

Jonas took a few minutes to look at all the statues that lined the circular walls. For the first time he noticed that at the bottom of each one was a mini altar and they all had melted candles that covered the base of the statue.

"Taleen?" asked Jonas.

"Yes?"

"I spoke with an elf once, well she was a half-elf, but anyway, she said that elves do not believe in gods. How can they not believe in the gods when we have proof of their existence?"

"What proof do we have?" Taleen asked.

"Our magic of course," Jonas replied, a little taken aback by her question.

"Well, the elves do not believe in gods, but they do believe in what we call our gods," she said.

"What do you mean?" he asked

"It's a matter of perspective, Jonas," Kiln interjected.

Taleen nodded her head in agreement. "Exactly. The elves believe that Ulren, Bandris, Shyann, and all the gods, including the Foresworn, are not really gods at all, but people who somehow achieved enough power to become god-like, powerful enough where people believe they are gods. The elves do not believe that our gods made all things, but that they themselves are a result of the true power."

"The Ru'Ach," muttered Jonas.

"Yes. They believe that our gods were once great people who somehow accessed the Ru'Ach and gained tremendous power. Most priests do not believe this. They believe that the gods created all things, including the Ru'Ach."

"What do you believe?" Jonas asked.

"Does it matter what I believe? Helikon is real, that I know. Was he made a god because he knew how to use power from the Ru'Ach, or has he always existed as a god, a creator of all things? Maybe he is a being of another world, another plane of existence. I do not know, Jonas, but either way it does not change who he is, or who I am. Helikon is a warrior god who fights for justice and courage, and I am a protector of these ideals. That is all I need to know. The question is…do YOU need to know more?"

"I do not know, Taleen. I shall think more on it."

"That is good. Such decisions should not be hastily made."

"What do you believe in, Kiln?" asked Taleen.

Kiln swung his piercing gaze toward her. "I believe in myself. That is the only constant in my life," he replied sharply.

"I see," she replied. "And Jonas, I did not know you were a cognivant. Can you tell me about it? I have never met anyone with that power."

"I do not know much myself. It surfaced several years ago when I was fighting against some mountain giants. I was able to mentally stop one of the giants clubs."

"So you can control objects?" Taleen asked.

"Yes, I guess. In my mind I can see the energy that makes up everything, and I can control it to some degree. But I'm still learning the extent of this power."

"And you can speak in people's minds as well?" Taleen asked.

"I guess. Today was the first time I've done that. I think perhaps I can only do that with another cognivant since that power had never surfaced before. There is much I do not know about this power."

"You are not alone in that respect, for it is such a rare ability. Are there any limits to it?" she asked.

"Yes, the more power I try to control and use, the more severe the headaches. In some cases they are so extreme that I pass out. But my meditative training with Kiln has helped strengthen my cognivant powers and lessen the pain when I use them."

Taleen looked at Kiln with interest. "Meditative training? I would like to hear more of this."

Suddenly a door opened to their left, ending their conversation. The sound of the opening door echoed against the large stone walls. A young man, maybe a year younger than Jonas, walked gracefully toward them. His short blond hair framed a thin tanned face. The short sleeves of his green cotton shirt exposed his muscular forearms. Loose fitting, black cotton pants, flowed around his legs as he walked. The boy's green shirt was long and laced at his waist with a black cotton belt. No weapons dangled from his belt but he looked like he didn't need any. They all stood up from the bench as the young man neared them.

"I am Kandris, a cavalier candidate to Ulren. It is a pleasure to have you here, cavalier." The young man bowed deeply to Taleen who nodded her head in acknowledgement.

The young man then turned his attention to Kiln. "And to you, sir." The boy tried hard to hide his excitement, his voice shaking a bit with nervous energy. "I have heard stories about you all my life."

"Some that are probably not true," replied Kiln, inclining his head toward the boy.

"I hope not, sir. There are many different tales swirling around the name of Kiln the General, not all of them tales to be proud of."

"And what do you make of the tales, young man?" Kiln asked with interest.

The young man smiled. "I think that lesser men are always trying to mar the reputation of great men, sir."

Kiln's cold features dissolved slightly, replaced by the hint of a smile. "Remember, Kandris, all men make mistakes, whether they are great men or not."

Kandris bowed his head in acknowledgement. "I will remember that, sir." He then pivoted smoothly to face, Jonas. "Jonas Kanrene, it is a pleasure to meet you." Jonas caught Kandris's eyes quickly glance down toward his chest. He looked confused for a moment but he quickly recovered, smiling kindly at Jonas. "You look like a cavalier."

"That I do," said Jonas.

Kandris nodded his head and his smile disappeared. "It is not my place to pry, sir. I apologize."

"You are not in the wrong, Kandris. It's not that simple, I'm afraid," Jonas said, trying to reassure the young warrior. "And I am no sir, just a few years older than you actually."

"Very well, and thank you. Well, if you will all follow me. I will take you to the council room." Kandris turned, walking back the way he had come.

The council room was large and empty except for six chairs sitting on a raised ledge on the far side. The wooden chairs were carved with intricate symbols and writing. Above each chair on the wall was an embroidered tapestry representing each of the benevolent gods of Kraawn.

The chairs were all occupied as they entered the room. Kandris bowed deeply to the six occupants of the chairs and then left the room quickly. Jonas recognized the old priest Rayall sitting in the chair below the symbol of Halyean. The old man smiled at them as they walked closer to the priests.

"Welcome to Annure, it is a pleasure to see a cavalier in our halls," said a middle aged man sitting in the middle chair. The four-pointed star above him marked him as a priest of Ulren. "I am Lyrus, high priest to Ulren." The man was tanned and his curly brown hair was streaked slightly with gray above the ears. His smile was warm and sincere. "You have met Rayall already. To my right is Tundis, high priest to Nomus, and Jeweleasiam, high priestess to Inis. On my left is Weelon, high priest to Bandris, and Lulaylin, high priestess to Shyann."

They all nodded as they were introduced.

"Thank you, high priest Lyrus, for agreeing to meet with us. As you know, I am Taleen, cavalier to Helikon. This is Kiln and Jonas. We have many questions that need answering and we came here as the likely source for those answers."

"I'm assuming that your questions concern Jonas," Lyrus reasoned.

All the priests stared at Jonas intently.

"They do," replied Taleen.

"Jonas, can you please tell me how you bear the armor and weapons of a cavalier and yet we know nothing of you?" Lyrus asked.

"I can, and I will sir," replied Jonas, taking a deep breath to prepare for his story. Jonas began his tale again. The council members all leaned forward in their chairs as the story progressed. He tried to judge their reactions as the story unfolded, but they were very good at masking their emotions. Finally, Jonas finished with the battle against the Greever. There was only silence in the room as the council members digested the tale.

"Jonas, may we see this symbol that you speak of?" asked Lulaylin, priestess to Shyann. She was older than the rest and she wore a silver hairpiece with Shyann's symbol etched into it. It covered her forehead and her long gray hair was pulled back behind her ears. Her gown was made from expensive green silk that matched her eyes perfectly. Lulaylin was beautiful for someone her age and Jonas was drawn to her sparkling green eyes. But once there, he saw an underlying intensity that did not match her appearance.

"You may," Jonas said as he began unbuckling his breastplate and setting it on the smooth polished stone at his feet. He then lifted the tight chain mail shirt over his head.

"Where did you get that armor?" Lulaylin asked.

"From Shyann's tomb," he replied, setting the light metal shirt on the ground.

Lulaylin stood up in her chair in shock. "That cannot be! No one has found her tomb in a thousand years!" she said as her voice rose in disbelief.

Jonas did not react to her outburst but looked at her sincerely. "I do not lie. I was led by a huge stag to her tomb underneath a giant oak tree. It was there that she gave me this armor and these weapons."

Lulaylin sat back down, but her eyes still reflected her shock. "That cannot be. You are not even a cavalier."

"It is true," replied Kiln. "I was there."

Lulaylin directed her fiery eyes toward Kiln. "Your loyalty and honor is in question General. Why would we believe an oath breaker?"

"Lulaylin!" bellowed Lyrus. "General Kiln is our guest. Do not show disrespect."

Kiln's face was calm and emotionless as he addressed the priestess. "You know nothing of my loyalty other than rumors and stories that have been told for over twenty years. Until you know the truth of it, I recommend you keep your ill-mannered comments to yourself." Kiln's eyes, cold as the tone of his voice, left no room for argument.

"Besides," replied Jonas. "I believe this mark will represent the truth where our words have not." Jonas lifted off his cotton shirt and set it next to his armor. He stood up straight and the six council members sat back in their chairs in shock.

"Come closer, Jonas," ordered Rayall. Jonas stepped closer to them all so they could clearly see the God Mark. He finally stepped in front of Lulaylin so she could view the mark for herself. His toned muscular torso was covered with the God Mark.

"And you say that you have powers like a cavalier?" asked high priest Weelon. The burly man was obviously once a warrior. He had that look, and his face was scarred in several places.

"Yes," said Jonas with some trepidation. "I can bring forth God Light, heal, detect evil, and I can wield God Fire, although I have not had much experience with any of those powers."

"The skills of a first rank cavalier," muttered Weelon to himself.

"Show us, Jonas, bring forth light," ordered Tundis, high priest to Nomus. His voice was soft and inviting. Tundis was a small man and his face reflected many years of working in the sun. His skin was tough and tanned and his long wavy black hair was speckled with gray. He wore a simple tan tunic with loose gray pants common to a farmer. Jonas could even see dirt stains covering his knees as if he had just come from his garden.

Jonas looked within himself and called upon Shyann's magic. He felt it boil up within him and he released it in a brilliant flare of light. The bright light appeared quickly causing the six council members to rock back in their chairs in surprise. As the light bathed them, any remnants of tension and disbelief disappeared in a flash. Jonas let it flare briefly before dispelling it. They all stared at him for several seconds, their shock apparent on their faces.

Taleen broke the silence. "When we healed Kiln, Jonas channeled his energy into me. I have never felt that much power. It almost consumed me. As you know, only a rare person can control the power needed to be a first rank cavalier. I believe that we are looking at our first true god picked cavalier."

"It is hard to imagine that being possible. We have never known that to happen. We have no record of it, nor have we ever seen a cavalier to Shyann," muttered Lyrus in disbelief.

"And yet we have a young man standing in front of us who can bring forth light, and he bears her mark on his chest. What else could it be?" asked Jeweleasiam, the beautiful priestess to Inis.

"And we have the word of a true cavalier that he wields great power. How else would he have it unless it was god given?" asked Weelon.

"May I see your swords, Jonas?" asked Lulaylin gently, her disbelief and frustration seemingly extinguished.

Jonas reached down, drawing forth a sword. He approached Lulaylin, handing it to her hilt first.

She grasped the bone handle and lifted it into the air. She closed her eyes and Jonas saw her lips moving slightly. Suddenly the blade flared brightly and receded just as quickly. Lulaylin opened her eyes and for the first time smiled warmly at Jonas.

"There can be no question. These blades were given to him by Shyann herself." She handed the blade back to Jonas. "Jonas, I am sorry for my outburst and for doubting you. It was just so hard to believe. Being allowed to see her tomb is a great honor, one that I wish was bestowed upon me. It was envy and doubt that sparked my emotional response. I am sorry. You are indeed a cavalier to Shyann. I am convinced." Lulaylin turned her eyes on Kiln and bowed her head slightly. "I must apologize to you as well, General. I spoke rashly and I hope you will forgive me."

Kiln simply nodded his head in acknowledgment but said not a word.

"I understand, priestess. I can hardly believe it myself," replied Jonas.

"Know this, young man. You are very much needed," Lulaylin continued. "Lyrus, please tell them what is happening."

Jonas looked around at all the faces before them. They now looked at him differently, no doubt was apparent in their expressions. "What did you do to my sword?" asked Jonas.

"I asked Shyann to tell me the truth, and she did. You are a cavalier. It is unprecedented, but true nonetheless."

"You spoke with her?" Jonas asked.

"No, not exactly. I asked her if the sword was hers, and she responded in confirmation," Lulaylin replied.

"Jonas, Taleen," interjected Lyrus. They both looked at the high priest as he sat forward in his chair. "There are no more cavaliers that we know of."

Taleen stepped back in shock as the disturbing news assaulted her. Kiln, who seldom showed emotion, was also visibly stunned by the horrible declaration. Jonas just stood, lowering his head in shock, his entire body deflating. It was too much to comprehend. The guardians of the righteous were dead. Who would protect the people against the darkness? The question lingered in Jonas's mind as Lyrus spoke again.

"An army marches toward Finarth as we speak. King Gavinsteal has sent out riders requesting aid. We have no cavaliers to send and we have not heard from any except you two. We only have three candidates that are close to finishing their training and they are still years away. Kandris, the young man you met, is furthest along and he still needs two winters, if he makes it all. The Kulam at Rohindrin has two candidates that are close, but they are still several years away. " Lyrus sighed deeply, his weariness finally surfacing.

"Do the people of Kraawn know about the dead cavaliers?" Kiln asked.

"Most do not," Lyrus said. "I suggest we keep it that way. It would not help matters if word got out that there are no cavaliers to protect them."

"King Olegaurd sent ten thousand men to Finarth four days ago. They should arrive at Finarth in several days," said Tundis.

"What would you have me do?" asked Jonas.

"Jonas, it is not the job of the council to direct a cavalier. It is up to Shyann's will. Have you received a calling?" asked Jeweleasium.

"No, that is why we came here. To get some answers."

"I, too, have received no calling," Taleen added. "I spent many weeks traveling across the Tundrens at Helikon's request. He sent me to help Jonas, but now I am unsure of our next quest."

"I will leave at first light for Finarth," Kiln announced. "They are in need of my skills. I think the cavaliers should accompany me to Finarth. Their gods may call them soon, but until then, their powers will be needed there."

"I concur with the general," Rayall spoke up. "If we had cavaliers here then I'm sure several of them would have been called to that conflict. I think that Jonas and Taleen should accompany Kiln to Finarth. We do not have the time to test Jonas any further. He will be needed there. There is one more thing I wish to speak of," he added. "Jonas is also a cognivant."

"A cognivant? Are you sure, Rayall?" asked Lyrus in disbelief.

"I am. I wish I had more time to help you understand your potential as a cognivant, but the truth of it is my powers are limited. I can read minds and that is all. What cognivant powers have you realized thus far, Jonas?"

"So far I am able to see the true make up of all things, the magic that makes up everything around us. This ability has given me the power to control objects."

"That is indeed a rare thing. Use that power wisely, young cavalier. That magic is old, and we know very little about it," Tundis cautioned.

"Jonas, do you get headaches after you use this power?" asked Rayall.

"I do. The more power I use, the more severe the pain."

"You may want to practice this power so you know what your limits are," Rayall said. "It would not be prudent to find the end of your strength during battle. It could prove disastrous."

Rayall's advice was sound and Jonas nodded his head in thanks. "I will think on that, high priest Rayall, thank you."

"I wish we could further test you and help you understand your power, but I think we are running out of time," said Weelon.

"Do we know what army it is that attacks Finarth?" asked Kiln.

"Yes, it is an army led by Lord Moredin, but we believe that he is backed by Malbeck's power. A second force is marching from Banrith Castle toward Tarsis as we speak," added Lyrus.

"Malbeck is back then?" asked Taleen.

"There can be no doubt. But we have yet to learn how this has happened," said Lulaylin.

"What aid will you need to get to Finarth?" asked Lyrus.

"Horses and provisions," replied Kiln.

"Will you be in need of an escort?" asked Weelon.

"No. We three will travel faster alone. I do not intend on taking the roads."

"Very well. I will have horses and provisions brought to the main gate at sunrise. We wish you a fast and safe journey," added Lyrus as he stood up, signaling the end of the meeting.

"Remember, it is very likely that you are both still being hunted. Be vigilant," cautioned Lulaylin.

"We will," replied Jonas. He looked at each of the council members and they nodded their heads in farewell. The trio turned and walked from the room without another word.

***

The White Unicorn was busy; patrons crowded around the bar and filled the many tables in the dining room. Hundreds of candles and oil lamps lit the area casting orange hues throughout the large bar. The crackling fire blazed and the flames danced as if they wanted to leap out of the fireplace. The sounds of laughter and idle conversation filled the large room making it difficult to hear the gossip that seemed to be on everyone's tongues.

Jonas, Taleen, and Kiln sat alone at a table close to the fire. Bomm had saved it for them for more than an hour before the trio came back from their meeting at the Kulam. They were hungry and ordered Bomm's recommendation, smoked mutton pie, oven baked and filled with onions, wild mushrooms, potatoes, mutton, and covered in gravy. They sipped cold water and discussed the new adventure ahead of them.

"Kiln, tell me of Moredin," Jonas asked.

"Moredin is the ruler of Stonestep, a bandit city far to the east. Stonestep is a staging base for every invasion into Finarth, Tarsis, and Annure. On the surface Moredin stays out of most politics, but under the surface he is ruthless, conniving, and does whatever he can to gain more power, land, and wealth."

"Who are his allies?" asked Taleen.

"None really. His kingdom is vast and surrounded by the nomad lands and Flatlands south of Mt. Ule. He usually allies himself with tribes from the Sithgarin and nomads from the Tarsinian Plains. He also has a decent relationship with Prince Bomballa of Numenell. Their relationship is one of convenience and they are not official allies," Kiln added before he took a long sip of his water, his eyes scanning the room instinctively.

Many of the patrons cast curious glances at the trio. Kiln hoped that Bomm had kept his mouth shut about who he was. He knew that Jonas and Taleen would be seen for what they were, but he did not want his identity known. Many patrons smiled, acknowledging the cavaliers, but none had the courage to approach them.

"Why would Moredin risk everything by attacking Finarth? What is in it for him?" asked Jonas.

Kiln returned his attention to them both. "I don't know. His chance of winning is slim if King Gavinsteal's allies arrive in time. Even if they didn't, Finarth's forces should have no problem repelling Moredin's army."

"Even with Malbeck's help?" Taleen asked skeptically.

"That I don't know. The only way to know is to scout Moredin's army. Find out how many men, cavalry, and siege machines exist, and if Malbeck has sent his minions there to help him."

Kiln looked around the room again. Something didn't feel right to the old warrior.

"Would Lord Moredin fight alongside orcs, boargs, and other monsters?" asked Jonas.

"I imagine so, especially if riches, power, and land were involved," replied Kiln as he leaned back in his chair, getting a better look at their surroundings. He felt like they were being watched, and Kiln never questioned his instincts.

Out of the crowd came a buxom serving girl carrying a large tray of steaming food. She smiled warmly at them, setting the tray down. Jonas's mouth began to water when he saw the food. Each plate contained huge slices of mutton pie. The crust was thick and slathered with gravy, mushrooms, and onions. Jonas quickly grabbed his plate and began to consume the delicious and hearty food.

"Can I get you anything else?" asked the rosy cheeked bar maid. She was pleasantly plump and her ample bosom was barely contained by her bodice. Her infectious smile was warm and made her average face seem attractive.

"No thank you. Thank Bomm again for the meals," added Taleen.

"I will indeed." The waitress quickly turned, disappearing into the boisterous crowd.

The three ate their food in silence. The succulent flavors were enough to halt their conversation.

As Kiln ate, he continued to monitor the crowd. The feeling was still there, the hairs on the back of his neck were standing up in warning.

Jonas looked at him with concern, his mouth full of mutton. "What is it?" he asked.

Kiln looked at him seriously as he set his fork down. He took a shallow drink of water before responding. "Something is wrong. I can feel it. Do either of you sense anything?"

Taleen and Jonas looked at each other, replying in unison. "No."

"Would you sense something if it wasn't directly evil?" asked Kiln.

"No. Our powers enable us to detect, or be warned, in Jonas's case, of true evil, evil that is deep and black, but we might not detect a normal person who chose to do an evil act. It is hard to say, it really depends on the person and the situation." Taleen took another sip of her water. Following Kiln's lead, she leaned back in her chair, away from the table's edge.

"I wonder why I didn't detect the gnolls we fought up in the Dragon's Spine?" Jonas mused as he drank from his mug.

"There could be many reasons. Maybe they were too far away, or maybe they were not directly a danger to you. A cavalier's power is very specific; each cavalier has different degrees of power as well as slight differences in how their power works. No two are the same," answered Taleen. "How did you end up fighting them if they were not a direct danger to you? Surely you would have been warned if they attacked you?'

"We found the gnoll tracks which led us to them. We attacked them as they ate at their fire," said Jonas.

"Without knowing their purpose?" Taleen asked with an edge to her voice.

"They were gnolls who stole my cattle," answered Kiln as if that were enough.

"Are all gnolls doomed because of their race?" challenged Taleen.

"Have you met a gnoll whose heart was not black?" asked Kiln.

"No, but that does not mean that one does not exist. Not everything in the world is black and white, General."

"Easy to say from one who can detect evil. For the rest of us, living in the realm of absolutes can keep us alive. It was a raiding party that would have eventually attacked. I learned long ago to take every advantage in battle, so I brought the fight to them before they could bring it to me and my men. By killing those gnolls as we did, I probably saved lives," Kiln said.

Kiln suddenly shifted his attention to his surroundings. Jonas and Taleen both noticed the change in his demeanor.

"You are making me uneasy. What is it?" asked Jonas.

"I don't know. Stay alert. My senses are not usually wrong," added Kiln.

Jonas slid his left hand down to one of his swords. The bone handle gave him some reassurance and made him feel a little better.

Jonas watched Kiln close his eyes for a few seconds and then reopen them. His posture had changed and so had his eyes. He had just entered Ty'erm. Jonas, too, closed his eyes and concentrated on his breathing. After a few seconds he opened his eyes. He was in the relaxed state of Ty'erm and in that state the room seemed quieter, and everyone was moving more slowly, at least in his mind.

Jonas scanned the crowd, looking for anything that warned his heightened senses. He was able to focus on separate conversations and shut out the other noises. Kiln was also scanning the crowd, looking for anything strange and out of the ordinary.

"Do you see anything?" asked Taleen who had brought both hands under the table closer to her weapons.

"Not yet," replied Kiln. "Wait," Kiln whispered as he looked to his left between two men standing about four paces away. It wasn't the men that caught his attention, but the man moving just beyond them. A dark haired man with an un-kempt beard moved toward them. It was his posture that triggered Kiln's instincts. He was moving with purpose, and his pace was accelerated.

Just then Jonas's eyes looked up, scanning the railing that lined the landing on the second floor. It was dark, but the many candles from the chandelier shed a finger of light onto the edge of the railing. Just enough to see the sparkling crossbow bolts slowly emerge from the darkness.

Instantly Jonas reacted, calling on his IshMian powers. "Crossbows! above!" he yelled, standing up quickly and raising his right hand. In his mind everything around him changed hues as he saw the spinning particles and the energy that moved them. Just like he had done when he practiced with the rocks, Jonas concentrated on the energy around them, drawing it into a translucent shield that covered the table in front and above them. He did this in a matter of seconds just as the bolts were fired. They hit the invisible shield, falling harmlessly to the ground. Everyone around them screamed in confusion, looking around trying to figure out what was happening.

Kiln instantly slid his chair out and drew his sword in one smooth motion. The dark haired assassin barreled through the two unsuspecting men and tried to lance Kiln with a sword that he had hidden in his long black cloak. Kiln side stepped the blade easily and flicked his razor sharp edge across the man's throat. The move seemed casual and effortless, but the result was devastating to the assassin. Blood sprayed from the gruesome wound and the man crashed face first into the table.

As soon as the blades were out, everyone around the three warriors scurried out of the way in panic. Kiln scanned the crowd looking for another attacker.

Taleen had leaped back, drawing her sword just as the man tried to skewer Kiln. She saw movement to her left and pivoted out of the way as a huge axe came crashing down onto the table, easily splitting the wood. She brought her sword down onto the attackers arm, severing it cleanly. The man jumped back screaming, but not before the deadly cavalier reversed her swing and drove the point of her blade into his heart. He fell backwards, disappearing into the frenzied crowd.

In a matter of seconds everyone around the trio had run frantically out of the way, leaving the warriors alone with swords drawn and glistening in the firelight.

Jonas saw the men from the landing stand up and reload their crossbows. There were three of them, but it was still too dark to make out their features.

Jonas quickly looked around for something that he could use against the dangerous crossbowmen. He didn't have his bow so that was out of the question. Or was it? Jonas saw two of the crossbow bolts that the assassins had fired lying on the ground in front of him. He quickly seized the bolts with his mind, lifting them in the air. He used his telekinetic ability to fling the bolts toward the men who were now leaning over the railing with reloaded weapons.

Jonas focused on two of the assassin's throats and the bolts smashed into their windpipes before they could fire their second volley. They dropped the crossbows and grabbed the feathered shafts that were buried in their necks. One fell back into the darkness of the landing, while the other fell over the railing to land hard on a table, shattering it into several pieces.

The third assassin got his shot off as his comrades died. The twang of the crossbow was followed by the *phhhhhht* of the bolt as it zipped through the air. It took Taleen in her right shoulder, causing her to stumble backwards against the rock fireplace.

Jonas didn't have time to see if she was okay, because four men with swords drawn were running at them. They were all hard-faced men, wearing black, loose fitting clothes. Jonas drew his blades and sprang towards them with Kiln at his side, attacking the assassins with deadly silence.

One man lunged at Jonas with his long sword while the other chopped downwards with a powerful stroke. Both of Jonas's blades worked independently. One slapped the lunge to the side while the other blocked the downward stroke. Jonas quickly brought both blades swinging back across each other towards the opposite opponent. His razor sharp weapons cut each man in the thigh and they stumbled backwards, bright blood gushing from the wounds.

Jonas silently thanked Kiln for the many lessons on how to fight more than one opponent at a time. It was one thing to face a skilled swordsman, but facing two or three at a time required a totally different skill set, techniques that now were paying off.

Moving forward, Kiln's left arm snaked sideways, hurling his hunting knife into the throat of the nearest attacker while he engaged the second man with his long sword. The nearest assassin's eyes opened with shock as the hunting knife buried itself to the hilt just under his chin. He fell backwards like a limp rag doll.

The other attacker quickly engaged Kiln, his long sword vainly trying to find any gaps in Kiln's defenses. The cloaked man parried a strike and flicked his blade toward Kiln's throat. Kiln stepped into the attack, pivoting sideways. He grabbed the man's sword arm at the wrist with his free hand and used his sword to slice him from his groin across his inner thigh, lacerating an artery. Kiln's face was right next the assassins, his cold eyes stared into the man's face as the fatal wound did its work. Kiln pushed him away and he fell to the ground, blood quickly pooling around him.

The two men that Jonas had been fighting fell backwards as their free hands instinctively grabbed at the deep lacerations on their legs. Jonas used the brief distraction to his advantage. He lunged forward with his right blade, skewering one of the men in the heart. The man grunted and fell backwards, but the second assassin was faster and he quickly got his blade up to block Jonas's second strike. But the retreating wounded man could not stop the third and the fourth strikes. Jonas fell into the attack quickly and had both blades cutting devastating wounds across the man's chest. The assassin groaned, stumbled to his knees, and fell across a table, upturning it in the process.

Jonas scanned the room for more attackers. His heart pounded and his hands began to shake as the energy of battle still surged through him. These were the first men he had killed, and despite the fact that they had tried to kill him, he felt strangely sad about it. He saw Kiln to his left doing the same, blood dripping from his sword. Now that he had time he glanced back towards the fire and saw Taleen holding herself up against the wall, one hand on her sword and the other holding the shaft that protruded from her shoulder. She smiled weakly at him as she saw his look of concern.

"I'm fine, make sure there are no more assassins," she ordered.

The bar was now clear of all patrons. Everyone had run outside and away from the danger. Jonas moved toward Kiln who was wiping the blood from his blade on the cloak of one of the assassins.

"What do you make of them?" Jonas asked.

"Assassins it would seem," Kiln replied nonchalantly.

Suddenly, armed men, wearing the Annurien colors, rushed into the bar. They wore metal breast plates embossed with the Annurien symbol. The men fanned out, holding their swords in front of them at the ready.

The commander approached Jonas and Kiln hesitantly, his eyes quickly scanning the room and assessing the situation. As he neared them he lowered his sword. He was beyond middle aged, maybe fifty winters, and had a large shaved head. Tall and muscular, he had the look of a veteran warrior.

"I am Dagmar, captain of the night watch. What happened here? "

"I am Kiln, and this is Jonas, cavalier to Shyann. We were attacked by assassins. Behind me is Taleen, cavalier to Bandris. She is in need of healing," replied Kiln.

"I will see to her," Jonas said.

Kiln nodded his head in approval. He knelt down next to one of the bodies to get a better look. The man wore no armor, just a thin black cloak, and his legs and torso were covered with a dark tunic and leggings. His face was young and unremarkable.

"I had heard that cavaliers were in town. It seems that the rumors of attacks are not mere rumors," added the red haired warrior. Dagmar motioned to his men. "Get the bodies out of here and get this mess cleaned up."

"Wait," Taleen said as she approached one of the bodies with Jonas right beside her. She was able to walk, but the pain from the bolt was evident in her strained voice. "Just a second, I want to check something." Taleen knelt near one of the bodies and removed the hood. She used her left hand to lift the man's eye lid and turned it inside out. Jonas had moved up next to her to see what she was doing. On the underside of the man's eye lid was a small tattoo of a spider. "Just as I thought."

"What is that?" asked Jonas.

Kiln and Dagmar moved closer to her as she stood up.

"That was Bor-Zan's mark. I believe you call her, Naz-reen. She magically marks her servants on the inside of the eyelid or the lip." Dagmar made the protective mark across his chest at the mention of the evil goddess's name.

"Why were we unable to detect them?" asked Jonas.

"We have the power to detect evil, Jonas, but there are many different shades of darkness, as there is of goodness. Is a man who steals bread to feed his family evil?"

"Of course not," Jonas said.

"But it can be a start. That is how Naz-reen slowly molds her followers. She takes ordinary men, men who might be good but grow up in situations of her making, situations that test their resolve. She slowly shapes them into the criminals and assassins that you see before you. We didn't detect them because they were not truly evil, at least not yet. There is definitely a gray area when it comes to detecting evil, and these men fell into that area. They wore no symbols, which would have given them away to us. I do not know exactly, Jonas, but I have learned over the years to always be prepared, as we are not invincible to our enemies. We would have detected a true follower of Naz-reen, like the one you fought outside of Finarth, because they would have had all that is good hammered out of them, until all that remained was a black corrupt shell. These men were forced to do her bidding, maybe even blackmailed, but they had not yet been fully corrupted. They were her lackeys. It is quite sad really."

"They were weak men. I would rather have died than to have succumbed to her powers," said Kiln.

"Still no gray area? Black and white, eh?"

Kiln caught her tone and looked at her briefly, his face showing no emotion, before returning his gaze to Dagmar. It was a rhetorical question and he didn't bother answering it.

"Captain, we are leaving the city in the morning. Please station several guards here tonight in case we are attacked again," Kiln ordered.

The captain did not hesitate. "Yes sir. I will place my six best men here."

Dagmar turned to issue his orders just as Bomm approached them from the counter. He was carrying an old crossbow in his hand and he looked worried. "Cavaliers, General, I am sorry about this attack. I have never had something like this happen in my establishment." Bomm set the crossbow on the table.

"It is not your fault, Bomm, we have had the misfortune of being hunted for awhile now, and I believe it will continue. I'm sorry that it happened in your fine inn," Jonas replied sincerely.

"Thank you, sir. Rest assured that I got one of the assassins as he tried to flee." Bomm smiled, tapping his crossbow.

"You got the third crossbowman?" asked Jonas.

"I did. He tried to run out the door and I shot him from behind the bar."

They all looked toward the door and, sure enough, several of the night guards were trying to remove a dark cloaked man with a feathered shaft buried in his back.

"Good work, Bomm," added Kiln.

Bomm smiled, lifting up his crossbow again. "I fought one term in the Annurien Legion many years ago. I guess I didn't forget everything that I learned. Don't worry about a thing. Go to your rooms and get some sleep. I will take care of everything down here. I will make sure that you are awakened before sunrise and that you get a good warm meal in the morning. I will also pack you some food for your journey."

"That is good of you, Bomm. Your generosity is much appreciated," Taleen said.

"It is you who are appreciated. We need you now more than anything." Bomm bowed as if royalty stood before him. "Now, I have much work to do to get this cleaned up, so if you will excuse me." Bomm turned and immediately began issuing orders to his staff. They were standing around dumfounded looking at the guards, the cavaliers, and corpses that littered the blood splattered floor.

Jonas looked at Taleen with concern. "Time to get that bolt out."

Taleen grimaced, smiling awkwardly. "I was hoping you would forget."

"What do I do first?" asked Jonas, knowing that she was joking. Jonas had heard that pulling a bolt or arrow from your flesh was extremely painful, and he did not relish performing the task on Taleen anymore than she did.

Taleen sat down on a chair. "First you pull the shaft out. Then you heal me as you did Kiln. And please do it fast."

"I will pull the shaft as Jonas heals," Kiln said, moving towards her. "It will be faster that way."

"Very well," replied Taleen. "Let's get this over with."

Kiln stood above her while Jonas knelt down and held her hands. Taleen squeezed his hands as Kiln gripped the shaft and put the other hand on her shoulder for leverage. "Ready?" he asked softly.

"Yes," Taleen replied through gritted teeth.

"I am," Jonas added. His eyes were already closed. Kiln tightened his grip and jerked the shaft out with one quick pull. The bolt held for a second and Taleen groaned in pain. Then it ripped free from her flesh and crimson blood gushed from the wound. Taleen leaned over in pain as Jonas flooded her with healing magic.

He felt the power push through him as he asked Shyann for her help. Kiln watched as Jonas's hands glowed a bright blue. The magic entered Taleen as Jonas concentrated on mending her shoulder. There was no damage to the bone so he was able to focus on mending the torn flesh, cartilage, and blood vessels.

Taleen stood up straighter as the wound sealed and the pain began to recede. Finally Jonas's work was finished and he opened his eyes. Taleen was staring at him with gratitude. "Very good, Jonas, your power is truly amazing. You healed my wound perfectly and you did it so quickly."

Jonas stood up, happy that he could help her. "I am glad that I could take away your pain."

Taleen got to her feet, testing her shoulder by spinning her arm. There was no pain, and it moved smoothly. Kiln set the bloody shaft on the table and looked at them both. "Let's get some sleep. We have a big day ahead of us."

Ten
War

Lord Moredin had seen many things in his life but the sight of the Banthra so near him was unnerving. The darkness of the beast lay upon everything and everyone like a dense fog. He felt the evil of the demon permeate his very bones as he glanced over at the Banthra who was standing several paces away in the shadows of his tent.

Several months ago the demon appeared and demanded he give his allegiance to Malbeck, allegiance that he had no choice but to give, for the alternative was death. Laying siege to Finarth was not something that he was looking forward to, but after looking at his new allies, he thought to himself that the venture could turn very profitable. The Banthra had brought in thousands of orcs, goblins, ogres, tribesmen from the flatlands, and even several hundred boargs. Combined with the thousands that he could summon and the thousands that would come from Prince Bomballa, the outlook for this coming war seemed bright indeed. Besides, it was just the prelude to Malbeck's advancing army, who, when he arrived, would destroy his enemies and reward his allies. At least that is what Moredin hoped. But did he really have a choice? He didn't think so.

The war council was assembled and the large spacious tent was filled with faces he knew, and faces he'd rather never see again. Ongessett, chief of the orcs, stood to his right looking down at the map sprawled out across the table. The orc war chief stood a full head taller than Moredin and his bulky mass looked half as wide as he was tall. He wore heavy plate mail interlinked with black leather. Any gaps in his protection were filled with charcoal gray chain mail. Ongessett's massive neck supported a misshapen skull with a protruding pig like snout and thick lips that curled up exposing yellow fangs. His dark beady eyes scanned the map and Lord Moredin could see him struggling to process its intricate details. Ongessett was intelligent as far as orcs go, but that certainly did not mean that he could comprehend all that was being discussed. Moredin was not considered a good man, but even he didn't like his present company.

The Banthra stepped closer to the table and Lord Moredin and the others shifted nervously away from it. The black knight wore dark armor covered with runes written in a language that Lord Moredin did not understand. The Banthra's helm was made from dark steel, like his armor, and covered with serrated spikes. The most frightening part of the black knight's visage was its eyes, two red glowing orbs of pure hatred that penetrated the black narrow eye slits. Other than the eye slits, the helm covered its entire face. There was not even an opening for its mouth.

Lord Moredin glanced at the others surrounding the table. The Banthra drifted closer and a blanket of evil draped over them, filling them with despair, fright, anger, and other dark emotions that penetrated their meager shells of humanity. The Banthras presence stained their very souls.

Prince Bomballa, leader of Numenell, held his ground at the table but his eyes betrayed his resolve. Numenell was the gateway city to the Flatlands and it was home to many bandits and raiders that used the city as a staging base for raids into Finarth and the lands of Annure.

His eyes darted nervously. The feeling of despair emanating from the black knight was obviously taking its toll on the prince. The tall black nomad was wearing his traditional flashy clothes, a bright red coat over a silky white low cut shirt. His deep purple pants were made of the same fine silk and the outfit was finished off with knee high boots made from expensive soft leather. He wore a purple hat with a long feather protruding from it. At his side was a jeweled rapier and dagger.

Moredin laughed inwardly at the outfit but he knew that looks could be deceiving. Bomballa was a deadly swordsman and Moredin had seen him slay more than one person who had underestimated him based on his outward appearance.

Also at the table was Arg'on, a gigantic black tribesman from the Sithgarin who was Lord Moredin's war leader. He was huge and heavily muscled and the only thing he wore was the traditional war skirt that was standard for his tribe. A crisscrossed leather harness held together by a square piece of steel in the center of his chest wrapped his muscular torso. His tribe's symbol, a desert hunting hawk, was embossed on the small steel plate. A giant heavy broad sword was lashed to his back and his tribal skirt was made from supple leather covered with thin plates of steel. Lord Moredin had never seen such a powerful and fearless looking warrior in all his life and he was glad that Arg'on was on their side.

Lastly there was Chief Grazzit, leader of the goblins. Grazzit was short, about as tall as a child who had seen twelve years, but his long arms gave him a wiry look. His thick skin was gray and patches of dark hair covered his body. The beast's face was human in appearance but the yellow eyes, narrow fangs, and pointed ears were all too goblin-like. Dark plate mail covered thick wool clothing and at his waist hung a curved short sword.

Lord Moredin had heard that the history of the goblins was somehow linked to that of the elves, that they were fallen elves that had turned evil. He glanced briefly at the goblin and decided that there could be some truth to the legends.

The Banthra stepped to the table and slowly spread his hand over the map. The black spiked gauntlet clicked ominously as he opened his long fingers.

"We will use the goblins first to expose their archers," hissed the Banthra. The demons voice was soft and guttural and it made the men and monsters alike fidget with apprehension. "How many warriors do you have, Grazzit?"

"Five thousand, my Lord," muttered the goblin. His voice was high pitched and he mumbled slightly due to the many teeth that filled his mouth.

"Lord Moredin, you will use the phalanx, sending your cavalry around to the west while Prince Bomballa leads a second group of cavalry from the east. Arg'on will stay in the center with Ongessett and the orcs. I will leave the hundred ogres under your command, Chief Ongessett."

"Very good, Lord," replied Ongessett. The orc's expansive chest gave his voice a deep, rasping baritone sound.

"We will flank them and crush them." The Banthra's speech was slow and calm, but it carried the weight of power, and darkness. To Lord Moredin it felt like someone was running a claw down his spine. The others felt it too for they glanced around the room nervously.

"Lord, what will your part be in the battle?" Moredin asked boldly.

The demon slowly turned its spiked helm toward Moredin. The black knight's voice sounded like a whisper on the wind and its eyes sucked any shred of confidence from Moredin's body. "I will be where I am needed."

"Will our spy do his job as expected?" asked Bomballa nervously.

"Yesssss," whispered the demon. "Everything will be ready."

***

The Finarthian army had marched hard for several days before they reached the Lindsor Bridge. Scouts had been sent out periodically to assess the progress of the approaching army. Every modrig had been briefed daily as the enemy advanced into their lands.

Fil, Calden, and several other warriors sat around their fire discussing the news. Their army was spread as far as they could see and thousands of sparkling fires covered the grassy plains just beyond the Lindsor Bridge. The warriors with Fil and Calden were new recruits. Jack was a tall lean warrior who had joined the king's forces a year ago. He was a kind quiet man who Fil had immediately taken a liking to. Lumis, his short haired blonde friend, had just joined the army several months ago. Lumis was stout and more square shouldered and definitely the talkative one.

"What do you think?" asked Lumis as he stoked the warm coals with a stick.

"What do you mean, what do we think?" asked Calden.

"About the orcs and goblins," replied Lumis. Scouts had come in just that day and informed the king that Lord Moredin now marched with over ten thousand orcs and goblins. And to their dismay, they had also sighted ogres and boargs in the enemy ranks.

"I think we will kill them just like the rest," muttered Fil under his breath. Fil's mood had changed the last couple of days. He had become somber and agitated, his fear being replaced by a cold resolve to enact his revenge. Fil wanted nothing more than to kill and destroy the army that was approaching.

"Yeah, I guess we will," added Calden, looking at his friend with concern.

"I've never seen an orc or goblin before, have any of you?" asked Lumis.

"I saw a dead orc once," said Jack. "My father and I were hunting at the base of the Tundrens and we came across a ripped and torn body of an orc. A bear had killed it. It was hard to recognize, but my pa said it was an orc. It was pretty big and thick."

"If it has a heart it can be killed," Fil said, looking up at Jack. "If it bleeds, it can die. Boargs are tougher than orcs, but I've killed them before, and I will kill more."

Lumis and Jack looked at Fil with interest. "You've killed a boarg before?" asked Jack.

Calden knew of Fil's story but Fil had not brought up what had happened to his village to anyone outside of his knight apprentice group.

"Yes. They massacred my friends and family." The intensity in Fil's eyes was unnerving.

"I'm sorry, Fil. I did not know," Jack responded sincerely.

Fil stood up abruptly. "I will get my revenge. Let them come." He reached down, picked up his spear, and walked away into the darkness.

They watched him leave before Lumis spoke up. "I didn't know that his family was killed. What happened?"

Calden added another log onto the fire. "Fil and his friend, Jonas, lost their entire village to boargs almost four years ago. He has not forgotten it."

"I imagine not, nor would I," Jack replied.

"What happened to his friend?" asked Lumis.

"I am not at liberty to say. But I will tell you that Jonas left the knight apprenticeship several years ago. We have not heard from him since."

"Why would he leave and give up the chance to become a knight? Doesn't make much sense," Jack said.

Calden snorted softly. "If you knew the circumstances you wouldn't be saying that." He offered no more information so they went back to staring into the fire.

After a couple of minutes Jack spoke up. "Are you scared?"
Calden and Lumis looked at each other, replying together, "Yes."

***

The trio had made it past Ta'Ron in good time. They passed through the city quickly, staying only long enough to learn that Lord Dynure had joined forces with his brother, King Olegaurd, four days ago, and was marching toward Finarth. Ta'Ron was a vassal city to Annure, and although not as large, still held a standing army of five thousand. The combined force would reach the Lindsor Bridge and join forces with the Finarthian army within the week.

The three rode hard across the grasslands staying clear of all major roads. The long journey was uneventful until they set up camp two days from Finarth. Kiln decided it was okay to light a fire so he went about collecting wood. They had run into no problems and since they were not traveling the roads they had not seen anyone else since they left Ta'Ron. Kiln figured it wouldn't hurt to have a fire for as long as it took to cook a warm meal. They could put it out after they warmed their bellies with good food and hot tea. As he collected small branches from the plentiful shrubs, Taleen set up their sleeping rolls, while Jonas tethered the horses to one of the thick shrubs that grew like weeds across the grasslands.

Jonas was tying off the rope when he heard a horse whinny in the distance. "What was that?" he asked, standing up quickly, his hand moving to one of his swords.

Taleen and Kiln got to their feet as well, looking towards the sound. In the distance, cresting a gentle hill stood a magnificent white horse. The sun was setting behind the hill, silhouetting the majestic animal like a fine painting.

The horse whinnied again, rearing up on its hind legs. Jonas looked closer and saw that the animal was wearing silver plate mail that covered its head and chest. The horse also had a saddle that was rigged with sparkling silver buckles.

Taleen looked at Jonas and smiled. "I think your steed has arrived," she said as Jonas stared at the horse in wonder.

"You think so?"

The horse was now running down the hill toward them. As it neared them, Jonas's breath caught in his throat. It was the most striking horse he had ever seen. Its bright white coat was perfectly smooth and shining like it had been recently washed and brushed. The horse's white mane bounced and fluttered in the wind as it galloped towards them.

There was not a speck of dirt on the animal. Its entire body was milky white, like freshly churned cream. The horse stopped ten paces away and looked right at Jonas. The plate mail on its chest was embossed with the silver and blue emblem of Shyann. The silver steel was mirror-like and it shone with brilliance. The black leather saddle was polished and lined with gleaming pieces of metal. Under the saddle lay a blue and silver cloth that rested over a blanket of sparkling chain mail. The horse snorted, nodding its head toward Jonas, seemingly beckoning him to approach. Jonas stood there awestruck.

"I think he wants you to come to him," muttered Kiln, who was also staring in wonder at the incredible animal.

Jonas slowly approached the white horse. It gazed at him calmly, standing perfectly still. As Jonas neared the animal he was surprised at how big it was.

Taleen was also awed by the animal's size and splendor. "That is the biggest, most magnificent horse I have ever seen," she said.

"He must be over twenty hands tall," added Kiln.

Jonas reached out, touching the horse on the head. Instantly Jonas felt a warmth flow through his hand. The horse turned and looked at him and Jonas clearly saw the intelligence in its deep black eyes. He gently stroked the animal's head, laying his other hand on the horse's muscular neck. Its glistening coat revealed rippling muscles forming the most perfect specimen of any steed Jonas had ever seen. He noticed that the saddle was covered with intricate artwork, embossed symbols of the gods, many of which Jonas recognized from the Kulam. Every piece of leather and shining metal that made up the saddle and harness had some sort of etching or carving. There was also a place for his bow and quiver.

Jonas's hands moved down the animal's side as he admired the horse's perfect form. The horse was so large that the saddle was level with his eyes. He noticed that there was a blue cloth rolled up behind the saddle and strapped down with black buckles. Jonas unbuckled the cloth, lifting it off the horse. It was turquoise blue and made from a soft and flowing fabric. He unfurled it, holding it out before him. The outer fabric was like wool, but much softer, and the inside was lined with another fabric, something similar to cotton. It was a fine cloak, edged with silver thread, and on the back of the garment was a magnificent embroidered oak tree. It was the very same symbol that covered Jonas's chest and the armor on the front of the horse.

"There can be no doubt, that horse is your cavalier steed," Taleen said.

Jonas smiled, flipping the cloak over his shoulders. There was a silver clasp with a blue sapphire in the middle. He clipped the clasp together and glanced up at Taleen and Kiln. "How do I look?" he asked with a big smile on his face.

"Like a cavalier," replied Kiln evenly.

Jonas turned his attention back to the horse who was still staring directly at him. "What do I call you? What would be a fitting name?" Jonas thought for a moment. Suddenly he smiled at himself. "I shall call you, Tulari," he said, "my mother's middle name. It is elvish."

"What does it mean?" asked Taleen.

"Honorable," replied Jonas.

"A fitting name for such a fine steed," added Kiln.

***

King Olegaurd was a tall man, lanky, with sharp features like the craggy edges of broken rock. His armor was polished silver and edged in gold. Draped over his shoulders was a cavalry cape the color of deep purple, and embroidered in gold thread was the Annurien emblem. His hair was cut short, infantry style, and he was mostly shaven except for a few days of stubble. The king's hair was dark brown and interlaced with silver. Thick bushy eyebrows edged his dark eyes, tired from hard riding and lack of sleep. But that did not take away the aura of power that emanated from him as he stepped into King Gavinsteal's command tent.

With him was his younger brother, Lord Dynure of Ta-Ron, who was a spitting image of the king, but with lighter hair and much less silver. He too was tall, and together they portrayed a sense of calm power.

They had ridden hard with their army and had arrived at the Lindsor Bridge just before sunset. Orders were dispatched and their men had set up camp in the large open fields that covered the Finarthian hills for miles. Moments later they were escorted to the command tent.

Inside, King Gavinsteal was looking over several maps with his commanders. In audience were General Kuarin, General Ruthalis, and General Gandarin, along with first lance, Tilvus, leader of the Finarthian Knights. All the men were in battle armor and dressed for war. Standing next to their father were Prince Baylin and Prince Nelstrom. They, too, were in full armor in preparation for the coming violence.

King Gavinsteal withdrew from the map and moved to greet the king. "King Olegaurd, Lord Dynure, we thank you for coming, your presence is of great value to us." The Finarthian king shook each of their hands in the warrior's grip.

"Of course, we came in all haste and I'm glad to see that we were not too late," replied King Olegaurd. His deep voice sounded like the rumbling of an angry mountain.

Lord Dynure spoke. "King Gavinsteal, please inform us what you know as we have received no other information from your messenger other than the fact that an army approaches bearing the banner of Lord Moredin. What else can you tell us?"

"Please, come and take a look at the map," the king replied as he beckoned to a servant who was standing calmly at the edge of the tent. "May I offer you some wine?" he asked.

"That would be most gracious," answered King Olegaurd. The servant went to a nearby table and poured several goblets of red wine.

"King Olegaurd, Lord Dynure, it is good to see you again. It's been too long and I dare say I wish the circumstances were different," Prince Baylin added as he greeted them both with firm handshakes. "You remember my brother, Prince Nelstrom."

"Of course," replied King Olegaurd with a nod to the younger prince.

"And General Ruthalis, Kuarin, and Gandarin," continued Prince Baylin as they all greeted each other.

"Yes, it is good to see you all," replied the Annurien king nodding to each of them as he took a goblet of wine offered by the servant. "Now, let us get to business so we can hope to get a few hours of rest tonight."

The commanders smiled briefly at that comment as they knew that most of the night would be spent planning, issuing orders to subordinates, and preparing for the coming battle. Little, if any, sleep would be gotten this night.

"Very good," King Gavinsteal began, "what we now know is that Lord Moredin's army is one day out on the east road to Stonestep," he said as he indicated the positions on the map.

"Do we have accurate numbers assessments?" asked Lord Dynure.

"No," replied Prince Baylin, "our best guess is that he has near twenty thousand troops, ten of which come from various Sithgarin tribes. Our spies and scouts have not been very successful as the enemy is using boargs to guard their perimeter. The beasts can sniff my men out a mile away," continued Baylin, frustration evident in his voice.

"Your court wizard?" questioned King Olegaurd. "If I recall correctly, Alerion was his name. Why has he not been used to get more information?"

"Indisposed at the moment," King Gavinsteal said. "I have him hunting down other more pertinent information."

"A blind army is a dead army," stated King Olegaurd bluntly.

"His absence is necessary," replied King Gavinsteal simply. There was a pause as if the Annurien king was expecting the king to continue, but he did not add any more information.

"They also have orcs, and possibly goblins," General Ruthalis added, filling the silence. The general was not very tall, but he was built like a warrior, lean and strong, his handsome face tanned from many days in the saddle under the hot sun.

"What could possibly force Moredin to fight alongside orcs?" Lord Dynure asked. "The man is a backstabbing dung eater but even he must draw the line somewhere. And how was he able to unite that many tribes to fight?"

"Something is binding them together," replied the first lance. Tilvus was pale, with plain features, but his mind was sharp and he was a natural at leading men.

Prince Baylin addressed the men. "We do not know what is binding them together, nor why he would openly attack us. His force sounds formidable, larger than I would have guessed he could bring together. But even if he defeats us here there is no way that he can take Finarth with his army, and surely he must know this."

"Perhaps, but maybe he does not mean to win," said General Gandarin. Gandarin was thick and his big head was covered with shaggy brown hair. His scarred face sported a bushy mustache and beard. Well known and respected, his presence resonated raw power and strong leadership. All eyes turned to him immediately.

"Meaning?" questioned King Olegaurd.

"Maybe they are just stalling. If the early reports from Alerion are accurate, then perhaps Malbeck's army is massing to attack Tarsis, and in order to keep any of us from going to Tarsis's aid, he occupies us here with another smaller force."

"We had thought of that," Baylin answered, "but it would take us over a month to march to Tarsis, and that is only if the weather holds before winter."

"Might be just a precaution though, a guarantee that Tarsis and Finarth could not aid one another," reasoned King Gavinsteal.

"So, Malbeck is back?" asked the stunned King Olegaurd.

"We do not know, but we suspect so," said King Gavinsteal wearily. "An army is massing near Banrith, and we have reliable information that the Banthras are back, or at least one was. And then we have reports that many of our cavaliers have been hunted down and killed." The king sighed in frustration.

"I know about the cavaliers, a great worry no doubt, but a Banthra? Are you sure?" asked Lord Dynure, his tone skeptical.

"We are. Airos, the cavalier, killed one, but unfortunately he died in the process," Prince Baylin said.

"Let us discuss what we should do here and now, not about what is our best guess." Prince Nelstrom spoke for the first time. "Tomorrow Moredin's army will be here. What are we going to do about it?"

King Olegaurd looked at Prince Nelstrom. His dark eyes narrowed momentarily as he took in the prince's curt words. Then he looked away and down at the maps on the table. "It is a foolish commander who ignores intelligence that has been gathered," he said slowly before turning his gaze to the other commanders. It was not often that someone spoke to the prince that way, but none of them seemed to be terribly concerned, except for Prince Nelstrom of course, who looked as if he might boil over. But before he could respond, the Annurien king continued. "The young prince is partly right, though. Let us plan for tomorrow, and then the living can worry about whether Malbeck is back or not."

***

Fil stood with his modrig facing the massive army assembling before them. The grasslands beyond the Lindsor Bridge were a perfect place for a battle. They were open as far as the eyes could see and covered with knee high grass. The colossal bridge was the only spot that an army could cross the river to approach the city of Finarth. It would have to be protected.

The Finarthian army, now combined with King Olegaurd's troops, had assembled early that morning as their scouts had reported the enemy army moving into position. Fil's modrig would be part of the infantry that stormed the center of the enemy ranks. King Oleguard and King Gavinsteal had met with their war commanders all night planning their attack. Fil had a fairly good idea of what the plan was. Tanus, their commander, had briefed them on their role in the battle. As the enemy army approached they would use their archers and the travel catapults.

Fil had not seen the catapults used before, but after looking at the hundred or so lined up beyond the bridge he easily surmised their role. Each one had a long arm that had a large stone as a counter weight to violently swing the opposite end into the air, launching the desired missile. They were built on huge wagons pulled by oxen.

As the enemy ranks were being bombarded with arrow and stone, the infantry would slowly advance with long spears and shields. King Gavinsteal would keep a reserve line in the back while the cavalry, led by the famous Finarthian Knights, would move in and flank the enemy. That was the plan anyway and Fil hoped that it would be successful.

The sun was just rising as the advancing enemy army stopped on the rise of a gentle hill. They were still a distance away but Fil could hear the goblins as they screeched and banged their shields. They spread out across the hill like a black wave ready to swamp them all. Fil could not see beyond the hill but he knew that there was more to the army than what they were seeing.

Calden stood next to him holding his long black spear tightly. "You ready for this?" he asked nervously.

"I am," Fil replied firmly, his desire for revenge burying any residual fear he felt as he viewed the approaching goblin horde. "Remember, they bleed, and die, like anything else."

Calden nodded his head, looking nervously toward the army of goblins before them. Fil glanced to his left and right at the thousands of stern fighting men quietly facing the enemy. They stood firm, their jaws clamped shut with resolve, their hands gripping long spears as if their lives depended on it. Maybe they would.

Suddenly a loud deep horn bellowed across the grasslands and the screaming goblins were racing down the hill toward them. It happened so quickly that Fil's heart seemed to leap from his chest. It was finally happening. He had trained for this, waited for this, waited for his chance to revenge his family and friends. And now it was upon him. He would not fail them.

Tanus rode his warhorse across the front of his modrig yelling for the men to hold their line. He was wearing his great helm, and the boarg horns protruding from it helped remind Fil of the revenge that was due.

Anger boiled within him and his knuckles turned white as he squeezed his spear shaft. His heavy shield was strapped tightly to his right arm but he barely felt the weight of it as he vividly recalled the death and destruction of his town.

The Finarthian army answered the goblin's charge with their own horns, signaling thousands of archers to let their deadly shafts fly. The arrows were so thick in the air that they momentarily blocked the sun's light. Fil then heard the sound of the catapults behind him as they unleashed their lethal barrage of stone.

He looked up into the sky, seeing huge flaming spheres fly over them and explode in flame as they landed in the goblin ranks. Hundreds of goblins fell victim to the flames and arrows in several seconds.

"What are those?" asked Fil, for it was obvious that the catapults had not launched stones.

Gandis, a veteran warrior to his left, answered him. "Flaming jugs of oil. When they hit, fiery oil engulfs whoever is unfortunate to be near."

Despite their losses, the goblins kept coming like a swarm of locusts. They were getting closer now and Fil could make out their distorted faces, fanged teeth, and yellow beady eyes. They were a mass of spindly bodies screaming wildly as they ran toward them with no discipline. Fil gripped his spear tightly, waiting for the order to advance.

He momentarily glanced up to the top of the hill to see another large group of hulking demi-humans emerge. They were much bigger than the goblins and thicker of limb. They must be orcs, thought Fil. He also spotted a handful of even larger foes, enemies that Fil recognized, for they were ogres.

Fil's attention went back to the advancing goblins as a high pitched horn blew; it was the signal for their advance. Fil angled his spear forward and started moving toward the enemy with determination. The entire infantry began to march toward the screaming goblins that were now only a couple hundred paces away. The infantry lowered their long spears even further and the second horn blew ordering them to move double speed. Slowly the infantry built up speed as they approached the goblin horde. A deadly line of glittering spear tips bobbed up and down as they moved at the quick step, a drill they had practiced hundreds of times.

One hand carried their famous infantry shields while the other carried their spears. The shields were basically round with one spot cut out on the top in a small half circle. It allowed the infantry soldiers to hold the shield in front of them and angle their spears out over them, giving each warrior a spot to rest the heavy spear and jab it forward into a mass of enemies. It was an effective technique and one they had drilled for many hours.

The wall of sparkling metal spear tips spanned to Fil's left and right farther than he could see. He screamed a battle cry, focusing on one goblin before him and listened for the signal.

Then he heard it.

A loud screeching horn sounded over the battle field and the infantry suddenly stopped in one big mass, shields came up in a solid wall of steel and spear tips angled out as the approaching goblins neared.

The two armies came together in a clash of bodies and steel. The sound was deafening but Fil kept his focus on the screaming beasts before him.

The goblins were propelled backward as they smashed against the solid shield wall. Thousands of the howling beasts were skewered by the razor sharp spears. The power of the wall came not from the first line, but the lines after them. The bodies of the men behind the first line supported each other and drove them forward as the goblins smashed into them. If someone in the first line fell then the man behind him moved into the position.

Spears jabbed forward again and again dropping the goblins by the hundreds. The Finarthian infantry slowly advanced, stepping over the growing number of enemy bodies.

Fil took his first goblin right in the throat and the momentum of its charge ran the spear point through the beast's neck and a full pace up the spear shaft. Fil was forced to drop the spear and the dead goblin to the ground, and draw his short infantry sword. Battle lust took over and he screamed maniacally holding his shield and sword before him.

The battle was fierce and the noise deafening. Men and goblins alike screamed in defiance and pain. Blood, sweat, and dirt flew everywhere as the battle progressed. The trained infantry kept their shield wall tight as they used spear and infantry swords to deadly effect.

Fil blocked a downward stroke from a goblin sword with his shield and used his immense power to shield charge the beast. He rammed the shocked goblin with his shield, taking the beast directly in the face. The goblin's head snapped back violently and Fil finished it off with a downward stroke of his heavy short sword. The blade took the goblin in the neck, showering them both with thick blood.

He felt Calden's shield bang against his as his friend tried to fend off two goblins and still maintain the integrity of the wall. Fil noticed that he had moved forward too fast creating a gap in the wall near his friend.

He shuffled backwards and locked shields with Calden, taking another powerful strike against his shield. The blow knocked him back and his arm stung from the force, but he gritted his teeth, jabbing his sword forward and down through the gap he created by angling his shield to the right.

They had practiced the very same maneuver hundreds of times and now that training was paying off. Their short infantry swords were not made for jabbing, but their short length and weight made them deadly if used correctly and in conjunction with their sword brothers. The idea was to create gaps in the shield wall and jab forward and down, or forward and left and right, allowing the weight of the sharp blade to cut into arms and legs. If the wall could be maintained then the tactic generally proved deadly to their enemies.

This was the first time that Fil saw its practice in reality, and he thanked his trainers silently as he felt his blade swing down and cut into the thigh of the goblin before him. The beast stumbled to its knee and Fil finished it off with a powerful slash across its neck.

As the goblin fell to its death, Fil noticed the sunlight had momentarily disappeared. He glanced up and saw, to his dismay, thousands of arrows on their downward decent.

He had just enough time to get his shield up before the arrows turned him into a pin cushion. Many men near and behind him weren't so lucky and their screams of pain and death sounded all around. He even heard the grunts and howls of goblins as they, too, fell victim to their own arrows. Three arrows pounded into his shield just as he saw a surviving goblin in front of him jab a spear at his unprotected belly.

Fil could do nothing but turn his body at the last minute, but it was enough. The tip of the goblin spear struck his leather armor a glancing blow and the deadly point slid by harmlessly, cutting a nasty gash across the hardened leather.

The goblin stopped its forward momentum but it could not pull its spear back for a second strike as Fil had slammed the hard edge of his shield down on top of the shaft, breaking it cleanly in two. Then he swung his heavy sword down on the goblin's arm, cutting it in half just as easily as the spear shaft.

There was a brief reprieve as the barrage of arrows killed many men and goblins alike, creating gaps between the two forces.

Fil looked to his right to see Calden battling two goblins. They had both survived the enemy arrows, but now, they and their nearby comrades, faced the enemy in disarray, their formation momentarily crumbling around them.

Fil could not believe that Moredin's forces launched their arrows into the fighting ranks while they fought so closely. Obviously they would kill some of their own troops in the process, which of course they had. But Fil did not have time to think any further on it as his friend battled for his life. He frantically looked for a way to help Calden, when his eyes glimpsed a discarded spear at his feet. Sheathing his sword, he picked up the spear.

He was getting ready to throw it when another goblin attacked him from the left. He used the spear like a staff, hitting the goblin's sword away and then reversing the swing, taking the goblin in the side of the head. The goblin grunted, stumbling as Fil spun the spear around quickly, lancing the off-balance beast in the side with the razor sharp point. The goblin fell away into the battling mass of men and beasts around him.

Fil turned in one smooth motion and hefted the spear back for a throw. He spotted Calden fifteen paces away struggling to keep the goblins at bay. He used his powerful arms and legs, throwing the spear as hard as he could. Fil's weapon of choice was the spear and not many could use it as proficiently as he. He had practiced with it every day and he could throw a spear farther and more accurately than any of the knight apprentices.

His practice had paid off, for the spear took one of the goblins in the side and the powerful throw launched the beast into the other goblin. Both creatures landed heavily on the ground and Calden cleaved the uninjured one with his short sword before the beast could untangle himself from his dead comrade. Calden glanced toward Fil and smiled before he was forced to engage another goblin.

Fil forced a frantic smile back as he glanced around at the chaos around him. He looked up and saw Tanus on his warhorse twenty paces away swinging his longer cavalry sword left and right, cutting into the enemy ranks, leaving a swath of death in his wake as he expertly led his horse through the mass of goblins.

Fil glimpsed a goblin sneaking toward Tanus from behind with a long spear in its hand. Fil looked around frantically for another spear but there were none to be found.

"Tanus, behind you!" Fil yelled.

Tanus glanced toward Fil, pivoting his horse around simultaneously. The warhorse shouldered several goblins out of the way but he wasn't quite fast enough as the goblin jabbed up with the long shaft. The spear point took Tanus in the shoulder, penetrating a gap between his protective plates and knocking him off balance.

Fil unsheathed his blade and charged toward his commander, screaming in rage as he went. At the last minute he lifted up his shield, barreling through a goblin that stood in his way.

Tanus landed hard on his back, the wind knocked from his lungs, his helm dislodged from his head. Gasping for breath, he struggled to stand and find his sword just as he saw the spear wielding goblin jump on top of him screaming in bloodlust. The goblin kicked him in the face so hard that he saw stars as blood and a few teeth flew from his mouth. Tanus lay flat on his back, trying to shake off the dizziness. The goblin howled with glee and reversed its grip on the spear so that the point was angling towards him. Tanus looked up as the spear tip descended. Everything slowed as he looked upon his own death.

Suddenly a soldier rammed into the goblin, launching the beast into the air. Tanus didn't waste any time getting up and grabbing his sword from the ground. He stumbled slightly as he shook off the fogginess and pain. After a few seconds he planted his legs firmly and stood up.

Fil stood next to him holding his blood smeared shield and sword.

"Nice timing," Tanus said, looking about the battle field.

"Thanks."

Blood ran freely from Tanus's shoulder and mouth but the wounds did not seem to affect him. He nodded and then quickly engaged the nearest goblin with a defiant roar.

Fil fought next to Tanus for what seemed like an eternity. Goblins stacked up around them as they slashed, stabbed, and cut their way through the beasts.

Fil's sword arm began to tire and his body was dripping sweat and blood. Suddenly another enemy horn sounded and Fil and Tanus looked around as they took advantage of the quick break from the fighting.

"What is that?" Fil gasped through deep breaths.

"The enemy is sending in their second line." Tanus glanced around for his horse and saw his steed close by. The well trained animal didn't leave his master's side even in the heat of battle.

Tanus ran to his horse, stumbling slightly, the exhaustion and loss of blood from the wound now taking its toll. Fil rushed to Tanus and caught him before he fell.

"Let me help you," he said as he guided Tanus to his horse and helped him into the saddle.

"My thanks," Tanus muttered as he scanned the scene from his higher vantage point.

"What do you see, sir?" Fil asked anxiously.

"As I thought, they are sending in their second line." Tanus pulled out a horn from the side of his horse's saddle and blew it three times. It was the signal to reform their modrigs.

Quickly the soldiers reformed their fighting lines and tried to reestablish their shield wall. The remaining goblins had retreated and reformed with the advancing orcs and humans that were marching towards them. The enemy was beating huge war drums as the lumbering orcs marched down the hill. The menacing sound was deafening and the men around Fil looked about nervously. But most of them were veterans and they held their ground, their iron resolve strengthening the will of the younger inexperienced soldiers near them.

A horn blew behind them and Fil glanced back to see their reserve line move into position. Fil understood their role perfectly. The reserve line would fill any gaps that broke in their own line. Simultaneously the cavalry would be attacking from the flanks.

Fil could not see King Gavinsteal anywhere but he suspected he would be leading the Finarthian Knights into battle. Fil looked around for

Calden and could not see him among the tired and bloody men nearby. He was exhausted and covered with the grime of battle.

"Drink from your water skins!" bellowed Tanus as he rode in front of his modrig. At his commander's words Fil noticed how dry his mouth was. He took a long pull from his water skin, relishing the taste as the cold water took away the cottonmouth coating his tongue. The water brought new vigor back into his tired body.

Fil looked down and picked up another fallen spear. The thick shaft in his hand felt comforting as he looked upon the approaching horde of orcs and humans. The booming of the drums corresponded to the thumping of his heart as the adrenaline of battle coursed through his body.

Behind the orcs, Fil could make out the upper bodies of the massive ogres ambling towards them. The pace of the drums quickened and the orcs picked up their pace.

Fil set his feet into the ground, lifted up his shield with his sword brothers, and held his spear in front of him as the orcs bellowed defiantly, racing towards them, howling for blood.

"Give them nothing but death!" screamed Tanus on his horse as he lifted his sword into the air. The wound in his shoulder had stopped bleeding but the injury still hurt. He shook off the pain, raised his war horn to his mouth and blew into it, giving the signal to move forward at the single step. The silent infantry slowly advanced toward the enraged orcs, spears and shields held before them.

The two forces crashed together making a noise like a thunder clap. The fighting was intense and the tired men fared poorly against the fresh enemy troops. The orcs were strong and powerful and they sensed that their enemy was tiring. Tanus saw his line starting to falter.

"Formation, get in formation!" he screamed, pivoting his horse expertly behind the ranks. All the warriors near him quickly got shoulder to shoulder again, their shields defending the sword arm of the soldier next to him.

The reserve line sent in fresh troops to fill the gaps and maintain the line. Orcs ran at the formation wall with no sense of control or organization. The trained men used their shields to block the attacks while their sword brothers jabbed and cut into the orcs with their short swords.

King Gavinsteal, dressed in full battle array and carrying a long glittering lance, rode his warhorse over the peak of the hill. Behind him were two thousand Finarthian Knights. His armor shone brightly in the afternoon sun and his royal sword was strapped to his broad back. The king was old but he knew the importance of leading his men into battle. His very presence would provide the resolve his warriors needed to defeat this large force invading their homeland.

The king looked down at the battle and saw that his infantry was holding the orcs back, but barely. His eyes narrowed in anger and his jaw clenched in frustration as he surveyed the scene before him. For every orc that died upon the line, another took its place. The reserve line was filling in the gaps perfectly but they could only maintain the formation for so long.

Dagrinal rode up next to the king and gazed at the battle below. "Should I give the signal, my Lord?" he asked. "King Olegaurd should be in place with his cavalry on the east side."

Upon the signal, both cavalries would ride in to flank the enemy army, each group representing the fearsome points of the "horn of the bull" attack. The powerful maneuver was designed to crush the enemy from all sides.

But something didn't seem right to King Gavinsteal. Where was the enemy cavalry? Surely they had some mounted warriors. Also, there was no sign of Lord Moredin or Prince Bomballa in the enemy ranks. Where were they? King Gavinsteal continued surveying the battle and the lands beyond, anxiously looking for some clues.

"My King, if we don't give the signal the infantry will be crushed. What are your orders?" asked Dagrinal again.

The king put his hand up to silence Dagrinal as he mulled over the decision, his eyes never leaving the battle below.

Prince Baylin rode up next to his father. His royal armor was polished brightly and his double headed battle axe was strapped to his back. The visor on his helm was up and his father noticed his worried expression.

"Are you thinking the same thing I am?" asked the king, turning to look at his son.

"I am. Where is their cavalry?" Prince Baylin asked.

"I don't know. I've been blinded all night and day. They have boargs patrolling their perimeter and none of my scouts have returned. The boargs continue to sniff them out," added the frustrated king.

"We have to assume that their cavalry is waiting for us to make our move and then they will try to flank us," replied the prince as he surveyed the battle.

"Where is Nelstrom?" asked the king, looking about for his younger son.

Prince Baylin now knew about Nelstrom not being his brother, but he said nothing to his father about it. He figured if he wanted to talk about it that he would bring it up when he was ready. For now, with all that was happening, the issue seemed trivial in the big picture of things.

"I don't know, father. I haven't seen him. But you must make a decision now or our infantry will be destroyed."

They all looked down as the ogres threw stones the size of human heads, punching holes in their infantry formation. The stones crushed several men at a time but the reserve line moved in to fill the gaps. The formation was holding but it was obvious they wouldn't hold much longer.

"Baylin, stay here with half an akron. Keep Graggis with you. Dagrinal, you and I will sound the horn for the advance. If you see their cavalry, sound the horn and we will retreat to a defensive position while you ride in with your five hundred and re-flank them."

"Yes, Father. May Ulren be with you," the prince replied.

"And you, my son," replied the king. "Dagrinal, give the signal."

The king hefted his long lance and dropped his visor down over his face.

***

Fil's arm was starting to tire. The orcs kept coming, ignoring the bodies of their brethren as they plodded through ground sodden with their blood. The Finarthian infantry stepped over their own dead bodies as they slowly pushed their formation forward.

A young man to Fil's left suddenly disappeared as a huge rock blasted him from the line. A screaming orc with a black sword jumped at Fil, trying to barrel his way through the shield wall.

Fil had learned from Tanus that orcs purposely keep their blades dirty, that they sheath them still covered in blood, in hopes that they will turn black and become infested with grime that caused infections. A cut from an orc's blade, even one that was minor, could be life threatening.

So he kept a wary eye on the orc's sword as he jumped in front of the beast, lifting his shield to block its forward attack. But he couldn't concentrate on that foe as another orc came at his sword arm. Long ago Fil had dropped his spear for his close formation sword, and he used it well. He slashed his sword across the attacking orc's forearm as the other orc grabbed the edge of his shield, trying to yank it from his grasp.

The orc was strong, but so was Fil. He gritted his teeth and dug deep for the strength to keep the shield up. The orc's face was close and he could smell its vile breath over the edge of the shield. The orc kept pulling on the shield and Fil's tired arm was starting to weaken.

Fil pictured his younger brother being ripped apart by boargs and his vision blurred momentarily as raw anger flowed through his body. He gritted his teeth as he came eye to eye with the gruesome monster. The beast's yellow eyes with their dark pupils pulsed with hatred. Its thick greenish skin resembled dried mud baking in the summer sun.

The orc growled, showing its long rotting canines. Its deformed head was bald, devoid of all hair except for a few patches that grew in random places.

The orc that Fil had cut on the arm dropped its sword and roared in pain, its forearm flayed open like a gutted fish.

"Time to die," Fil whispered to the orc in front of him. He couldn't hold the shield any longer, so he simply let the orc pull it. As the orc yanked the shield back, Fil used that momentum to lunge forward with his forehead, ramming the boney part of his skull into to the face of the orc, shattering its pig-like nose and several teeth. The impact was jarring but Fil maintained his balance, skewering the dazed orc right through the throat.

Suddenly he heard the cavalry horn. He quickly looked up and to the sides to see the knights storm down the hillside. The thundering horses shook the earth as the knight's long glittering lances sparkled in the sun.

The men around him cheered with newfound energy as the charging knights sent hope into the tired infantry. Fil's battle lust returned and he, too, cheered as new strength coursed through his body. His sword felt lighter as he lifted it to defend his land.

The knights' lances tore into the orcs, killing hundreds of them instantly. Many lances were lost on the initial charge, either breaking on shields or piercing enemy warriors and falling to the ground with their victims. It wasn't long before the knights were using their close formation weapon, the long cavalry sword.

The Finarthian Knights were known for their horsemanship and their skills were quickly displayed with deadly precision. They maintained their formation as they cut through the orcs, swinging their cavalry swords left and right, destroying the screaming monsters. Each horse was perfectly positioned to give them room to fight but also to maintain the line without any breaks. They had trained long and hard with their steeds until their movements became nearly instinctive.

King Olegaurd's cavalry reacted to the signal horn as well. He and his brother, Lord Dynure, led fifteen hundred Annurian cavalry into the right flank. The orcs and ogres were in utter chaos. They were being attacked on three sides now as the 'horns of the bull' drove them back up the hill. Hundreds died as the unstoppable maneuver slowly closed in on the desperate creatures that couldn't escape.

Dagrinal kept close to his king, his spinning sword defending his liege with lighting speed. The swordsman glanced to his left, making sure that King Gavinsteal was still close.

The king swung his massive sword with one hand, his powerful arm easily cleaving his sword into whatever unfortunate creature got close. But his movements were slowing already, his age taking its toll on the battle hardened warrior.

Dagrinal urged his horse on, expertly moving it closer to the tiring king. He roared defiantly as he lanced an orc through the eye and looked up for his next victim.

A huge ogre lumbered near on their right. The beast was twenty paces away and he carried a large stone in his hand.

"Lord, look out!" shouted Dagrinal as he frantically drove his horse forward. The ogre heaved the stone overhand with a loud grunt just as the king swung his horse toward the beast with his sword raised high.

The stone took the king's horse in the neck, snapping its spine instantly and sending the king flying backwards into the air.

"To the king!" yelled Dagrinal as he leaped from his horse and ran to King Gavinsteal. One burly orc raced forward with a wicked looking axe lifted over his head. The beast growled and started to swing its axe downward towards the unconscious king's head when a flying dagger took the orc in its open mouth.

Dagrinal followed his knife, jumping over the king, straddling his inert form and swinging his long sword in a deadly dance, keeping the attacking orcs away. Enemy blood covered his plate mail and Dagrinal clenched his jaw firmly, gazing through the eye slits of his helm at the enemies surrounding him. "Come on! This kill will not be that easy!" yelled Dagrinal as more orcs attacked him viciously, hoping to kill the downed king and the man now guarding him.

One lunged forward trying to skewer the swordsman but Dagrinal was too fast. He swatted the sword away with a lighting quick parry and sent his sword swinging left and right so fast that the orc didn't even register the fact that its stomach was just sliced open. The orc's eyes bulged while he frantically tried to hold his intestines inside his stomach cavity. Dagrinal kicked him in the face and lanced another orc in the throat. "Come on you dung eaters, my blade thirsts for more blood!" Dagrinal yelled in defiance as he parried another attack and sliced open an orc's leg.

Third lance, Lathrin, hearing Dagrinal's call, spurred his horse forward and rammed the remaining orcs away from the downed king. He swung his sword downward, slicing open the skull of one orc while Dagrinal leaped on top of another fallen beast, stabbing him through the heart.

Just then a ring of knights moved in to form a protective shield around their king.

"Get the king out of here!" yelled Dagrinal.

"I have him!" cried Lathrin over the screaming and yelling of the battle around them. Dagrinal lifted the king up as Lathrin reached down and grabbed a hold of the king's sword belt. As Lathrin lifted up hard, Dagrinal heaved the king's body over the back of Lathrin's horse. Dagrinal swatted the horse on its hindquarters as Lathrin spurred it to the back of their line, towards the safety of the royal tent.

Suddenly Prince Baylin's horn blew, signaling the appearance of the enemy cavalry. Seconds after that another loud horn blew, one that Dagrinal did not recognize. It was an enemy horn and he quickly found his horse, leaping back up into the saddle. Dagrinal's heart sank as he saw a wave of enemy cavalry rise up over the crest and gallop towards them like a thunderous earthquake. In front of the horses ran several hundred boargs. But that wasn't all. As enemy cavalry moved in from both sides, thousands of tribesmen sprinted over the hill towards them, yelling their war cries.

Dagrinal quickly grabbed his horn and blew the signal to retreat and regroup.

***

Fil had no enemies to kill as the remaining orcs backed away from the deadly infantry. He lowered his exhausted sword arm, panting heavily. He tried to lick his dry lips but his mouth and tongue were devoid of any moisture.

Just then he heard the horn that signaled their forces to retreat and regroup. The infantry officers sounded their horns again and the trained fighting force slowly retreated backwards in formation.

The thundering of horses drew Fil's gaze up the hill and what he saw drained the blood from his face. Thousands of enemy cavalry stormed down the hill towards them. In front of them ran several hundred boargs. At the sight of the hated creatures, Fil's heart began to beat faster. He clenched his jaw, his long-held rage at the boargs pulling him out of formation towards the oncoming beasts.

"Fil!" Calden screamed.

Fil stopped, recognizing the voice. He turned to see Calden running towards him. He was covered in blood and he had a vicious cut running down the side of his left cheek.

"Fil, you can't beat them by yourself! Get back in line!" He grabbed Fil's arm, cutting through Fil's trance.

Fil shook his head and looked at his friend. Sweat soaked Calden's head and dripped freely down his dirt covered face. The sight of his friend alive brought Fil out of his killing rage. "You're right. I lost it for a moment."

More horns blew and both the warriors looked around to see what was happening. Their own cavalry was expertly moving backwards and regrouping in two separate formations to the infantry's left and right. They were angled outwards to deflect the incoming enemy cavalry while the infantry stayed in the center to fight face to face with the fearsome tribesmen.

"Here they come, get back in formation!" yelled Tanus.

Both the men ran back, joining forces with their infantry. The Finarthian infantry stood still, shields and swords locked together in a massive wall of determination, strength, and experience.

The screaming tribesmen raced down the hill yelling the names of their own gods. As they neared the infantry line Fil noticed their dark bare skin covered with black and red paint. Most did not wear any armor except metal and leather skirts. They carried short stabbing javelins and long curved swords. This fearsome group of fighting men screamed and raced down the hill with abandon, joining the remaining orcs as they neared the Finarthian infantry.

Prince Baylin raced his five hundred horses down the hill to reinforce the cavalry just as the enemy cavalry neared them. The enemy cavalry would have crushed the knights if they had not reacted so quickly. Their skill and experience as a fighting force enabled them to retreat and reset their cavalry against the vulnerable part of their own infantry. Now the enemy cavalry was racing towards a set line of determined knights rather than the backs of a surprised group of soldiers.

The prince lifted up his long lance, shaking it toward the approaching enemy. "Show them the strength of our steel! For your king!" he roared.

All the knights shook their lances or swords, yelling as loud as they could. The prince lowered his visor and spurred his horse forward. Instantly, five hundred knights launched forward towards the rapidly approaching enemy.

***

The Annurian Knights were not faring as well. The enemy had crested the hill closer to them, not giving them time to fully reestablish their perimeter. But they were skilled and brave knights who had fought in many battles. They held their ground as the enemy crashed into them.

Hundreds of Annurian Knights died quickly on the long lances of the enemy, but they didn't break or flee. Lances were dropped and cavalry swords banged against shield and sword alike.

King Olegaurd leaned over in his saddle, slicing his long sword across the leg of a horsed rider. The man screamed and frantically brought his sword down to block the next attack, but the king met the man's blade and rolled his razor sharp edge over the weapon, ramming the point into the surprised man's chest. The warrior fell off his horse without a sound.

King Olegaurd had lost his lance after it snapped under the pressure of taking a horsed rider in the chest. Now that he had a few seconds, he reached up to the leather harness that lashed his buckler to his back and yanked it down, bringing the small round shield around to his front where he inserted his forearm into the straps. He cinched them down quickly and looked around at the chaos.

The small shield, or buckler as it was often called, had the diameter of his forearm and allowed him to use the reigns and block various attacks from the saddle. They were designed specifically for horsed combat and the Annurien Knights were experts in their use.

The cavalry skirmish was not going well for the Annuriens. They were being overwhelmed with superior numbers as the enemy had broken their ranks. It was now a free for all as Annurien Knights fought for their lives.

Lord Dynure rode up to his older brother, his face covered in sweat and splattered with crimson stains. He too had lost his lance and now held his long cavalry sword.

He nodded in greeting, no words needed to be said as they understood their situation.

"Stay with me, Brother," King Olegaurd said softly, but with quiet intensity.

And with that he urged his horse forward toward the enemy line, his brother to his left, both with swords raised and fire in their eyes.

***

The black tribesmen barreled into the formation line taking many Finarthian men to the ground. The line broke immediately as the power and sheer numbers overwhelmed the already tired infantry.

The fighting became disorganized and fierce. The Finarthian reserves moved in to defend their brethren against the formidable warriors.

Fil jumped over a fallen comrade, swinging his sword down and through a tribesman's neck who was preoccupied with defending himself from another attack. Wrenching his sword free of the dead man's spine, Fil frantically defended himself against an onslaught of attacks.

The desert warriors were everywhere and it was all Fil could do to defend himself. He would block one attack with his shield while using his short sword to deflect any other blows. He began to feel the cold clutches of fear as he glanced left and right and saw his comrades in similar states.

Suddenly he felt a jabbing pain in his right side. He had turned quickly just as a curved sword lanced through his side from behind. The pain was quick and intense but Fil was forced to ignore it as he turned toward the new attacker. The warrior's sword was stuck in Fil's side and Fil had turned so quickly that it had ripped the sword from the man's hand. Fil roared with fury, swinging his sword down, cutting through the screaming man's arm just above the elbow. Fil followed the attack with a reverse swing, slicing through the man's unprotected abdomen.

Fil didn't even have time to pull the sword free from his side as more tribesmen attacked him. Luckily the sword had just cut through skin and some muscle so no vital organs were damaged. But the pain was immense as Fil fought; the sword bouncing and moving around inside his flesh. He gritted his teeth and embraced the pain as he fought for his life.

Suddenly a horse barreled its way to the front of the line, its rider swatting aside enemy warriors as he went. The rider swung his long sword down with a lightning quick strike that ripped open the back of the man who was attacking Fil.

Fil glanced up at the new rider and saw a dark haired man with steel gray eyes staring back at him. The man smiled, amazing Fil with his apparent confidence that seemed to surround him like a warm blanket. The warrior's eyes shone with a focused intensity that reflected certain death to any who faced him.

Fil gave silent thanks that this warrior was on their side as the newcomer resumed his attack on the enemy ranks. He expertly maneuvered his horse left and right, cutting down any enemy that neared him. His long sword was a blur of green magical energy as he attacked the tribesmen, while staying in the center of the line at all times.

"To me, warriors, hold the center!" the dark haired man bellowed above the sounds of war.

The remaining Finarthian infantry fought and struggled to get near the horseman and reestablish the line.

Fil sidestepped a clumsy attack by one of the tribesmen whose sword glanced off his shoulder guard. He rammed his knee hard into the tribesman's exposed stomach and the man keeled over, gasping for breath. He then brought the pommel of his sword down on top of the man's head and he fell to the ground unconscious.

Fil looked up from the downed man and saw the horseman ride near him just as a massive spear took the stranger's mount in the throat. The spear was huge, made from a crudely shaped sapling.

The horse stumbled to the ground, the spear sinking several feet into its chest. Something big had thrown that spear and Fil's nightmares were realized as he looked up and saw a huge ogre lumber through the ranks of the tribesmen to finish off the rider.

Fil yanked out the sword in his side, grimacing from the pain just as the ogre moved towards the downed horse.

The rider had jumped free and rolled across the bloody ground to come up standing with sword and dagger held before him. "Finally a challenge," the swordsman said to himself, loud enough for Fil to hear.

Fil marveled at the warrior's amazing agility as he stumbled in to help him. The ogre glanced toward Fil as he tried to sneak in towards its tree trunk legs. The beast was as tall as two short men and its legs were stout and thick with muscle.

Fil sliced his short sword across the ogre's leg but the blade did little damage to the thick skin. The beast roared, swinging its thick arm down and hitting Fil squarely in the chest, the immense strength of the blow breaking his ribs. He was thrown backward like a rock from a catapult, landing fifteen paces away. Though he was able to maintain consciousness, the pain was so intense that he could barely move. He felt his broken ribs move around inside him as he struggled to get up.

Kiln balanced himself on the balls of his feet as the ogre lumbered toward him. The ogre looked down at him as it attempted to kick him with its massive leather boot. The beast's foot was as big as a small boulder. Kiln leaped to the side and sent his blades into motion. His weapons sliced into the ogre's foot and calf twice before the ogre could even register the pain. His magical blades sliced through the thick skin easily, furrows of red appearing on the beast's legs as Kiln danced around the slow behemoth.

The ogre roared in pain as it set its foot down and tried to reach out with its hands to crush the little human. But Kiln was a blur of razor sharp steel and he lunged under the hands, slicing his long sword across the beast's abdomen simultaneously ramming his dagger into the left thigh of the ogre. The dagger sunk in deep and the ogre roared in pain as it reached down to yank out the weapon. Kiln dove between the ogre's legs, coming up in a roll just behind the huge creature. His long sword sliced left and right, cutting through the tendons located on the back of the beast's knees. Again, the ogre howled in agony, dropping to the ground, while Kiln, simultaneously leaped into the air, driving the point of his sword down and through the ogre's back, penetrating its lungs and heart. The warrior left his sword in the beast, landing lightly on his feet.

Fil held his body still and watched the swordsman carve the large ogre into meat. He didn't want to move because of the pain and he was afraid an enemy warrior would see him and attack. Fil knew that in his state he would be hard pressed to defend himself.

The dead ogre fell face first onto the bloody ground with Kiln's long sword jutting from its back, quivering in the air.

Kiln spun around toward the enemy warriors and yelled again. "Men of Finarth, hold the line!"

The soldiers responded with renewed courage and strength and they began to fight their way to the swordsman. Fil watched in amazement as the line began to reform and move towards the dark haired warrior. But the pain was too much and his vision began to blur. The ogre's fist had done tremendous damage and it was difficult to breath. He fought to stay conscious but it was no use. His head sank to the ground and his body lay sprawled among the dead as he finally succumbed to the darkness.

Rorum, a young infantry soldier, felt a sharp sting to his thigh as he pivoted his body away from the curved blade of the attacking tribesman. The tribesman had swung hard, the momentum of his swing pushing him off balance as Rorum spun by him. He then sliced his short sword down and across the tribesman's sword arm. The cut was deep and the enemy warrior screamed, staggering to his left where another Finarthian warrior finished him off.

The young soldier, and several other infantry soldiers, had fought their way to the dark haired stranger who had rallied the men and strengthened the line. More Finarthian warriors found the strength and courage to fight their way to this man, and they now stood before him, exhausted but determined. They had formed a break in the enemy's ranks but the fighting still continued all around them.

Kiln reached down and ripped out his sword from the back of the dead ogre. He glanced back and saw the men behind him, looking at him with uncertainty.

"Who are you?" asked Rorum through deep panting breaths.

Kiln glanced at the young warrior as he turned around to face the men. "I am Kiln!"

Then he looked forward and saw enemy soldiers converge on them screaming their battle cries. He grabbed his bloody dagger from the ground and focused his attention on the rapidly approaching tribesmen. He swung his sword from side to side. "If they want death!" he yelled, lifting his sword into the air. "Let them come!"

The men behind him yelled in unison, raising their crimson swords in defiance. Kiln smiled and ran forward to meet the enemy.

***

Jonas and Taleen sat high on their mounts scanning the battlefield below. They had followed the sounds of the battle and had ridden over the crest of a nearby hill. Below them, accompanied by the sounds of blasting horns and pounding war drums, raged a huge battle. The enemy riders had just attacked the flanks of the Finarthian cavalry.

Kiln, who had viewed the dire scene with them, had immediately spotted the desperate situation forming in the center of the infantry. He explained that if the center broke, enemy soldiers would surround and destroy them. Jonas had reluctantly followed Kiln's orders and stayed behind while Kiln urged his mount down into the melee. Kiln told them that they would be needed to combat more dangerous foes, the priests of Naz-reen or Gould, or worse, a Banthra.

So Jonas and Taleen scanned the battle before them trying to figure out how they would best fit in. It didn't take long for the cavaliers to sense the evil that was approaching through the ranks of enemy warriors.

"Jonas, do you feel it?" asked Taleen as she scanned the enemy ranks.

"I do," Jonas answered, gazing out over the battle looking for the source of this malevolent feeling. "There," he said, pointing towards a group of horseman that were maneuvering toward the Finarthian cavalry.

Their steeds had already sensed the dark force before them and both animals pranced, urging their riders forward.

Taleen looked at Jonas and nocked an arrow to her long bow. "May Helikon be with you," she said with a nod of her head.

"And may Shyann guard your back," Jonas responded, drawing forth one of his sabers. The cavaliers raced down the hillside towards the unearthly threat, eager to confront the evil that was corrupting their land.

Prince Baylin swung his mighty axe as if it were a toy. The razor sharp axe head dealt death to every enemy who neared him. His powerful legs controlled his horse expertly as he swung his battle-axe left and right with one hand. He lost all sense of time as he methodically cut down his enemies. Though he bled from several wounds, he didn't register the pain as his mind and body became immersed in the heat and pandemonium of battle.

The prince's battle frenzy was interrupted, however, by a sudden cold force that seemed to weigh him down, draining the warmth and energy from his body. He glanced frantically about trying to locate the source of this oppressive feeling that had so rapidly assaulted him, chilling his very bones.

His knights, too, were enveloped in the same dark miasma, their minds and bodies imprisoned by weakness and fear. Baylin saw his knights, and enemy warriors, part to give way to a trio of dark warriors mounted on even darker steeds, drifting through the ranks like a suffocating fog. Clad in black armor, the warriors and their horses emanated such evil energy that no nearby mortal could withstand it, turning their resolve into mindless terror.

The leader of the black triad caught Prince Baylin's eye. Like the others, he wore dark plate mail the color of charcoal and his wicked helm jutted curved horns and spikes. What really drew the prince's attention, however, were the warrior's glowing red orbs that bore into his own, subjugating his will and causing his body to shake with uncontrollable fear.

Elsewhere, Graggis fought with the energy of a god, his mighty axe piling up bodies around his warhorse. He roared in defiance as he cut his way toward a giant black warrior riding a chestnut warhorse. He had spotted the muscle bound warrior and knew that this man was Arg'on, Lord Moredin's war commander, a legendary warrior who was known for his strength and ferocity.

Graggis swung his magical axe down on top of the head of a nearby horseman, creasing his helm so badly that it drove the edges of the metal into the man's broken skull. The path to Arg'on was now open and Graggis urged his horse forward.

Arg'on carried a massive two-handed sword that he swung easily with one hand. The black tribesman yanked his sword from the breast of a knight and pivoted his horse towards the new threat.

"Well met, Arg'on," Graggis said evenly as his horse pranced eagerly in front of the huge black warrior. All the men fighting around them seemed to sense the contest and consciously moved away to give them room.

"Are you someone I should know?" asked the tribal warrior in the common tongue. He spoke it well and his accent was barely noticeable.

"You should always know the name of the man who is going to kill you so you can buy him a drink in the afterworld," replied Graggis, smiling broadly.

"Then stop talking and tell me your name so that I may pray for your soul after I kill you and cut out your heart," Arg'on responded calmly.

"I am Graggis," and without further hesitation he spurred his horse forward, swinging his mighty axe in a powerful downward stroke.

Arg'on brought his sword up to block the blow but at the last second Graggis redirected his strike expertly to hit the tribesman's horse. It was Graggis's immense strength that enabled him to change the momentum of the stroke so quickly.

The magical blade easily sank through the steed's armor, slicing through the animals shoulder muscle. The horse reared up, stumbling backwards before it pitched side long to the ground.

Arg'on jumped off the horse and landed hard on his side, but he was a tough warrior who had survived many battles. Few men could match his strength. He rolled backwards and came up quickly to face the horseman with the axe.

Graggis quickly dismounted from his horse and stood in front of the tribesman. He couldn't help but think what a great specimen of a man this tribesman was. He was tall and heavy, with iron hard muscle. The warrior wore a metal-laced skirt that was cinched tightly around his narrow waist. His legs and arms were so corded with muscles that he almost looked deformed. He held his huge blade easily with one hand, his face a picture of confidence.

"I wouldn't want anyone to think that I had an unfair advantage in killing you," Graggis said as he attacked the tribesman with fury.

The fight was intense. Both warriors were skilled and strong. They traded blow for blow for several minutes, the power of each strike echoing across the battlefield. They had similar styles, both used to crushing their opponents with strength and speed, but after several minutes of hard fighting, Graggis noted a difference.

The tribesman was undisciplined in his fighting, accustomed to using his strength and power to destroy anyone who stood against him. Graggis, however, had been trained as a Finarthian Knight, trained by Master Borum, the greatest weapons master around, and they had learned not only discipline, but tactics that were beyond most common warriors.

Graggis noticed that Arg'on held his sword with his right hand only, making him a bit slow in defending his left flank. Graggis swung his axe left and right and looked for an opening. But the man was fast and strong as an ox. When their weapons met the earth around them shook. Graggis had never met a man whose strength equaled his own, until now. But Graggis now knew the tribesman's weakness and he worked to exploit it. Arg'on swung his huge sword down, Graggis brought his axe up to block the attack. Just as the warrior retracted his blade, Graggis tossed his axe to his left hand and attacked the tribesman's left flank with lightning speed.

Arg'on recovered quickly, and frantically deflected the axe blade. But Graggis's attack had been a ruse. As he attacked the tribesman's left flank with his axe, he swung his gauntlet covered right hand into the side of the powerful warrior. His fist struck the tribesman solidly in the kidney.

Normally such a blow would cause little damage, for the tribesman's waist was protected by thick muscle. But he had never before encountered a man with such strength.

The blow crushed his kidney and he keeled over from the pain, bracing his fall with his sword arm. He gritted his teeth through the pain and looked up to fend off the deadly axe man. But all he saw was the razor sharp edge of Graggis's axe as it split his astonished expression in two.

The huge tribesman fell heavily to the ground. "I'll take a pint of Annurien mead when you see me next," Graggis said as he yanked his blade clear of the grisly mess.

Back at the infantry's center, Kiln had become the point of a wedge of the small group of Finarthian infantry that had followed him into the enemy ranks. He let the undisciplined tribesmen break themselves on the wedge point, forcing them to the sides of the formation where more Finarthian warriors were there to meet them.

He stopped advancing and held the point as he fought one enemy after another. He knew that if he advanced too far the enemy would surround them and crush them. He put some faith in the Finarthian commanders and hoped that they would see the wedge and move in to support them.

Kiln spun and pivoted as his blades cut into the enemy warriors. No one could touch him as he moved effortlessly, killing any tribesman that neared him. Rorum and the others fought furiously next to him. Kiln's very presence seemed to give the men new hope, and they fought on, well past the point where their sword arms and lungs should have given out.

Prince Baylin had never been more afraid. He couldn't move as the deadly trio moved closer to him. The lead warrior spurred his black horse forward and the prince shifted his gaze to the horrible animal.

It was huge, a full pace bigger than any warhorse Baylin had ever seen, with a coat that was thick and covered with sweat. Its long black mane was tangled with knots, but it was the animal's eyes and mouth that made Prince

Baylin realize that this was no ordinary horse. Glowing red eyes, like those of its master, peered out over a mouth that opened to expose long razor sharp teeth embedded in gums the color of congealed blood.

"Do you know what I am?" hissed the Banthra. The Banthra's voice drifted towards the prince and danced around in his mind as he struggled against the magic that was paralyzing him.

Prince Baylin redirected his gaze to the warrior and used every ounce of inner strength to answer the demon. "You are a Banthra, a fallen cavalier corrupted by magic," replied the prince as he swallowed the knot growing in his throat.

The Banthra hissed again and the big black horse shifted uneasily beneath him. "And you are Prince Baylin, next in line for the throne of Finarth, a position that you will not be filling."

At that moment a dazzling white light burst forth from the fighting men behind the prince. Two huge horses parted the milling mass of warriors, completely washing the area with a light that shone with the brilliance of the sun. The warhorses carried magnificent warriors wearing gleaming silver plate mail and glittering steel helms that hid their identity.

The Banthra hissed loudly as it shifted in the saddle. The demon's horse growled menacingly and pranced backwards a few steps. The riders that flanked him also moved uneasily in their saddles, retreating several steps away from the light. These riders were dark clerics of the Forsworn and each wore similar armor and spiked helms, both cursed by the dark magic of the three evil gods.

Jonas and Taleen urged their horses forward as their light flared even brighter, sending rays of hope into the fighting men around them. Enemy warriors moved away, the light from the cavaliers frightening them into a panic. Finarthian soldiers around them looked up in awe as they gazed at the cavaliers. As the light washed over them, all fear and fatigue evaporated. They stood taller, gripping their weapons with new strength and confidence.

Jonas drew forth his second saber, not needing his hands to control his magnificent mount. Tulari took him directly towards the Banthra.

Taleen pulled back the string of her powerful bow and sighted the arrow as her horse approached the evil warriors without the slightest bounce. The ability to fire a bow from a riding horse was a skill reached by few, and even amongst cavaliers it was rare.

"Cavaliers!" hissed the Banthra.

The two priests gripped their long lances angling their sharp tips toward the approaching threat. The shafts of the lances were smooth and black and the steel points were as long as a short sword, dark in color with a sharp edge that sparkled like silver in contrast to the black metal. Just as they brought their weapons to bear, two arrows slammed into one of the priests, both hitting him in the chest. The magical bolts sunk in deep and the priest's enchanted armor could not protect him against Taleen's blessed arrows. He fell from his horse, landing heavily on the ground.

As the cavaliers galloped past the prince, their white light blanketed the area, evaporating the oppressive fear that had immobilized him. In control of his body again, the prince quickly moved his horse away from the Banthra as Jonas flew at the demon, both sabers held before him.

The Banthra hissed angrily as the God Light washed over him. He drew forth a deadly looking battle axe that was bladed on one end, opposed by a long spike on the other.

Jonas's heart pounded in his chest as he drew near the black knight. He screamed Shyann's name, pushing away his fear and urging Tulari forward. Jonas did not have much combat experience, and facing a Banthra as an untried cavalier had filled him with fear. But he remembered his training with Kiln, and he thought of his connection with Shyann, forcing the uneasy thoughts away.

Taleen expertly sheathed her bow on Kormac's side and drew forth her sword as she closed the distance to the second priest. He lifted his lance and whispered several words of power. The lance head glowed red shooting forth a stream of red orange flames toward her.

Her horse pivoted at the last minute, the flames shooting by her, but singing the side of her horse and her right leg. Taleen grimaced, her God Light shining brightly as she brought her sword down towards the evil priest. He backed away from the light, lifting his magical lance to block the blow. Taleen swung her sword expertly, attacking the retreating priest left and right, trying to score a killing blow.

As Tulari rammed into the demon horse, Jonas didn't waste any time in attacking. His twin sabers worked independently as Tulari guided him perfectly around the Banthra. Jonas had never been on a horse such as Tulari and he had no idea what the horse was capable of. Luckily he didn't have to know. Tulari needed no guidance as he positioned Jonas perfectly as the two combatants traded blow for blow.

But the dark warrior's horse was no ordinary animal. The beast used its massive head to bash Tulari in his flanks, trying to get him off balance so its master could destroy the cavalier. But Tulari's size and strength allowed him to shake off the blows, hammering his own head and shoulders into the beast. The Banthra wielded its axe to fend off the attacks as both animals danced left and right, tearing up grass and dirt, trying to gain an advantage.

Prince Baylin was an experienced warrior and he didn't waste his good fortune. He rejoined the fight, fighting off any enemy cavalry that neared the battling cavaliers. It wasn't long before Dagrinal galloped up to the prince on his tired warhorse, his sword wet with enemy blood. "Lord, I tried to get near you when the Banthra approached, but I was surrounded by enemies," the weary warrior said as the chaos of battle whirled around them.

"Thankfully the cavaliers intervened. I could not even move against that abomination," the prince replied as he scanned the battle field.

Both men pivoted their warhorses back and forth as they spoke, ready to attack their foes and hoping the cavaliers had changed the tide of battle in their favor.

Things were looking better. The center was holding, although the prince was not sure how. The cavaliers had given the men a jolt of hope and the fighting seemed to be swinging in their favor.

"Is that Jonas?" asked Dagrinal in astonishment.

"I don't know. I can't tell under that horned helm he is wearing. I don't recognize the female cavalier either," replied the prince as four boargs leaped over the heads of several nearby fighting men and ran towards the two warriors. The animals moved with lighting speed and Dagrinal and Prince Baylin lifted their weapons to defend themselves as their horses positioned them to face the charge.

Jonas and the Bantrha maneuvered their huge horses side by side, exchanging blow for blow, their magical weapons meeting in a shower of sparks.

In one close exchange, the Banrtha was able to reach down and grasp Jonas's leg with its gauntleted hand, and at the same time deflect one of Jonas's swords. The Banthra's fist glowed red, sending a burst of burning energy into the cavalier.

Jonas screamed and Tulari bolted backwards away from the demon. His leg was badly burned but he didn't have time to heal himself for the Banthra quickly attacked again. The demon came in with its axe raised, ready for a killing blow.

Jonas saw the blow coming and instinctively used his IshMian powers, stopping the blade in mid-swing, immobilizing the demon's entire arm in energy that only he could see. Jonas worried about using the power so early in the fight, as the toll in doing so could be too great, causing him severe headaches, and in some cases debilitating him. But the blow came so quick that Jonas had no choice.

The puzzled Banthra had little time to try and figure out why his axe wouldn't move. Jonas took advantage of the brief pause and lunged with his right saber, driving his blade deep into the shoulder of the Banthra.

The demon hissed and dropped the axe to the ground as its steed jumped back from the attack. The Banthra then lifted both hands and screamed several words of power that Jonas did not recognize. Jonas sensed what was coming and used his mental powers to quickly create a swirling shield of energy in front of him. An observer would have seen an iridescent wall of bluish magic swirling before him.

The Banthra's flames shot forth from his hands, hitting the wall with an explosion. The power was immense and it was all Jonas could do to maintain the mental shield. His head pounded from the pain of using his powers to hold back the burning flames conjured by something as powerful as a Banthra. But he clenched his teeth and willed the energy wall to hold. He could feel the heat of the magical fire through the shield, but none of the deadly flames struck him.

Taleen was struggling against the dark priest. The evil priest used his lance perfectly, deflecting every blow that Taleen sent his way, but he was tiring. Taleen kept at it furiously, her God Light gradually draining the energy from the dark warrior.

Then the priest used his warhorse to give him some time, forcing the animal to rear up and attempting to bring its front hooves down on top of Taleen. Her steed reacted quickly, perfectly maneuvering away just in time. The deadly hooves didn't find their mark, but it gave the priest a few precious moments to cast his spell.

He muttered a few words and threw something to the ground between them. A massive black spider suddenly appeared before her. The bulk of the creature was several paces wide and each leg at least two paces long. Nearly the height of a horse, its ugly hairy head was at eye level with her. The spider clicked its long sharp mandibles together and leaped into the air towards Taleen.

All she could do was scream and raise her sword to try and deflect the nasty creature. Kormac, her horse, quickly jumped away from the attack. The spider just missed her, but several of the long hairy legs had hooked into her cape, pulling her down from her saddle. She swung her sword in a deadly arc as she flew through the air, slicing one of the legs off as she landed hard on the ground, which momentarily knocked the wind out of her. But she frantically regained her composure and scrambled back up to her feet.

The spider hissed from the pain but moved in quickly for the kill.

Jonas and the Banthra were locked in magical combat. Finally the Bantrha's flames ceased and Jonas released the mental shield. The Banthra hissed in frustration as it pivoted its horse back and forth, trying to figure out a way to destroy the troublesome cavalier.

Jonas's head felt like it was going to explode and he slumped over briefly in his saddle, but he managed to push the pain away and concentrate on the deadly foe before him. He could not risk the use of his IshMian powers again, fearing that he would lose consciousness. So he spun both his blades in the air and urged Tulari forward to meet the Banthra with cold steel.

The Banthra drew a dark blade that was strapped to the side of his steed's saddle and met the cavalier's charge. Both animals came together hard, their strong bodies pounding into each other again, trying to position their riders in an advantageous position. The warriors' blades came together again and again as they both fought for an opening in the other's defenses.

Jonas's opening came when Tulari used his incredible strength and agility to counter the demon horse's attack. The steed lunged forward with its thick armored head but Tulari pivoted to the side and bashed the demon horse on the side of the neck, causing it to stumble. The Banthra was forced to grab the horse's mane with its free hand to keep from falling from the saddle.

Jonas capitalized on the distraction, swinging his left sword down in a powerful strike, completely cutting off the demon's sword arm. He followed up the attack by lunging forward with his right sword, piercing the Banthra's armor and spearing the black knight through the chest. The demon horse leaped backwards, ripping Jonas's sword from his grip.

The Banthra screamed shrilly and brought its only hand down to the handle of the weapon that was buried to the hilt in its chest. The sword sizzled deep in the demon's chest as it seared the howling Banthra. The demon's hand also burned as it grasped the hilt of the blessed weapon, trying to yank it clear. Gray smoke drifted from the burning wounds bringing forth a horrid stench, like rotting flesh baking over a fire.

Jonas, remembering what had happened to his town, to his mother, to Gorum, the baker, brought forth all his anger and called on his God Fire. He felt the energy course through his body, his hand bright with a bluish glow. Jonas centered his hatred on the Banthra and sent the magical energy towards the screaming black knight. The blue flames burst forth with such power that they completely covered the demon and its horse. Jonas gritted his teeth and ignored his pounding head as he channeled more energy into the Banthra. He was close to losing consciousness by the time the blue flames consumed the demon, leaving nothing but a pile of ash with his unscathed saber lying perfectly in the middle.

Taleen was not faring as well. The spider scurried forward quickly trying to destroy the downed cavalier. She retreated, using her sword to maintain a defensive wall against the spider's vicious attack. The spider, using its many legs like sharp spear points, attacked her with quick precision.

She frantically called on Helikon and brought forth her God Light, concentrating on making it brighter, hoping to blind the creature. She glowed so brightly that the spider could not penetrate the light. The creature backed up slightly, dropping its ugly head to shield itself from the burning magic.

Taleen used this brief reprieve to strike the spider across the head with her blade, the razor sharp edge slicing through one of the creature's eyes. But the spider was quicker than anything Taleen had previously encountered. Two legs, like spears, blindly shot out, one deflecting off her breast plate, but the other managed to pierce the plate that protected her thigh, shattering her knee cap. Taleen stumbled to the ground as the spider leaped on top of her, eager to destroy the woman and the searing light.

Jonas, hearing Taleen's scream, brought himself from his tired daze and jerked his attention from the charred remains of the Banthra just in time to see a bolt of red flame strike him cleanly in the chest. He flew off his horse and landed hard on his back. The flames had burned his exposed skin but his magical armor had protected most of his body. He struggled to stand and saw the second priest riding towards him, his magical lance angling toward the ground, the tip again glowing red.

Jonas's head still pounded, and his body felt like it weighed three times its weight, but he didn't have the time to fight this enemy sword to sword and he didn't know what kind of trouble Taleen was in. So, again, he called upon Shyann to help him in pushing aside the pain and giving him the strength to use his powers. He felt renewed energy infuse his mind and body as he used his cognivant powers to lift the saber from the ground and send it flying towards the priest. The sword struck the evil priest's chest so hard that he flew off his horse and was launched five paces backwards.

Jonas stumbled over, relieved to see that the priest was dead, his sword buried deep in his chest. He stumbled again as his head swirled from the pain of his exertions. Concentrating on the state of Ty'erm, his mind focused slightly, just enough to take in his surroundings.

Frantically he looked for Taleen and saw her fall onto her back as a huge spider fell upon her. Jonas couldn't use his God Fire as he had no idea if it would consume Taleen as well. So he concentrated on the massive form of the spider and drew forth his mental powers one last time. He knew that if he exerted anymore mental energy that he very well could pass out. But he also knew that Taleen's life may depend on his IshMian abilities.

Again, he focused on the particles that surrounded the spider's bulbous abdomen and used them to squeeze the creature.

Taleen screamed again and that was all Jonas needed to bring forth all his mental power together on the bloated form of the spider. The pressure of the particles around the spider came together like a loud clap, and the creature's abdomen exploded in a shower of blood and entrails.

Taleen felt another leg pierce her side just as the spider exploded all over her. She painfully scrambled out from underneath the gore and tried to stand, but her injured knee gave out on her.

Jonas stumbled toward her, nearly falling beside her. "Are you okay?" he asked, panting heavily.

"Yes, I'll be fine," she said, her teeth clenched in pain. "I just need to heal myself."

Jonas nodded as speaking was too difficult. He focused all his remaining energy on standing up to protect her as she prayed. Swaying slightly, he dropped to his knee again to keep from falling. The use of his cognitive abilities combined with the exertion of using magic had weakened him severely.

The fighting coursed nearby but luckily no enemy ventured too close, afraid of attacking anyone who could defeat a Banthra.

After a few seconds Taleen stood up next to him, her wounds healed. "Now it's your turn," she said with concern. "You look burned and exhausted."

"I am; I don't think I have the energy to heal myself, my head feels like it's going to explode."

"Let me heal you and then we'll see if we are needed elsewhere," Taleen said, placing both hands on Jonas and asking Helikon for his power again.

In the meantime, a huge boarg had vaulted upon Dagrinal's horse, wrapping all four limbs around the animal's muscled neck. Clawed hands dug into exposed flesh as its long fangs searched for an opening in the horse's armor. The boarg snapped its jaws again and again but couldn't break through the horse's armored chest. But it didn't need to, for the weight of the boarg alone drove the horse to its knees, and Dagrinal didn't wait to see if the boarg would finish off his warhorse. He leaped off the animal's back and brought his sword down across the boargs right arm, which was firmly clenched around the horse's body. His sword cut in deep and the boarg finally released its grip, rolling backwards off the animal. It roared in fury, swinging its huge head from side to side as if to shake off the pain. The enraged animal then barreled forward hoping to crush the human in its powerful arms.

Dagrinal whipped his blade back and forth, cutting several deep gashes into the advancing boarg. Still, its fury and pain propelled it forward. Just as it was about to leap on Dagrinal, however, several arrows took the animal in the side, one skewering its neck perfectly. The boarg pitched to its left and then fell over dead.

Dagrinal glanced to his left and saw two cavaliers galloping toward him on their magnificent mounts, both holding their long bows. Dagrinal smiled broadly as he recognized Jonas under the horned helm. He took a moment to look for his prince and saw Lord Baylin several paces away swing his blood coated battle axe through the neck of a dying boarg. The prince flipped his sweat soaked hair from his face, having lost his helm early on in the battle. When he spotted Dagrinal and the cavaliers, he maneuvered his steed quickly toward the trio as the battle continued around them.

"Well met, Jonas. It is good to see you," Dagrinal said with a wide smile as he remounted his warhorse. "You look well, to say the least," he added as he gazed at his armor and horse in open admiration.

Suddenly an enemy horn blasted through the noise of the battle. As they all looked toward the sound, they saw another enemy force rise above the hill. Fifteen armored hill giants lumbered down the hillside with long heavy strides, carrying huge war hammers as big as a man. The ground shook as each meaty leg moved them closer. Their black breast plates were painted with Gould's white eye.

The remaining enemy cavalry disengaged from the fight and rode toward the giants. The remaining enemy infantry did the same, leaving a dazed and tired Finarthian force scattered across the field.

"In Ulren's name," whispered Dagrinal. "How do we fight armored hill giants?" The prince surveyed the scene quickly. There were several hundred horsed knights left, and maybe a hundred infantry nearby. Fighting continued farther down on both flanks, but their forces were busy trying to hold back the horde of orcs and tribesmen.

They would be alone against this powerful group.

"Look, Prince," Jonas said as he urgently pointed towards the giants.

Prince Baylin looked again toward the enemy, and saw, crested on the hill, several men on horseback. Two were obviously warriors of Gould since they bore his mark, the other wore a black billowing robe and cape lined with red.

"Two knights of Gould," Taleen said, answering their unasked question.

"And the other?" asked the prince.

"A dark wizard to the Forsworn," she whispered.

Jonas looked around frantically. He saw many Finarthian warriors slowly retreating backwards as the huge giants, now followed by enemy cavalry and infantry, thundered towards them. Even the knights looked around with uncertainty, their horses prancing nervously underneath them. Jonas had to admit, the site of attacking hill giants wearing armor and carrying huge steel war hammers was nerve racking. They were so big and their weapons equally so that it looked like they would hammer their way through them with ease.

Tulari stood still and tall, fearlessly waiting for his master to make a decision. Jonas took strength from his steed, and digging deep within himself to find the courage and power he needed, he sent his prayers to Shyann, praying for the power needed to confront this force. He felt her energy infuse him as he called forth his light and rode Tulari before the men, his horse prancing back and forth as he spoke. But no one on that battlefield had ever heard a voice like his before. Jonas had no idea how he did it, but he spoke with the power of a god, his words carrying strength, courage and hope.

"Men of Finarth! I am a first rank cavalier to Shyann! Raise your weapons, and stand beside me to face this threat!" His voice echoed across the battlefield and it slammed into the men like a hammer wielded by Ulren himself. All fear and uncertainty seemed to dissolve from them and they stood up straight, gripping their weapons with newfound strength. "This is your land, and they stain it with their blackness!" Jonas felt Shyann's power flow through him and fuel his words.

His voice was so amplified that even Taleen looked on with awe, his words infusing even her with increased vigor, courage, and the desire to destroy the enemy before them. She was no longer fearful, nor were the men around her.

"Knights! Form up with me, with your prince, and fight for your land and your families!" Jonas shouted. "Shyann is with us on this day!"

The remaining knights galloped into formation behind Jonas; some still held their long lances, but most had discarded them long ago for their cavalry swords. Their eyes shone with determination, their weapons held before them, Jonas's light and voice saturating them with courage.

Graggis rode from the crowd and approached his prince, who also stood wide eyed as Jonas finished his speech.

"For your king! For Finarth!" Jonas yelled, raising one of his sabers in the air and turning Tulari towards the approaching enemy, his entire body glowing brightly.

"By the gods, I have never heard anything like that," Graggis said in amazement.

"Nor I," replied Prince Baylin as he directed his horse forward to lead his men. The magic in Jonas's words spurred him forward confidently. He was not afraid, he would die this day if need be, and he would die next to his men, fighting for the land that he loved.

Dagrinal, Graggis, and Taleen followed close behind him. Soon they were all lined up next to Jonas, and behind them was a line of Finarthian cavalry, followed up by a line of infantry, all of whom stood tall, proud, and confident as they looked toward the huge giants.

"Knights! All with lances ride behind me! Target the giants!" yelled the prince. Ten knights holding long razor sharp lances spurred their horses forward to take up positions behind the prince. Prince Baylin glanced at Jonas and smiled. "Very impressive, Jonas, I feel like I have the strength of ten men. I pray it is not an illusion."

"My Lord!" yelled a young warrior to their left. They all turned to see a young soldier carrying two lances struggling toward them. He was covered in dirt and blood and limped badly on his right leg. The boy's face had the smoothness of youth, but his eyes revealed a maturity that was likely gained by the blood shed of battle.

"Good work," the prince replied as the young man handed him and Dagrinal each a lance.

They were interrupted by the sudden shaking of the ground. They looked toward the advancing line and saw that the giants had started to run, their long strides keeping pace with the cavalry that rode on their flanks. The ground rumbled as each pounding step brought them closer.

Jonas glanced quickly toward the top of the hill. Sure enough the three minions of Gould were still there.

"Warriors of Finarth! Victory is won through courage!" The prince yelled. He lowered the tip of his long lance and spurred his horse forward.

The warriors behind them screamed 'For Finarth!' and followed their lord.

Twelve glittering lances led the three hundred defenders toward the enemy who was storming toward them with great speed.

Taleen brought forth her light to join Jonas's, and their combined energy made the bright sun look small in comparison. Jonas urged his horse forward and Tulari's great speed pushed him to the front of the line and beyond the bouncing tips of the lances. Jonas heard Taleen yell at him from behind, but the pounding of the horse's hooves and the giant's feet drowned her words.

He had a plan.

"Tulari, run like the wind!" he yelled, sheathing his sword and leaning forward in his saddle. Tulari surged forward, in a blur of speed and power, shooting toward the enemy. As Jonas flared his light brighter he could see the giants hesitate slightly as they squinted their eyes against the glare.

Then he called on more of Shyann's power.

"Shyann!" he screamed, channeling an immense amount of her energy into his right hand. His fist burst with an intense blue flame, the power of the flames building within him until he felt they would consume his very being. Though he was relatively inexperienced in the use of this magic, he could feel that if he didn't release the power soon that it would burn him to a crisp.

When he was close enough that he could almost smell the giants, he released his God Fire in a powerful burst of blue flame. The running giants saw the shooting flames and tried to veer away, but their formation was too tight, and all they succeeded in doing was tripping each other up and distracting them from the Finarthian lances that were quickly approaching.

Jonas's flames hit two giants directly, blasting them from their feet and taking a score of their own infantry out behind them. The intense blue flames burned hotter than any known fire, creating a searing hole in the enemy ranks through which Jonas rode unharmed. Anything caught in the path of his God Fire was blown aside in a pile of ash.

Jonas erupted out the other side of the enemy ranks and continued up the hill toward his real targets, the trio of dark riders.

Taleen saw Jonas's plan evolve before her eyes, but she could not keep pace with Tulari. No steed could. She screamed his name, hoping to deter him from his present course of taking on the vile minions of Gould on his own, and urged her horse to run faster. Jonas had blasted a hole through the enemy ranks but the hole was beginning to close quickly as the astonished giants stumbled to resume their attack. Her path to Jonas was closed, so she held her sword before her like a spear and targeted the nearest giant who stood in her path.

Taleen's steed brought her toward the giant with lightning speed. At the last moment, she veered to the behemoth's left. She had prepared herself for the sharp change in direction and leaned sharply over in her saddle, swinging her silver sword across the giant's arm. It roared in pain as her blade opened its forearm from elbow to hand.

The giants had slowed their pace as they tried to recover from Jonas's attack. That's when the Finarthian defenders slammed into them. Five of the giants died instantly as the sharp lances hit them with tremendous force, spearing them through their chests. But the tremendous force of the clash sent many of the knights sprawling into the air, their horses broken and dying as they collided with the huge creatures.

Meanwhile, Taleen pushed through the giants into the other enemy fighters. Orcs and tribesmen alike fell to her blade as her bright light blinded them from her deadly attack. Her powerful steed pierced the lines of enemy soldiers, scattering aside infantry and horses alike. She continued her surge through the enemy ranks, swinging her sword mercilessly down upon any hapless soldier she encountered.

She looked up briefly to see Jonas, his light shining impossibly bright as he flew up the hill toward the followers of the Forsworn. She growled in frustration, urging her horse forward.

She had to get to Jonas. He would need her.

Back in the melee, Prince Baylin's lance took a giant in the throat just as the beast had raised its huge club to crush him. The giant had been too slow and the prince's lance sliced through its thick neck. His momentum, however, propelled him right into the giant's chest, snapping his poor horse's neck and sending the prince flying through the air. He quickly tucked his head as he smashed into the dying giant's armored chest. He felt the sharp pain of broken ribs as he hit the ground hard, scattering a group of enemy infantry. Though dazed and in pain, he knew that he had to move or he would die. His broken ribs sent sharp pains shooting through his body, but he forced himself to bury his agony as he roared in defiance. Spinning his legs beneath him he leaped to his feet with remarkable speed for someone his size, simultaneously grabbing the leather strap that held his battle axe and un-slung the weapon.

Others were fighting frantically around the downed prince.

Dagrinal leaned forward in his saddle and held his lance firm as his warhorse barreled into the enemy ranks. It took many years of practice to become proficient at holding a lance steady as one's horse charged ahead. Dagrinal was the elite of the Finarthian Knights. He was able to manipulate his body to counteract the galloping motion of the horse, keeping the silver tip of his lance on target. At the last minute Dagrinal steered his horse to the right just as he angled the lance tip to his left, spearing the giant right through its chest armor and taking Dagrinal past the astonished beast.

The lance snapped as Dagrinal rode by, but the tip had pierced the giant's heart. He couldn't see the beast stagger around before it fell dead to the ground since his horse took him right into the enemy infantry. He roared, "Finarth!", as he used the sharp end of the broken lance to take an orc in the face, then he dropped the useless weapon and drew forth his long sword.

The fighting was chaotic; everyone was fighting for their lives. Graggis had never been a warrior who fought with finesse. His method of attacking the giant before him was impulsive and direct. He charged his horse right toward a giant, hoping to throw it off balance and finish it off with his axe. But this giant, being on the far right flank, was not nearly as disoriented as the rest, and quickly lifted its war hammer, thrusting it forward into the charging horse's lowered head.

The head of the huge weapon smashed into the horse's nose. The heavy hammer, the immense strength of the giant, and the power of the impact, caused Graggis and his horse to launch backwards as if they had hit an invisible wall of steel. The horse's head collapsed under the impact, snapping its neck with a loud crack.

Graggis and his dead horse were thrown back, landing hard on the grassy ground. The air was driven from his lungs but he struggled to get up as he fought for his next breath. The giant, meanwhile, recovered more quickly from the massive impact.

The thundering of heavy footsteps directed Graggis's gaze toward the giant that was now standing above him, its hammer raised in the air, ready for the downward descent that would crush him. But before it could strike, a young Finarthian warrior flung himself at the giant and stabbed the thing in its thick muscled leg. The blade barely broke the skin, but the attack distracted the giant enough to give Graggis a split second to recover.

As he sucked in desperately needed air, he saw the enraged giant pivot, swinging its huge hammer down onto the boy. Everything seemed to be in slow motion to Graggis as he saw the look of shock and horror on the boy's face. It was the same boy who had brought the prince and Dagrinal the lances. The monsters hammer slammed into the young warrior, crushing him into the ground.

Graggis roared in anger as he gripped his magical axe. "Now it's your turn!"

The giant looked down at him with a confused expression on his face, as if trying to understand his words. But the giant's expression changed to one of pain when Graggis bolted forward and swung his axe in a mighty swing at its unprotected ankle. The attack was so quick that the giant didn't have any time to respond. In a blur, Graggis went to work on the giant's ankles like he was downing a tree, and he might as well have been, considering the size of the beast's massive legs. Graggis's immense strength, fueled by his anger, drove the magical axe head through tough skin and muscle to stop dead at the beast's strong ankle bones.

The giant bellowed in pain as it toppled to its knees. As the beast fell, however, it was able to reach out with its right hand and seize Graggis around the waist, lifting him in the air. Though the hill giant's hands were not able to totally encircle Graggis's thick waist, its grip was so powerful that it was able to grasp and hold him securely in the air. Even though the giant was on its knees, Graggis was still several paces from the ground. Graggis struggled, but it was no use, the giant's fingers squeezed harder. Luckily Graggis's armor was protecting his flesh, but even that was beginning to bend under the sheer power of the beast.

The giant, groaning from the pain in his ankles, brought Graggis closer to his face. "You hurt Toglin, now you die," the giant growled, its deep voice covering him with breath that stunk of rotting flesh.

Fortunately for Graggis, giants were not too bright. The injured giant had overlooked the fact that Graggis was still holding his deadly axe.

"This is for the boy!" Graggis growled back as he lifted his enchanted axe with one hand. Most men could not wield an axe that size with one arm only, but Graggis was not like most men; he was as strong as dwarven steel, and right now, as angry as a wounded bear guarding her cubs.

By the time the giant processed the angry human's words, Graggis's axe had cleaved the stupid beast's face. The giant convulsed several times before it fell backwards, releasing its deadly grip on Graggis. Graggis landed hard on top of the giant's chest. He stumbled to his feet and stood tall upon the dead giant's chest. He reached down, gripped the axe handle, and placed his booted foot on the dead giant's chin. The axe head was buried deep in the giant's skull, but he pulled hard and the axe broke free from the grisly wound.

As soon as he had retrieved his axe, he looked up and saw four orcs running toward him. Glancing quickly around him he saw that the fighting had turned to complete chaos; everyone, man and beast alike, was fighting wildly to try and stay alive.

Graggis growled, and yelling maniacally he leaped off the dead giant to meet the orcs. The boy had saved him, and his death had caused a fire to burn inside him, a fire that needed more blood before it could be extinguished.

As the chaos of battle continued, Jonas was rapidly approaching the dark trio on the hill. Tulari's effortless strides quickly narrowed the distance between them. He drew forth his long bow. From his magical quiver he could draw an endless supply of arrows, another gift from Shyann, one he had realized a few days earlier as he and Taleen practiced their bows one evening before the sun had set. He nocked an arrow, and though he was still some distance from his target, he took aim.

This was no ordinary weapon. He pulled back the string and leaned forward in the saddle, in harmony with Tulari's movement, his light still pulsing bright with Shyann's power.

The two clerics of Gould drew their swords and spurred their horses down the hill to meet Jonas's attack.

Jonas smiled and released the arrow, and a heartbeat later he followed it up with a second. The arrows whistled through the air with incredible speed, a trail of blue tracing their path.

The first arrow took the astonished cleric between the eye slits on his black helm. The tremendous force of the blow shot him out of the saddle and he landed dead on his back.

The second arrow took the other cleric in the shoulder, the force spinning his body sideways. But he was skilled and experienced and he was able to hold onto the reins of his warhorse.

Jonas quickly nocked another arrow and pulled back on the string as the black cleric neared him, his sword held low in his undamaged arm. Before the cleric was close enough to attack him, Jonas's third arrow slammed into the man's chest, burying itself deep, the power of the bow launching the man through the air to land heavily on his back. He struggled momentarily, the glowing blue arrow quivering slightly in his chest, and then he went still, death overtaking him.

Taleen was fighting with all her skill and power, but her sword arm began to tire as she furiously fought back the horde of orcs and tribesman who swarmed around her, trying to extinguish her light and yank her from the saddle.

She desperately asked Bandris for the strength to keep fighting, and she felt his answer as new power began to surge through her body. She grinned, yelling Bandris's name as she renewed her attack, slicing her sword down, left and right, killing the enemies surrounding her. Kormac, her tireless steed, used his massive body to throw enemies off balance, giving Taleen the upper hand as she expertly carved her way through them.

She didn't escape unscathed, however. One of the orc's blades managed to slice across her calf. She grimaced in pain and kicked that same foot out, connecting solidly with the beast's nose, crushing it and sending blood into the air. Taleen then quickly brought her sword down on the dazed orc's head, splitting its skull all the way to its broken nose. The Orc fell away and disappeared into the crowd of enemies.

Elsewhere on the battlefield, Prince Baylin used the end of his battle axe like a spear and rammed the spiked end into a rushing orc's face. He quickly yanked the point out of the dead orc and spun to his left, swinging his mighty axe in a wide arc, taking a tribesman on the shoulder. The prince roared as fury and adrenaline rushed through his body. The tribesman fell to the ground as other enemies swarmed around the fighting prince. But he continued to fight like a demon possessed, roaring in defiance, his eyes lit with fire as he attacked the enemy before him.

Suddenly the prince felt a sharp pain in his back. He screamed and spun around, yanking a sword from a tribesman's hand. As he spun he sent his axe flying through the air into the neck of the surprised warrior. The man's body slumped to the ground as his head flew through the air to land among the fighting warriors.

Then he felt another pain on the back of his leg, causing him to fall to his knees. Holding his axe with one hand, he swung the mighty weapon blindly as he tried to spin his body around. The blade hit an orc's knee, shattering it and causing the howling monster to fall to the ground.

Baylin dug deep for the strength to fend off the foes moving in from all directions. He again yelled, "Finarth!" and jumped to his feet, swinging his battle axe and cutting into the orcs and tribesmen that surrounded him. He saw no Finarthian warriors nearby.

He was alone for this fight.

Taleen had finally broken through the rear of the enemy ranks. Her legs and her horse had sustained some minor cuts but nothing that needed healing immediately. She saw Jonas, his light marking him like a beacon, near the top of the hill, a lone rider there to meet him. She urged Kormac forward and he followed her demands instantly, launching them up the grass covered hill.

As Jonas moved closer to the horsed man he could better make out his features. He wore a black cape that was lined in red cloth and it had a sinister look to it as it billowed in the breeze behind him. His horse was as dark as night and its coat glistened like black blood. The man's long dark hair fluttered in the breeze, and his piercing green eyes shone with confidence. He carried no weapon other than a long staff made from some dark wood, with a carving of Gould's eye at the end. The center of the eye was white, in stark contrast to the black wood.

Jonas drew another arrow from the quiver at his side and nocked it to string. The man did not move even as Jonas drew the powerful bow back. As Tulari closed the distance between them, Jonas saw the man smile just as he released the shaft.

His arrow shot toward the wizard with great speed, but just as the arrow was going to take the man in the chest, it stopped, and flew back at him with the same tremendous velocity.

It all happened in the blink of an eye and Jonas could do nothing as his own arrow took him in the chest. The pain was intense and the force of the arrow knocked him from Tulari's back. He landed hard, the shock of the attack causing his light to disappear.

Jonas gasped in pain as he struggled to get up, his own arrow shaft buried deep just below his right shoulder. His lung had been punctured and he was struggling for air as blood filled his chest. He got to his knees as he coughed up blood onto his hands. He heard, rather than saw the horse gallop up to him.

"A repel spell, one of my favorites," the evil wizard said calmly.

Jonas glanced up, slowly regaining his footing, sharp pain shooting through his right arm and chest. His right arm hung useless. Despite the intense pain, he calmed his mind and drew one of his blades with his left hand.

The man laughed as Jonas struggled to steady himself. "Go ahead, young cavalier, attack me. Even your mighty weapon will not save you now."

Jonas felt his strength slowly dissipate as his lung continued to fill with blood. Healing himself would be impossible while the arrow was still embedded deep in his flesh, and he did not have the strength to pull it free. He was running out of time, and he knew it.

He narrowed his eyes, concentrating on the man's face. He was middle aged, his hair was peppered with gray and his tan skin wrinkled like tough leather. A dark moustache folded into a long trimmed beard decorated his chin. His green, deep set eyes were pools of malice.

Jonas was desperate, but as he focused on the wizard's eyes, he had an idea. He continued to focus on the man's eyes, wrapping his energy around his brain. He had never used his cognivant powers in this way before, but he could think of no other option. He entered the state of Ty'erm to conquer his pain and center his focus. Then he entered the man's mind, wrapping it with tendrils of energy, constricting the tendrils with the power of his own mind. It all happened in a few heartbeats. The wizard didn't know what hit him.

How does that feel? Jonas asked within the man's mind.

The wizard grimaced with pain as he brought his hands to his head. His horse pranced underneath him as he struggled to stay in the saddle. Moaning with pain he dropped his staff.

Jonas's vision blurred briefly as the pain in his own head intensified from the use of his powers. The wizard was powerful, and it was taking everything Jonas had to continue the attack. But he forced himself to use any power he had remaining to concentrate on the task. He stumbled to his knees but kept his head up, focusing on the man before him, trying at all cost to crush the wizard's mind.

Suddenly two arrows slammed into the wizard's chest, one after the other. The impact forced the man to fall backwards from his saddle and land hard on his side. As the wizard fell the mental link between the two was broken.

Jonas was on all fours trying to stay conscious as the pain from his effort exploded in his head. He was exhausted, both physically and mentally, and he desperately needed to rest.

He looked up at the man sprawled out on the ground before him. He could clearly see the blue feathered arrows embedded in the man's chest, and that quick vision forced a brief smile through the pain. The wizard's repel spell must have dispersed when he attacked the man's mind.

"Are you okay, Jonas?"

Jonas recognized Taleen's worried voice behind him. He looked up just as she rode next to him. He forced a painful smile to reassure her.

"I'm injured badly. I need healing…quickly." He coughed up more blood as he fell to his back, his own feathered arrow protruding from his chest

"In Bandris's name, what happened?" Taleen cried as she quickly dismounted and rushed to Jonas's side.

"Remove the arrow and heal me and I'll be happy to tell you," Jonas gasped.

Back among the hordes, Prince Baylin swung his axe in frantic strokes, hoping to keep the enemy away from him long enough to give someone time to come to his aid. His arm was tiring and he stopped momentarily as he noticed the orcs were no longer advancing.

Just then a huge orc pushed through the ring of enemies to stand before the tired prince. The enemy warriors, including the tribesmen, looked to the colossal monster for their orders. The orc wore thick plate mail that covered his muscled body. He was abnormally wide, which gave him the look of a walking boulder. In his right hand he carried a thick wood handle capped with a long chain. At the end of the chain was a heavy spiked ball of steel. The weapon, called a morning star, was large and cumbersome, but the massive orc carried it with ease. The beast's yellow eyes narrowed with malice as it stepped closer to the exhausted prince. "You are Prince Baylin," the orc growled. "I am Ongessett, war leader of the orcs."

Prince Baylin was bleeding from several wounds and his arms felt like they were weighted down by rocks. He took a deep breath and stood up tall, holding his magnificent axe before him. "I do not banter with orc scum," he growled back, launching his body forward, the sharp point of his axe leading the way.

Ongessett lifted his morning star, one hand grasping the handle while the other grasped the chain near the ball, using the thick chain like a staff to block Prince Baylin's weapon. The orc chief moved quickly for someone so large. He stepped back as he deflected the prince's axe with the thick chain of his awesome weapon. The orc continued the momentum of his parry, attempting to bring the heavy spiked head of the weapon down on top of the prince.

Prince Baylin continued forward, the heavy spiked ball slamming into the ground near him leaving behind a deep divot. He shifted his grip on the handle of his axe and rammed the razor sharp blade into the orc's chest. But he could not find a seam in the beast's armor and his blade slid across the armor harmlessly. The orcs armor was clearly enchanted as it so easily turned aside the prince's powerful axe.

The orc growled, bringing its left mailed fist down on top of Prince Baylin's head. He tried to dodge the powerful blow but his tired body wasn't reacting. But the orc's fist missed Baylin's head and crashed instead into his shoulder. The power of the blow popped his shoulder from its socket. He screamed in pain and stumbled to the ground. Frantically he glanced up, struggling to get away, but all he saw was a large steel toed boot crash into his face. Teeth and blood erupted from his shattered jaw as he flew backwards to land heavily on the trampled ground. His vision blurred and darkness enveloped him as he heard the Orc chief's words.

"Do not kill him."

Then all went black.

The fighting throughout the battlefield was intense. Dagrinal used all of his skill to stay alive. He had no idea how long he was fighting when suddenly an orc before him shuddered in death and was launched to the side like a rag doll. Standing in the beast's place was Graggis, his bloody axe held before him. He was covered in dirt and blood but he did not seem hurt. Within moments they had killed any enemy nearby.

"Where is the prince?" stormed Dagrinal over the cacophony of the battle.

"I know not! I lost him when we hit the giants!" roared Graggis in reply. "We must find him!"

Suddenly a horn sounded above the din of battle.

"That was not ours!" yelled Dagrinal.

As they spoke they noticed the decimated enemy troops start to pull away, leaving an exhausted Finarthian force standing amongst the dead. Dagrinal and Graggis pushed their way through the tired soldiers.

"The prince, where is the prince!" yelled Dagrinal. The exhausted soldiers could barely stand up, but they immediately began searching for their prince. The men parted as Dagrinal and Graggis quickly moved through the ranks, looking for some sign of Prince Baylin amongst the living, or the dead.

Graggis found the body of the boy that had saved him. His face and upper body were crushed and his neck was unnaturally twisted. Graggis knelt by the boy and gently closed his eyes. "You're a brave boy, and I count myself lucky to have fought next to you. I look forward to buying you a drink in

Ulren's great hall." Graggis shook his head sadly before he stood up and looked up the hill towards the retreating enemy forces.

"It looks like they are retreating for the day," Graggis said.

"I think I know why," replied Dagrinal softly. He held up a weapon for Graggis to see. In his hands was Prince Baylin's axe. "I found it over there," Dagrinal continued, indicating to his right, "but there was no sign of his body."

"You think he was captured?"

"That would be my guess. The absence of a body means that he is not dead on the field. And if they captured him then they must want him alive, at least for now," added Dagrinal as he grabbed a nearby soldier. The warrior was tired and covered in blood, but other than that he was not injured. "What is your name?" asked Dagrinal.

"Fulren, sir."

"Fulren, find third lance Lathrin and inform him that Prince Baylin is missing. Have him search the nearby area."

The man's face reflected his shock at the grim news, but his posture straightened as the importance of the mission infused him with new energy.

"Yes, sir! Right away!" The warrior sprinted away, searching the ranks for Lathrin.

Graggis grabbed Dagrinal hard on the arm. "Dagrinal, if he is captured…" Graggis did not finish the statement. "We must get him back. There is no telling what they will do to him."

"I know, my friend, I know."

Just then two horses galloped toward them. It was Jonas and Taleen. Jonas was tired but Taleen had healed him completely. Even the hole in his armor was gone. They were both covered in blood, luckily only a small amount of it was their own.

"Why are they retreating?" asked Jonas.

Both men gazed at the horse with open admiration.

"I don't know, but I'm glad to see it happening," Graggis replied. "Well met, Jonas. It is good to see you so well."

"And you, Graggis. This is Taleen, cavalier to Bandris." Taleen nodded her head in greeting.

"Taleen, I shall thank Bandris for your sword," Dagrinal said smoothly, quickly redirecting his gaze to Jonas. "Jonas, the prince has not been found, and his weapon was lying among the dead."

Jonas sat back in his saddle at the distressing news. Prince Baylin had done a lot for him and he respected the man immensely. The news made him sick, the thought of what the enemy might do to him if he were captured caused his stomach to churn with anxiety. He clenched his teeth in anger.

"Then let us withhold the pleasantries and find him."

The large tent of the king had been set up in a lightly forested glen far enough from the battlefield to be secure, but close enough that the progress of the battle could be relayed quickly to the king and other commanders whose job was more logistical than physical. The king's tent was made up of heavy red cloth held up by long straight pine trees. It stood out from the rest of the encampment and it was surrounded by the king's personal guard. Four burly soldiers holding halberds stood before the entrance. They moved aside quickly as they saw Dagrinal, Graggis, and the two cavaliers move briskly toward them.

The spacious tent was empty except for a huge table in the middle surrounded by ten heavy wood chairs, and the king's sleeping furs that were stacked up in the corner on a large mattress of goose feathers. King Gavinsteal sat on the edge of his bed while a priest of Ulren removed the bandage on his head. The king's wound had disappeared, the priest obviously having done his job. The king looked up as they approached.

"My King, how are you feeling?" asked Dagrinal with concern.

"I am fine, just a nasty gash and a bad headache, nothing serious," the king said as his gaze moved to Taleen and Jonas. He smiled broadly. "Jonas, it is you. My men told me that two cavaliers had arrived killing the Banthra and the Naz-reen priests. That is good news! I am very glad to see you."

"Likewise, King Gavinsteal, I'm glad you are well. Are you in need of any healing?"

The king glanced at the old priest by his side. "No, Hondris here has taken care of me. The gash is no longer and my head is now beginning to clear, but I thank you nonetheless. Hondris, this is Jonas, and by the looks of it he is a cavalier to Shyann." The king's last words were stated as a question.

"I am, my Lord, sanctioned by Annure and Shyann herself. It is a pleasure to meet you, Hondris, priest of Ulren."

"The pleasure is mine, young cavalier," replied the old man as he turned to face Jonas.

"When we have more time I would like to hear what has happened with you. But right now we have a war to win," the king said as he stood up from his bed.

"Very good, sir. Lord, this is Taleen, cavalier to Helikon. She has come to help where she may."

The king slowly approached Taleen and extended his hand. "Thank you, Taleen. Helikon? Are you from the west, beyond the Tundrens?" the king asked, shaking her hand warmly.

"I am, King Gavinsteel. I am from Osrigard. Helikon sent me here to help Jonas."

"Very good, your presence gives me hope. Thank you for being here," he said sincerely.

"Thank Helikon," replied Taleen, releasing the king's grip.

King Gavinsteel smiled broadly at the beautiful warrior. "I will do that," he said, sitting down in a large wood chair and looking around for his son. "Where is Baylin, where is my son?"

Dagrinal looked down at the ground momentarily before returning his gaze to his king. He felt to blame for not staying closer to the prince during the battle and he had a hard time looking his king in the eye. The king spent his life reading men, and he could see the pain and sorrow in Dagrinal's eyes before he even said anything.

"My Lord, we found Prince Baylin's axe among the dead," Dagrinal said, reaching behind him as Graggis handed him the prince's axe. Dagrinal held the axe before him as the king stood up slowly, his eyes wide with shock.

"Did you find his body?" asked the king, his voice shaking slightly.

"We did not, my Lord. He may have been captured," answered Dagrinal.

The king stood up straighter at the news that is son might be alive. He walked briskly forward and took his son's axe from Dagrinal's grasp. "Then he must be alive. We must find him! Send out a messenger now, I will pay whatever price they demand."

"Very well, my Lord," replied Dagrinal as he glanced at Graggis. Graggis nodded his head and walked from the room to find a messenger.

The king sat back down and tried to push the grave news away and focus on the task at hand. He laid his son's axe on the table and looked at it momentarily before he spoke. "How did we fare, Dagrinal?"

"We did well, my King, considering. Jonas killed the Banthra which helped us greatly. It is even possible that the army will not continue to fight without the Banthra and the Naz-reen priests."

"And if they do? How many men have we lost?"

"The numbers are still coming in, but I believe we've lost more than a third of our infantry and at least an equal amount of our cavalry."

The king shook his head sadly and sighed deeply, the pain of those losses sitting heavy on the tired monarch. "What of the enemy?"

"I do not know. Most of our scouts have not returned. The ones that did reported that a large army still rests beyond the hills past the Lindsor Bridge. I would imagine that most of the orcs and ogres that are still alive will not fight without the Banthra there to force them. There are still a few hill giants, but who knows who controls them. We cannot be sure of anything at this point."

"Sir, if I may interrupt?" asked Jonas.

The tired king looked at Jonas. "Go ahead, Jonas. You've earned the right to be rid of formality in my tent. What is it?"

"Sir, we have brought someone with us who may be able to help."

Just as Jonas spoke, Graggis returned through the tent flaps followed by Kiln. Though Kiln was covered with blood but he walked with no sign of injury.

"My Lord, I have sent out your messenger. And I have found someone that wants to see you," Graggis said, bowing his head.

King Gavinsteal stood, nodded his thanks to Graggis, but kept his wide eyes fixed on Kiln, who stood facing the monarch, his own face struggling to mask a maelstrom of emotions.

Jonas shifted his feet uneasily, not sure how this meeting would go.

King Gavinsteal walked over to Kiln, and placing his hand on his shoulder, he forced a smile from his tired and sad face. "My friend, it has been far too long," he said slowly. "I did not think I would ever see you again."

Kiln subtly nodded his head, giving the king a slight smile. "Uthrayne, it is good to see you as well. I have grown bored in the mountains and I have sulked long enough," he said softly. "It is time I put my grievances aside and return to the world of the living. I thank you for your letter, and your words."

The warriors around the duo looked about uneasily, uncomfortable at witnessing such a personal encounter.

"I wronged you, my friend and I have carried this guilt for over twenty years. There has been only one action in my life that I have regretted, and it was what I did to our friendship."

Kiln nodded his head in acknowledgement. "Women have a way of making fools of men, my Lord," replied Kiln, putting emphasis on the words, *my Lord*.

The king tried to force a smile, but the strain of the recent news regarding his son hindered his effort, and Kiln knew that something was wrong.

"What is it, Uthrayne?" he asked with concern.

"My friend, my son Baylin is lost, probably captured by the enemy. I need you Kiln, now more than ever."

The king walked over to the large table and spread some maps out on it. Just then Prince Nelstrom strode into the tent wearing his typical black clothing and burnished black steel chest plate. His long dark cape billowed behind him as he moved quickly to the table. "Father, I heard you had been injured. It is good to see you are well," he said as he quickly surveyed the room. His eyes swept past Jonas but returned briefly, recognizing him easily.

"I see that we have guests. Jonas, how good to see you. You look like a cavalier. Are my eyes betraying me?"

"No, they are not," Jonas said curtly.

"When did you arrive?"

"Just today. This is Taleen, cavalier to Helikon," Jonas replied smoothly. Jonas could still feel something about this man that he did not like. He couldn't place it but his spine tingled slightly whenever he was around.

Prince Nelstrom nodded his head toward Taleen and smiled. "I did not know that cavaliers were so beautiful."

Taleen kept her face a blank mask and simply nodded her head in greeting. From anyone else those words would have been a compliment, but even though Taleen did not know Prince Nelstrom, the words he spoke sounded like the hiss of a snake to her. She clearly felt that his words were condescending and she made no effort to mask those feelings.

The room was uncomfortably silent for a few seconds before the king spoke. "My son, this is Kiln, who I think needs no introduction. He arrived today with Jonas." Prince Nelstrom crossed over to Kiln and reached out, shaking his hand in the warrior's grip. As the two shook hands the Prince's master swordsman mark could clearly be seen on his right hand.

"I have heard much about you. You are a legend," the young prince said. "I would be honored if you would cross blades with me when time permits."

Kiln glanced down at his son's hand, although the only people that knew that Prince Nelstrom was of Kiln's loins were the king, Jonas, Dagrinal, and Graggis, basically everyone that was standing in the room. Kiln smiled, his eyes sparkling at the prospect of a challenge as he noticed Prince Nelstrom's master swordsman's mark. "It would be a pleasure. I'd love to see if that mark has been well earned."

"I can assure you that it has."

"Where have you been?" asked the king.

"I was fighting with the right flank, Father," replied the prince.

Dagrinal glanced at Graggis skeptically, but no one saw the brief exchange. They both knew that the prince had not taken part in any of the fighting. The young man was a skilled swordsman, but fighting in the dirt and mud, next to common soldiers, was beneath him. Everyone knew it, but no one said a word.

"My son, Baylin is missing, we believe him to be captured," the king announced, sitting down heavily to look at the maps.

Prince Nelstrom sat down next to him. "Are you sure, Father?" he asked with concern.

"No, but we did not find his body. I have sent out a messenger to Lord Moredin to barter for his return."

"That is good. We will get him back if he is indeed taken, I have no doubt," replied the prince, his tone rather unconvincing.

The king looked at his youngest son for a few moments before shifting his gaze to Kiln. "We have much to prepare for. Kiln, you are needed now. Volnos, my high commander was slain today. It is a great loss to us. Would you offer your services to Finarth in its time of need? No oath need be taken."

"I will," replied Kiln evenly.

Suddenly a man in long robes hurried through the king's entrance. It was Alerion, the king's wizard. He looked haggard and his brow was covered with sweat. He carried a wooden staff ending in a blue stone held firmly on the end with silver wire. "My Lord," he said as he walked toward the king. "I am sorry to barge in on you like this but I have urgent news."

The warriors shifted away from the table to make room for Alerion.

"No need to apologize, Alerion. Here, take some water first." The king offered, pouring the wizard a glass of water from a ceramic jug on the table. "Now, what is it that brings you to my tent in such haste?"

"My Lord, I have dire news. I have learned positively that Malbeck has been resurrected. But that is not the most troubling news as it was already suspected." Alerion stopped to take another sip of water. "Malbeck's energy has been floating in limbo for over a thousand years. Your ancestor killed his physical body only."

"Then what brought him back?"

"The Shan Cemar."

"What! That is not possible. The Shan Cemar is just a legend." The King stood up in surprise.

"No, my Lord, the Shan Cemar is real, and it is now in the hands of the Dark One."

"What is the Shan Cemar?" asked Jonas.

Alerion turned toward Jonas and noticed him for the first time. "Jonas, it is good to see you. I'm glad that you are well, and it seems the gods have favored you," Alerion said, looking Jonas up and down with new respect. "The Shan Cemar is an ancient elven book that holds their most powerful words of magic. The book is so old that even the elves did not know its location; it was hidden thousands of lifetimes ago to keep the power safe. Wizards have been searching for the manuscript for a long time. It has somehow been found, giving Malbeck more power than you can possibly imagine. With that book he has access to all the ancient elven words that can unlock the true power of the Ru'Ach."

"How do we stop him?" asked Jonas, a grim look on his face.

"I don't know."

An oppressive silence filled the tent as those inside contemplated this new development.

Finally the king spoke up. "One step at a time. We have a threat here to face first, and we have my son to find. Then we can worry about Malbeck."

"My Lord. I'm afraid that this army is just a ruse to keep you busy while Malbeck destroys Tarsis. As we speak, Tarsis smolders and boargs roam the lands searching and destroying any scouts that King Kromm has sent out."

As the king listened to this new revelation, the blood seemed to drain from his weary face. He collapsed heavily on the edge of his bed.

"You mean Tarsis is destroyed?" asked Dagrinal.

"Yes. King Kromm escaped at the last moment with a small force of followers. He is being pursued by Malbeck's minions as we speak."

"How do you know this?" asked Graggis.

"Graggis, your skills are with the axe, mine are with magic. The means by which I found this information is irrelevant. The fact is, Tarsis is no more, and King Kromm fights for his life."

"And that very same army that took Tarsis is sure to be moving south toward us," added Taleen.

"We will be flanked on two sides." Jonas said what everyone was thinking.

The king rubbed his long beard in thought. "Kiln, what would you suggest?" asked the king, his tired eyes almost pleading.

All eyes turned towards the famous war commander.

Kiln stepped close to the table and gazed down at the big map positioned there. "It would take Malbeck's army over ninety days to march from Tarsis to Finarth and that is in the most advantageous conditions. Winter will be approaching by then and it is hard to say how that will affect his plans. Will he force march his army during the winter? Will he hold up and let the snows pass? We will have to keep careful watch on his forces. We should send out our best scouts now. I would suggest that you take your army back to Finarth to prepare for a siege and a long, hard winter. Finarth has never been taken, and that is where we should make our stand."

"If Malbeck brings the Shan Cemar to our doorstep, then I do not think we can stop him," Alerion said somberly.

Kiln narrowed his eyes in thought. "There must be something that can fight the power of the Shan Cemar. No army is undefeatable."

"There is one thing," added the wizard.

"What, Alerion? What can defeat Malbeck?" asked the frustrated king.

"I was told by my source that the only thing that may defeat Malbeck is an IshMian whose veins pulse with the blood of Finarth."

"That sounds like a riddle," interjected Prince Nelstrom. But he did not miss the looks that Kiln, Taleen, and Graggis, sent Jonas's way.

The king did not miss the looks either. "What? Why are you all staring at Jonas?" asked the king.

"King Gavinsteal, Jonas is an IshMian," said Taleen.

"Really? Jonas, you are definitely full of surprises. But what does the riddle mean, the blood of Finarth?" asked the king.

"My Lord, it sounds like that phrase would have some connection to the royal family of Finarth, which would exclude Jonas," reasoned Alerion.

"King Gavinsteal, are there any members of the royal family that are IshMian?" asked Jonas.

"The only members of the royal family are standing in this tent, and none of them have the powers of an IshMian," the king answered.

"There must be something we are missing," Kiln pondered thoughtfully.

"Alerion, What do you make of the riddle? Is it possible that Jonas could be the IshMian that your source spoke of?" asked the king.

"I do not know, my Lord. I have relayed all I was told. If Jonas is an IshMian, then he could be that man. I know of no other IshMian with powers that might enable him to defeat the Dark One. On the other hand, *the blood of Finarth* part of the riddle does not seem to apply to him at all. Even if he is this man, I do not know how he might defeat the powers of the Shan Cemar. I will think on this riddle further and see if I can find anything related to *the blood of Finarth*."

"IshMians are extremely rare and the gods seem to have a plan for Jonas. It is very possible that Jonas may be who your source was speaking of," Taleen said.

"Jonas, I know I cannot give you orders as a cavalier, but will you stay and fight with us?" asked the king.

Jonas did not hesitate in his response. "My Lord, I have not yet received a calling. If my calling is to stay and fight then my steel will be yours, but if I am called, then I cannot argue with Shyann's will. She knows best where I may be of use."

"Very well. Dagrinal, send out scouts and spread the word that we leave at first light back to Finarth. Kiln, Jonas, and Taleen, will you three stay awhile so we can talk? I need your council on this dark day."

"It would be my pleasure," replied Kiln.

"Sir, there are men to be healed and I would like to find my friend, Fil. Do you know where I can locate him?"

"You are correct, Jonas. I'm embarrassed I did not think of my wounded first. Both of your healing powers would be appreciated. We can talk at another time. I think Fil is with Tanus's modrig. They should be camped to the southeast."

Jonas bowed his head slightly. "Thank you my Lord, until tomorrow."

"It was a pleasure to meet you, King Gavinsteal," replied Taleen with a slight nod.

"The pleasure was mine, cavalier. Thank you for your help," the king nodded in reply.

She turned and followed Jonas out of the tent. They strode through the tent flaps to their horses. Jonas climbed onto Tulari who was standing patiently outside. Several of the nearby guards were staring at them and their magnificent horses with open admiration. Taleen mounted her steed as well and they slowly trotted southeast.

As they made their way through the various camp sites, many men stood up and acknowledged their presence with a smile or a simple greeting. It was obvious to them both that their presence was uplifting to the entire army.

It was a strange feeling for Jonas and he wondered how long it would take him to get used to it. He openly expressed his feelings to Taleen.

"It feels strange to have everyone look at me with awe and respect. I am so accustomed to the opposite reaction."

"It will happen wherever you go, Jonas. I am still not accustomed to it, and I don't know if I ever will be."

"I guess that is a good thing. Who were you before you became a cavalier?" Jonas asked as he snuck a peak at her beautiful profile.

"I was the daughter of a blacksmith. He raised me like I was his son, taught me how to wield a sword and ride a horse. He was a stern strong man whom I loved very much."

"What happened to him?"

"He was killed when our village was raided by goblins. After that I joined King Allryan's army and fought for him for eight years." Taleen paused as her memories came flooding back.

"I am sorry, Taleen. I didn't mean to bring back unpleasant memories."

Taleen looked at him and smiled. "Do not fret, Jonas. It's just been a long time since I thought about my father. Anyway, I rose quickly through the ranks as a soldier and I decided to try my skills as a cavalier. It took me five years but I was granted the rank of cavalier by Helikon six years ago."

"What about your mother? Do you have any siblings?"

"My mother died during child birth, along with my sister."

"I see. I'm sorry. It seems we both have had difficult pasts," Jonas commented.

"I guess so. But my father loved me and he cared for me the best he could. I was better off than many," Taleen reasoned.

Jonas thought about her words knowing full well the truth of them. Even he, who led a very difficult life, realized at a young age that no matter how hard your life seemed, it could always be worse. He, too, had it tough, but he did have a loving mother who did her best to care for him. Jonas changed the subject. "Did many women serve with you? We don't have many female warriors here."

"There are not many, but I would not say it is rare. Women are allowed to fight but few can pass the training."

Jonas looked at her again and marveled at her beauty. She noticed him staring and didn't look away.

"Have you ever been married?" Jonas asked softly.

"No. The life of a cavalier is not fit for marriage," she replied with no hint of emotion.

"Is it forbidden?" Jonas asked.

"No, it is not forbidden," Taleen replied as she looked at Jonas.

Jonas looked away and pretended to scan the camp fires for Fil. A lone rider galloped toward them and pulled up short. He was wearing plate mail and a helm similar to Jonas's, except the horns were those of a boarg.

Jonas shivered involuntarily as memories came flooding back to him. It was hard for him to picture a boarg, or even hear the name, without thinking of his mother's brutal death. The warrior was bloody and he held his shoulder as if he were injured. He lifted his visor and smiled warmly at the two cavaliers.

"Greetings, cavaliers, word of your presence has quickly spread through the ranks. My name is Tanus and I am a captain in the king's army."

"Hello, captain, my name is Jonas Kanrene, cavalier to Shyann."

"And I am Taleen Gothar, cavalier to Bandris." Taleen figured it was easier to use the western name for her god so as not to cause confusion.

"I am glad you are both here. Is it true that you battled a Banthra and several priests of the Forsworn?" Tanus asked, crossing his chest at the mention of the dark gods.

"It is true. Jonas killed the Banthra and helped me slay the priests," stated Taleen. "Sir, are you hurt? Do you need healing?"

"I took a goblin spear to the shoulder. I had it patched up to stop most of the bleeding. I'd rather have you save your energy for my men if you are up to it. I have many men more severely wounded."

"It would be our pleasure. After we heal who we can, would you be able to lead us to a friend of mine? I believe he is in your modrig?" asked Jonas.

"What is his name?"

"Fil Tanrey, he is a knight apprentice."

"Ah yes. Fil saved my life today. He was hurt badly but nothing life threatening, thank the High One for that. He is brave and strong. I am glad he is on our side."

Jonas felt a twinge of worry and pride as he thought about his friend. "Please, take me too him. I must see him and heal him immediately," Jonas said eagerly.

"Very well. Follow me."

Tanus led the two cavaliers through the camp; the men's faces, reflected in the many campfires, showed a mixture of emotions. Some looked tired and haggard, others seemed happy to be alive, or solemn at the loss of their brethren. But all stood and greeted the cavaliers with a nod or a smile as they rode by.

When they neared a large cream colored tent, Tanus dismounted and tethered his horse. Taleen and Jonas both followed his lead, though they had no need to tether their own mounts.

Tanus stared openly at Tulari as the giant horse stood passively, and Jonas couldn't help but feel immense pride for his new steed.

"That is the most magnificent animal I have ever seen," Tanus said as he admired the huge animal.

"Thank you, Tanus. His name is Tulari, and you're right, he is magnificent in many ways."

Tanus broke his gaze from the animal and led the two warriors into the tent that housed the wounded. The first things Jonas noticed were the sounds and odors. It had been many years since he had seen the results of a battle, and even then he had only seen the dead. But here he was looking at the wounded. It didn't take him long to realize that witnessing the survivors of a battle may be worse than seeing the dead. The dead didn't moan or cry out in pain. The sounds of the wounded and dying were something that Jonas would not forget. But it was the smell that would stick with him. The interior odor was a mix of sweat, blood, infection, and vomit that assaulted Jonas's nose. The tent was filled with makeshift cots lined with the many wounded. Surgeons and their apprentices moved quickly among the men, cleaning their bandages, and stitching their wounds. There were men unconscious, men moaning in pain, and even some men screaming as surgeons cut, sewed, or sawed. It was a gruesome scene that Jonas would not forget.

"How many other tents are there for the wounded?" Jonas asked.

"One or two for each modrig. The injured are organized into three groups. A black mark on their forehead means they will probably not survive, a red mark means they are seriously injured and they need treatment immediately, and a blue mark means their injuries are minor and they can be looked at later. The few priests that we have will try to heal the severely injured first, but we just don't have enough magical healers to go around."

As Tanus led them through the injured men Jonas began to make out the colored marks painted on each man's forehead.

"Jonas!"

The familiar voice broke Jonas's trance as he was looking at the helpless men around him. Tanus had led them to a cot where Fil lay nursing his wounds. His skin was pale and he had a bandage wrapped around his bare chest.

Jonas smiled happily as he gazed at his friend. "Fil, are you okay? Where are you hurt?" Jonas asked anxiously.

"I was stabbed in the side and then an ogre broke some ribs and cracked my breast bone." Fil struggled to sit up, his face strained as pain shot through his body.

Jonas laid a restraining hand on him, easing him back down to a prone position. "Take it easy, my friend, all in good time."

"It is so good to see you, Jonas," Fil said through a forced smile. He looked at Jonas more closely, his eyes moving across Jonas's immaculate sparkling armor, and the beautifully crafted swords strapped at his side. The blue and silver symbol of Shyann danced in the candle light.

"Ulren's star, you did it, you're a cavalier," Fil said in amazement.

"I am, my friend, but let me heal you first and we can talk in detail once you feel better."

"You can heal now? I knew you would do it, Jonas."

"I can do many things now. Now hold still. You will feel some heat and your body will feel warm as I mend your wounds. But it will not hurt."

"Okay, go ahead. I am ready."

Jonas reached down and put both of his hands on Fil's chest. He began to pray silently, calling on Shyann for the power to heal his friend. His hands began to glow blue as he sent the healing energy into Fil.

Jonas searched Fil's body for the injuries and saw his breastbone was indeed cracked and he had seven broken ribs, one dangerously close to lacerating his lung. Jonas went to work on mending the bones, any ruptured blood vessels, tendons, and the surrounding tissue. Then he went to work in eliminating the infection that was building up in Fil's side. The wound was shallow and he sealed it quickly. After a few minutes Jonas opened his eyes to see Fil staring at him with wonder.

"That felt incredible. Thank you, Jonas. I feel perfect," Fil said. He leaned up in bed and bent his body to test it for pain. He smiled broadly as he got out of bed. "I feel no pain. I'm a little sore but I feel much better. You completely healed me! Amazing!" He rambunctiously grabbed Jonas in a big bear hug and held him tightly. "I've missed you, my friend! We have much to discuss. But first, who is this beautiful lady beside you?"

"My name is Taleen, and I'm a cavalier to Bandris," Taleen said with a warm smile.

Fil noticed for the first time her immaculate armor and he reddened in embarrassment. "I am sorry, Taleen. I was so excited to see Jonas that I did not notice you were a cavalier. Please forgive my lack of respect."

Taleen reassured Fil with a brilliant smile. "You are forgiven, Fil Tanrey. Besides, even a cavalier likes to hear compliments from time to time," Taleen added. Her smile was infectious and seemed to make the tough warriors around her blush.

"It is nice to meet you, Taleen. And let's just say that you are both a wonderful sight. I had heard that two cavaliers had arrived and destroyed the Banthra, but I had no idea it was you, Jonas."

"It was. We arrived today with Kiln. He held the center line today."

"Kiln is here?" asked Tanus, clearly shocked at the mention of the great swordsman's name.

"He is with the king now. He has taken over as high commander," replied Jonas.

"Is Kiln dark haired with gray eyes and fights like a demon?" Fil asked skeptically.

"That is him. Have you seen him?" asked Jonas.

Fil smiled as he thought about the fight today. "I have. I fought with him today. He came in on his horse and kept the line together. I have never seen anything like it. We were crumbling and getting scattered and he barreled in and took control, killing anything that came at him. He diced up the ogre that almost killed me like it was nothing more than a tiny goblin. He rallied the men and held the center, wading into the screaming tribesmen with no hint of fear. I couldn't believe it; he just cut into them like they didn't exist, leaping and spinning from one enemy to another, leaving dead bodies wherever he went. The enemy was so thick around him that I could no longer see him. I thought he had been killed, until our men, encouraged by his bravery, fought their way through the enemy ranks and found him fighting for his life. I passed out before that, but that is the story that I heard. Everyone is talking about him, but I don't know how many knew that he was Kiln, the legend."

"That sounds like, Kiln," Jonas said with a smile.

"Jonas, we need to start healing these men," Taleen interrupted.

Jonas looked at her and at the wounded and dying men around them. "Yes, you're quite right. Fil, let us talk later. Taleen and I must heal as many of these men as we can. We will take care of the most urgently wounded first, and then we will heal you, Tanus. Your men will need you healthy in the trials to come."

"Very good, Jonas. Thank you for helping my men, both of you," Tanus said.

"You're welcome. I will find you later to tend to your wound. Fil," Jonas said, turning his gaze to his friend. "How will we find you later?"

"You can find my camp farther on the south side. I will have a warm cup of tea waiting for you," Fil said.

"I am looking forward to it."

"Taleen, I'm glad to have met you," Fil said. "I hope you accompany Jonas to our camp site so that we may talk more."

"It would be my pleasure, Fil," replied Taleen with a nod.

"Sir, do you need me for anything or am I free to go to my camp?" Fil asked Tanus.

Tanus smiled and shook his head. "No, you've done enough. You saved my life today and I thank you for that. Go ahead, get some rest. You've earned it."

Fil nodded his head and looked one more time at Jonas, smiling widely before walking out of the tent.

Jonas and Taleen spent the better part of two hours healing as many men as they could. They were both exhausted as they drug themselves from the tent to their horses and made their way towards Fil's camp. They couldn't heal all the men in one night. The energy expended took its toll on their bodies and they had to rest. A warm meal and a soft bed were needed now. But Jonas had to see Fil and that is where they headed.

They found Fil's camp easily enough and it wasn't long before they had their tired bodies resting on their sleeping blankets in front of a warm crackling fire. A full belly, a cup of warm tea, and the camaraderie of friends did wonders for Jonas's bone-weary body.

Jonas and Taleen talked with Fil for as long as their tired bodies would allow. Fil and Jonas had a lot to catch up on and the words flowed from their mouths. They were both very happy to see each other, but it wasn't long after they got there that Jonas began to tire, his fight with the Banthra and the healing finally wearing him out, finally overcoming the excitement of seeing his friend. Taleen was also exhausted and Jonas took notice of her heavy eyelids fluttering beyond the dancing flames of their campfire.

"Fil, my friend, Taleen and I are both exhausted and we need to get some sleep. We have much to do in the morning," Jonas said.

"Oh yes, of course. Do you want to lay your bed rolls here at my fire?"

Jonas was just going to accept when a lone horseman approached them from the darkness. The bright moonlight and many campfires enabled the rider to maneuver through the campfires to find them. The man was one of the king's knights.

"Cavaliers, the king has prepared a tent for you. There is warm water, food, and drink waiting. Would you like me to escort you there or send a rider for you later?"

"We will go now. Thank you for the offer," replied Jonas.

"It is my pleasure. I am glad that you both are with us." The warrior looked to be older than fifty winters. His face was covered with course whiskers, some of which were gray. He was powerfully built, and his thick wavy hair gave him the look of a lion.

Jonas and Taleen mounted their horses which had been standing nearby.

"Fil," the veteran warrior spoke up. "I heard that you fought well today. Tanus said you saved his life. Good work, son."

"Thank you, Renagar," Fil replied seriously.

Renagar addressed the two cavaliers who were both ready to leave. "Follow me, if you please."

"I'll find you tomorrow, Fil." Jonas smiled at his friend as he turned his horse to leave.

"Thank you for inviting me to your fire, Fil. I am glad to have met you," added Taleen.

"I'll see you both tomorrow," Fil said, watching them ride away into the night.

Their tent was not large but the interior was spacious since it had little furniture. It had been placed near the king's own tent, for which Jonas was grateful, in case the monarch might need them. Inside were two beds hastily made from furs, thick cotton blankets, and soft pillows. Just the sight of them made Jonas's eye lids feel as if they were made of lead. A small table, covered with trays of meats, cheeses, and fruits was set up in the middle of the tent. They were also provided a large copper wash basin filled with steaming water. King Gavinsteal had also taken into consideration Taleen's privacy and had his men construct a screen framed with wood with blue dyed cotton forming the panels.

They used the wash basin to wash away the grime of battle, and after eating their simple but nourishing meal, they finally dropped their tired bodies down onto their soft beds. They fell asleep quickly, exhaustion permeating their bodies.

Jonas slowly opened his eyes as a bright light shone before him. He squinted and held up his hand to block out what felt like the sun's rays shining right in his face.

After a few moments the light disappeared and Jonas opened his eyes fully, revealing Shyann before him. She was standing on the edge of a cliff, with her back to Jonas, and she was wearing black leather breeches and a matching black sleeveless shirt. Her whole body seemed to be bathed in white light.

Jonas looked around and noticed that he was standing on a mountain and Shyann was looking down at something below.

She turned her head, smiling warmly at him. "Jonas, come here. I want to show you something."

Her voice was the same as before, melodic and entrancing, and it warmed his very soul. Jonas slowly approached and stood next to her, looking at her beautiful features the entire time.

She turned and looked at him, but her face was a mixture of pain and sorrow. "Jonas, Look down," she ordered.

Jonas followed her gaze and saw that they were standing above a huge city that was burning, smoke billowing from every corner. There were thousands of orcs and goblins camped along the perimeter and Jonas could see many still plundering the area. The city was obviously in ruin.

"Is it Tarsis?" he asked.

"It is, Malbeck has taken the city and King Kromm is now being hunted in these very hills."

"Is he alone?"

"No, he has a small group of his elite guard with him, but Malbeck will find him. He is sending out his hunters as we speak. That is why I need you."

"You want me to go to the king and bring him to Finarth?"

"I do. There will be forces hunting him and his family that even Kromm, the mighty warrior king, cannot face. Take Fil and Taleen with you. You will need help in this

venture. Jonas, King Kromm and his family must not be captured. The king is necessary to the survival of these lands."

"What can one man do against the Shan Cemar?"

"To win this war we will need a culmination of what many men can do. The power of one, combined with the power of others, is a force that is hard to break. This is the ultimate difference between good and evil, men working together for a common cause. Evil harbors resentment, greed, and other emotions that eat their power away from the inside. It is a time for heroes, Jonas."

"How will I find him, my Goddess?"

"Remember, Jonas, call me Shyann. I was once just a farmer and a hunter like you." Shyann smiled warmly now. "Tulari will lead you there."

Shyann's eyes suddenly lit up with shock, as if she were watching something terrible happen. "Jonas, you must awaken! Treachery is happening in the king's chamber! Hurry or it will be too late!"

A bright flash of white seared Jonas's eyes......

......And he awoke with a jolt, his eyes wide and his body fully awake. He leaped out of bed and noticed that he was already wearing his armor and both his swords were strapped at his side. He didn't stand around pondering how that happened but ran out of his tent, yelling for Taleen as he went. "Taleen, to the king's chamber!"

Jonas was long gone as Taleen awoke quickly, grabbing her sword next to her. She was already wearing her chain mail shirt but she didn't bother taking the time to put on her plate mail.

Jonas raced towards the king's tent and noticed the guards at the entrance were all lying on the ground. He didn't stop to see if they were hurt or just spelled, barreling through the drape that covered the entrance and calling on his light simultaneously. He drew both his blades so quickly that it looked as if they leaped into his hands. His light bathed the entire interior and nothing of darkness could escape the magic.

A tall figure stood over the king's bed and the man turned as Jonas's light filled the room. It was Prince Nelstrom and he was holding a bloody dagger.

But Jonas's light wasn't touching the prince. He was surrounded by a shadow that seemed to pulse around him, just like Jonas's light, but dark and heavy with evil. Jonas's light hit the darkness and was repelled.

Prince Nelstrom's eyes were glowing red and his features seemed to grow and elongate, until he was two heads taller than Jonas with long legs and arms. The fingers holding the knife grew as well, becoming long and tipped with short talons. His features were still that of the prince, but different, demonic in appearance. The bloody dagger in his hand slowly grew in length until it became the same long sword that he always wore at his side.

"It is too late, cavalier," hissed Prince Nelstrom, spitting out the last word like it was poison. "The king is dead."

"But you still live, something I will remedy shortly," Jonas growled, stepping further into the room, his twin blades glowing faintly, as if they were waiting to explode into action.

"I'm afraid that killing me will not be that easy. Do you know what I am?" The prince asked, advancing slowly towards Jonas. His long arms and legs carried him smoothly a few steps closer.

Jonas noticed that he was wearing the exact armor and clothes of Prince Nelstrom. It had somehow grown and stretched to fit his new size.

"You are a man who sold his soul to the Forsworn. You are weak. You are nothing," Jonas responded.

The prince laughed as he started to circle Jonas, his aura of darkness still holding back Jonas's light. "I am much more than that. Right now your cavalier friend and many others are trying to get into this tent. But they can't. I have magically sealed it off. It is just you and me, something for which I have been patiently waiting."

"As have I, traitor," Jonas whispered through clenched teeth. He willed his mind into the state of Ty'erm and readied himself for battle. All his senses were sharp and his finely honed muscles twitched, eager to spring forth and crush the murderous traitor. The king was a great man, and now he was dead, killed by his own corrupted son, at least that is what Prince Nelstrom believed. Jonas knew that Prince Nelstrom did not know that his real father was actually Kiln.

Again the prince laughed, refocusing Jonas's attention. "I have more power than ever. My Lord Malbeck has shared with me some of the power of the Shan Cemar. That is why you could not detect me, cavalier. We have new power, power that was hidden for many years, but it is ours now and you cannot stop us. I am Malbeck's right hand, the hammer that will crush Finarth so that I may rule this land in his name and the power of the Forsworn will cover the lands."

"Your heart is now dark and corrupted with the stench of the Forsworn. They hold no power over me," replied Jonas sternly, flaring his light again, trying to break through the prince's defenses, but to no avail.

"Oh but they do. They have been watching you for a long time; even before you were born they were watching you."

"What are you talking about?" Jonas demanded.

The demon prince laughed again. "Do you know what happened to your father?"

"He left us when I was born. He did not want a cripple as a son," Jonas said, a little bit shaken by the direction of the conversation.

"You were a cripple because the Forsworn made you so. Gould the tormentor had known about you before you were even born. Your mother was poisoned during her pregnancy hoping to kill her and you."

"You lie," spat Jonas, gripping his swords tighter. Jonas used his powers to weave the energy around him into an invisible shield. His powers were growing stronger and it only took him a couple of seconds to spin the molecules around him into a translucent shield of energy.

But Jonas knew that he had to use his powers sparingly, for the headaches that came with their use could incapacitate him, something that would be his doom when facing a foe like the one before him.

The demon prince snickered knowingly. "We had assumed your mother would die, killing you along with her, but she was much stronger of spirit than we thought. She was sickened; however, the poison deformed you. Your father was strong of body, but not of spirit. Gould used his servants to force him to leave and then they took him as Gould's slave."

"You mean my father did not leave us on his own accord?" Jonas asked shocked.

"Correct, and we thought you as good as dead, a mistake which I'm here to remedy."

"You should have killed me then, I will not be so easy to defeat now. My heart is pure. You cannot corrupt me with your seeping blackness."

"When the Forsworn realized that you were still alive, they had Malbeck the Dark One, my master and their sword on this plane of existence, order your death."

"But the High One sent Airos to protect the town and me," replied Jonas as he thought about Airos's sudden arrival. "But Airos did not know exactly who I was, only that he needed to help fight off the threat that attacked my town. His death helped me survive and I believe now that Shyann shielded me on that dark night." Realization of Airos's sacrifice and the simmering plot to destroy his family hit him like an ogre's fist. "But why me?" Jonas asked more to himself than anything.

The demon prince spat on the ground and hissed. "You already answered that question. You are IshMian, a rare power that threatens my masters. More importantly, your heart is pure and incorruptible; a rarity in men and a potential threat to the powers of darkness, but it is a weakness, cavalier, for you cannot truly accept the power of the Forsworn. "

Now it was Jonas's turn to laugh. "Power? They hold no power! They only exist because they feed off of the weaknesses of men. Your Forsworn are parasites that have no power of their own," Jonas countered, swinging his swords left and right.

The demon prince crouched, hissing angrily like a snake, his long blade bursting in red flames. Then he whispered a few words and orange flames suddenly burst from his left hand. Jonas stood his ground as the flames slammed into his mental barrier and rushed to either side of him. He smiled as the flame's heat did not touch him. The fire subsided, revealing Jonas unharmed, holding his swords at his side.

Jonas used his mind to send the translucent shield forward like a battering ram. The energy wall hit the demon prince hard, slamming him against the back of the tent. Strangely, when he hit the tent wall it looked like he had crashed into stone. Whatever magic the demon had used to seal the tent turned the walls into something hard and unbreakable.

Jonas quickly charged forward as the demon prince smashed into the wall. Releasing the energy of the shield he used his leading blade to hastily block the demon's fire sword, but his second blade scored a hit on the demon's leg, causing a deep cut across its thigh. Nelstrom hissed and kicked his leg out impossibly fast. His powerful foot struck Jonas in the abdomen and sent him reeling backwards.

Kiln had taught Jonas many things, one of which was how to deflect the power of a blow by not fighting against it. And Jonas's agility almost equaled Kiln's, allowing him to move like an acrobat. So Jonas went with the blow, leaping backwards at the last moment, deflecting some of the power of the strike. He rolled backwards over his head and came to his feet quickly.

The prince wasted no time and attacked him furiously with his fire blade. The struggle became a blur of blades as the two master swordsmen used all the skills they had. They spun and danced, their magic blades leaving traces of fire and blue light as they whirled through the air. The demon's long arms and legs allowed him an advantage, but Jonas's skill with two blades allowed him to keep the demon's steel away from his flesh.

The demon prince pushed Jonas close to a wall, hoping to pin him against it, but Jonas sensed the wall's presence and frantically fought to keep from being cornered. Nelstrom's foot struck out again, so fast that Jonas could not avoid it, striking him in the thigh, the power of the kick forcing him to stumble backwards.

The demon prince saw his opening and swung his fire blade downward towards Jonas's head. But Jonas, too, was fast and he quickly brought both blades up in a cross to block the powerful stroke. The power of the strike sent sparks everywhere, severely jolting Jonas's strong arms. It felt like he had caught a falling boulder.

The blades held together and the prince stepped in close to Jonas's face. Jonas used all his strength to hold the blade still as the demon leered down at him. He strained and gritted his teeth as the flaming steel inched closer.

As the demon's head moved closer, he opened his fanged mouth, spitting burning flames at Jonas's face. Jonas screamed as the fire seared him but he did not let go of his swords for he knew that the demon's fire sword would cleave him in two. He felt his skin bubble and the pungent smell of his burnt hair assaulted his senses.

Jonas closed his eyes and drew on his cognivant powers again. Using these powers was always tricky. He had to balance the need against the power of his opponent and the energy he would expend in using it. Against a powerful opponent like the one he faced now, he risked incapacitating himself. But if there was a time to use those powers, it was now. He called on the energy around him and wrapped it around the demon prince. Instantly the flames went away and Jonas used his mind to lift the demon in the air and throw him across the room to smash again into the wall of the tent.

Jonas stumbled from the agony, trying to open his eyes. The pain was immense. He had been burned so badly that his eyes were sealed. His head pounded from the cognitive energy used to fling the powerful demon against the wall.

From a distance, Jonas heard the demon laugh as he struggled to maintain his balance. His heart beat quickly as he fought to get control of himself through the pain and fear. Jonas could heal himself but he didn't know if he had time before the demon attacked again.

Then he heard Shyann's voice in his head and all fear went away. *"Hold tight Jonas. Do not fear. I am here with you. Use your mind."*

Jonas's mind cleared and all fear evaporated in a rush of energy. He opened up his mind and used his powers as a cognivant to see the area around him. In his mind's eye he could make out the particles of everything around him, including the demon prince who was now just before him with his sword raised above his head. Everything shone with different hues of light but it was enough to give Jonas an idea of distance, size, and shape.

Prince Nelstrom smiled wickedly as he brought his fire blade down with all his strength at the blinded cavalier. But the blade struck the ground hard as Jonas had moved aside with impossible speed and agility.

The prince tried to get his blade up but the cavalier was too fast. As Jonas sidestepped the powerful swing, he swung his right hand blade down onto the exposed arm of the demon, slicing easily through its flesh. As the demon's sword arm fell to the ground, he watched in horror as the cavalier spun like a dancer, the momentum of the spin sending his left sword whirling by his face, slicing through his throat. The prince's neck parted easily on Jonas's blade, and he stumbled backwards from the blow.

Jonas, his eyes still burned shut, saw the demon prince move backwards holding onto his slit throat with his one good arm. But he would not be so easily killed. In his mind's eye, Jonas saw the demon work some dark magic. Two bolts of energy shot forth from the demon's hand but the bolts did not hit the cavalier. Instead they landed on either side of him creating two huge spiders from the crackling energy. Jonas could not see the spiders perfectly but he could make out their shape and size. They were as big as a man, similar to the spider that Taleen had fought on the battlefield.

Both spiders instantly attacked him. They leaped with incredible speed and slammed into the invisible wall that Jonas had quickly formed with his mind. One landed heavily on its back while the other maintained its footing, sending long clawed legs into the barrier as it tried to reach the retreating cavalier.

Jonas asked for Shyann's help and brought forth burning blue flames that erupted from his right sword. He pointed the blade at the spider that was attacking the invisible barrier and sent a column of flame into the hideous beast. He had to drop the wall to let the flames out and he hoped that the spider on its back would take a few moments to recover.

The flames struck the spider with a flash, quickly incinerating it. Its squeal of pain was quickly extinguished as it was transformed to a smoldering pile of ash.

The second spider was quicker than he had expected, attacking Jonas simultaneously with four spiked claws. He stumbled backwards and used his right sword to deflect the first three attacks, but the last lightening quick claw shot through his defenses piercing his thigh just below the metal skirt that protected his hip and groin. The spider retracted the leg and attacked again as Jonas screamed from the pain and stumbled backward.

Jonas knew that he had to finish this spider off quickly or the demon might soon join the fight. He did not know if the demon prince had survived his attack but he had to assume he had.

The spider was a blur of red energy in his mind's eye. He used his two blades frantically to keep the beast at bay while he used his mind to concentrate on the hunting knife that was sheathed at his side. The spider did not see the knife coming as it was focused on trying to get through the deadly blades that blurred before it. Jonas used his mind to send the knife into the large right eye of the spider. Green gore burst from the wound. Screeching in pain, the spider backed up, trying to use several legs to knock the knife free.

Jonas had never used his power to levitate his own body but he had to try. His head was pounding with the exertion of using his powers but he put his trust in Shyann and forced himself to focus and draw forth whatever energy he had left within him.

He was able to use his power to leap high into the air, wrapping his body in energy and lifting himself well above the spider, then quickly releasing the energy to slam his body into the injured creature. His feet hit first followed closely by both blades. His feet slammed the spider down into the stone while both swords plunged to the hilt into the soft hairy body. Jonas ripped both blades outward, slicing open the abdomen and showering the floor with its entrails. Simultaneously he jumped off the dead spider, landing on his shoulder and rolling quickly up to his feet, both swords held before him.

He mentally scanned the room for another attack. He was tired and severely injured, but in the state of Ty'erm he was able to block the pain and focus on what needed to be done. His head ached badly but in his meditative state he could handle more pain than normal. He pushed his strength to its limit, knowing that it would mean life or death.

Various colors assaulted his mind as he tried to makes sense of what he saw in the room. He could make out the two dead spiders, their color in his mind now a darker red as their bodies cooled in death. He could *see* the king's bed and the softly glowing blue outline of the dead ruler.

Prince Nelstrom was choking on his own black blood as his spiders were attacking the cavalier. He tried to whisper the healing word that his master had taught him, a secret word found in the Shan Cemar. All that came out was hissing and gurgling as his ripped throat showered the ground with his blood.

One of his innate abilities as a follower of the Forsworn was that he could call on Naz-reen's servants at will, once a day. So he didn't need to say words of magic to bring forth the spiders. He simply willed them to arrive and they would, but to heal himself he needed to speak, to use words of magic like a wizard.

His red eyes boiled with rage as he felt his life's energy begin to leave his body. But he was not dead yet, his magical body was able to handle injury and pain beyond that of any human.

He used the last bit of his energy to run forward, grabbing his sword off the ground with his only arm. His eyes focused on the cavalier with hatred and fury and he ran toward Jonas just as he had finished off the last spider. The demon prince attacked Jonas from the side, hoping to drive his dark blade deep into his body.

Jonas detected a glimpse of energy from the corner of his eye and turned quickly to meet the attack. He felt a searing pain lance through his side in the seam below his breastplate. No normal blade could puncture Jonas's chain mail shirt under his armor, but this was no normal blade; it was a dark blade cursed by the Forsworn, and its magic was powerful. The blade pushed through the chain mail shirt, and through his abdomen, bursting out his back.

Jonas screamed in pain as the demon prince held the blade inside his body, twisting it left and right as the flames burned his soul. Jonas's arms were flayed out to his sides, but he still held his swords in both hands. He whispered a prayer to Shyann as the pain enveloped him, nearly causing him to drop his swords.

"I am here, Jonas," Shyann whispered in his mind as she shielded him from the pain.

Instantly the pain went away and Jonas spun his swords in both his hands so the points were facing down. The demon used his sword as leverage lifting Jonas's body off the ground with one arm just as Jonas raised his blades high, and slammed both points downward through the demon prince's chest and into his lungs and heart. Simultaneously he called on his God Fire, sending the flames roaring down the blades and into the body of the screaming demon. The flames burst inside the prince and shot forth from his ears, eyes, and open mouth, until his entire body was glowing with God Fire from the inside. Suddenly Prince Nelstrom burst into flame and disappeared in a shower of fire and ash.

The only thing left on the ground was his armor.

Jonas crashed hard into the ground and fought to maintain consciousness. The pain was minimal as Shyann still shielded him, but he did not have the strength to pull forth the dark blade or heal himself. He lay on his side, the cursed blade buried deep in his flesh, his face burned like a blackened piece of roasted meat, his long curly hair scorched and burned to his scalp. His head swirled with exhaustion and he barely held onto consciousness.

He heard the faint sound of rushing footsteps nearby but didn't have the strength to view the scene in his mind. But through the black haze he thought he heard Taleen's frantic voice.

"Kiln, do not touch the blade, it is cursed. Let me do it!" There was a pause. Then he heard Taleen whisper close to him. "Jonas! Bandris help me! Jonas, do you hear me?"

His senses were blurry with sounds and smells whirling around in his mind. Finally, the pain from his injuries slammed into him like the gust from a dragon's wing. Jonas's head swam and his body finally succumbed to his terrible wounds. The last thing he felt was the dark blade being pulled from his body. Then he felt Taleen's hands on his abdomen and nothing more.

Eleven
The Mission

Jonas awoke slowly as several voices gradually brought him from a deep sleep. As his eyes adjusted to the light he could see Taleen and Fil standing before him. He was lying in a bed of soft furs in the tent that King Gavinsteal had arranged for them.

Then it all came back to him in a flood of memories. The king was dead, slain by his own son who had sold his soul to the Forsworn. But as he recalled the terrible battle with the prince and the severe injuries he had sustained, his heart lifted with joy as he realized that he was seeing the world from his own eyes.

Jonas slowly reached up and touched his face for any sign of scarring. Taleen leaned in close to him as she sat on the edge of the bed. Her red hair seemed to outshine her gleaming silver armor. Jonas was again overwhelmed by her beauty, and the vision was such a contrast to the terrible images of his recent memories.

"There are no scars, Jonas. I healed you but you were so exhausted that you've slept for over a day. I'm glad I was there or you surely would have perished within moments of sustaining those horrible wounds." Taleen smiled warmly as his hands moved to his scalp and his eyes widened in surprise. "You don't look so bad bald, Jonas. I'm sorry, your hair was so badly burned that we just shaved it clean. But you'll never guess what was left behind."

Fil moved closer and smiled reassuringly at Jonas as he sat on the other end of the bed. Jonas's senses finally came back to him as he looked at his two friends.

"You should see it, Jonas. It is amazing," Fil said with open admiration.

"What are you talking about?" Jonas asked, bewildered.

"I think you pleased Shyann, Jonas. She left you a gift," Taleen said as she brought a mirror to his face.

Jonas lifted himself up in bed and looked into the mirror. It took him a second to get used to the bald headed face reflected there, but he had to admit that he didn't look half bad. Then he saw the mark, the gift that they were talking about. His heart swelled with pride as he rubbed his hand over the symbol on his forehead. It was a scar, but no ordinary scar. Burned into the skin was the shape of a great oak tree, the symbol of Shyann. It was as if someone had branded his forehead with the symbol and then stained it blue.

The mark did not have the jagged edges you might expect from a normal scar, they were raised and smooth, perfect in every way. Jonas stared at it for several seconds.

"It is beautiful," he said quietly.

"So what happened in there, Jonas?" Taleen asked. "We tried to get into the tent but the walls had been magically turned to stone."

Jonas sat up in bed, feeling much better and rested. "When I ran into the tent I saw Prince Nelstrom kill the king. And then he transformed into this powerful demon, spawned by the power of the Forsworn." Jonas shuddered at the memory. "I thought he had killed me."

"He nearly did. We ran in as soon as we could and saw the remains of the spiders and the pile of ashes that must have been him. His armor was piled up near you," Taleen said. "Jonas, I was so scared. You should have seen yourself. I was not sure I could heal you."

The tent flap opened and everyone looked over to see Kiln approach them with purpose. He was wearing full battle armor and covered with the grime of battle.

"Jonas, good, you are awake. You had us worried for a while."

Jonas looked at Kiln solemnly. "Kiln, I'm sorry about the prince. He had been corrupted; his heart was black and was beyond help."

Kiln put up his hand to silence him. "Jonas, he was my son in blood only. I never knew him." Kiln turned to both Fil and Taleen who stood staring with their mouths open. Neither of them was privy of the fact that Prince Nelstrom was Kiln's son, or the details about Kiln and the scandal between Cassandra and King Gavinsteal. "I know neither of you knew this. We have kept it a secret for a reason and even though he is dead I'd like the secret to remain. Can I count on you both to stay silent?"

"Of course," Taleen answered.

"I will say nothing," Fil said.

"I'm sorry Kiln. In my exhaustion I had forgotten that they did not know," Jonas apologized.

"It is okay. Do not fret Jonas, about your actions or your words," Kiln continued. "Who knows what cracks were formed in his heart to let that evil in," Kiln sighed and shook his head sadly. "I wish I could have known him. Maybe my presence would have changed things." He then appeared to force those thoughts from his mind and as he lifted up his head, smiled broadly. "I'm just glad you are alive. You did what you had to do. It is unfortunate you did not arrive earlier or maybe the king would be alive. The kingdom of Finarth is without a ruler now, and at a time when a strong ruler is most needed."

"Can you assume that role until a solution is found?" asked Jonas.

"Aye, I will, and gladly. The commanders voted me to act as regent until we find Prince Baylin."

"And if we don't?" Taleen asked.

"We will solve that problem when we come to it. I am a man of war, not politics. I would like to hear what happened in that tent, Jonas. It pained me severely to know that we could not enter to help you. We had no idea what was happening and feared the worst."

Jonas looked at them all as they gazed back at him, eager to learn what happened in the tent. So Jonas told them, not skipping a single thing, including what the demon prince had told him about his family and about what Shyann had instructed him to do. They listened raptly and when he finished Fil spoke up first.

"Jonas, I can't believe that your family has been a target for that long. Do you believe what he said?"

"I don't know, Fil. Just the idea of it makes me boil with rage. And if it is true then what happened to my father? I need to find out. I will find out," Jonas said adamantly.

"That is how Naz-reen works. She weaves her webs slowly until she snares her victims," Taleen muttered. She looked at Jonas seriously. "Jonas, if you do find your father you must be prepared for the worst."

Jonas looked away in thought. "I have thought about that. But I need to know." After a few seconds of silence Kiln addressed Jonas directly.

"Jonas, it will hurt us that you will not be fighting with us. We have been slowly retreating back to Finarth but Lord Moredin has been attacking us with hit and run tactics the entire time. We do not know if he is being directed by Malbeck himself, one of his minions, or if he just decided to fight us on his own. Nevertheless, Lord Moredin is not making our retreat back to Finarth easy." Kiln glanced at Fil and Taleen. "But your mission to save King Kromm and bring him back is sanctioned by Shyann and I will not interfere with it. When will you three leave?"

"You mean I get to go with them?" Fil asked enthusiastically.

"Yes, Fil. You heard Jonas. Shyann wants you with him. I relieve you from your duties here and expect you to watch over him."

"With my life," Fil said seriously. Jonas smiled at his friend. It warmed his heart that Fil would be coming with him. Jonas had a feeling that his friendship and his spear would very much be needed on this mission.

"And I will be accompanying you as well. I have received no other calling, which means that Shyann's wishes are in league with Bandris's."

"That is good. Jonas, I have one favor to ask of you before you leave," Kiln asked.

Jonas did not hesitate in his response. "Of course, anything, Kiln. I owe you much".

"I am going on a mission tonight, and I would like you by my side."

"I will be there. What kind of mission?"

"Let us discuss it in more detail later. I must return to my men. Meet me in the king's tent at dusk."

"I will be there," Jonas said.

"Good, I will see you soon." Kiln smiled one more time. "I am proud of you, Jonas. You suffered a mortal wound in that fight and yet you persevered and managed to defeat that demon. It fills my heart with pride that Shyann has rewarded your courage and skill with another mark. There is no doubt that you are something special." With a smile Kiln added, "I would not want to face you myself."

"Yes, but you are over fifty winters old," Jonas laughed.

Kiln smiled wryly. "I'll see you soon." He turned and walked from the tent.

Fil watched him leave before he turned and spoke to Jonas. "There is something about him, like a volcano ready to explode. I would not want to fight him, even if he is over fifty winters old."

"Nor I, Fil. He is utterly fearless, and I cannot imagine someone skilled enough to best him. Now go get ready. We have a meeting very soon."

Fil's smile took up his entire face as he stood up and walked from the room, eager to begin the mission.

Kiln sat at the heavy wood table in the king's tent looking over several maps when Jonas, Taleen, and Fil entered. Sitting with him were several commanders, third lance Lathrin, fourth lance Dagrinal, and three others that Jonas had not yet met. The first warrior, Gandarin, was a second rank general of five akrons. The tall lean man, sporting a graying beard and mustache, and still wearing his dirt and blood encrusted plate mail, stood as the trio entered. Jonas immediately perceived an aura of strength and power in this man, a man obviously accustomed to commanding others.

The other two men were also second ranking generals and they looked equally disheveled. General Kuarin and General Ruthalis wore similar armor but that is where the similarity ended. General Kuarin was short and thick around the waist, a powerful muscular man. His chin was covered with a gray braided goatee and his head was completely shaven. General Ruthalis was of medium height and build with a thin waist and a handsome, tanned face. His shoulders were wide and his exposed arms were muscular.

Each of the generals wore a gold colored cape to mark their rank. Kiln introduced Jonas and Taleen to the three men. They all looked tired, their eyes red and puffy from lack of sleep.

Also sitting at the table was Alerion, the wizard. He sat, silently staring at the three, stroking his pointy beard in thought.

Jonas, Taleen, and Fil stood before them. The two cavaliers were attired in their full battle gear, the armor and clothes perfect and clean.

Everything from their breast plates down to their buckles and belts shone and sparkled with brilliance.

Fil stood next to them wearing his infantry chain mail under a gray tunic. He carried a stout spear in one hand and he wore a short infantry sword at his waist. He shifted uneasily as he looked around the room at all the important men. He was part of an audience with two cavaliers standing before Kiln, the legend, and Finarthian generals discussing an important mission of which he would be a part. He smiled openly but then quickly masked his smile, replacing it with a more serious demeanor, one more typical of a warrior standing before his commanders.

"Jonas, thank you for coming, we have something important to discuss," Kiln announced.

General Gandarin then spoke. "Cavalier, I am glad that you are well and I would like to thank you for your efforts in trying to rescue my king from the treachery that has befallen him." His powerful voice loudly resonated in the large tent.

"Thank you, General. I just wish I could have arrived sooner. I am sorry that I could not save him. And I am also sorry for the treachery that has befallen the kingdom."

General Gandarin waved his hand in a gesture of dismissal. "You did your best, young cavalier. I am glad that you slew King Gavinsteal's murderer. I've known something was wrong with Prince Nelstrom for years. I think the Forsworn have been working on him for a long time and finally his heart and soul could not fight them anymore. What you killed in that tent was not my prince, but a shell of his former self. You killed a demon that used to be Prince Nelstrom," he said sadly.

"General, I think you are right," Taleen agreed. "Of all the Forsworn, this incident stinks of Naz-reen. She works slowly, over many years, bending someone's will until they break and become her puppet. I, too, believe that is what happened to the prince. Moreover, Jonas fought two Urlikes, agents of Naz-reen that take on the shape of a giant spider. There can be no doubt that Naz-reen had her claws into the young prince for many years," she concluded.

General Gandarin shook his head sadly.

"Enough of this," General Ruthalis interjected. "High Commander Kiln informed us that you will not be with us much longer, and that you are taking one of our warriors with you, one who is already developing a reputation among the veterans."

Fil tried not to smile as he concentrated on maintaining his warrior appearance.

"Yes, General Ruthalis. I received my calling last night. I am to take Taleen and Fil with me to Tarsis and find King Kromm and what is left of his army and bring him back here before he is caught and killed."

"I see. Did Shyann inform you where he was located?" General Ruthalis asked.

"No, but she told me Tulari, my steed, will guide me to him. I was informed that King Kromm's presence will be needed here if we are to defeat the Dark One."

"Well, I can certainly say that *any* presence will be helpful, especially a mighty warrior like King Kromm. I'm disappointed that we will be losing both our cavaliers but I'm sure that Shyann has her reasons for taking you from us. Jonas, Kiln has informed us that you will be accompanying him on his mission tonight. I am glad that you agreed, your presence will help ensure our success."

"My sword is yours," Jonas replied easily, bowing slightly.

"Jonas, we have found Prince Baylin, and he is still alive. I plan on getting him back and killing Lord Moredin in the process," Kiln interjected.

"What happened to the messenger?" Taleen asked.

"His head was returned to us with his genitals stuffed in his mouth," replied Kiln.

"Sounds like the work of a Dykreel agent," Taleen muttered, openly disgusted by such barbarity. Dykreel, the third ranking Forsworn, had an affinity for the implementation of torture and his followers were experts at the craft of pain and suffering. The three generals all crossed their chests with Ulren's four pointed star at the mention of the dark god's name.

"Kiln, how do we know that Prince Baylin is still alive?" Jonas asked.

"Alerion has magically located him, and he is alive," replied Kiln. "Jonas, your presence will be needed in case there are any other surprises from the Forsworn. I do not know if Prince Moredin is acting alone or if there is another Banthra with him. There may be other agents of the Forsworn with him as well. We just don't know. But we need Lord Moredin dead to halt their attacks on us as we retreat to Finarth. We are losing too many men and the retreat is taking too long. It will be done tonight."

"And I will be at your side," Jonas confirmed.

"I am glad you agree to come with me," Kiln said. "I just hope we arrive in time to find the prince alive. Alerion, will you please explain to Jonas how this will work."

Alerion looked at Jonas and spoke for the first time. "The spell I will be using is a teleportation spell. I have enough power to teleport four people only. I will get us three inside the tent where the prince is being held. From there we will have to work fast. When Moredin is killed and the prince is freed I will teleport the four of us back."

"Alerion, I thought that in order for a teleportation spell to work you had to have been to the location where you are going. Have you seen Lord Moredin's tent?" asked Taleen.

"You are correct, cavalier. And no, I have not seen Lord Moredin's tent. But I have scryed his tent and learned its location and lay out. That is how I learned that Prince Baylin is still alive and located there. The spell shouldn't pose a problem."

"Scryed? The word is unfamiliar to me," Jonas said.

"Scrying is a magical means to find someone, to spy on them. It is very taxing and you need to have an article that belonged to the individual you are trying to find. The spell is very useful, but it requires a lot of energy," answered the wizard.

"I see. What if we appear in his tent and Lord Moredin is not alone?" asked Jonas.

"Then your swords and my magic will have to be enough," replied Alerion matter-of-factly.

"When will we do this?" asked Jonas.

"Late tonight, when he should be alone and asleep," replied Kiln.

"Very well, I will be ready," Jonas said.

"I will send a messenger to your tent when the time is upon us," added Kiln. "Now go, get some rest. We have other plans to discuss and not enough time in the day to discuss them."

Jonas, Fil, and Taleen turned and walked from the tent as the military leaders continued to discuss strategy and peruse the maps on the table.

The three comrades talked for hours around the campfire as they waited for the messenger to come. The sounds and smells of the Finarthian army blanketed the hills around them. Yesterday had been a bloody day of hardship as they tried to retreat back to Finarth. Lord Moredin's men, including thousands of tribesmen, made constant hit and run attacks on the retreating army. Kiln was forced to stagger their retreat in groups, several akrons moved back while others stayed and protected the retreating groups. They did this all day. It was very tiring and casualties were high on both sides.

Most of the men were sleeping while the trio stayed up and discussed the adventure ahead of them.

"I wonder why it is so important to find King Kromm and bring him back?" Jonas said as he stirred the fire with a stick.

"I'm not sure. Not being from here, I am unfamiliar with who he is or the history of these lands. But Shyann must have her reason," Taleen replied thoughtfully.

"I have heard men talk of the king of Tarsis," added Fil as he looked at both his companions. "He is always spoken of with respect and awe. He is known by all warriors as a warrior king, unstoppable in battle and strategy. Men speak of him as if he is a god. It is said that he can fight all day and never tire and his colossal size makes a boarg shake with fear. It is likely he will be needed here to help King Baylin."

"If he was already defeated in Tarsis then why would his help be needed here?" Jonas asked.

"We do not know what happened in Tarsis," Taleen answered. "There are many variables in war, Jonas. Maybe he was surprised, maybe there were spies within Tarsis, maybe he finally made a mistake, or maybe the army that faced him was just too powerful. Maybe we will need to combine all the strength of Tarsis, Finarth, and their vassals, to defeat the Dark One."

"Why can't Shyann just tell you why Kromm is needed? I fail to understand the games gods play," Fil asked.

"It is easy to feel that way, Fil. Perhaps she is being ambiguous for a reason, to protect Jonas."

"How do you mean?" Fil asked doubtfully.

"What if he, or we, are captured by agents of the Forsworn. They will do whatever they can to learn of Kromm's importance. If we don't know the exact reason then we cannot divulge the information, no matter what they do to us."

Jonas stirred the hot coals with his stick as he thought about what Taleen had said. "I'm sure that this mission's purpose will be revealed to us as she sees fit. There must be a good reason…"

Some commotion to their left interrupted them and all three turned their attention to a rider who appeared from the darkness. He was a Finarthian Knight riding a large chestnut warhorse.

"I'm sorry to interrupt, cavalier," the man said, addressing Jonas. "The high commander is ready for you now. If you will please follow me."

Jonas looked at his friends and stood up smoothly. Tulari, understanding that it was time, rode from the darkness to nuzzle his head on Jonas's shoulder.

"May Bandris be with you," Taleen said as she shook his hand in the warrior's grip.

Jonas shook her hand and smiled warmly. "I'll be fine. I'll be with Kiln."

"You're watching his back, but who will be watching yours?" asked Fil as he, too, shook Jonas's hand.

"Why, Shyann of course." Jonas smiled at them both, mounted his horse, and with a soft touch of his heel, Tulari was off into the night, leaving his two friends staring into the darkness.

There were only three people in the king's chamber, Kiln, Jonas, and the Finarthian wizard, Alerion. Alerion had explained to them the process but Jonas was a little apprehensive. Disappearing and then reappearing in an enemy tent wasn't something that most people did. Stepping into the unknown concerned him. But he would be ready to fight next to his friend if need be.

Alerion drew the two men in close to him so he could explain the spell and what they could expect from it. "Now, we are hoping that he will be alone. I have scryed him several times at this time and he was always asleep. But I dare not scrye him again for it weakens me and I need to rest afterward. I will need my strength to cast the teleportation spell and I want to make sure I'm strong in the event that something goes wrong." Kiln and Jonas simply looked on and waited for the wizard to continue. "When I cast the spell you will feel somewhat dizzy and a bit weightless. After several seconds of darkness, your eyes will see your new destination. It happens rather quickly and is painless, but it may take a few seconds to feel normal after the dizziness. Do you both understand?"

Jonas and Kiln nodded. Kiln was wearing black leather pants and a light chain mail shirt under his black tunic. His wrists and thighs were protected with metal and leather bands and he wore his long sword and dagger at his belt. His eyes reflected nothing but concentration on the task at hand.

Kiln looked at Jonas. "You ready?"

"I am," replied Jonas.

"Remember, stay back and alert in case I need you. I will take care of Moredin. If there are minions of the Dark One in that room, take them out. If not, then find the prince while I kill Lord Moredin." Kiln redirected his gaze to Alerion. "Whatever happens protect yourself. You are the only one who can get us out. If it looks like things are going badly then teleport us back, but only if Jonas and I can't handle what we find. Do you understand?"

"I do. Are you ready?" asked Alerion.

Jonas and Kiln looked at each other as they gripped their weapons. Jonas nodded in affirmation. "We are," answered Kiln.

Alerion began to chant. The words sounded elvish to Jonas but he wasn't quite sure. Jonas was watching Alerion as the wizard closed his eyes and recited the words of power.

After a few moments of chanting everything got a little blurry, just as Alerion said they would. Jonas brought both his hands to his swords and whispered a silent prayer to Shyann just as everything went black. His eyes were open but he couldn't see anything. He felt light, as if he was nothing but air. The sensation lasted for several moments.

Suddenly light came flaring back to him as his eyes adjusted to his new surroundings. His head spun a little but thankfully he regained his senses in a matter of seconds.

Then it struck him. If Moredin was sleeping in his tent, then why was there so much light in the room? As his brain quickly processed this information, he instantly dropped his mind into the state of Ty'erm.

The answer to his question was quickly revealed. The situation appeared in slow motion. He saw Kiln to his left and Alerion to his right. But standing right before them was Lord Moredin, Prince Bomballa, a huge orc, and a dark cleric of Dykreel. Jonas recognized the red spiked halo that was painted on the black breastplate that the cleric wore, the mark of Dykreel, master of torture and pain. They were standing around a table going over what looked like battle plans. The surprised looks on their faces clearly told Jonas that they were not expecting guests.

Kiln and Jonas exploded into action, launching forward like striking adders, their blades leaping into their hands. A part of Jonas's mind heard Alerion muttering behind him, preparing another spell, but it was a distant sound as he concentrated on the task at hand.

Lord Moredin's eyes opened widely in surprise as he frantically jumped back from the table while trying to draw his long sword. He screamed for help at the top of his lungs. "Guards! Help! We're under attack!"

Prince Bomballa, wearing his typical garish outfit of teal and purple, reacted with lightning speed, his thin rapier materializing in his hand as he jumped backwards to create more space between him and his attackers.

The gigantic orc was slower, the surprise of the appearance of three men in the tent still registering in his tiny brain. But he was Ongesett, chief of the orcs, and he was a warrior tried in many battles. He stumbled backwards and reached for his heavy morning star that was leaning against the table near him.

Kiln assessed the three men quickly and perceived Prince Bomballa as the most serious threat. In a blur of motion his arm flashed to the side, hurling his dagger at the flashy clothed warrior. Simultaneously he leaped onto a nearby chair with his left foot, jumped onto the table with his right, launching into the air directly toward the stumbling Lord Moredin. Kiln's long sword arced through the air, leaving a trailing path of green light as his blade sought its target.

As Kiln and Jonas sprang into action, Alerion heard commotion behind him as Lord Moredin yelled for help. He had two choices, abandon the mission and teleport them back, or somehow seal off the tent so that Jonas and Kiln could do their job without guards storming in and overwhelming them all.

Thinking of his prince, he chose the latter. Alerion concentrated on a spell until he remembered the necessary words of power to bring forth the magic that he needed. He began to chant, focusing on saying the words exactly, and after a few seconds he released the energy of the spell with a wave of both hands and the final word, "Fulstarris", the word for fire.

Lord Moredin's eyes went wide with terror as he tried to get his blade up to deflect the impossibly fast warrior that was flying through the air at him. All he could do was trace the arc of green light with his eyes as he felt a tight, hot pressure, and then a release at his throat. Lord Moredin's head flung backwards, tenuously hanging on by pieces of skin and flesh, his life blood showering the legendary swordsman as he landed lightly on his feet.

Jonas moved with liquid grace, leaping at the surprised cleric, both swords spinning their dance of death. The cleric unsheathed a coal black blade with a wickedly curved edge. He got the blade up just in time to block Jonas's first strike. Sparks flew as the two magic blades clashed. Jonas knew that the cleric's blade had been forged with dark magic and that the slightest cut would cause damage and pain to him, but be deadly to others. The dark cleric was not wearing his helm but he was protected by his cursed armor. Everything he wore had sharp edges and spikes, any of which could be used as a weapon. His gauntlets were covered with spikes as were his wrists, shins, and greaves. His skin was pale and his eyes burned with madness. He looked almost skeletal except for the straggly black hair that draped his scalp. But he was a powerful cleric and a warrior of Dykreel. He would not be defeated easily.

Jonas's second blade just missed the cleric's head as the dark warrior ducked under the deadly sword. The cleric then punched his spiked gauntlet at Jonas's exposed stomach.

Jonas had been moving forward on the offensive as the unexpected punch flew out. But few were as quick and agile as Jonas. At the last second, he pivoted his body at a seemingly impossible angle and the cleric's fist glanced off his cuirass. Jonas, trained by Kiln, moved instinctively with little thought of his next move. Kiln had taught him that for every action there is a reaction, and for every reaction there is an action. Every move has a counter and every counter has another counter. Jonas had trained daily so that his body would react appropriately to all situations.

His training paid off as his body moved without thought. He stepped forward, past the punch, and rammed his elbow into the face of the stunned cleric. The man's head snapped back violently as his nose shattered under a spray of dark blood. Jonas was just about to finish him off with a reverse swing of his lead blade when the cleric bellowed a word of power.

"Kularc!" he screamed as he fell backwards. Instantly a wall of energy struck Jonas like a hammer and he flew backward landing on his back. But Jonas went with his momentum, rolling backward and coming up lightly on his feet. The wind was knocked from him and he took a couple of seconds to catch his breath.

As Alerion finished his spell, a huge wall of fire erupted at the entrance to the tent. The wall was four paces high and five paces wide. Alerion used his hands to control the fire, continuing the magical wall of flame all the way around the perimeter of the tent. He kept the flames just beyond the reach of the thick canvas that made up the tent. The last thing he wanted was for the tent to burn and drop on top of them. There was no way any guard could reach them as long as the flames stayed intact, a relatively easy task for the powerful wizard. And Alerion knew that they would not risk firing arrows into the flames because of the risk of hitting their lord.

Alerion turned around quickly to see how he might continue to help the two warriors. His eyes widened with fear as he gazed upon a huge orc running toward him swinging a spiked ball on a chain.

Kiln felt an object hit his back followed by a sharp pain just as Lord Moredin's lifeless body hit the floor. He spun around to see Prince Bomballa standing behind him.

"I thought I'd give you your dagger back," the black man said with a smirk.

Kiln reached back over his left shoulder and felt a knife embedded there. It was a shallow wound for his chain mail shirt had deflected most of the power. The prince must have deflected the blade, or even caught it. This warrior would be no easy kill thought Kiln as he reached back and pulled the blade out, showing no sign of pain.

"I appreciate your concern. I'd hate to lose my favorite knife," Kiln replied, his face still and cold.

"You are Kiln," Bomballa said, "thought to be the best swordsman ever to walk Kraawn."

"You are about to find out the truth of those words," Kiln replied smoothly. Bomballa smiled in retort and attacked the swordsman with his thin rapier. The man was lightning fast, and his light sword enabled him to move even faster. Kiln spun both his blades, creating a whirling wall of razor sharp steel. Their swords met again and again, neither warrior able to score a hit.

Jonas had moved to attack the dazed cleric when he saw the massive orc out of the corner of his eye. The beast was bearing down on the weaponless wizard, its huge morning star spinning, making a loud whirling noise that could be heard above the burning flames.

Jonas had to quickly slow the orc and then dispatch the cleric. He concentrated on the energy in front of the orc, creating an invisible wall. The orc's morning star hit the wall first, bounced back, and smacked the creature in the chest. The beast stumbled backwards, a look of utter confusion on his face.

Alerion had already begun his own spell right as the orc's morning star hit the invisible wall and bashed him in his own chest. He didn't wait to ponder his luck as he unleashed the spell at the confused orc.

"Zithara Um Toric!" he screamed as he directed a crackling bolt of lightning from his fingers into the chest of the astonished orc. The sizzling bolt struck the giant orc solidly in the chest, arcing back and forth across its metal armor. The power of the bolt sent the orc stumbling backwards where it tripped and fell hard on its back. The smell of burnt flesh and hair permeated the tent as the chief of orcs cooked inside his armor.

Jonas turned back to the dark cleric just as the warrior of Dykreel regained his footing. Jonas wanted to end this fight quickly so he called upon Shyann to bring forth his God Fire. The energy built up quickly within him until it felt like he would explode. He pointed his right sword at the cleric and unleashed the power, directing a cone of blue flame that completely engulfed the cleric.

The cleric must have simultaneously called on the power of Dykreel, for the flames parted around him as he held his sword in front of him like a shield. Jonas stopped the flames and the man stood before him, unharmed and smiling wickedly.

"You will need more than that to stop the might of Dykreel," he muttered, his voice low and dark.

"I don't need magic to stop you. My swords will suffice." Jonas spun his blades in unison and attacked the cleric. The cleric brought up his blade defensively and fought hard to keep Jonas's deadly blades away from him, but Jonas was relentless in his attack.

He flicked his left blade across the pale cheek of the cleric opening up a shallow cut, the red blood from the wound standing out sharply against the pale skin. The cleric grimaced and jabbed his sword forward, toward Jonas's groin. Jonas turned, stepping back and reversing his right sword to block the stroke. As Jonas deflected the blade, he flicked his left sword across the other cheek of the enraged cleric, opening up another thin cut.

The cleric growled in anger, lifted his sword, and started a powerful downward stroke. But the attack never finished. Jonas quickly lanced his left sword forward into the exposed part of the cleric's armpit, where his shoulder plate fastened to his chest plate. The thick wool under the cleric's armor provided no protection against Jonas's sword.

Jonas drove the sword in deep, right through his lungs and heart. The cleric's eyes widened in surprise and pain, his sword held high above his head. Jonas withdrew the razor sharp steel quickly just as the evil cleric dropped his sword behind him. A thin trickle of blood oozed from the perfect narrow slit under his arm, and then he fell to the ground.

Kiln fought furiously to keep the razor sharp sword away from his flesh. The man was a master swordsman; there was no doubt. Bomballa had backed Kiln up next to the flames and Kiln grimaced as he felt the heat from the magic fire singe his back.

Alerion had brought forth the fire to keep the guards at bay, but unfortunately it was becoming a problem for Kiln as well. But Kiln concentrated on every move that the man made, trying to find his weakness. When two master swordsmen meet in battle, there are many things that can decide the outcome of the fight. The variables are endless, conditioning, similarity of styles, and ability to control one's emotion to name just a few.

Kiln was an expert swordsman, but his real skill came in reading his opponent. In the state of Ty'erm, emotion never controlled him. He could focus on every move and every counter. Kiln also knew that no one had better stamina then he. Years of training gave him complete confidence in his abilities to defeat another master swordsman.

After several minutes of trading blow for blow, Kiln began to notice Bomballa's weakness. He favored his right hand and he signaled a left flank attack by slightly raising his left hand. It was very subtle and most people would never have noticed it.

Kiln smiled inwardly as he waited for the signal and his opening. It wasn't long before it came. Bomballa's left arm lifted up slightly and Kiln moved in fast. It was a dangerous maneuver because if he was wrong he would be lining himself up for a forward thrust and the wound would be fatal.

But he wasn't wrong. Bomballa lifted his left hand and simultaneously swung his blade toward Kiln's left flank. Kiln read the move ahead of time and stepped aside and toward the surprised warrior, ramming his dagger deep into Bomballa's unprotected stomach as his thin rapier hung uselessly over Kiln's right shoulder. Kiln was close to Bomballa's ear as he twisted his long dagger. Bomballa grunted in pain as his eyes opened wide in shock.

"Sorry to ruin your expensive silk," Kiln whispered into the dying man's ear. Kiln pulled his blade from Bomballa's stomach and he fell to the ground with a thud.

He looked up to see Jonas move toward him, his blades red with blood. They both scanned the room as Alerion quickly ran to them, his long robes billowing at his feet.

"Where is the prince?" yelled Kiln over the sound of the roaring flames that surrounded them.

"There," answered Alerion as he pointed to a corner of the tent blocked off by a hanging crimson tapestry. "We must hurry; the tent is starting to catch on fire."

Sure enough the flames creating the magic barrier were starting to spread up the tall sides of the tent. All three ran over to the tapestry and flipped it open. Lying on a wooden table was Prince Baylin, completely naked and tied down with thick leather straps. His eyes were closed and he was not moving. He was covered with cuts, bruises, and blood, but it was not those wounds that caused the men to stop in horror and gaze in mute shock, but the grisly wound at his crotch, or at least where his crotch should have been. His manhood was completely cut off, leaving behind a bloody wound.

"In Ulren's name, look what they did to him," muttered Alerion.

"Is he still alive?" asked Jonas in horror.

"I don't know. But it's time to go, the fire will consume the tent soon and I don't want to be here when that happens," the wizard replied.

Kiln quickly cut the straps holding the prince to the table and lifted him over his shoulder. "Get us out of here wizard," ordered Kiln.

His words went unheard for Alerion was already beginning his spell. Jonas heard the words clearly but then everything became a blur as his head spun. The world went black and they all disappeared from the tent leaving nothing behind but four dead bodies.

***

Malbeck the Dark One sat casually on the Tarsinian throne. The magnificent chair was made of white stone that looked to be carved from one piece of rock. It was simple, large, and powerful, a fitting chair for the king of Tarsis, a warrior king of tremendous size and strength.

But King Kromm was somewhere in the Tundrens, running for his life, and Malbeck, the destroyer of Tarsis, sat on the white throne; the darkness of his very presence was in stark contrast to the white marble.

Malbeck, too, was a large man, over eight feet tall, but thin and muscular, with short, glossy black hair that draped a hard chiseled face. His eyes were pure white, which made it difficult to gaze at him without looking away. His lips had a bluish tinge to them, like the rest of his body, as if he were perpetually cold, and his teeth came to sharp points. He wore tight black breeches made from the skin of a black dragon. The black thick leather boots he wore were plated with dark steel. His muscled chest and arms were bare and he wore a black cloak that framed his huge shoulders and fanned out to cover most of the throne.

He was a demonoid, part man and part demon, twisted by the magic of the Forsworn. In his right hand he held the Spear of Gould, a powerful weapon given to him by his master, Gould the Tormentor. The shaft was made from light steel, polished black. The tip was a sharp silver point about as long as a man's forearm. At the base of the spear tip was a round disk the size of a large fist, and engraved in the middle of this disk was the white eye of Gould.

In Malbeck's left hand he held a small book bound with old worn leather, the Shan Cemar, the ancient elven text that held the secrets for tapping into the energy of the Ru'Ach. Whoever held the book held vast amounts of power, power that Malbeck planned to use as he spread the Forsworn's darkness across Kraawn.

Leaning against the white throne of Tarsis was Malbeck's battle-axe. The twin blades each curved to deadly points, and carved into the flat blades were depictions of demons and other denizens of the lower planes. The handle, made from the same light steel, was wrapped with the tough scaled skin of a black dragon.

Malbeck shifted slightly as the large double doors to the throne room opened. Gullanin, Malbeck's follower and a powerful wizard in his own right, entered the throne room and prostrated himself before his master. The man was old and frail, and he wore a silver skullcap engraved with Gould's white eye.

Behind him were three high priests to the Forsworn, Janrick, high priest to Gould, Cuthare, high priest to Dykreel, and Kane, high priest to Naz'reen. They, too, bowed before their master.

"What is your report?" asked Malbeck, his low voice deep and resonant.

"My Lord, Tarsis is in ruin and the Tarsinian army is destroyed," replied Gullanin.

"What of Kromm?" interjected Malbeck.

"He escaped with a small group, but we know he is near, he can't have gotten far," Gullanin replied quickly.

"We must find him and kill him." Malbeck turned his milky white eyes toward the high priests. "Are you ready to serve me in this task?"

Janrick stepped forward and bowed his head. "Of course, my Lord, what would you have us do?"

Malbeck smiled wickedly and stood up from the throne. His form was impressive, strong arms, chest, and shoulders, tapered to a thin waist surrounded by rippling muscle. "Hunt him down and rip his heart out."

Janrick shifted uneasily and looked sideways at Gullanin who stepped back away from him, as if to distance himself from something diseased.

"How would you like us to do this?" Janrick asked.

"With your own teeth and claws of course," Malbeck replied, taking one big step toward them.

Cuthare and Kane stepped back from their lord, unsure of what was happening, his words making no sense. Janrick held his ground but looked about nervously.

"My Lord, I'm not sure what you mean," said Janrick.

"You will serve the Forsworn in the ultimate way, by giving up your life to their service."

Janrick, Cuthare, and Kane started to back away slowly, their eyes going wide with fear and surprise.

"But my Lord, we brought you back, we have served you well…" stammered Kane.

"You did not bring me back, Gullanin did. And yes, you have served me well, which is why I am giving you this reward. You will become the Hounds of Gould, and serve him in this task." Malbeck approached the trio slowly as he whispered a few words of power. The priests were backing away from Malbeck when they froze in mid-step, unable to move.

"Gullanin, please cut their throats," whispered Malbeck as he began another spell. His words whispered around the trio as they struggled to free themselves from the powerful spell. Their eyes widened with fright at the Dark One's words.

Gullanin unsheathed a razor sharp blade and approached Janrick from behind. He did not hesitate as he brought the sharp edge across the immobilized priest's throat. Janrick's blood squirted from the deep cut and splattered onto the stone floor. Malbeck's spell held Janrick's body upright as his blood continued to pool at his feet. Cuthare and Kane suffered the same fate and then Gullanin stepped back from the dying trio.

Malbeck continued to chant.

The words were not familiar to Gullanin, probably ancient words from the Shan Cemar. He tried to concentrate on the words, tried to remember them, but they seemed to waft around the room and then disappear from his mind.

Malbeck's staff was glowing brightly as he came to the end of his spell, his voice a crescendo of power. Suddenly the tip of the staff flared brightly and three beams of light shot forth to strike the pools of blood that had formed at the feet of the dying priests. Almost immediately the light disappeared, leaving behind three pools of blood, sizzling and boiling.

All three of the bodies fell to the floor with a dull thud as the blood began to boil and froth even more. Gullanin stepped back and watched the transformation as the three pools expanded and boiled more violently. As he watched, the boiling blood began to take form, growing from the ground, emerging from the crimson pools. The three forms pulsed with life, growing slowly into a writhing rust colored mass that grew to the size of a small horse. Four clawed legs began to push from the flesh, as a head that resembled a dog strained forward, stretching the translucent skin.

Gullanin retreated farther away as the beasts took on a more defined shape.

"Have no fear, Gullanin. You have served me well and they will not harm you," Malbeck said as he moved closer to the writhing shapes.

Gullanin stopped and looked at the beasts more closely. Their glistening skin had transformed into a more solidified look, huge and muscular, their skin rough like stone but the color of rusted steel. They were shaped like a large cat crossed with a bull, with strong powerful legs that tapered to padded feet tipped with black claws the size of knives. Their heads were dog-like, but much larger, with thick powerful jaws lined with black teeth. Their red eyes were sunk into a knobby forehead that was covered with a ridge of sharp spikes that went all the way down their spine. The spikes on their heads were as long as a man's forearm, tapering down in size the farther down the spine they went.

The three beasts stretched and opened their mouths, emitting low, deep growls. They pivoted their red eyes toward Gullanin, causing him to step backwards even more. Malbeck approached them, reaching out with his left hand. One of the beasts moved toward him, its black claws clicking on the hard stone. Its chest puffed out as it growled, sniffing Malbeck's hand. The beast curled its lips exposing sharp teeth dripping saliva. Malbeck stroked the beast's head as the other two gathered around him. They sat on their haunches and then began to whine as if they were pets seeking attention from their master.

"The Hounds of Gould, Gullanin. Do you like them?"

"They are magnificent, my Lord," replied the wizard uneasily.

"Do you have the article that I requested?"

"I do, my Lord." Gullanin reached into his robe and pulled forth a gold crown glittering with jewels. "The crown of Tarsis."

"Good. Bring it forth," ordered Malbeck.

Gullanin approached the Dark One cautiously, the Hounds of Gould eyeing him hungrily. As he walked by them he detected a strange smell, like burnt hair. The beast's red eyes bored into him. Gullanin shivered slightly as he handed the crown to Malbeck, then shuffled away from the hounds.

"Now, my beasts, smell the crown and get his stench." Malbeck brought the crown to each beast and held it to their noses. They sniffed the metal and licked it with their rough tongues. "Hunt him down and kill him, and then return to me. Gullanin?"

"Yes, my Lord."

"How many Gould-Irin orcs do you have?"

"One hundred, my Lord."

"Good. I want you to lead fifty of them into the Tundrens. Use this amulet to follow the Hounds of Gould. Make sure that Kromm and what is left of his followers are slain." Malbeck handed Gullanin a red stone hanging from a black chain. "The amulet will give you control of the beasts and allow you to track them. Make sure that King Kromm and everyone with him is killed."

"As you wish, my Lord."

***

As soon as they had materialized back in the king's tent, Kiln, with the injured and incapacitated prince on his shoulder, ran to the soft bed in the corner of the room. He gently laid the naked and bloody prince down and looked to Jonas for help.

"Jonas, can you help him?" he asked with concern.

Jonas had immediately followed Kiln to the bed and knelt next to the unconscious prince. "In Shyann's name," he whispered as he surveyed the wounds. There were several long pink scars on his abdomen and more than a handful of open and bleeding lacerations on his arms and legs. His face was bloody and bruised and his lips were torn and bleeding in several spots. He had obviously been repeatedly and severely beaten. Also, burned in the middle of his forehead was Dykreel's brand, a circle of spiked wire. But the worst of the damage was to his groin. They had cut off his manhood leaving nothing more than a bloody stump of flesh. Jonas had never seen anything so horrible.

"Is the prince alive?" asked Alerion as he quickly moved next to the bed.

"Yes, he is breathing. But he has been tortured and severely wounded. By the looks of it they completely slit open his abdomen and then healed the wound with magic, just enough to stop the bleeding. Kiln, what are we to do? Those evil vermin have taken his…"

"Heal him, Jonas," Kiln interrupted. "Bring him back from the darkness. But cover his body first." Kiln's voice was low and dripping with anger at the vile deed that had been done to such a good man.

Jonas was shaking with anger as well. How could someone do this to another human being? It was incomprehensible to him, and the dark deed just added fuel to the fire that was burning deep in Jonas's soul. Dykreel, dark god of torture and pain, the third ranking Forsworn had marked this man, and that act alone was a violation of all that is good. Nothing would dampen the flames of vengeance. And Jonas knew that Kiln felt the same way. He could see it in the hard set of his face and in his ice cold eyes. As Jonas looked at him, an understanding was shared between them. Nothing would stop either one of them from stamping out the evil that was responsible for this act.

"Heal him, Jonas," Kiln repeated.

Alerion draped the prince's body with a light red blanket as Jonas laid both his hands on the mortally wounded prince. Jonas closed his eyes and prayed to Shyann, asking for her power to heal this man who embodied all the qualities of goodness.

He felt her power rise deep from within him and he channeled it into his hands. Instantly they glowed blue and he released the healing magic into the prince's ravaged body. Tendrils of magic surged into the prince, searching out all that was corrupted. Shyann's magic first sought out the prince's forehead, drawn to the evil mark that was burned there. The magic healing tendrils were like hunting dogs sniffing out their prey. The magic grabbed hold of the mark and wrestled with the dark magic there in.

Kiln and Alerion saw smoke rise from the scar as it glowed brightly. But Jonas's eyes were closed and he didn't see the reaction. He felt it. Dykreel's darkness tried to hold on but Jonas gritted his teeth and sent a strong burst of light into the mark, chasing the shadow of darkness from Prince Baylin's body.

Then Jonas found the other wounds, and there were many. The cleric of Dykreel had slit open the prince's abdomen and pulled sections of his intestines out while he was still alive. Then the torturer replaced them and healed the wound, just enough to keep him from bleeding to death. This had been done several times and Jonas cringed thinking about the pain that Prince Baylin had gone through. Jonas could see the damaged and bruised sections deep in his abdomen. He worked quickly to heal the area and sealed all the lacerations on his body, after first pushing out the salt that had been poured on the wounds to maximize his suffering.

Lastly he went to work on the Prince's groin. There was nothing he could do for the missing flesh so he simply did his best to heal the wound with the least amount of scarring. Jonas knew that an opening would be needed for the prince to relieve himself of his fluids, so he found that spot and sealed the flesh around it. Finally Jonas opened his eyes, took a deep breath to steady his body before standing up from the prince's inert form.

Prince Baylin's chest was rising in slow deep breaths and his flesh was no longer pasty white. The scar on his forehead was gone and it looked as if he had never been burned.

"He will be okay, but I think he will need to rest for a while," Jonas said softly.

"The damage that the prince sustained was not just physical. The mental trauma alone will likely keep him unconscious, at least for a while," Kiln said, looking at Alerion and Jonas both. "We will speak to no one of this, do you both understand? No one must know of his injuries."

"I understand," replied Alerion gravely.

"I will tell no one," added Jonas. Kiln nodded his head as if to seal the oath they both took.

"You both have exerted a lot of energy, now go get some sleep, I will stay with the prince," Kiln said as he sat on the edge of the bed and pulled the blanket all the way over his prone body.

"Very well, Kiln." Jonas was indeed tired. He had been fighting constantly for two full days and it was time to get some rest. "Please inform me if you need anything," he said as he turned to leave.

"And me as well, Commander," added Alerion as he left the room on Jonas's heels, leaving Kiln and the prince alone in the dimly lit tent.

Kiln looked down at the unconscious prince. "I'm sorry, young king. But don't worry, you will get your justice, and I will be standing right beside you."

The morning came quick. They had a new task before them, one filled with uncertainties and danger, but also hope. Their task was to find the warrior king, Kromm, who was fleeing for his life in the mountains around Tarsis with what was left of his followers.

Tarsis had been destroyed by Malbeck the Dark One, and his forces were now moving on Finarth. Jonas knew that something was hunting King Kromm with the sole purpose of destroying him, and this something was probably of another world, something that only a cavalier could face. They had to find the king and bring him back; it was necessary for the survival of the land, although Jonas had not yet been told why.

King Baylin Gavinsteal and Kiln would be preparing the defenses for Finarth while Jonas, Taleen, and Fil went on this mission. They could wait no longer, it was time to leave.

Their nighttime mission had been successful. Lord Moredin was dead and they had rescued the prince. Hopefully the retreat would now go unhindered since Lord Moredin and the other enemy commanders were now dead. It would take Malbeck many months to reach Finarth and the winter season would slow them as well, giving Finarth the time needed to prepare for a long drawn out siege. Also, no one knew if Malbeck would stop along the way to plunder other cities like Cuthaine, a free city just outside of Finarth's borders and in Malbeck's path. Either way, the people of Finarth had a lot of work to do, as did Jonas. He had to find the King of Tarsis and bring him back.

All three of the warriors were saddled and ready to ride. Kiln had given them all provisions and the necessary supplies for the long journey.

Fil had a hard time masking his excitement. He sat proud and tall on a sturdy warhorse that Kiln had given him. He was wearing his chain mail shirt draped with a charcoal gray tunic and black breeches and he carried his traditional footman's short sword and dagger, as well as a stout long spear. He was ready for this mission.

Jonas and Taleen sat on their cavalier mounts. Everything sparkled in the morning sun as their huge warhorses pranced about, eager for their mission. Tulari would be leading them, and he shook his head back and forth in anticipatory eagerness for the adventure.

Jonas was wearing his polished helm, the deer antlers jutting from both sides like a noble stag. Endowed with magic, the magnificent piece was almost weightless. Jonas sometimes forgot he was wearing it. It felt a little different now that he had no hair, but that would grow back, creating a softer bed for the helmet.

The edges of the God Mark that had been burned into his forehead could be seen under his helmet. The blue symbol was slightly raised, like a scar, its lines smooth and its edges straight. Jonas often brought his hand up to touch it, marveling at the feel of the gift that Shyann had given him for his service. He did not need a religious symbol on a chain around his neck; his symbol was embedded in his flesh, where it would never go away.

A small crowd of men were out to watch the departing trio. It was an hour before dawn but word had spread throughout camp and many of the men had come to wish them well.

Kiln was there, along with Alerion and several knights with whom Jonas had traveled. Graggis stood like a block of stone holding his huge battle axe. He nodded his head to them as they made eye contact.

Dagrinal was standing next to him in full battle armor, casually resting his hand on his long sword. Jonas smiled and Dagrinal smiled back, nodding his head in farewell.

Suddenly the men around them parted and began to cheer, "Finarth! Finarth!" as an armored man moved through them with purpose. It was the prince, now the King of Finarth, and he approached the trio dressed in full battle armor.

The men were yelling and cheering for their king. Rumors had spread quickly of his rescue but no one had yet seen him. He looked tired but he had healed fully and he moved with determination. He moved close to Jonas and looked up at him. They shared something briefly, a knowing, and a silent thank you. Words about what happened did not need to be spoken. It was understood and it did not need to be discussed.

"Thank you, Jonas, and good luck. May Bandris guard you and bring you back safely with the help you seek."

Jonas leaned down and gripped the young king's hand. "Just hold out long enough to give me time to get back," he said with a wry smile.

"It will be done," replied the king, his soft voice emanating power.

Something had changed within the man; Jonas could see it, could feel it. His face was hard and cold, and he looked like a volcano ready to erupt. Something had died within him and something else was born, and growing.

Jonas turned his gaze to Kiln who stood next to the king. He reached down from Tulari's back and gripped his hand firmly.

"Be careful, Jonas. I still need a training partner and no one is good enough with a blade. Bring yourself back," he said seriously.

"I will," he answered back as Tulari took the lead and moved forward in anticipation.

Taleen's and Fil's horses followed and they moved off through the meadow. Jonas looked back at the group, who were silently watching them depart, and yelled. "May Shyann be with you!"

Epilogue

Allindrian angled her hand out slightly and flicked her wrist, the subtle move slicing open the orc's throat just after she had skewered the monster to the left of its windpipe, right through the artery that snaked up its neck like a thick ropey vine.

The orc fell back into the throng of enemies without a sound.

Allindrian whipped her head around to survey the situation. She had only a few moments before more orcs were upon her, but it was enough.

Their retreat from Tarsis was turning into a rout. Chaos surrounded them as King Kromm and maybe a hundred knights battled for their lives.

They had barely made it out of the city alive and when they emerged from the king's secret tunnel several hundred paces from the city's western wall, they were set upon immediately by the enemy.

They had been fighting for their lives ever since.

Eight hours ago, in the dead of the night, Allindrian had heard something, her elven hearing more acute than that of the humans around her. Her private room was near the king's chambers, and she knew that something was amiss, as the sound was out of place.

The walls of Tarsis had been breached, impossible, but nonetheless true. Malbeck's army had descended upon the city like the plague, slaughtering all of those who were caught unaware, and eventually even those who had had the time to rise from their warm beds and arm themselves. There were just too many of them and the Tarsinian Knights had been caught completely by surprise. They'd had no time to prepare a proper defense. It was a blood bath.

Allindrian was able to rouse King Kromm and his family and escape through the secret tunnel with a small group of castle guards.

Allindrian dodged another strike from an orc's axe and shuffled backwards, cutting the beasts arm off at the elbow. They had to move; if they stayed there fighting, eventually they would be overrun by sheer numbers.

Several knights fought next to her with shield and sword. She jumped back and the trained knights closed the gap, offering her the reprieve she needed to race up the slight hill on which they were fighting.

The terrain consisted of rolling hills covered with huge old timber, interspersed with low growing shrubs and a mixture of mosses and grass. Winter was approaching and the typically dense forest was opening up, its greenery tucking away from the quickly dropping temperature. Soon the mountains would be covered with snow.

There were pockets of fighting all around her and it only took her a few moments to find King Kromm. The giant monarch stood near a stand of trees swinging his mighty sword in great arcs of steely death. He was flanked by a hundred of the elite knights and Allindrian knew that behind them would be his family, and probably Addalis, his court wizard.

When they had emerged from the escape tunnel they had found pockets of resistance all throughout the forest. Some of the Tarsinian soldiers had escaped and the king had wasted no time in uniting the forces and establishing a quick defense.

Kromm's son, Prince Riker, was coming of age and beginning to fill out, looking like his massive father. The young man could fight if he needed to but Allindrian would bet with confidence that he was safely hidden behind the king and protected by Addalis and the prince's mother, Queen Sorana, who was a decent blade wielder in her own right.

More orcs were scrambling up the hill toward the king, and as Allindrian looked down through the trees she saw even more black armored beasts scurrying upward.

She swore under her breath, racing the last thirty paces toward the king. Several orcs leaped from behind a few nearby trees and came at her with black steel. But her silver blade danced left and right and she spun by them in a blur, hardly slowing as both orcs fell to the ground, eyes wide with shock, trying to register how such a small form could be so deadly.

It took only moments to reach the guard behind the main fighting force. Her guess was correct. Queen Sorana was standing alert, sword in hand as if expecting at any moment for the wall of knights to break and the orcs to overrun them. Her beautiful full eyes were wide with fright but her stance was determined. Her long blond hair was pulled back, gathered with a leather thong, and then braided down to mid back.

Standing next to her was her son, Riker. He, too, held a blade and his height made him recognizable immediately. He was almost as tall as his father, but his build was slighter, taking after the more petite stature of his mother. Even so, his figure was impressive at such a young age.

Six armed knights formed a perimeter around the two, while Addalis was glancing left and right looking for attacking orcs. The fighting was so chaotic that no one knew when or where the enemy would appear.

"Addalis!" Allindrian yelled as she jumped over a log to land in the midst of them.

Addalis quickly ran to her as did the queen and the prince. "Allindrian! What do we do?" He questioned frantically.

They had all been running and fighting for the better part of the day and the constant struggle was starting to takes its toll. Everyone's nerves were strung tight and it was clear to Allindrian that they were beginning to lose hope.

"We must retreat! Many more orcs are converging on us now! If we stay, we die!"

"How will we escape? They are upon us!" yelled the queen over the clashing of metal near them.

The fighting was so loud that they didn't even hear the sound of approaching men. Kromm moved toward them with haste, flanked by General Farwin who had luckily escaped with the king in the middle of the night.

The king was dripping with sweat and covered with the blood of his enemies, yet his blue eyes still shone with the lust of battle. His giant two handed long sword was held low in one hand, dripping dark crimson from its shiny surface. The battle king was seven feet tall and covered with rippling muscle, dense and powerful, the kind of muscle built from constant warfare.

General Farwin held a shield and long sword and he breathed heavily from the relentless fighting. His dark hair was laced with many strands of silver. He was not a young soldier anymore and Allindrian wondered how much longer he could keep up the fighting.

"King Kromm, we must get you away, and now! More orcs are storming the hill and they will reinforce the group you now fight!" Allindrian yelled again.

"How many, Blade Singer?" asked Kromm, his voice deep and masking any emotion he might be feeling.

Allindrian had never seen someone so calm and deadly in battle before, at least no human. The man had been swinging that massive sword all day and he still looked like he could crush an ogre with his bare hands. His focus never faltered. Allindrian was impressed, and that was no easy feat.

"Hundreds, and it will be thousands soon after."

"Father, what should we do?" Riker asked.

"We have few options and none of them are desirable," Kromm said.

"My Lord! More are upon us!" screamed a soldier as he ran from the fighting men behind them. He stumbled from exhaustion and General Farwin caught him before he fell. "Hundreds of the vermin are racing up the hill," the soldier stammered as he righted himself and stood up straight before his king. "And I saw several ogres in the distance!"

"Ogres! In Ulren's name, my husband, what can we do," Queen Sorana cried, her eyes flicking to her son and back to her husband. Kromm did not miss the look and he gritted his teeth in anger. He would not let anything happen to his son, or his wife, they had to get away at all cost.

"We will keep a force here to protect your backs while you flee into the mountains, it is the only way!" Allindrian yelled.

"I cannot leave my men to die!" Kromm yelled in frustration.

"My Lord Kromm, it must be done, you know we have no other options," General Farwin said as he gripped the king's muscled arm tightly, making him understand. Kromm stared at his general, his eyes hard and filled with anger for the decision that he must make.

Kromm would normally never leave his men. He would fight, and die, next to them. But this time he had his family with him. He could not stay behind knowing they were alone in the mountains being hunted by Malbeck's minions. He knew that deep down every one of his personal guards would lay down their lives for him, and his family, as he would do the same for them. Sometimes leaders had to make difficult decisions. This was one of those times. "See to it," Kromm ordered reluctantly.

And with that, things were set into motion.

Before the orcs could be reinforced by the others, the knights pressed forward with reckless abandon.

But the maneuver was expertly executed under the direction of General Farwin. It seemed reckless, and it was, but it had a purpose, and the knights under his leadership knew it. They had fought hundreds of battles together and they had complete trust in their sword brothers and their officers. They followed his orders without question.

They pushed forward and moved into a tight formation, shields and swords cutting down orcs as they crashed into the steel wall of bodies. Slowly they moved down the hill, pushing the orcs back and getting closer to the enemy reinforcement that would surely crush them.

General Farwin was yelling orders at the rear the entire time.

Simultaneously, as the formation shrunk into a tight V shape, men would move behind the formation and disengage completely to run back up the hill to join their king.

About thirty or forty men had disengaged from the formation when the enemy reinforcements appeared through the trees.

General Farwin was behind the formation standing on a downed tree. "Hold!" he screamed over the fighting.

Fifty men instantly stopped their forward momentum as hundreds of orcs raced toward them to reinforce their brethren. Tarsinian steel came down again and again with deadly efficiency at the orcs before them. But as one fell back another took its place, and it wouldn't be long before there would be two or three replacing the one fallen.

They were doomed. The vast numbers would enable them to flank their small formation and crush them. General Farwin looked around frantically, trying to come up with something that would slow the advance of the orcs to give his king enough time to get away. He looked back up the hill towards his king and saw Addalis running at him. "What are you doing?" Farwin asked. "You should be running with the king!"

"Allindrian is leading them away as we speak. I have a plan to slow them down," Addalis said through panting breaths as he stood up straight and tried to calm his breathing.

"A spell?" General Farwin questioned.

Addalis nodded. "Be ready to leave with me directly," Addalis said as he took two calming deep breaths.

"I will not leave my men."

"Kromm ordered it," was all Addalis said before he began his spell. He closed his eyes, lifted both his arms wide, and recited the ancient words, the words that would allow him to access the power of the Ru'Ach.

Suddenly a thick greenish mist materialized on both sides of the fighting formation. It appeared quickly and began to spread out in both directions.

"What is it?" yelled General Farwin.

"Stinking cloud! It will hold on both sides of the formation; hopefully the orcs will avoid it and funnel towards the center."

"Where they will be met with Tarsinian steel," Farwin reasoned.

They fought in the center of a natural gully so it came to reason that the orcs would take the easiest route to them, and the cloud would just give them another nudge towards the center rather than tempt them to flank the knights.

It all depended on who the beasts had leading them, if anyone. Regardless, it would at least give them some more time.

The thick green mist covered the forest floor on either side of the fighting men and sure enough the plan was working. The enemy reinforcements came howling up the hill and they joined their brethren with steel and claw. It tripled the numbers they were fighting, but at least they would not be flanked.

Some orcs attempted to breach the mist but were repelled quickly as they inhaled the poisonous mixture. It would not kill them but the stink was so severe that they stumbled from the noxious fog, coughing and vomiting and struggling for clean air.

"Let's go, General, we need to catch up to them," Addalis said as he turned to go.

Farwin hesitated, looking back at his men who were fighting for their lives.

"General, their sacrifice is for their land and liege, you know they would make the conscious choice if they were able," Addalis reasoned.

Addalis felt for the man, as he too felt for the men that would die so they could live. But he had not built close relationships with the men below them as had the general, and he knew that that connection, built over years of combat together, would be a strong pull to keep him with his men. It would be heart wrenching for General Farwin to leave them.

"General, would you not die to save your king?" asked addalis.

Farwin turned toward him again, his eyes pleading, begging for him to come up with a solution to his problem. "Yes, without reservation."

"And so would they. Your king ordered you to leave your men; he will need you in the trials ahead of us, do not let Kromm down," Addalis said.

And that was all it took.

General Farwin turned toward his men and raised his bloody sword in the air. "For Kromm!" he screamed. "For Tarsis!"

And his men, fighting for their lives, took up the cheer.

Addalis and General Farwin raced up the hill to the sounds of Kromm's name echoing through the trees.

The End...

Now Available...

Book two, *The Rise of Malbeck*
And
Book three, *Glimmer in the Shadow*

Look for them at www.*TwiinEntertainment.com*

About the author

Jason McWhirter has been a history teacher for seventeen years. He lives in Washington with his wife, Jodi, and dog, Meadow. He is a certifiable fantasy freak who, when he wasn't playing sports, spent his childhood days immersed in books and games of fantasy. He'd tumble into bed at night with visions of heroes, dragons, and creatures of other worlds, fueling his imagination and spurring his desire to create fantasies of his own. When he isn't fly fishing the lakes and streams of the Northwest, or wine tasting and entertaining with his wife and friends, he spends his spare time sitting in front of the computer writing his next novel or screenplay.

Glossary

Ru'Ach: An elven word used to describe the source of all life…thought of as a river of energy that created all things.

Ekahal: An elvish wizard

IshMian: Elven name for a cognivant, a person gifted with mental powers. Little is known of this power but the gifts range from telekinesis, and ESP, to mind control.

Ty'erm: Sharneen term used to describe a meditative state.

Akron: Military term that means a thousand men.

Modrig: Military term that means five hundred men.

Ludus: Military term that means two hundred and fifty men.

Pandar: Military term that means fifty men.

Nock, or Nocking: The *nock* is the end of the arrow that has a crevice for the string. To nock an arrow is to put an arrow to string.

Made in the USA
San Bernardino, CA
03 June 2017